The t..... ....**was**
und... .... **..e to**
be **..en.**

It w.s odd. All day so far he'd seemed like a force of n.ture—albeit in a pristine suit—and now that ju. even the tiniest part of that armour had been di.c.rded she was suddenly confronted by the fact that he was a man. And a rather attractive one at that

His dark hair was short, but not severe, and now she knew he had Italian blood in him she could see it in the set of his eyes and his long, straight nose. The mouth, however, was totally British— tightly drawn in, jaw tense as he grimaced at some unwelcome news and hung up on the caller without saying goodbye. He brought the phone down from his ear and stared at it so hard that Ruby thought it might burst into flames.

That was when he looked up and spotted her, sitting where she'd been for the last ten minutes, and it took .im by total surprise. She allowed her lips to curve into the barest of smiles and held his gaze. For some .ason she liked the fact her presence sometimes .uffled him.

TAMING HER
ITALIAN BOSS

BY
FIONA HARPER

MILLS
BOON

Published in Great Britain 2014
by Mills & Boon, an imprint of Harlequin (UK) Limited,
Eton House, 18-24 Paradise Road, Richmond, Surrey, TW9 1SR

© 2014 Fiona Harper

ISBN: 978-0-263-91290-6

23-0614

Harlequin (UK) Limited's policy is to use papers that are natural, renewable and recyclable products and made from wood grown in sustainable forests. The logging and manufacturing processes conform to the legal environmental regulations of the country of origin.

Printed and bound in Spain
by Blackprint CPI, Barcelona

As a child, **Fiona Harper** was constantly teased for either having her nose in a book or living in a dream world. Things haven't changed much since then, but at least in writing she's found a use for her runaway imagination. After studying dance at university, Fiona worked as a dancer, teacher and choreographer, before trading in that career for video-editing and production. When she became a mother she cut back on her working hours to spend time with her children, and when her littlest one started pre-school she found a few spare moments to rediscover an old but not forgotten love—writing.

Fiona lives in London, but her other favourite places to be are the Highlands of Scotland and the Kent countryside on a summer's afternoon. She loves cooking good food and anything cinnamon-flavoured. Of course she still can't keep away from a good book or a good movie—especially romances—but only if she's stocked up with tissues, because she knows she will need them by the end, be it happy or sad. Her favourite things in the world are her wonderful husband, who has learned to decipher her incoherent ramblings, and her two daughters.

For my readers,
from those who have been with me
since the beginning to those who are
picking one of my books for the first time.
I'm grateful to every one of you.

CHAPTER ONE

'YOU WANT ME to give you a job?'

The woman staring across the desk at Ruby didn't look convinced. The London traffic rumbled outside the first-floor office as the woman looked her up and down. Her gaze swept down over Ruby's patchwork corduroy jacket, miniskirt with brightly coloured leggings peeking out from underneath, and ended at the canvas shoes that were *almost* the right shade of purple to match the streaks in her short hair.

Ruby nodded. 'Yes.'

'Humph,' the woman said.

Ruby couldn't help noticing her flawlessly cut black suit and equally flawlessly cut hair. She'd bet that the famous Thalia Benson of the Benson Agency hadn't come about her latest style after she'd got fed up with the long stringy bits dangling in her breakfast cereal and convinced her flatmate to take scissors to it.

'And Layla Babbington recommended you try here?'

Ruby nodded again. Layla had been one of her best friends at boarding school. When she'd heard that Ruby was looking for a job—and one that preferably took her out of the country ASAP—she'd suggested the top-class nannying agency. 'Don't let old Benson fool you for a moment,' she'd told Ruby. 'Thalia's a pussycat underneath, and she likes someone with a bit of gumption. The two of you will get along famously.'

Now that she was sitting on the far side of Thalia Benson's desk, under scrutiny as if she were a rogue germ on a high-chair tray, Ruby wasn't so sure.

'Such a pity she had to go and marry that baronet she was working for,' Benson muttered. 'Lost one of my best girls *and* a plum contract.'

She looked up quickly at Ruby, as if she'd realised she'd said that out loud. Ruby looked back at her, expression open and calm. She didn't care what the nanny provider to the rich and famous thought about her clients. She just wanted a job that got her out of London. Fast.

'So...' Ms Benson said in one long drawn-out syllable while she shuffled a few papers on her desk. 'What qualifications do you have?'

'For nannying?' Ruby asked, resisting the urge to fidget.

Benson didn't answer, but her eyebrows lifted in a what-do-you-think? kind of gesture.

Ruby took a deep breath. 'Well...I've always been very good with kids, and I'm practical and creative and hardworking—'

The other woman cut her off by holding up a hand. She was looking wearier by the second. 'I mean professional qualifications. Diploma in Childcare and Education, BTEC...Montessori training?'

Ruby let the rest of that big breath out. She'd been preparing to keep talking for as long as possible, and she'd only used up a third of her lung capacity before Benson had interrupted her. Not a good start. She took another, smaller breath, giving herself a chance to compose a different reply.

'Not exactly.'

No one had said it was going to be a *great* reply.

Thalia Benson gave her a frosty look. 'Either one has

qualifications or one hasn't. It tends to be a black-or-white kind of thing.'

Ruby swallowed. 'I know I haven't got any *traditional* childcare qualifications, but I was hoping I could enlist with your new travelling nanny service. Short-term placements. What I lack in letters after my name I make up for in organisation, flexibility and common sense.'

Benson's ears pricked up at the mention of common sense. She obviously liked those words. Ruby decided to press home her main advantage. 'And I've travelled all over the world since I was a small child. There aren't many places I haven't been to. I also speak four languages—French, Spanish, Italian and a bit of Malagasy.'

Ms Benson tipped her head slightly. 'You've spent time in Madagascar?' The look of disbelief on her face suggested she thought Ruby had gone a bit too far in padding out her CV.

'My parents and I lived there for three years when I was a child.'

Benson's eyes narrowed. *'Inona voavoa?'* she suddenly said, surprising Ruby.

The reply came back automatically. How was she? *'Tsara be.'*

Benson's eyes widened, and for the first time since Ruby had walked through the office door and sat down she looked interested. She picked up the blank form sitting in front of her and started writing. 'Ruby Long, wasn't it?'

'Lange,' Ruby replied. 'With an *e*.'

Benson looked up. 'Like Patrick Lange?'

Ruby nodded. 'Exactly like that.' She didn't normally like mentioning her connection to the globetrotting TV presenter whose nature documentaries were the jewel in the crown of British television, but she could see more than a glimmer of interest in Thalia Benson's eyes, and she really, *really* wanted to be out of the country when good old Dad got back from The Cook Islands in two days' time. 'He's my father,' she added.

The other woman stopped messing around with the form, put it squarely down on the desk and folded her hands on top of it. 'Well, Ms Lange, I don't usually hire nannies without qualifications, not even for short-term positions, but maybe there's something you could do round the office over the summer. Our intern has just disappeared off to go backpacking.'

Ruby blinked. Once again, someone had heard the name 'Lange' and the real person opposite them had become invisible. Once again, mentioning her father had opened a door only for it to be slammed shut again. When would she ever learn?

'That's very generous, Ms Benson, but I wasn't really looking for a clerical position.'

Thalia nodded, but Ruby knew she hadn't taken her seriously at all. From the smile on the other woman's face, she could tell Thalia was wondering how much cachet it would bring her business if she could wheel Ruby out at the annual garden party to impress her clientele, maybe even get national treasure Patrick Lange to show up.

That wasn't Ruby's style at all. She'd been offered plenty of jobs where she could cash in on her father's status by doing something vastly overpaid for not a lot of effort, and she'd turned every one of them down. All she wanted was for someone to see *her* potential for once, to need her for herself, not just what her family connections could bring. Surely that wasn't too much to ask. Unfortunately, Ruby suspected Ms Thalia Benson wasn't that rare individual. She rose from her side of the desk, opened the office door and indicated Ruby should return to the waiting area. 'Why don't you take a seat outside, and I'll see what I can do?'

Ruby smiled back and nodded, rising from her chair. She'd give Thalia Benson fifteen minutes, and if she hadn't come up with something solid by then, she was out of here. Life was too short to hang around when something wasn't working. Onwards and upwards, that was her motto.

Everything in the waiting area was shades of stone and heather and aubergine. The furniture screamed understated—and overpriced—elegance. The only clue that the Benson Agency had anything to do with children was a pot of crayons and some drawing paper on the low coffee table between two sectional sofas. When Thalia's office door closed, Ruby shrugged then sat down. She'd always loved drawing. She picked up a bright red crayon and started doodling on a blank sheet. Maybe she'd go for fire engine–red streaks in her hair next time they needed touching up....

She spent the next five minutes doing a pretty passable cartoon of Thalia Benson while she waited. In the picture, Thalia dripped sophistication and charm, but she was dressed up like the Child Catcher from the famous movie, locking a scared boy in a cage.

As the minutes ticked by Ruby became more and more sure this was a waste of her time. The only thing she needed to decide before she left was whether to fold the drawing up and discreetly stick it in her pocket, or if she should prop it on the console table against the far wall so it was the first thing prospective clients saw when they walked in the door.

She was holding the paper in her hands, dithering about whether to crease it in half or smooth it out flat, when the door crashed open and a tall and rather determined-looking man strode in. Ruby only noticed the small, dark-haired girl he had in tow when he was halfway to Thalia Benson's office. The child was wailing loudly, her eyes squeezed shut and her mouth wide open, and the only reason she didn't bump into any of the furniture was because she was being propelled along at speed in her father's wake, protected by his bulk.

The receptionist bobbed around him, trying to tell him

he needed to make an appointment, but he didn't alter his trajectory in the slightest. Ruby put her cartoon down on the table and watched with interest.

'I need to see the person in charge and I need to see them now,' he told the receptionist, entirely unmoved by her expression of complete horror or her rapid arm gestures.

Ruby bit back a smile. She might just stick around to see how this played out.

'If you'll just give me a second, Mr…er…I'll see whether Ms Benson is available.'

The man finally gave the receptionist about 5 per cent of his attention. He glanced at her, and as he did so the little girl stopped crying for a second and looked in Ruby's direction. She started up again almost immediately, but it was half-hearted this time, more for show than from distress.

'Mr Martin,' he announced, looking down at the receptionist. He stepped forward again. Ruby wasn't sure how it happened—whether he let go of the girl's hand or whether she did that tricksy, slippery-palm thing that all toddlers seemed to know—but suddenly father and child were disconnected.

The receptionist beat Mr Tall and Determined to Thalia's door, knocking on it a mere split second before he reached for the handle, and she just about saved face as she blurted out his name. He marched into the room and slammed the door behind him.

Once he was inside, the little girl sniffed and fell silent. She and Ruby regarded each other for a moment, then Ruby smiled and offered her a bright yellow crayon.

Max looked at the woman behind the desk. She was staring at him and her mouth was hanging open. Just a little. 'I need one of your travelling nannies as soon as possible.'

The woman—Benson, was it?—closed her jaw silently and with one quick, almost unnoticeable appraising glance she took in his handmade suit and Italian shoes and decided to play nice. Most people did.

'Of course, Mr Martin.' She smiled at him. 'I just need to get a few details from you and then I'll go through my staff list. We should be able to start interviewing soon.' She looked down at a big diary on her desk and started flipping through it. 'How about Thursday?' she asked, looking back up at him.

Max stared back at her. He thought he'd been pretty clear. What part of 'as soon as possible' did she not understand? 'I need someone today.'

'Today?' she croaked. Her gaze flew to the clock on the wall.

Max knew what it said—three-thirty.

The day had started off fairly normally, but then his sister had shown up at his office just before ten and, as things often did when the women in his family were concerned, it had got steadily more chaotic since then.

'Preferably within the next half hour,' he added. 'I have to be at the airport by five.'

'B-but how old is the child? How long do you need someone for? What kind of expertise do you require?'

He ignored her questions and pulled a folded computer printout from his suit pocket. There was no point wasting time on details if she wasn't going to be able to help him. 'I came to you because your website says you provide a speedy and efficient service—travelling nannies for every occasion. I need to know whether that's true.'

She drew herself up ramrod straight in her chair and looked him in the eye. 'Listen, Mr Martin, I don't know what sort of establishment you think I run here, but—'

He held up a hand, cutting her off. He knew he was steamrollering over all the pleasantries, but that couldn't be helped. 'The best nanny agency in London, I'd heard.

Which is why I came to you in an emergency. Have you got someone? If not, I won't waste any more of your time.'

She pursed her lips, but her expression softened. He hadn't been flattering her—not really his style—but a few timely truths hadn't hurt his case. 'I can help.' She sighed and Max relaxed just a little. She'd much rather have told him it was impossible, he guessed, but the kind of fee she was measuring him up for with her beady little eyes was hard to say no to. 'At the very least, let me know the sex and age of the charge,' she added.

Max shrugged. 'Girl,' he said. 'Older than one and younger than school age. Other than that I'm not quite sure. Why don't you take a look and see what you think?'

The woman's eyes almost popped out of her head. 'She's here?'

Max nodded. Where the hell else did the woman think she'd be?

'And you left her outside? Alone?'

He frowned. He hadn't thought about that for one second. Which was exactly why he needed to hire someone who would. Anyway, he hadn't left Sofia completely alone. There had been the flappy woman…

Ms Benson sprang from the desk, threw the door open and rushed into the waiting area beyond her office. There, colouring in with the tip of her tongue caught at one side of her mouth, was Sofia. Max suddenly noticed something: the noise had stopped. That horrible wailing, like an air-raid siren. It had driven him to distraction all day.

'Here…try purple for the flower,' a young woman, kneeling next to Sofia, was saying. Sofia, instead of acting like a child possessed with the spirit of a banshee, just calmly accepted the crayon from the woman and carried on scribbling. After a few moments, both woman and child stopped what they were doing and lifted their heads to look at the two adults towering over them. The identical expression of mild curiosity they both wore was rather disconcerting.

Max turned to the agency owner. 'I want her,' he said, nodding at the kneeling woman who, he was just starting to notice, had odd-coloured bits in her hair.

Benson gave out a nervous laugh. 'I'm afraid she doesn't work here.'

Max raised his eyebrows.

'Not yet,' she added quickly. 'But I'm sure you'd be better off with one of our other nannies who—'

He turned away and looked at the strange pixie-like woman and the little girl again. For the first time in what seemed like weeks, although it had probably only been hours, Sofia was quiet and calm and acting like the normal child he vaguely remembered. 'No. I want *her.*'

Something deep down in his gut told him this woman had what he needed. To be honest, he really didn't care what it was. It was twenty-five to four and he had to get going. 'What do you say?' he asked the her directly.

The woman finished colouring in a pink rose on the sheet of paper she and Sofia were sharing before she answered. She flicked a glance at the agency owner. 'She's right. I don't even work here.'

'I don't care about that,' he told her. 'You have all the skills I want. It's you I need.'

She blinked and looked at him hard, as if she was trying to work out whether he was serious or not. Normally people didn't have to think about that.

'What if the job isn't what *I* need?' she asked. 'I don't think I should accept without hearing the terms.'

Max checked his watch again. 'Fine, fine,' he said wearily. 'Have it your way. We'll interview in the car. But hurry up! We've got a plane to catch.' And then he marched from the offices of the Benson Agency leaving its proprietor standing open-mouthed behind him.

[illegible faded text from previous page showing through]

CHAPTER TWO

IT TOOK RUBY all of two seconds to drop the crayon she was holding, scoop up the child next to her and run after him into the bright sunshine of a May afternoon. God did indeed move in mysterious ways!

And so did Mr...whatever his name was.

Those long legs had carried him down the stairs to street level very fast. When she burst from the agency's understated door onto one of the back roads behind Oxford Street, she had to look in both directions before she spotted him heading towards a sleek black car parked on a double yellow.

She was about to run after him when she had a what's-wrong-with-this-picture? moment. Hang on. Why was she holding his child while he waltzed off with barely a backward glance? It was as if, in his rush to conquer the next obstacle, he'd totally forgotten his daughter even existed. She looked down at the little girl, who was quite happy hitched onto her hip, watching a big red double-decker bus rumbling past the end of the road. She might not realise just how insensitive her father was being at the moment, just how much it hurt when one understood how extraneous they were to a parent's life, but one day she'd be old enough to notice. Ruby clamped her lips together and marched towards the car. No child deserved that.

She walked up to him, peeled the child off her hip and

handed her over. 'Here,' she said breezily. 'I think you forgot this.'

The look of utter bewilderment on his face would have been funny if she hadn't been so angry. He took the girl from Ruby and held her out at arm's length so her legs dangled above the chewing-gum-splattered pavement. Now it was free of toddler, Ruby put her hand on her hip and raised her eyebrows.

He was saved from answering by the most horrendous howling. It took her a few moments to realise it was the child making the sound. The ear-splitting noise bounced off the tall buildings and echoed round the narrow street.

'Take it back!' he said. 'You're the only one who can make it stop!'

Ruby took her hands off her hips and folded her arms. '*It* has a name, I should think.'

He offered the screaming bundle of arms and legs over, but Ruby stepped back. He patted the little girl's back, trying to soothe her, but it just made her cry all the harder. The look of sheer panic on his face was actually quite endearing, she decided, especially as it went some way to softening that 'ruler of the universe' thing he had going on. He was just as out of his depth as she was, wasn't he?

His eyes pleaded with her. 'Sofia. Her name is Sofia.'

Ruby gave him a sweet smile and unfolded her arms to accept the little girl. She still didn't know whether following this through was a good idea, but the only other option was working for her dad. He'd flipped when he'd found out she'd given in her notice at the vintage fashion shop in Covent Garden.

Considering that her father didn't pay an awful lot of interest the rest of the time, Ruby had been shocked he'd noticed, let alone cared. He was usually always too busy off saving the planet to worry about what his only child got up to, but this had lit his fuse for some reason.

According to him, Ruby needed a job. Ruby needed to grow up. Ruby needed to stop flitting around and settle to something.

He'd laid down a very clear ultimatum before he'd left for the South Pacific—get a proper job by the time he returned, or he'd create a position for her in his production company. Once there, she'd never escape. She'd never get promoted. She'd be doomed to being *What's her name? You know, Patrick Lange's daughter*…for ever.

Sofia grabbed for Ruby as her father handed her back over, clinging to her like the baby lemurs Ruby had got used to seeing in the Madagascan bush. A rush of protective warmth flooded up from her feet and landed in her chest.

She looked up at the man towering above her. 'And, before I get in that car, we might as well continue with the information gathering. I'd offer to shake your hand but, as you can see—' she nodded to Sofia, who'd burrowed her head in the crook of her neck '—it's in use at the moment. I'm Ruby Lange. With an *e*.'

He looked at her blankly, recognising neither her name nor the need for a response. 'And you are?' she prompted.

He blinked and seemed to recover himself. 'Max Martin.'

Ruby shifted Sofia to a more comfortable position on her hip. 'Pleased to meet you, Mr Martin.' She looked inside the dark interior of the limo. 'Now, are we going to start this interview or what?'

Max sat frowning in the back of the limo. He wasn't quite sure what had just happened. One minute he'd been fully in charge of the situation, and the next he'd been ushered into his own car by a woman who looked as if she'd had a fight with a jumble sale—and lost.

She turned to face him, her eyes large and enquiring as

she looked at him over the top of Sofia's car seat, which was strapped between them. 'Fire away,' she said, then waited.

He looked back at her.

'I thought this was supposed to be an interview.'

She was right. He had agreed to that, but the truth of the matter was that, unless she declared herself to be a drug-addicted mass murderer, the job was hers. He didn't have time to find anyone else.

He studied his new employee carefully. The women he interacted with on a daily basis definitely didn't dress like this. It was all colour and jarring patterns. Somehow it made her look very young. And, right there, he had his first question.

'How old are you?'

She blinked but held his gaze. 'Twenty-four.'

Old enough, then. If he'd had to guess, he'd have put her at a couple of years younger. Didn't matter, though. If she could do the job, she could do the job, and the fact that the small bundle of arms and legs strapped into the car seat was finally silent was all the evidence he needed.

He checked his watch. He really didn't have time to chit-chat, so if she wanted to answer questions, he'd dispense with the pleasantries and get on with the pertinent ones. 'How far away do you live?'

For the first time since he'd set eyes on her, she looked surprised.

'Can we get there in under half an hour?'

She frowned. 'Pimlico. So, yes… But why—?'

'Can you pack a bag in under ten minutes?'

She raised her eyebrows.

'In my experience, most women can't,' he said. 'I don't actually understand why, though.' It seemed a simple enough task, after all. 'I believe it may have something to do with shoes.'

'My parents dragged me round the globe—twice—in

my formative years,' she replied crisply. 'I can pack a bag in under five if I have to.'

Max smiled. And not just the distant but polite variety he rolled out at business meetings. This was the real deal. The nanny stopped looking quite so confrontational and her eyes widened. Max leaned forward and instructed the driver to head for Pimlico.

He felt a tapping on his shoulder, a neatly trimmed fingernail made its presence known through the fabric of his suit sleeve. He sat back in his seat and found her looking at him. 'I haven't agreed to take the job yet.'

She wasn't one to beat about the bush, was she? But, then again, neither was he.

'Will you?'

She folded her arms. 'I need to ask *you* a few questions first.'

For some reason Max found himself smiling again. It felt odd, he realised. Not stiff or forced, just unfamiliar. As if he'd forgotten how and had suddenly remembered. But he hadn't had a lot to smile about this year, had he?

'Fire away,' he said.

Was that a flicker of a smile he saw behind those eyes? If it was, it was swiftly contradicted by a stubborn lift of her chin. 'Well, Mr Martin, you seem to have skipped over some of the details.'

'Such as?'

'Such as: how long will you be requiring my services?'

Oh, those kinds of details. 'A week, hopefully. Possibly two.'

She made a funny little you-win-some-you-lose-some kind of expression.

A nasty cold feeling shot through him. She wasn't going to back out already, was she? 'Too long?'

She shook her head. 'I'd have been happy for it to be longer, but it'll do.'

They looked at each other for a couple of seconds. Her eyes narrowed slightly as she delivered her next question. 'So why do you need a nanny for your daughter in such a hurry? I think I'd like to know why the previous one left.'

Max sat bolt upright in his seat. 'My daughter? Sofia's not my daughter!'

The nanny—or *almost* nanny, he reminded himself—gave him a wry look. 'See? This is what I'm talking about… *details.*'

Max ignored the comment. He was great with details. But nowadays he paid other people to concentrate on the trivial nit-picky things so he could do the important stuff. It worked—most of the time—because he had assistants and deputies to spring into action whenever he required them to, but when it came to his personal life he had no such army of willing helpers. Probably because he didn't have much of a personal life. It irritated him that this mis-matched young woman had highlighted a failing he hadn't realised he had. Still, he could manage details, sketchy or otherwise, if he tried.

'Sofia is my niece.'

'Oh…'

Max usually found the vagaries of the female mind something of a mystery. He was always managing to put his foot in it with the women in his life—when he had time for any—but he found this one unusually easy to read. The expression that accompanied her breathy sigh of realisation clearly said, *Well, that explains a lot.*

'Let's just say that I had not planned to be child-minding today.'

She pressed her lips together, as if to stop herself from laughing. 'You mean you were left holding the baby.… Literally.'

He nodded. 'My sister is an…actress.'

At least, she'd been trying to be the last five years.

'Oh! Has she been in anything I've heard of?'

Max let out a sigh. 'Probably not. But she got a call from her agent this morning about an audition for a "smallish part in a biggish film". Something with...' what was the name? '...Jared Fisher in it.'

The nanny's eyes widened. 'Wow! He's really h—' She shut her mouth abruptly and nibbled her top lip with her teeth. 'What I meant to say was, what a fabulous opportunity for her.'

'Apparently so. She got the job, but they wanted her in L.A. right away. The actress who was supposed to be playing the part came down with appendicitis and it was now or never.'

Secretly he wondered if it would have been better if his little sister had sloped despondently into his office later that afternoon, collected her daughter and had gone home. She'd always had a bit of a bohemian lifestyle, and they'd lost touch while she'd travelled the world, working her way from one restaurant to another as she waited for her 'big break'. But then Sofia had come along and she'd settled down in London. He really didn't know if this was a good idea.

Maybe things might have been different if they'd grown up in the same house after their parents had split, but, while he'd benefited from the steadying influence of their English father, Gia had stayed with their mother, a woman who had turned fickle and inconsistent into an art form.

They had grown apart as teenagers, living in different countries, with totally different goals, values and personalities, but he was trying to make up for it now they were more a part of each other's lives.

Gia always accused him of butting his nose in where it wasn't wanted and trying to run her life for her, but she always said it with a smile and she was annoyingly difficult to argue with. Perhaps that was why, when she'd turned up at his office that morning with Sofia and had begged him to help her, her eyes full of hope and longing, he hadn't been able to say no.

'And what about you?' he asked. 'Why do you need a job in such a hurry?'

She rolled her eyes. 'It was either this, or my father was threatening to make me work for him.'

'You don't want to work for the family firm?'

She pulled a face. 'I'd rather jump off the top of The Shard! Wouldn't you?'

Max stiffened. 'I now head up the business my father built from nothing.'

An unexpected stab of pain hit him in his ribcage, and then came the roll of dark emotion that always followed. Life had been much simpler when he'd been able to bury it all so deep it had been as if it hadn't existed. 'There's something to be said for family loyalty,' he added gruffly. 'For loyalty full stop, actually.'

She looked a little uncomfortable, but waltzed her way out of the awkward moment with a quip. 'Well, I'm quite prepared to be loyal to your family. Just as long as you don't ask me to get entangled with mine. Parents are fine and all that, but I'd rather keep them at a safe distance.'

Max couldn't help but think of his mother, and he decided not to quiz Ruby any further on her motives. It wasn't going to alter whether he hired her or not for a couple of weeks. If this had been for a more permanent fixture in his life, it might have been a different matter.

'So, why do you need a travelling nanny?' Her face lit up. 'Are we going to Hollywood?'

She sounded just like Gia. Max resisted the urge to close his eyes and wish this were all a bad dream, that he'd wake up in bed, his nice, ordered life back.

'I'm taking Sofia to stay with her grandmother,' he said. It was the only possible solution. All he had to do now was convince his mother of that. 'I can't possibly babysit a toddler for the next fortnight, even if I knew how to. I have three weeks to turn around an important work situation and I can't take any time off.'

The shock of realising he'd have to cope with Sofia on his own while Gia was away had been bad enough, but then his biggest client had phoned, slinging a spanner in the works. Now he couldn't afford even an hour off work, let alone a fortnight. He needed time to think. Space. Peace and quiet. And Sofia brought none of those things with her in her tiny, howling package.

Hopefully he'd get Sofia installed at his mother's, then he'd be able to fly back and be at his desk first thing Monday, only half a day lost. It had been Gia's idea, and, while he didn't relish having to take time out to deliver Sofia, at least his sister's moment of destiny had come on a Friday morning. He'd stay overnight to make sure they all settled in and leave the nanny with his mother. He'd thought of everything.

The girl gave him a sideways look. 'So work is important to you? More than family?' She didn't look impressed.

Max gave her one of his patented you-don't-know-what-you're-talking-about looks. *Of course* family was important! That was why he had to seal this deal. He was determined to carry on and finish what he and his father had started together, to ensure that his dad's dream was fulfilled.

'I'm a thirty-something bachelor with a riverside apartment that has split-level floors with no railings, stairs with no banisters and no outside space except a balcony with a hundred-foot drop to the Thames. Do *you* think it would be the responsible thing to allow a child to live there?'

He could see her wrestling with herself, but finally she shook her head.

'Taking her to her grandmother's is the most sensible and practical thing to do—for everybody.'

He looked up. They'd crossed the river now and could only be minutes from her home. If she said no he'd just drop her off and they'd never see each other again. And he'd have to wrestle a screaming Sofia all the way to her grandmother's on his own.

'So, Miss Lange with an *e*, will you take the job?'

She inhaled and held the breath for a few seconds before glancing up at her building, then she let the air out again. 'I have one last question.'

'Which is?'

The corners of her mouth curled up, as if she couldn't quite believe he hadn't mentioned this himself. 'You really are a big-picture kind of guy, aren't you?'

Yes, he was. 'How did you know?'

'There's another detail you've forgotten, a rather important one. If I'm going to be your travelling nanny, I kind of need to know where we'll be travelling to.'

Ah, yes. Another good point. He cleared his throat. 'Italy,' he said. 'We're going to Venice.'

Ruby's hand shot out, her long slender fingers stretched towards him. 'Done.' He half expected her to spit in her palm, but she just looked steadily at him.

He encased her smaller hand in his own, feeling the warmth of her palm, the softness of her skin. Something tiny but powerful tingled all the way up his arm. He shook her hand. 'It's a deal,' he said, his voice rumbling in his own ears. 'You're hired.'

But as he pulled his hand away he started to wonder if he knew exactly what he'd got himself into.

CHAPTER THREE

RUBY SHOULD HAVE realised when the limo driver gingerly put her hastily packed canvas rucksack into the boot that this journey was going to be different. She was used to travelling, used to crowded terminals in international airports teeming with the whole spectrum of human life. She was used to queuing just to buy a bottle of water and browsing the endless shops filled with travel gadgets in order to fill the time. She was used to playing 'hunt the chair' in the departure hall, and dozing on it with her jacket for a pillow when she found one.

She was not used to hushed and elegant lounges in small city airports, free food, drink and entertainment. Even though her father could easily afford to fly business class everywhere, he refused to, preferring what he called 'real' travel. If he wasn't squished into Economy or standing at a three-mile queue at Immigration it wasn't a real trip. Of course, the public loved him for it. Privately, Ruby had always wondered why dust and the ubiquitous Jeep with dodgy suspension were more 'authentic' than air-conditioned coaches these days, but she wasn't daft enough to argue with him. He was disappointed in her enough already.

She sighed. It had been better when Mum had been alive. Even though she'd done exactly the same job, travelled along with him and presented the programmes alongside him, she'd always been good at hugs and sending postcards and presents to boarding school to let Ruby know that just because she was out of sight, it didn't mean she was out of mind. Her father was no good at that stuff. And after she'd died he'd channelled his grief into his work, meaning he lost himself in it more than he ever had done before.

Ruby found herself a spot on the edge of a designer sofa in the lounge and reached for the bowl of macadamia nuts on the table in front of her, only scooping two or three out with her fingers and popping them quickly into her mouth, then she returned to doodling on a paper napkin with a pen she'd pulled out of her bag.

It was supposed to have been easier once the journey got under way. She'd thought that at least the 'travelling' part of being a travelling nanny would be inside her comfort zone. *Wrong again, Ruby.* And she didn't even have anything work-related to do to keep her mind off her awkwardness, because Sofia, obviously exhausted by the sheer graft of tantruming half the day, was stretched out on the plush sofa with her thumb in her mouth, fast asleep and completely unaware of her surroundings.

Her new boss didn't make it any easier. He'd hardly made eye contact with her since they'd left her flat, let alone talked to her. He was a right barrel of laughs.

She filled the short time they had by quickly sketching him as he remained, granite-like and motionless, hunched over his laptop; the only parts of him moving were his eyes and his fingers. She used only a few lines to get the back of his head and his jaw right, leaving the strokes bare and uncompromising, then settled down to reproducing the wrinkles on the arms of his jacket, the soft shock of dark thick hair that was trimmed to perfection at his nape.

Thankfully, once the flight was called and they had to head to the gate and board the plane, Ruby started to feel a little more normal. Jollying a freshly woken toddler along kept her occupied. It wasn't that difficult. Sofia was a sweet

child, even if the quiet curiosity hid a will of steel, like her
uncle's. Poor child must have been scared and upset when
she'd seen her mother disappear out of Max's office without her. It was no wonder she'd screamed the place down.

As the plane began its descent to Marco Polo airport
Ruby began to feel the familiar quiver of excitement she always got at arriving somewhere new. She'd always wanted
to visit Venice, had even begged her father to go when
she'd been younger, but he hadn't been interested. It was
a man-made construction, built on stilts in the middle of a
lagoon, and the city itself had few open green spaces, let
alone rare wildlife—unless you had an unusual passion for
pigeons. Ruby didn't care about that. She liked cities. And
this one—*La Serenissima*, as it used to be known—was
supposed to be the jewel of them all.

It was a disappointment, then, to discover that they
weren't going to be arriving in Venice by boat, as many
visitors did. Instead Max had ordered a car to take them
along the main road towards the city of Mestre, which then
turned onto the seemingly endless bridge that stretched
from the land to the city across the lagoon.

Sofia began to whine. Although she'd had that brief nap
at the airport, the poor little girl looked ready to drop. Ruby
did her best to calm her down, and it helped, but what the
child really needed was someone she knew. She might have
taken to her new nanny, but Ruby was still a stranger. As
was her uncle, Ruby guessed. The sooner she was reunited
with her grandmother, the better.

The car pulled to a halt and Ruby looked up. Her face
fell. Usually, she liked catching the first glimpse of a new
place, seeing it as a far-off dot on the horizon, and getting
more and more excited as it got closer and closer. This evening, she'd been so busy distracting Sofia back from the
verge of another tantrum, she'd missed all of that. They'd
arrived at a large square full of buses. They were in Ven-

ice at last, and yet this didn't look magical at all. The Piazzala Roma looked very much like any other busy transport hub in any busy city.

People were everywhere. They spilled off the large orange buses that seemed to arrive and leave every few minutes, dragging luggage behind them as they set off on foot, maps in hands; or they queued wearily and waited for the buses to empty so they could clamber inside and head back to the mainland.

The driver started unloading the bags. Ruby took her rucksack from the boot before this one had a chance to be snooty about it, then reached inside and unclipped Sofia from her car seat. The little girl grizzled softly as she clung round Ruby's neck. They walked a short distance to a waiting motor launch on the side of a nearby canal. But Ruby was too busy trying to work out if the sticky substance Sofia had just wiped onto her neck was tears or snot to really pay attention. The boat driver nodded a greeting to Max, and then started up the engine.

For the next few minutes they took a dizzying route through the narrow canals—the equivalent of back streets, she supposed—and she could hardly see more than whitewashed or brick walls, oddly placed ornate windows high up in them, or the odd washing line strung with underwear, waving like unconventional bunting above their heads. But then they emerged onto the Grand Canal and Ruby was glad she was sitting down, with Sofia's weight anchoring her to her seat in the back of the boat, because she surely would have thumped down onto her backside if she'd been standing up.

She'd never seen so many beautiful buildings in one place. All were ornately decorated with arches and windows and balconies. Some were crested with intricate crenellations that reminded her of royal icing fit for a wedding cake. Others were the most beautiful colours, the old stone

worn and warmed by both the salt of the lagoon water that
lapped at their bases and the soft sun dangling effortlessly
in a misty sky.

She was still sitting there with her mouth open when the
boat puttered to a stop outside a grand-looking palazzo. Instantly, two uniformed men dashed out of an ornate wooden
door and onto the small, private landing stage, complete
with the red-and-white-striped poles, and collected their
bags and helped them from the boat. One tried to relieve
Ruby of Sofia, but the little girl wouldn't have it. She clung
so hard to Ruby's neck that Ruby almost choked. She had
to make do with letting one of the men steady her as she
clambered, a little off balance, onto the small stone jetty.

Ruby looked up. The building was very elegant. Traditional Venetian style, its tall windows topped with almost
church-like stonework. Surely nobody real could live anywhere quite so beautiful?

Max must have decided she was dawdling, because he
huffed something and turned.

She shook her head slightly. 'Your mother lives *here*?'

He thought she was being slow again. She could tell by
the way he was looking at her, a weary sense of disbelief
on his features. 'Of course my mother doesn't live here.
It's a hotel.'

Maybe it was because she was tired and Sofia felt like
a lead weight, or maybe it was because this had probably
been the strangest day of her life so far, but she bristled.
'You said we were taking Sofia to see your mother. You
didn't say anything about a hotel.'

'Didn't I?'

'No, you didn't,' she said darkly, and then muttered
under her breath, '*Details*, Mr Martin.'

He waited until they had walked through the lobby and
were whooshing upwards in a shiny mirrored lift before
he spoke again. 'This is the Lagoon Palace Hotel. Sofia is

tired.' He nodded in her direction, where the child was still clamped onto Ruby's shoulder like an oversized limpet. It was the first time he'd even given a hint he'd remembered his niece existed since she'd taken over. And, consequently, the fact he'd even noticed Sofia was exhausted took Ruby by surprise. 'It'll be a lot less fuss if we settle in here this evening and go and see my mother in the morning.'

Ruby opened her mouth to ask why, then shut it again. A flicker of a look had passed across his features, tensing his jaw and setting his shoulders. She was only too well acquainted with that look. Some people rushed into their parents' arms after a separation, but other people? Well, sometimes they needed a chance to mentally prepare themselves.

She just hadn't expected Max Martin, who seemed to have life buttoned up and marching to his tune, to be one of her fellow throng.

The inside of the Lagoon Palace was a surprise. Ruby had expected it to be full of ornate furniture, antiques and brocade, but the style was a mix of classic and contemporary. The original features of the building were intact, such as the tall marble fireplaces, the plasterwork and painted ceilings, but the decor was modern, with furnishings in bold, bright colours and rich textures.

The suite Max had booked had a main living area overlooking the Grand Canal and a bedroom on either side. A low, modern sofa in cherry-red velvet faced the windows and two matching armchairs sat at right angles. The end tables were a funky organic shape and the walls were the same colour as the furnishings. Other than that it was all dark wood and pale creamy marble.

Ruby stood in the middle of the living area, mouth open, taking it all in. 'I was expecting something a little more... traditional,' she said to Max as she dropped her rucksack on the floor and let Sofia down from where she'd been carrying her. Sofia instantly thrust her arms upwards, demanding to be picked up again.

Ruby sighed and did as commanded. She needed a moment to get her bearings and having a wailing child wouldn't help. So far she'd felt totally at sea, and she had no idea whether she was looking after Sofia the right way. For all she knew, she could be mentally scarring the child for life.

Her uncle might not have noticed, but she needed to start acting, and thinking, like a real nanny. Tomorrow they'd be meeting Sofia's grandmother, and, if she was anything like her son, she'd be sharp as a tack, and she definitely wouldn't be oblivious to Ruby's shortcomings. The last thing she wanted was to lose this job before it had even started.

'I don't like clutter,' Max said. He took a moment to look around the suite, as if he hadn't really taken it all in before. 'While it's not exactly minimalist, it's as unfussy as this city gets.'

Sofia began to grizzle again, so Ruby carried her across to one of the bedroom doors and looked inside. There was a huge bed, with a sofa with burnt orange velvet cushions at the foot, and large windows draped in the same heavy fabric. Obviously the boss's room. She retreated and checked the door on the opposite side of the living area. It led to a spacious room with twin beds, decorated in brown and cream with colourful abstract prints on the walls. She assumed she'd be sharing with Sofia, at least for tonight.

She was relieved to see each room had its own en suite. It was odd, this nannying lark. Being part of a family, but not really being part of a family. There were obviously boundaries, which helped both family and employee, but Ruby had no idea where to draw those lines. Still, she expected that sharing a bathroom, trying to brush your teeth in the sink at the same time as your pyjama-clad boss, was probably a step too far.

Not that she wanted to see Max Martin in his pyjamas, of course.

For some reason that thought made her cheeks heat, and she distracted herself by lugging Sofia back into the living room, where her new boss was busy muttering to himself as he tried to hook up his laptop at a dark, stylish wooden desk tucked into the corner between his bedroom door and the windows.

'I'm going to put Sofia to bed now,' she told him. 'She ate on the plane, and she's clearly dog-tired.'

Max just grunted from where he had his head under the desk, then backed out and stood up. He looked at Sofia, but didn't move towards them.

'Come on, sweetie,' Ruby cooed. 'Say night-night to Uncle Max.'

Sofia just clung on tighter. Eventually he walked towards them and placed an awkward kiss on the top of the little girl's head. Ruby tried not to notice the smell of his after-shave or the way the air seemed to ripple around her when he came near, and then she quickly scurried away and got Sofia ready for bed.

She put Sofia to bed in one of the twin beds in their room. In the bag her mother had packed for her, Ruby found a number of changes of clothes, the usual toiletries, a few books and a rather over-loved stuffed rabbit.

'Want Mamma,' the little girl sniffed as Ruby helped her into her pyjamas.

Ruby's heart lurched. She knew exactly how that felt, even though her separation from her mother was perma-nent and at least Sofia would see hers again very soon. But at this age, it must feel like an eternity.

She picked Sofia up and sat her on her lap, held her close, and pulled out a book to read, partly as part of the bedtime ritual, but partly to distract the child from missing her mother. She also gave her the rabbit. Sofia grabbed on to the toy gratefully and instantly stuck her thumb in her mouth and closed her eyes, giving out one last shuddering breath before going limp in Ruby's arms.

Not even enough energy for a bedtime story. Poor little thing.

Ruby put the book on the bedside table and slid Sofia under the covers before turning out the light.

Ruby knew what it felt like to be carted from place to place, often not knowing where you were or who you'd been left with. She was tempted to reach across and smooth a dark curl away from Sofia's forehead, but she kept her hand in her lap.

Usually, she threw herself into each new job with gusto, immersing herself completely in it, but she had a feeling it would be a bad idea for a travelling nanny. This was a two-week job at most. She couldn't get too attached. Mustn't. So she just sat on the edge of the bed watching Sofia's tiny chest rise and fall for what seemed like ages.

When she was sure her charge was soundly asleep, and she wouldn't disturb her by moving, she crept out and closed the bedroom door softly behind her. The living room of the suite was steeped in silence and the large gurgle her stomach produced as she tiptoed towards the sofa seemed to echo up to the high ceilings. It was dark now, and the heavy red curtains were drawn, blocking out any view of the canal. Ruby longed to go and fling them open, but she supposed it wasn't her choice. If her boss wanted to shut himself away from the outside world, from all that beauty and magnificence, then that was his decision.

She could hear her employer through his open bedroom door, in a one-sided conversation, talking in clipped, hushed tones. She glanced over at the desk, where he'd already made himself quite at home. The surface was covered in sheets of paper and printouts, and a laptop was silently displaying a company name that floated round the screen.

Martin & Martin.

Ruby changed direction and wandered over to take a better look. Amongst the printed-out emails and neat handwritten notes there were also half-rolled architectural plans—for something very big and very grand, by the looks of it.

So Max Martin was an architect. She could see how that suited him. He was possibly the most rigid man she'd ever met. Anything he built would probably last for centuries.

She couldn't help peering over the plans to get a better look at the writing on the bottom corner of the sheet.

The National Institute of Fine Art.

Wow. That was one of her favourite places to hang out in London on a rainy afternoon. And she'd seen a display last time she'd visited about plans for a new wing and a way to cover the existing courtyard to provide a central hub for the gallery's three other wings.

Max's voice grew louder and Ruby scuttled away from the desk. She'd just reached the centre of the room when he emerged from his bedroom, mobile phone pressed to his ear. She did a good job of trying not to listen, pretending to flick through a magazine she'd grabbed from the coffee table instead, but, even though she was trying to keep her nose to herself, it was obvious that Max was the front-runner for the institute's new wing, but the clients had reservations.

She finished flipping through the glossy fashion mag and put it back down on the table. To be honest, she wasn't sure what to do now. Did being Sofia's nanny mean she just had to hole herself up in the bedroom with her, never to be seen or heard without child in tow? Or was she allowed to mingle with other members of the family? Seeing as this was her first experience of being a nanny she had absolutely no clue, and seeing as this was Max's first experience of hiring one—even if he had been the kind of person to dole out information without the use of thumb-screws—he probably didn't know, either.

He turned and strode towards her, frowning, listening intently to whoever was on the other end of the phone.

Ruby looked up at him, expecting maybe a nod, or even a blink of recognition as he passed by, but she got none. It was as if he'd totally forgotten she existed. So she became more comfortable studying him. He looked tired, she thought as she watched him pace first in one direction and then another, always marking out straight lines with precise angles. The top button of his shirt was undone and his tie was nowhere to be seen.

It was odd. All day so far, he'd just seemed like a force of nature—albeit in a pristine suit—and now that just the tiniest part of that armour had been discarded she was suddenly confronted by the fact he was a man. And a rather attractive one at that.

His dark hair was short but not severe, and now she knew he had Italian blood in him, she could see it in the set of his eyes and his long, straight nose. The mouth, however, was totally British, tightly drawn in, jaw tense as he grimaced at some unwelcome news and hung up on the caller without saying goodbye. He brought the phone down from his ear and stared at it so hard that Ruby thought it might burst into flames.

That was when he looked up and spotted her sitting where she'd been for the last ten minutes, and it took him by total surprise. She allowed her lips to curve into the barest of smiles and held his gaze. For some reason she liked the fact her presence sometimes ruffled him.

He shoved his phone back in his pocket. 'Is there anything you need?'

His tone wasn't harsh, just practical.

'I was wondering what to do about food.' Her stomach growled again, just to underline the fact. She refused to blush.

He had only just stopped frowning at his phone call, and now his features crumpled back into the same expression, as if he'd forgotten hunger was an option for him, and he was taking time to remember what the sensation was like. Eventually, he indicated a menu on the sideboard. 'Have what you want sent up.'

Ruby nodded. She'd been hoping he'd say that. 'Do you want anything while I'm ordering?'

'No…' His gaze drifted towards the array of papers on the desk and he was drawn magnetically to it. He picked up a sheet and started reading a page of dense text.

Ruby wasn't quite sure if he'd finished saying everything he'd been going to say, but she guessed he'd forgotten he'd actually started talking, so she went and fetched the menu. When she ordered her club sandwich she did it discreetly, so as not to disturb him, and just before she put the phone down she quietly ordered another. He hadn't touched the food on the plane, and she hadn't seen him eat anything all afternoon. He had to get hungry some time, didn't he?

If he did, he showed no sign of it. His eyes stayed on his papers while his fingers rapped out email after email on his laptop. She watched him out of the corner of her eye, slightly fascinated. He was so focused, so intense. He seemed to have an innate sense of confidence in his own ability to do what needed to be done.

To be honest, she was a little jealous.

She'd tried a number of jobs since dropping out of university but none of them had stuck. She wanted what Max had. A purpose. No, a calling. A sense of who she was in this world and what she was supposed to be doing while she was here.

A knock on the door a few minutes later heralded the

arrival of her dinner. She opened the door and tipped the room-service guy, then wheeled the little trolley closer to the sofa.

What she needed to do right now was stuff her face with her sandwich, before her stomach climbed up her throat and came to get it. That was the problem, maybe. She could always see the step that was right in front of her, the immediate details—like taking the job this afternoon—but when it came to the 'big picture' of her life it was always fuzzy and a bit out of focus.

She poured a glass of red wine from a bottle she'd ordered to go along with the food and took it, and the other sandwich, over to her boss. He didn't look up, so she cleared a little space at the corner of papers and put the plate down. The wine, however, was more tricky. The last thing she wanted to do was put it where he'd knock it over. Eventually, she just coughed lightly, and he looked up.

'Here,' she said, handing him the glass. 'You looked like you could do with this.'

For a moment he looked as if he was going to argue, but then he looked longingly at the glass of Pinot Noir and took it from her. As he did, just the very tips of their fingers brushed together.

'Thank you,' he said.

Ruby held her breath, then backed away silently. Her face felt hot and she had the sudden urge to babble. She always did that when she was flustered or nervous, and suddenly she was both.

Max, however, didn't notice. It was obvious he was as cool and calm and focused as he'd always been. He put the glass down near the back of the desk and carried on typing the email he'd been working on. Her cheeks flushed, Ruby retreated to the far end of the large sofa and ate her sandwich in silence.

When she'd finished her dinner, she stood up and replaced the empty plate on the trolley, then she hovered for a moment. He hadn't touched either the food or the wine. She wanted to say something, but she didn't know what; then she interrupted herself with a yawn. It was almost ten and it had been a long day. Maybe she should just go and get ready for bed.

Still, as she made her way towards her bedroom door she lingered, fingers on the handle, her eyes drawn to the silent figure hunched over his laptop in the corner. It was a long while before she pressed down on the metal fixture and pushed the door open.

As she got undressed in the semi-dark, careful not to wake the sleeping child, she thought about Max and all his quiet dedication and commitment. Maybe he was rubbing off on her, because suddenly she wanted to rise to the challenge in front of her.

She knew it seemed as if she'd come by this job almost by accident, but maybe that was just fate sending her a big, flashing neon sign? *This way, Ruby...* Maybe being a nanny was what she was meant to do. Hadn't Max said she was exactly what he needed? And Sofia already seemed very attached to her.

She held her breath as she slid in between the cool cotton sheets and pulled the covers up over her chest. Maybe this was her calling. Who knew? But for the next week— possibly two—she'd have her chance to find out.

Max looked up from his plans and papers and noticed a club sandwich sitting on the edge of the desk. How long had that been there? His stomach growled and he reached for it and devoured it in record time.

Ruby must have put it there. He frowned. Something about that felt wrong.

And not just because taking care of him wasn't part of her job description. He just wasn't used to being taken care of full stop, mainly because he'd carefully structured his life so he was totally self-sufficient. He didn't need anyone to look after him. He didn't need anyone, at all. And that was just as well. While his father had been his rock, he hadn't been the touchy-feely sort, and work had always kept him away from home for long hours. And his mother...

Well, he hadn't had a mother's influence in his life since he'd been a teenager, and even before the divorce things had been...explosive...at home.

A rush of memories rolled over him. He tried to hold them at bay, but there were too many, coming too fast, like a giant wave breaching a sea wall in a storm. That wall had held fast for so many years. He didn't know why it was crumbling now, only that it was. He rubbed his eyes and stood up, paced across the living room of the suite in an effort to escape it.

This was why he hated this city. It was too old, full of too much history. Somehow the past—anyone's past—weighed too heavily here.

He shook his head and reached for the half-drunk bottle of wine on the room-service trolley and went to refill his glass. The Pinot had been perfect, rich and soothing. Just what he'd needed.

He didn't want to revisit any of those memories. Not even the good ones. Yes, his mother had been wonderful when she'd been happy—warm, loving, such fun—but the tail end of his parents' marriage had been anything *but* happy. Those good times were now superimposed with her loud and expressive fits of rage, the kind only an Italian woman knew how to give, and his father's silent and stoic sternness, as he refused to be baited, to be drawn into the game. Sometimes the one-sided fights had gone on for days.

He took another slug of wine and tried to unclench his shoulder muscles.

His relationship with his mother had never been good,

not since the day she'd left the family home in a taxi and a cloud of her own perfume. He hadn't spoken to her in at least a year, and hadn't seen her for more than three.

He looked down at his glass and noticed he'd polished it off without realising. There was still another left in the bottle....

No. He put his glass down on the desk and switched off his laptop. No more for tonight. Because if there was one thing he was certain of, it was that he'd need a clear head to deal with his mother come morning.

CHAPTER FOUR

MAX WALKED OUT of his bedroom then stopped, completely arrested by the sight in front of him. *What the heck?*

And it wasn't the spray of cereal hoops all over the coffee table or the splash of milk threatening to drip off the edge. Nor was it the sight of his niece, sitting cross-legged on the carpet and eating a pastry, no sign of a tantrum in sight. No, it was the fact that the nanny he'd hired yesterday bore no resemblance to the one who was busily trying to erase the evidence of what had obviously been a rather messy breakfast session.

She froze when she heard him walk in, then turned around. Her gaze drifted to the mess in the middle of the room. 'Sofia doesn't like cereal, apparently,' she explained calmly. 'And she felt the need to demonstrate that with considerable gusto.'

He blinked and looked again.

The voice was right. And the attitude. But this looked like a different girl.... No—woman. This one was definitely a woman.

Gone was the slightly hippy-looking patchwork scarecrow from the day before, to be replaced by someone in a bright red fifties dress covered in big cartoon strawberries. With the full skirt and the little black shoes and the short hair swept from her face, she looked like a psychedelic version of Audrey Hepburn.

Hair! That was it!

He looked again. The purple streaks were still there, just not as apparent in this neater style. Good. For a moment there, he'd thought he'd been having a particularly vivid dream.

'Good morning,' he finally managed to mutter.

She raised her eyebrows.

Max covered up the fact that the sight of all those strawberries had made him momentarily forget her name by launching in with something she'd like—details. 'After breakfast we're going to visit Sofia's grandmother.' He paused and looked at the slightly milk-drenched, pastry-flake-covered child in front of him. 'Would you be able to get her looking presentable by ten?'

The nanny nodded. 'I think so.'

'Good.' Max felt his stomach unclench. 'My mother is not someone who tolerates an untidy appearance.' And then he turned to go and fire up his laptop, but he could have sworn he heard her mutter, *'What a shocker...'* under her breath.

The water taxi slowed outside a large palazzo with its own landing stage leading up to a heavy front door. They'd travelled for maybe fifteen minutes, leaving the Grand Canal behind and heading into the Castello district of the city.

The building was almost as large at the hotel they'd just left, but where its plaster had been pristine and smooth, this palace was looking a little more tired round the edges. Green slime coated the walls at the waterline, indicating the height of the high tide. Some of the pink plasterwork had peeled off at the bottom of the structure leaving an undulating wave of bare bricks showing.

There were grilles over the ground-floor windows, and the plaster was peeling away there, too, but up above there were the most wonderful stone balcony and window boxes overflowing with ivy and white flowers. The overall effect was like that of a grand old lady who'd had a fabulous time at the ball but had now sat down, a little tired and flustered, to compose herself.

Ruby's eyes were wide as she clung onto Sofia to stop her scrambling ashore before the boat was properly secured.

Max must have read her mind. 'This is Ca' Damiani and, yes, my mother lives here. But she doesn't occupy the whole thing, just the *piano nobile*.'

Ruby nodded, even though she had no idea what that meant.

'A lot of these grand old buildings have been split up into apartments,' he explained as he hopped from the boat and offered to take Sofia from her. 'In buildings like these the floor above ground level was the prime spot, where the grandest rooms of the house were situated—the stage for all the family's dramas.' He sighed. 'And there's nothing my mother likes more than a grand drama.'

His voice was neutral, expressionless even, but she could see the tension in his jaw, the way the air around him seemed heavy and tense. This was not a joyful home-coming, not one bit.

Ruby clambered out of the boat and reached for Sofia's hand, and then the three of them together walked off the dock and up to a double door with a large and tarnished brass knocker. Ruby swallowed as Max lifted it. When it fell the noise rang out like a gunshot, and she jumped. She did her best not to fidget as they waited.

After a short wait the door swung open. Ruby would have expected it to creak, from the age of it, but it was as silent as a rush of air. The woman who was standing there was also something of a surprise. Ruby had expected her to be tall and dark, like Max, but she was petite and her blond hair was artfully swept into a twist at the back of her head. She wore a suit with a dusky pink jacket and skirt and, just like every other Italian woman Ruby had ever met, carried with her an innate sense of confidence in her own style. Not a hair on her head was out of place.

Ruby looked down at her strawberry-patterned skirt. She'd chosen her best vintage dress for today in an attempt to emulate that effortless style, but now she feared she just looked like a sideshow freak instead of *la bella figura*. She held back, hiding herself a little behind Max's much larger frame.

His mother looked at him for a long moment.

No, Ruby thought, she didn't just look. She drank him in.

'Well, you have finally come, Massimo,' she said in Italian, her voice hoarse.

'I've told you I prefer Max,' he replied in English. 'And it was an emergency. Gia needed me. What else could I do? I wasn't going to run out on her, on my family, because things got a little difficult.'

The words hung between them like an accusation. Ruby saw the older woman pale, but then she drew herself taller.

'Oh, I know that it is not on my account that you are here,' she said crisply. 'As for the other matter, I named you, Massimo, so I shall call you what I like.' She glanced down and her face broke into a wide and warm smile. 'Darling child! Come here to your *nonna*!'

Sofia hesitated for a second, then allowed herself to be picked up and held. Ruby guessed that Max's sister must be a more frequent visitor here than he was. After a couple of moments Sofia was smiling and using her chubby fingers to explore the gold chain and pendant around her grandmother's neck. She seemed totally at ease.

When she'd finished fussing over her granddaughter, Max's mother lifted her head and looked at him. 'You'd better come inside.'

She retreated into a large hallway with a diamond-tiled floor and rough brick walls. There were hints of the plaster that had once covered them, and most of the moulded ceilings were intact. However, instead of seeming tumble-down, it just made the palazzo's ground floor seem grand and ancient. There were a few console tables and antiques, and a rather imposing staircase with swirling wrought iron banisters curved upwards to the first floor.

His mother started making her way up the staircase, but when she turned the corner and realised there was an extra body still following them, and it wasn't just some-one who'd helped them unload from the boat, she stopped and walked back down to where Ruby was on the floor, ballet-slippered foot hovering above the bottom step, and let Sofia slide from her embrace.

'And who do we have here?' she asked, looking Ruby up and down with interest. Ruby's heart thudded inside her ribcage. Not the sort of girl who usually trailed around after her son, probably. Well, almost definitely.

'This is Sofia's nanny,' Max said, this time joining his mother in her native language. 'I hired her especially for the trip.'

'Ruby Lange,' Ruby said and offered her hand, hoping it wasn't sticky, and then continued in her best Italian, 'It's lovely to meet you.'

Max's mother just turned and stared at her son, tears filling her eyes, and then she set off up the staircase again, this time at speed, her heels clicking against the stone. 'You have insulted me, Massimo! Of all the things you could have done!'

Max hurried up the stairs after his mother. 'I've done nothing of the sort. You're making no sense at all.'

He'd reverted to English. Which was a pity, because when he spoke Italian he sounded like a different man. Oh, the depth and tone of the voice were the same, but it had sounded richer, warmer. As if it belonged to a man capable of the same passion and drama as the woman he was chasing up the stairs.

Ruby turned to Sofia, who was looking up the staircase after her uncle and grandmother. Once again, she'd been forgotten. Ruby wanted to pull her up into her arms and hug her hard. She knew what it was like to always be left behind, to always be the complication that stopped the adults in your life from doing what they wanted. 'What do you say, kiddo? Shall we follow the grown-ups?'

Sofia nodded and they made their way up the stairs. It was slow progress. Sofia had to place both feet on a step before moving to the next one. Her little legs just weren't capable of anything else. When they got halfway, Ruby gave up and held out her arms. The little girl quickly clambered up her and let her nanny do the hard work.

Well, that was what she was here for. Or she would be if Signora Martin didn't think she was so much of an insult that she threw Ruby out on her ear. Max hadn't been wrong when he'd mentioned drama, had he?

When she got to the top of the stairs the decor changed. There was wood panelling on the walls and the ceilings were painted in pastel colours with intricate plasterwork patterns. Every few feet there were wall sconces, dripping with crystals. If this explosion of baroque architecture and cluttered antique furniture was what Max had meant when he'd called Venetian style 'fussy', she could see his point.

The 'discussion' was still raging, in a room just off the landing. The space must have been huge, because their voices echoed the same way they would in a church or a museum. His mother's was emotive and loud, Max's steady and even. Ruby was glad her soft shoes didn't make much noise and she crept in the direction of the raised voices, Sofia resting on her hip.

'You're never going to forgive me, are you?' his mother finally said softly.

Ruby crept a little closer. The room had double doors, which were still standing where they'd been flung open, and she peeked at the interior through the gap next to the hinges.

Max's mother closed her eyes and sadness washed over her features. 'That's why you brought the nanny, wasn't it? You think I'm not fit to look after my granddaughter on my own. Was I really such a terrible mother?'

This was getting too personal, Ruby realised. It was time to back away, leave them to it. She'd just have to find somewhere to hide out with Sofia until the whole thing blew over. Surely there must be a kitchen in this place somewhere?

She retreated a couple of steps, but she'd forgotten that she was much less nimble with Sofia increasing her bulk and she knocked into a side table and made the photo frames and lamp on it jangle.

There was silence in the room beyond. Ruby held her breath. A moment later Max appeared in the doorway and motioned for her to come inside. Ruby would rather have drunk a gallon of lagoon water, but she really didn't have much choice. She hoisted Sofia up into a more comfortable position, tipped her chin up and walked into the room.

It was a grand Venetian salon, with a vast honey-coloured marble fireplace and trompe l'oeil pillars and mouldings painted on the walls in matching tones, with mythic scenes on the walls in between. A row of arched windows leading onto a stone balcony dominated the opposite side of the room, and three large green sofas were arranged in a C-shape, facing them. But the sight that Ruby was most interested in was the stiff figure in the pink suit standing in the middle of the room.

'Ruby isn't here to usurp you, Mamma. I hired her partly to help me bring Sofia over here with minimum fuss, but also because I thought she could help you. Why should you have to cancel your social engagements, alter your plans, for the next couple of weeks because of Gia's work problems?'

The other woman's features softened a little, and she looked a little ashamed. She turned to face Ruby and held out her hand. Ruby let Sofia down and the little girl ran to the window to look at a speedboat that had just shot down the medium-sized canal beyond.

'Serafina Martin.' She smiled warmly and shook Ruby's hand firmly but very briefly. 'But everybody calls me Fina. I apologise most sincerely for not welcoming you to Ca' Damiani when you first arrived, but I do so now.'

Ruby replied in her best Italian. 'Thank you, Signora Martin, for your welcome and for opening your home to me, if you do decide you could do with my help. I'm afraid this is my first job as a nanny so I've been thrown in at the deep end.' She glanced at Max, who was watching her carefully. 'You'll probably have to help me more than I'll help you.'

A small flicker of approval, and maybe relief, passed across the other woman's features. Fina tilted her head. 'Your Italian is very good.'

Ruby kept her smile demure. 'Thank you.'

Fina's gaze swept over her dress and then up to her head. 'But your hair is not. Purple?'

She shrugged. 'I like it.'

For the longest moment Fina didn't move, didn't say anything. She didn't even blink, but then she smiled. It started in her eyes and moved to just lift the corners of her mouth. '*Bene.* What do I know? I am old and out of touch, probably, and I like a woman who follows her own path.' And then she turned and swept out of the room. 'Come, Massimo! We have to decide what you are going to do about this child.'

Max stared at his mother. 'What do you mean you want me to stay here, too?'

That hadn't been the plan at all. The reason he'd brought

Sofia here was because now was definitely not the moment to take an impromptu holiday. He couldn't let everything he and his father had worked for slide.

His mother did that infuriating little wave of her hand, suggesting he was making a mountain out of a molehill. 'You made a very good point,' she said airily. 'I do have plans this week, including earning a living. I can't take time off at this short notice.'

Max's jaw dropped. 'You have a *job*?'

She turned her head to look at him. 'Why is that so hard to believe? Yes, I have a job. I work for a real estate company in the mornings, helping them dress and present their luxury properties.'

He shook his head, hardly able to believe it.

'You are straying from the point, Massimo. It is not important where I work, but how we are going to do the best for Sofia.'

He frowned. 'I know that, Mamma. That's why I came to you in the first place. It just isn't possible to keep her in London with me. There's a work issue that's at a very crucial point and I can't give her the time and attention she deserves.'

'You know I adore having Sofia with me, but do you think I keep this place running because money falls from the sky? I also have urgent work to do.'

He shot a glance across at his travelling nanny. She was kneeling on the carpet, helping Sofia build a house out of colourful blocks. Max didn't know where they'd come from. His mother must have had them stashed away somewhere. 'But that's why I brought Ruby.' He'd thought of everything, made it simple and easy. Why was his mother turning this into a problem when there was none?

'The poor child is upset and away from her mother. When I'm not here, she needs to be with someone she knows.'

She looked the picture of innocence, perched on the edge of a green damask sofa. The high windows let in the soft light of the May morning, basking her in an almost saintly glow.

'But she doesn't know me, either.'

His mother frowned. 'I thought Gia had said that you were in regular contact now.'

'We text, mainly,' he mumbled. 'And she comes into the city to have lunch every couple of months, but she doesn't usually bring Sofia with her.'

He rather suspected she deliberately chose the days Sofia was at nursery, so she could come up to town and have a few hours to herself. She very kindly always picked the best places, and always let her brother pay.

'Texting is not communicating! It is not the same as a smile or a hug or a warm word. One cannot build relationships through one's phone.'

He shrugged and his mother did another one of her famous hand gestures. Not the little elegant hand-flap, this one. Both arms flew above her head and she stood up and walked over to stare out of the windows onto the canal below. 'Then this is the perfect opportunity for you to get to know her. You really should. She is your only niece, after all.'

If that wasn't an example of his mother's own brand of circular logic, he didn't know what was.

'But she cries every time I look at her,' he said, more than a little exasperated. 'I try to talk nicely to her but it doesn't seem to make any difference. I'd stay if it were different, but it's hardly the best thing for Sofia to leave her with me on my own if that's the case.'

'But you won't be on your own,' his mother said, far too silkily for his liking. 'You'll have Ruby.'

They both transferred their gazes to the travelling nanny. Ruby, who must have sensed two pairs of eyes on her, stopped what she was doing and looked up at them from under her fringe. Max had a lightning stab of revelation. Ruby had already proved very useful when it had come to Sofia, perhaps she could be more useful still. Perhaps he could enlist her as an ally. He sent her a silent message with his eyes.

Ruby's lips twitched. 'It's true,' she said, looking at his mother. 'She does cry most of the time when she's near him. They don't know each other at all. He's not even sure how old she is.'

His mother reached across and slapped his leg. Quite hard, actually. 'Massimo! Honestly!'

She turned to look at Ruby, and Max had the feeling he was being pointedly ignored for the moment. 'She'll be three in a month,' his mother said in Italian, and then she and Ruby had a brief exchange about when Sofia's birthday was and what sort of things she liked to do. He was quite surprised at how good the nanny's Italian was, to be honest. He hadn't even known she spoke it. Just went to show his instincts about her had been right, even if she did make each day look as if she'd raided a different fancy dress shop.

However, when Ruby and his mother started getting into what time was bedtime and favourite snacks, he decided that enough was enough. He stood up and walked closer to them. 'Can we just get back to the matter in hand?' he said, maybe a little abruptly.

Both women stopped talking and looked at him. They wore identical expressions. Max had the horrible sinking feeling that maybe he'd been right about Ruby being a good ally. He just wasn't sure she was his.

'I need to know this kind of stuff, actually,' she told him. 'And you weren't much help.'

Details.

He could almost hear Ruby's mental whisper that followed.

That was enough to set his mother throwing her hands in the air again. When she'd calmed herself down by walking over to the fireplace and back again, she fixed him with a determined expression. Max knew that look. It meant she'd made up her mind about something, and budging her from that viewpoint was going to be about as easy as asking the whole of Venice to pick up her skirts and move a little further out into the lagoon.

'I have made a decision,' she announced. 'I would like nothing more than to have my lovely granddaughter here for a visit.'

He let out a breath he hadn't been aware he'd been holding. 'Thank you, Mamma.'

His mother drew herself up and put on her most regal air. 'But I will allow it on one condition.'

What?

'I won't take Sofia unless you stay, too,' his mother told him, folding her arms across her chest. 'You cannot live your life cloistered away in that stuffy office of yours, communicating to those you love through bits of technology. It's high time you lived up to your family responsibilities, Massimo.'

Max almost choked. *His* family responsibilities? That was rich!

He opened his mouth to argue, but didn't get very far. He became aware of a small but insistent tugging on the left leg of his trousers and looked down to find his niece standing there. She was trying to pull him in the direction of the pile of blocks on the rug near the fireplace.

His mother just smiled at him. 'She's not crying now, my darling son, and you said you'd stay if she stopped.' She looked over at her granddaughter. Warmth and joy flared in her eyes. 'It seems I am not the only one who has made my mind up about this—Sofia has, too.'

CHAPTER FIVE

MAX AND HIS MOTHER had had a long conversation out on the balcony, ironing out the details of her ultimatum. When they returned, Fina knelt down on the carpet beside Ruby and Sofia and joined in their game of piling up bricks into tall towers for Sofia to knock down again.

Fina smiled and laughed, totally absorbed in her granddaughter, while her son stood, towering and silent on the fringes of the room. Ruby shot him a sideways look and found him staring back at her. She swallowed. She felt a little guilty that she'd ended up unwittingly providing Fina with leverage to use against him, but not guilty enough to regret she'd done it.

Despite Fina's superior manner and haughty words, Ruby had seen the way she'd looked at Max. That was a mother hungry for her son's company and, just like a child who'd settle for negative attention when they couldn't get praise, in desperation she'd taken whatever she could get.

Funnily, Ruby warmed to Fina for that. She wished her own father looked at her that way sometimes, but she'd never once got the impression from him that he was hungry for more of her company. No, he'd seemed perfectly content to push her out of the nest at an early age.

'I'd better go and check out of the hotel and get our bags,' Max finally growled.

Ruby stood up and brushed her skirt down. 'I'll help you.' That was the least she could do.

He scowled at her, indicating she'd done enough already. She ignored it and followed him as he headed out of the door. She had to trot to keep up with him as he marched down the corridor and down the sweeping staircase.

'So, what's going on?' she finally asked. 'I presume we're staying, for a short while, at least.'

Max sighed. 'My mother and I have come to an…arrangement.' He shuddered slightly, as if the idea of compromise was an abhorrent concept.

He was doing it again: failing to fill her in on the important stuff. 'Which is?'

Max stopped on the stairs and turned, hands still in pockets. 'My mother has agreed she will care for Sofia when she's free, with your help, of course, but only if I stay for a minimum of seven days. Otherwise she's happy to escort us all to the airport where we can catch the next plane back to London.'

Ruby's face crumpled into a bemused smile. 'She'd really do that?'

He grunted and set off again. 'You have no idea how stubborn my mother can be when she puts her mind to it.'

Ruby didn't reply to that. The only response that came to mind was that maybe he was more like his mother than he realised, and she'd got herself into enough trouble already with him this morning.

She studied the back of his head carefully as she followed him down the stairs. Did he really not get that this ultimatum had nothing to do with his sister's childcare issues and everything to do with Fina wanting to repair the gaping breach in her family? Ruby had also gone to extreme lengths to get just a crumb of her father's attention in her teenage years, and she understood completely why Fina had done it.

'And what about the Institute of Fine Art? The plans?'

He turned as he reached the ground floor, looking surprised.

'Couldn't help overhearing you on the phone last night. And then there are the drawings littered all over the suite...'

Max ran a hand through his hair as they emerged from the palazzo onto the dock and wearily took in the grand and crumbling buildings around them. 'I'm in Venice...' he said, and she sensed he was quoting his mother verbatim. 'The most beautiful city in the world. What better inspiration could I have?'

Thankfully, Max discovered his mother hadn't disposed of the little motor launch that had once been his grandfather's. By the looks of it, she'd kept it in immaculate condition. The varnish wasn't peeling and the navy paint on the sides was fresh and thick. He jumped in, stood behind the small windscreen and slid the key into the ignition to start it up. Ruby, unmissable in that damn strawberry dress, clambered in hesitantly then plopped down on the seat at the back. He put the boat in gear and set off through some of the narrower canals.

He'd spent every summer here as a boy, even before his parents' divorce, and it amazed him that, even though he hadn't driven a boat here in more than two decades, the old routes and back-doubles came to him easily. His passenger didn't say much. She spent most of the journey to the Lagoon Palace looking up at the tall buildings, her mouth slightly open, eyes wide. It was only when they moored the boat a short distance from the hotel's private jetty, where only the dedicated shuttles from the bus and train stations were allowed to dock, that Ruby began to talk again.

'So, what are the finer points of your agreement with your mother? You can't have spent that long arguing about it without going into details.'

He sighed as he led her up a narrow cobbled *calle* between buildings and out onto a wider one that led to the foot entrance of the hotel. He'd known he wouldn't be able to win his mother over to his plan from the moment he'd stepped out onto the balcony with her. He had, however, managed to broker a deal that meant his stay here would be on his terms.

'I have conceded to spend a couple of hours each morning with Sofia while my mother is at work and to attend a family dinner each evening.' He couldn't help the slight tone of disgust in his voice at the word 'family'.

She kept up pace, slightly behind him. 'And what did she concede?'

'That I should have the rest of the time to work on my design and do my business.'

'Will that do?'

He stared straight ahead and looked grim. 'It will have to.' As they entered the hotel through the street entrance he sighed. 'What's the alternative? At least this way I'm only tied up for seven days, instead of two weeks or more in a totally unsuitable apartment. Aside from the fact you'd be trying to stop Sofia breaking her neck every moment of the day, I've only got one bedroom.'

Ruby swallowed and her face grew just a little closer to the shade of her dress. 'No, I can see that would be a...' she swallowed again '...problem.'

'I don't know why she does these things. For some reason my mother isn't happy unless she's creating havoc in everyone else's lives as well as her own.' He shook his head.

They'd arrived at the suite now, and the next quarter of an hour was spent packing up their belongings. And then they checked out and headed back to the boat. Max carried his bag, his laptop case and his document tube, and she took care of her own rucksack and Sofia's bag.

He decided to take a less direct, but maybe more scenic,

route back. If she'd liked the little crumbling buildings of
the back canals, she'd love some of the palazzos on the
Grand Canal. He pointed a few of them out to her, telling
her a few of the famous stories connected with them, many
of which he guessed had been embellished over time with
a healthy drop of the Venetian love for drama and spectacle. She chatted back, asking him questions and laughing
at the more ridiculous tales, so it kind of took him by surprise when she suddenly said, 'I don't think she's done this
to cause trouble, you know. I think she just wants to spend
time with you and, yes, she's gone about it a back to front
kind of way, but she's not asking anything terrible, is she?'

He didn't say anything. Just stared straight ahead. Suddenly he didn't feel like playing tour guide any more.

He should have remembered this one was different, that
she wasn't like his employees at the firm, that she liked to
say things she shouldn't and be inquisitive. None of them
had ever dared to comment on his personal life. But then
he'd never given any of them a personal tour of Venice,
either.

He thought about what she'd said and let out a low growl
of a laugh.

'What?' she asked, never one to miss an opportunity to
stick her nose in.

'Now, maybe, my mother seems like that,' he said
gruffly, 'but she's a hypocrite.'

Despite the bustle and noise of the city—the purr of outboard motors, the noise of the seagulls and pigeons and the
ever steady hum of a million tourists' exclamations—the
air around them went very still. He'd shocked her into silence, had he? Well, good.

'She deserted my father and left him broken-hearted. He
never got over it. So don't talk to me about family loyalty.'

He turned to look over his shoulder, wanting some grim
satisfaction in seeing her squirm, but instead he found

her looking at him, her eyes large and warm. He looked away again.

'How old were you when she left?' she asked softly, almost whispering.

He forgot to ask how she'd guessed, too caught up in a sideswipe of memories that left him gripping the steering wheel so hard it burnt his fingers. 'Fourteen,' he answered hoarsely. 'She said she didn't want to disrupt my education, so she took Gia and left me in London.'

There was a hint of uncertainty in her voice this time. 'That was thoughtful, wasn't it?'

He made that same almost animalistic sound that could pass as a laugh again. 'It was an excuse. I'm too like my father, you see. Or I was. He died five months ago.'

There was a shuffling noise behind him. He couldn't resist a quick glance. Now he'd got what he'd wanted. Her cheeks were flushed red and she was looking down at her flat little black ballet pumps.

'Don't get sucked in,' he warned her. 'She's not what she seems. Nothing is what it seems in this city.'

Nothing is what it seems in this city.

Ruby heard the words inside her head as she stood outside the library door.

It was pure Venice, wasn't it? To have a proper room designated as a library in your palazzo, not just a flat-pack bookcase stuffed under the eaves in your poky little attic flat. Max had decided to use it as his office while he was here, and he was inside now. She could hear him tapping away on his laptop keyboard, along with the odd rustle of paper.

Not even you, Max Martin, she thought, as she knocked softly on the door. Or should that be *Massimo*?

All she got in response was a grunt. She took it as an invitation.

Max didn't look up straight away when she pushed the door open and slid inside to stand with her back pressed against the wall, hands tucked behind her. The library was small compared to some of the other rooms in the apartment, but it shared the same high ceilings and leaded windows. Two of the four walls were filled with bookshelves, and Max sat at a desk placed up against the dark green silky wallpaper of one of the other walls.

It had been a whole twenty-four hours since she'd seen him doing exactly the same thing in the hotel suite, but somehow she felt as if she were looking at a completely different man.

She'd thought him a robot, a machine, but she'd seen the bleakness in his eyes when he'd talked about his family that morning. There was a lot more inside there than met the eye. Maybe even a man with true Italian blood coursing through his veins, a man capable of revenge and passion and utter, utter devotion. The fact that the wounds of his childhood still cut deep, that he could neither forgive nor forget, showed he was capable of more than this grey, concrete existence. But like some of the crumbling buildings of this city, all that emotion was all carefully hidden behind a perfectly built façade.

He pressed the enter key with a sense of finality and turned to face her.

'I've just put Sofia to bed, and I wondered if you'd like to go and say goodnight? She's asking for you.'

His chair scraped and he moved to get up. Ruby pushed away from the wall and clasped her hands in front of her. She cleared her throat. 'I have something to say before you go.'

He stopped moving and looked at her.

She inhaled and let it out again. 'I'd like to apologise for what I said earlier. I didn't mean to butt in.'

She'd expected his face to remain expressionless, but she saw a subtle shift in his features, a softening. 'Thank you.'

He made to go forward and her mouth started off again before she could ask herself if it was a good idea or not. 'I know what it's like, you know. My relationship with my father has always been difficult. But I pretend I don't care, that it doesn't get to me. That it shouldn't matter after all these years...but it does.'

She was rambling, she knew she was. But she couldn't seem to shut up.

'So I just wanted to say that I won't comment on your family any more and that I'll try and be a little bit more professional in the future.'

He'd been right. She should keep her nose out. Not in the least because this silent, dedicated man was starting to tug at her heartstrings, but also because she was just the nanny, and getting sucked in definitely wasn't part of her job description.

He nodded and glanced towards the door. 'I'd better go and see Sofia before she falls asleep.' And then he walked down the wide corridor without looking back.

Ruby sagged back against the library wall and looked up. She hadn't noticed before, but painted cherubs were dancing on the ceiling, blowing flutes and twanging harps. For some reason, she got the feeling they were mocking her.

If there was one room Max hated more than any other in his mother's house, it was the dining room. Most people were left speechless when they walked inside for the first time, at least for a few moments, then the exclaiming would begin.

Apparently, his great-grandfather had had a fondness for whimsy, and had commissioned an artist to paint the whole room so it resembled a ruined castle in a shady forest glade. Creepers and vines twined round the doorway and round the fireplace. Low down there were painted stone blocks, making the tumbledown walls, and above, tree trunks and leaves, giving glimpses of rolling fields beyond. It even carried on up onto the ceiling, where larks peered down and a pale sun shone directly above the dining table. It was all just one big lie.

The table only filled a fraction of the vast space, even though it seated twelve. Max sat down at one of the three places laid at one end and scowled as his mother sat at the head and Ruby sat opposite him. He hadn't liked being manoeuvred into this whole arrangement and he wasn't going to pretend he liked it any more than he was going to pretend they were sitting in a real forest glade enjoying the dappled sunshine. He was just going to eat and get out of here. The plans he'd left on the desk only a few minutes ago were already calling to him.

'My family were successful merchants here in Venice for five hundred years,' his mother told Ruby as they tucked into their main course. 'But now I live more simply and rent the other parts of the house out.'

Max saw Ruby's eyes widen at the word 'simply'. As always, his mother had no grip on reality, and no awareness of how other people carried on their lives. He tuned the conversation out. His mother was busy regaling Ruby with stories from the annals of their family history, both triumphant and tragic. He'd heard them a thousand times, anyway, and with each telling the details drifted further and further from the truth.

Then his mother ran out of steam and turned her attention to their guest. Well, not guest…employee. But it was hard to think of Ruby that way as she listened to his mother with rapt attention, eyes bright, laughter ready.

'So, tell me, Ruby, why did you decide to become a nanny?'

Ruby shot a look in his direction before answering. 'Your son offered me a job and I took it.'

Fina absorbed that information for a moment. 'You didn't want to be a nanny before that?'

Ruby shook her head.

'Then what were you?'

Max sat up a little straighter. He hadn't thought to ask her that during their 'interview'. Maybe he should have. And maybe Ruby was annoyingly right about *details* being important on occasion.

Ruby smiled back at his mother. 'Oh, I've been lots of things since I left university.'

He leaned forward and put his fork down. 'What course did you take?'

'Media Studies.'

Max frowned. 'But you don't want to work in that field, despite having the qualification?'

She pulled a face. 'I didn't graduate. It was my father's idea to go.' She shook her head. 'But it really wasn't me.'

His mother shot her a sympathetic look. 'Not everyone works out the right path first time.'

Max snorted. If these dinners had been his mother's plan to soften him up, it was backfiring on her. Every other word she uttered just reminded him of how she'd selfishly betrayed the whole family. She might not have been a Martin by birth, but she'd married into the institution, and if there was one rule the family lived by it was this: loyalty above all else.

If his mother had heard the snort, she ignored it. 'You must have had some interesting jobs,' she said to Ruby, smiling.

Ruby smiled back. 'Oh, I have, and it's been great. I've made jewellery and I worked in a vineyard.'

'In France?' Fina asked.

Ruby shook her head. 'No, in Australia. I did that the year after I left university. And then I just sort of travelled and worked my way back home again. I tended bar

in Singapore, worked on a kibbutz in Israel. I did a stint
in a PR firm, I joined an avant-garde performance company—that was too wacky, even for me—and I've also
busked to earn a crust.'

His mother's eyebrows were practically in her hairline.
'You play an instrument?' she asked, taking the only salvageable thing from that list.

Ruby gave her a hopeful smile. 'I can manage a har-
monica and a bit of tap dancing.'

Lord, help them all! And this was who he'd thought was
exactly what he needed? No wonder his sensible plan was
falling to pieces.

'And will you stay being a nanny after this? Or is it on
to the next thing?' he asked.

She shook her head. 'I don't know. I know this sounds
stupid, but I see the way my father loves his work, and I
want to find something that makes me feel like that.'

His mother leaned forward. 'What does your father do?'

Ruby froze, as if she realised she'd said something she
shouldn't. She looked up at them. 'Oh, he makes nature
programmes.'

'What? Like Patrick Lange?' his mother exclaimed, clap-
ping her hands. 'I loved his series on lemurs! It was fas-
cinating.'

'Something like that,' Ruby mumbled.

Now it was Max's turn to freeze. *Lange?*

'Your father's Patrick Lange?' he asked, hardly able to
keep the surprise from his voice. The man seemed such
a steady kind of guy. Max could hardly believe he had a
daughter like Ruby.

She nodded and returned to eating her pasta.

'How marvellous,' his mother gushed and then the smile
disappeared from her face. 'Oh, I'm so sorry about your
mother, Ruby. It was such a tragedy. She was such a wonderful woman.'

Ruby kept her head down and nodded.

Max racked his brains. There had been a news story… Oh, maybe fifteen years ago? That was it. Martha and Patrick Lange had always presented their nature documentaries together until she'd contracted some tropical disease in a remote location while filming. She'd reassured everyone she was fine, that it was just a touch of flu, and had carried on, reluctant to abandon the trip. By the time they'd realised what it was, and that she'd needed urgent treatment, it had been too late. She'd died in an African hospital a week later.

Max watched Ruby push her pasta around her plate. He knew what it was like to lose a parent, and it had been bad enough in his early thirties. Ruby could have only been… what? Nine or ten?

'Anyway,' Ruby suddenly said, lifting her head and smiling brightly. 'I'd like to find my perfect fit. My niche.'

His mother, who had finished her meal, put her knife and fork on her plate and nodded. 'There's no sense in doing something if your heart isn't in it.'

There she went again. He'd just about forgotten about being angry with her for a moment, distracted by Ruby's sad story, but she had to dig herself another hole, didn't she? It just proved she would never change.

His mother must have noticed the expression on his face, because she stopped smiling at Ruby and sent him a pleading look. He carried on eating his pasta. She tried to smile, even though her eyes glistened in the light from the chandelier.

'Well, maybe being a nanny will be your niche. You're a natural with Sofia.'

'Thank you, Fina.' Ruby smiled, properly this time, and the gloom of her previous expression was chased away. How did she do that? How did she just let it all float away like that, find the joy in life again?

'Massimo wanted to be an architect since he'd got his

first set of building blocks,' his mother said. Her face was clear of the hurt he'd seen a few moments ago, but he could hear the strain in her voice. 'He always wanted to follow in his father's footsteps.' She turned to him. 'He would have been so proud to know you'd secured the commission for the Institute of Fine—'

Max's chair shot back as he stood to his feet. 'Don't you dare presume to speak for my father,' he said through clenched teeth. His insides were on fire, yet his skin felt as cold as ice. 'In fact, I'd rather you didn't mention him at all in my presence.'

And then he turned and strode from the room.

CHAPTER SIX

MAX STARED AT SOFIA, who was currently sitting on one of his mother's sofas, staring at him expectantly. Gone was the sunshine of the previous day, replaced by a low, drizzly fog. It would probably clear up by the afternoon, but that didn't help him now.

There would be no walk this morning, no playing ball games in the street or a nearby square. Unsurprisingly, there weren't many parks in Venice, so children had to make do with whatever outside space the city presented to them. He tried to rack his brains and think what he'd done as a boy on his visits here, but most of his memories were of when he was older, involving boats or other children.

Ruby walked into the room. He hadn't seen her since last night, and had almost got used to the bright strawberry-covered dress. Her attire was once again completely different, but somehow it seemed less of a jump this morning. Today she looked like a groupie from a rock band, with skinny jeans, a black T-shirt and a multitude of necklaces and bangles. Her dark, purple-streaked hair also seemed to be standing up a little more than usual.

'Good morning,' she said.

Max nodded.

Ruby must have seen the panic in his eyes, because she smiled that soft little I'm-trying-not-to-make-it-look-as-if-I'm-laughing-at-you smile. He gave up any pretence of competence.

'What do I do?' he asked, gesturing towards the windows.

She shrugged. 'Do something she likes to do.'

Marvellous suggestion. Great. That was the whole point. 'But I don't *know* what she likes to do.'

He searched around the room. His mother didn't have many toys, just a few in the bottom section of an antique sideboard. He opened the door and started to rummage. When he was halfway through pulling things out, most of them puzzles and board games far too old for his niece, he felt a light touch on his shoulder. He twisted his head and found Sofia grinning at him. 'Dat!' she announced firmly, pointing to a cardboard box.

Max reached for it and opened the lid. It contained the brightly coloured wooden blocks that Sofia had been playing with yesterday. As he stared at them, the way they were worn, how the paint had been knocked off some of the corners and edges, he realised they'd once been his. Sofia nodded, walked over to the large rug that filled the middle of the room and sat down on it, waiting.

Well, at least he knew what to do with bricks, even if they were this small. He started arranging them into a small structure, but Sofia wasn't happy with that. 'Build pinsess!' she said firmly, tugging at his shirtsleeve.

Max looked at her. 'Huh?'

'Build pinsess,' she repeated, looking at him as if he should have no trouble obeying her command. He looked up at Ruby helplessly.

'I think she's saying "build princess".'

He was still lost.

Ruby chuckled. 'I think she wants you to build her a fairy-tale castle.'

Max looked down at his rather square, half-finished

house. Great. Now the Institute of Fine Art weren't the only ones who weren't pleased with an original Martin design.

'What does a fairy-princess castle look like?'

Ruby got down on the rug beside them and started gathering bricks. 'The basics are there,' she said. 'You just need to embellish a little.'

She leaned forward to pick up another brick and Max caught the scent of her perfume. He would have expected her to wear something bold and eye-watering, like too-sweet vanilla or pungent berries, but it was a subtle mix of flowers and spices. It made him forget where he'd been about to place the next brick.

He shook himself and found somewhere, even though he was sure he'd had a different spot in mind when he'd picked the thing up.

They finished the main structure then added turrets and a drawbridge. Ruby even went and found a blue scarf from her luggage and they circled it round the castle like a moat. Sofia took a role as site manager, instructing the adults where she wanted the next tower built and letting them know in no uncertain terms when their efforts didn't meet her expectations.

'She's reminding me of someone else I know,' Ruby muttered under her breath.

Max hid a smile. Seriously, he was not that bad.

She reached for a red triangular brick at the same time he did and their hands bumped. She pulled back and rested her bottom on her heels. 'No, you have it. You're the expert.'

He picked it up and dropped it into her hand. 'This isn't a job I can accomplish on my own. I think the finishing touches require some definite feminine input to come up to our patron's high standard.'

She grinned back at him. 'She is a bit of a slave driver.' And then she put the brick above the main gate, making a porch, instead of the obvious place where he would have put it on top of the central turret. When she'd finished she stood up and brushed the carpet fibres off her black jeans.

'Where are you going?' he asked, realising he was disappointed she was leaving.

He told himself it was because he needed her there as backup, that he didn't want to be left alone with Sofia. What if she started crying again?

'It's lunch time,' she said, smiling. 'I think Sofia is getting hungry.'

Max checked his watch. So it was. He'd forgotten how much he'd loved these blocks as a boy, how many rainy days just like this one he'd spent in this room, building forts and skyscrapers and alien space stations.

He stood up and surveyed the creation they'd made together. Despite its flouncy, OTT design, he was quite proud of himself. And Ruby and Sofia, obviously. This really was a spectacular castle. He'd enjoyed himself, remembered just how much joy could be had from building and creating when the pressure wasn't on. And he'd enjoyed the good-natured banter and arguments about which door should go where and just how ridiculously high Sleeping Beauty's tower should be. Instead of feeling burdened and irritated, he felt...

It took him a while to name the sensation. Probably because it had been absent from his life for so long.

He felt relaxed.

'That's you relieved of duty for the morning, then,' Ruby said and held out her hand for Sofia and asked her if she'd like lunch in Italian. Sofia nodded vigorously and began to tell Ruby exactly what she'd consent to eat. The list consisted of mainly chocolate and flavours of ice cream. Ruby just smiled and led her away and Max was left staring at Sofia's castle.

The smile slowly slid from his face. The tiny rainbow-coloured castle might have turned out well, but he still had no idea how to add the same flair to his design for the institute. He stuffed his hands in his pockets and trudged back to the library. For some reason, he didn't think turrets and a moat would be a hit with his clients.

Rather than the pearly mist of the day before, which had draped the whole city in soft, off-white tones, the next morning was bright and loud and colourful. Instead of setting the blocks up in the living room, Max led Ruby and Sofia outside to the dock.

A minute later they were zipping through canals heading for somewhere Max said was a prime spot for what he had in mind. Ruby stared at the 'equipment' he'd brought with them that sat in the bottom of the boat. She guessed they must be doing fishing of some kind, because there were a couple of buckets, some nets and a line of dark wire, wrapped round a plastic reel, with a weight and a hook at one end.

She looked down at the toddler in her arms. Didn't fishing require patience and silence? She wasn't sure how much of a good idea this was.

She didn't have the heart to mention that to Max, though. All traces of the frown that had been permanently etched into his forehead since she'd first met him had disappeared, and he looked calmer, more relaxed, as he drove the little boat through narrow and wide canals, manoeuvring it expertly with only a slight twist of the wheel here and there.

They moored alongside a wide path beside a smallish canal. They were deep in the heart of the city, far enough off the beaten track to have left most of the tourists behind. Max hopped out of the boat and held out his hands for the tackle. Ruby passed him Sofia first, and reminded him to hold her hand tightly. She then picked the buckets and nets up and placed them on the edge of the stone path before clambering out herself.

'What now?' she asked, slightly breathlessly.

Max stared at the opaque green water. 'Now we put our line down and see if we can catch any crabs.'

'Crabs?' That wasn't what she'd been expecting at all.

He nodded. 'Every Venetian child knows how to fish for crabs. At certain times of year, when young ones have shells that are still soft, they are considered a local delicacy.'

'Are you sure Sofia's going to—?'

'I don't know,' he said frankly. 'But why don't we give it a try?'

There wasn't much Ruby could say to that, so she stood by and lent a helping hand where she could, holding on to Sofia while Max carefully explained to her what they were going to be doing and started to put some bait on the hook. He didn't let Sofia touch that bit of the line, but lowered it slowly into the dark water, allowing her to hold on to the plastic reel, but keeping his hands over hers.

They waited for a short while and then he slowly drew the line up again. Nothing. Ruby waited for Sofia to start fidgeting, but she seemed to be fascinated. She clumsily helped Max unreel the line again, frowning in concentration.

Ruby almost laughed looking at the pair of them. She didn't know why she hadn't seen it before, but the family similarity smacked her right between the eyes. The same dark eyes, same cheekbones. They even pursed their lips in the same manner as they stared at the dark twine hanging in the water.

After a minute or so, Max helped Sofia wind the line up again, and this time a tiny green-and-brown mottled crab was hanging from the end. It was hanging on with grim determination, as if it had decided it was *his* dinner on that hook and he wasn't giving it up for anybody.

Sofia squealed. Ruby shot forward, meaning to comfort her, but she realised when she saw the little girl's eyes shining that the noise had been one of delight, not fear. In fact, Sofia was so pleased with her catch that she reached out to grab it as Max tried to gently shake it from the line into a bucket he'd filled with canal water.

Then came another squeal. This one high-pitched and urgent. It seemed Sofia had been a little too enthusiastic, and the crab had thought her a little too tempting, because it had clutched on to her with its free pincer. Ruby quickly darted in and shook it away, but Sofia's eyes filled with tears and she looked at her hand in horror. 'Naughty!' she said vehemently. 'Bad fish!'

Ruby scooped her up and gave her a hug, then bent to kiss the red patch on her finger. The skin wasn't broken and she was probably more surprised and offended than in real pain. She pulled back and smiled at the little girl. 'He just liked you so much he didn't want to let go,' she told her.

Sofia's eyes grew wide. 'Fish *like* me?'

Ruby nodded. 'He's a crab, not a fish, and, yes, I think he thought you looked very tasty.'

Sofia screwed up her face and chuckled heartily. 'Silly fish,' she said leaning over the bucket and peering at her catch. 'No bite Sofia. Kiss.' And she puckered up her lips and bent over farther. Ruby caught her quickly before she got any other ideas.

'Why don't we see if we can find him a friend?' And she indicated where Max was waiting with the crabbing line.

Sofia grinned. 'Want lots and lots friends.'

So that was what they did for the next forty-five minutes—found lots and lots of friends for the little green-and-brown crab. Ruby and Max worked as a team, keeping a firm hold on Sofia when she got over-excited and tried to lean too far over the water, and dealt with crabs and bait when needed. After the first handful of attempts they settled into an easy rhythm, giving them lulls in the action while the bait dangled in the water.

Ruby took an opportunity to look around at the buildings. She wished she had her sketchpad with her—and a free hand—so she could draw them. 'There are so many wonderful shapes to be seen in this city,' she said, sighing. 'What's that called?' She showed Max the building on the far side of the canal, where the stonework around a window curved to a point at the top.

'It's an inflected arch,' he said.

'It makes me think of far-off lands and tales of Arabian nights.'

'It's interesting that you say that, because a lot of Venetian architecture has Eastern influences. Merchants travelled to the Byzantine Empire and traded with the Moors and they came back and combined those shapes with the European gothic architecture to create a unique style.'

She pointed to another building. 'And what about those ones? They're beautiful. At first it just looks like intricate shapes, but then you can see that the fussier patterns are actually made up of intersecting circles.'

He turned to look at her and didn't say anything for a few moments. 'You have a good eye for shapes.'

She shrugged and then bent down to help Sofia shake another crab off her line into the bucket. 'Thank you. I like to draw sometimes. I suppose it's just something I've picked up.'

Max took the line from his niece for a moment and worked out a few tangles before giving it back to her. 'Is that what you've been doing when I've seen you scribbling away in that notebook of yours?'

She nodded. She hadn't realised he'd noticed. 'It's just a hobby. Nothing impressive, really.'

'You haven't thought of making a career out of it?' He gave her a dry smile. 'Seeing as you've tried everything else?'

'Ha, ha. Very funny. Go for the easy target, why not?' Everyone else did.

'Seriously, if you love it so much, why don't you do something with it?'

She tipped her head to one side. 'You mean, like you did?'

'I suppose so.'

She looked down at the water below them, at the way the light bounced off the surface, moving constantly. 'I don't think I'd be able to do what you do. It's very structured and disciplined. When I draw, I just go with the flow. I see something that interests me and I capture it. I'm not sure you can make a career out of that.'

'You have plenty of discipline,' he said. 'Look at the way you are with Sofia. And sometimes you need that creative spark to liven all that structure up.' He let out a long sigh and stared at the buildings across the water.

'More fish! More fish!' Sofia shouted, jumping up and down so hard she almost toppled into the canal. Ruby kept a firm hand on her as she shook the most recent catch into the bucket to join his friends. Sofia did it so vigorously that Ruby was sure the poor thing must have a concussion.

When Sofia was happily dangling the line in the canal again, Ruby looked at Max. 'What's up?' she asked. 'Was it something I said?'

He sighed again and crouched down to look at where Sofia was pointing at some silvery fish swimming near the surface of the water. 'No. It's something I said.'

She waited for him to stand again.

'It's a commission for the Institute of Fine Art,' he told her. 'I've worked for months on a preliminary design that I'm really proud of, but the board say they're not sure about it.'

Ruby shook her head. She couldn't believe that. The designs she'd glimpsed were amazing. They were totally

Max, of course. No frills. No fuss. Nothing ostentatious. But there was an elegance to the simplicity. A pared-back beauty. 'Why on earth not?'

He shrugged. 'I think the actual phrase they used is that they want more "wow factor".'

A screech from around knee level interrupted their conversation. Ruby hadn't noticed it while she'd been talking to Max, but the bucket was now almost full and the crabs were scrambling over each other in an attempt to climb out.

Max knelt down next to his niece. 'It's time to put them back now,' he said matter of factly and tipped the bucket over to let a stream of crustaceans, legs flailing, fall back into the salty lagoon water.

'No!' The exclamation was loud and impassioned and followed immediately by a stream of hot tears. 'Want friend! Want friend!'

Ruby grabbed for the bucket and righted it. Only three crabs remained in the bottom.

Sofia stopped shouting and sniffed. 'Want take fish home.'

Ruby crouched down beside her, put an arm round her shoulders and joined her in looking into the bucket. She might be wrong, but she thought one of the three crabs left might be the little one they'd caught first. 'We can't take them back to Grandma's, sweetie. They belong here in the water. It's their home. We just picked them out to say hello for a little bit.'

Sofia let out a juddering sigh.

'Why don't we put the last ones back one by one and say a nice goodbye to them?'

Sofia frowned. 'Come back 'morrow say hello?'

Ruby smiled. 'If you want.'

The little girl nodded. Ruby looked inside the bucket and then up at Max. 'How do we...?'

Quick as anything his hand plunged into the bucket and

he pulled out a crab. 'There's a trick to it. If you hold them at the back of the shell like this, they can't reach to pinch you.'

He held the crab up for Sofia to see. She puckered up her lips. 'Kiss fish?' she asked.

Ruby's heart just about melted.

'Not too close,' she said softly, imagining what Fina would say if her precious granddaughter came home with pincer holes in her lips. 'Just blow a kiss.'

Sofia blinked then puffed heartily on the crab, who was so shocked it stopped waving its legs around angrily and went still. A deep rumble started in Max's chest then worked its way up out of his mouth in the most infectious of chuckles. Ruby looked up at him, eyes laughing.

'That's a first,' he said, smiling, and then he gently plopped the crab back into the canal.

They followed the same routine with the next crab, too, but when they came to the last one, Ruby asked, 'Can I pick it up?'

Max nodded. He put the bucket down on the cobbles and took hold of Sofia while Ruby took off her watch and stuffed it in her jeans pocket. She inhaled, then dipped her hand into the cold water and aimed her forefinger and thumb for the parts of the shell the way she'd seen Max do it. It wriggled away a couple of times, but then she gripped more firmly and lifted the crab out of the water.

'I did it!' she exclaimed. 'For a moment there I didn't think I was— *Ow*!'

A searing pain shot through her finger, making her eyes water. She blinked the moisture away, slightly breathless, to find an angry little crab attached to her hand. She was sure it was scowling at her.

'Ow, ow, ow...' she yelped and started shaking her hand backwards and forwards. Anything to make it let go!

Eventually the force of the swinging must have got the crab, either that or it lost its grip on her wet hands, because it shot off, landed on the paving stones a couple of feet away then scuttled to the edge and flung itself into the canal.

'Ow,' Ruby said again, just to make her point, even though her attacker probably neither heard nor cared.

She looked down as her finger started to throb. That had definitely *not* been the original crab with the delicate little pincers that hadn't punctured Sofia's finger. This one had been mean and angry, and blood was now seeping from a hole in her skin.

'Here, let me look,' Max said and swiftly caught up her hand.

Ruby would have expected his examination to be practical and thorough, and it was, but she hadn't expected it to be so gentle. She looked at him, head bowed over her hand as he ran his fingers over the area surrounding her war wound, and for some reason the sight of his dark lashes against his cheek made her feel a little breathless.

Sofia hugged her left leg. 'No cry, Ruby. Fish no want let go.'

Despite the thudding of her pulse in her index finger, Ruby couldn't help but smile. She looked up to find Max doing the same, but his face was very close. She blinked and sucked in a breath.

'Kiss better!' Sofia commanded.

Ruby would have been okay if she hadn't realised he was holding his breath, too, that he seemed to be stuck looking at her the same way she was looking at him.

'Go on, Uncle Max! Kiss better.'

Slowly Max raised her hand, not taking his eyes off her until the moment he bent his head and softly pressed his lips to where Ruby's finger was throbbing. The sensation spread out from that finger, through the rest of her body, until she couldn't breathe, couldn't move. Max seemed to be similarly affected, because even though he'd lowered her hand again he still held it between his warm fingers.

Sofia tugged Ruby's trouser leg, seeking a response she hadn't yet got. 'Him no want let go.'

Ruby swallowed. 'I know, sweetheart.' And as she spoke the words she slid her hand out of Max's and looked away to where the crab had plopped into the water.

'I think it'll be fine,' he mumbled, then busied himself collecting up the fishing equipment and putting it back in the boat.

CHAPTER SEVEN

MAX SPENT THE REST of the afternoon in the library with the door shut. He tinkered with his plans for the institute until his eyes were gritty and his brain was spinning. It didn't help that every time he wasn't 100 per cent immersed in what he was doing he kept having strange flashbacks.

He kept seeing Ruby's slightly swollen and bleeding finger. Inevitably that led to memories of looking up into her eyes. He hadn't noticed their colour before. Warm hazel. Not green. Not brown. But a unique pairing of the two that was slightly hypnotic. He hadn't been able to look away, hadn't been able to let go. And then he'd gone and kissed her finger. What had all that been about?

Okay, he knew *exactly* what that had been about. He might not have been in the mood to date since his father's death, finding himself drawn to his own company, filling his hours with work, but he was no stranger to desire.

He stopped tweaking a design for a staircase he had up on his computer screen and deleted all the last fifteen changes he'd made. It had been better before. Now it was *more* boring, if that was even possible. He'd seen a hundred different staircases like it in a hundred different buildings.

He pushed back from the desk, stood up, began to pace.

He needed something different. Something unique.

Like those eyes...

No. Not like those eyes. They had nothing to do with it.

For heaven's sake! It wasn't even as if Ruby was any-thing like the kind of women he usually went out with, the kind he'd hardly noticed he'd stopped seeing: cultured, so-phisticated, beautiful.

He sighed. And next to Ruby they seemed like clones churned out by a production line.

In comparison, she was strangely easy to be with. There was no game-playing. No second-guessing whether he'd accidentally said the wrong thing because he was being subjected to some secret test. If Ruby thought he'd over-stepped the mark, she just told him in no uncertain terms.

There was a knock at the door and he stopped pacing and faced it, grunted his permission to enter. A moment later his travelling nanny popped her head round the door. 'Your mother wanted me to let you know that dinner is served.'

She looked down and away, as if she was feeling awk-ward. When she looked up again, a faint blush stained her cheeks.

The air grew instantly thick. Max nodded. 'Thank you,' he managed to say. 'I'll be along in a minute.'

She smiled hesitantly and shut the door again.

Max ran a hand through his hair and swore softly. Was he imagining it, or had she got prettier since that after-noon?

He went over and sat back down at his desk. He clicked over to his email and read a few messages to distract him-self, although what they contained he couldn't have said. When he felt a little more his usual self, he rose and went to the dining room, lecturing himself en route.

You have no business noticing her eyes, warm hazel or otherwise. She's your employee. Get a grip and get over it.

Thankfully, he was sitting opposite his mother this eve-ning at dinner, and Ruby was off to one side, so he didn't catch her gaze while they ate their...whatever it was they ate. He kept his concentration on his plate as his mother once again pounced on their guest as both willing audience and source of conversation.

'Maybe being a nanny will be your niche after all,' she told Ruby. 'You're a natural with Sofia, and she's already very fond of you.'

Ruby smiled at her. 'Thank you. I'm loving spending time with her, too, and spending time in Venice. This really is the most remarkable place.'

Fina's chest puffed up with pride in her home. 'You've never visited before?' she said.

'No. I always wanted to, though.'

Fina clapped her hands. 'Well, then we must make sure we don't work you too hard, so you get time to see some of the sights! But the best time of day to see the city is the hour leading up to sunset, don't you think, Massimo?'

Max let out a weary sigh. 'I suppose so.'

Ruby smiled and sipped her glass of water. She'd refused wine, seeing as she was still on duty. 'I'm sure it is, but I may have to wait until my next visit for that. By the time I've got Sofia bathed and in bed, it's nearly always dark.'

Fina rose from the table to go and fetch the dessert from the sideboard. 'Then Massimo must take you before he goes back to London. Don't worry about Sofia. I'm sure her *nonna* can manage bedtime alone for one night.'

They both turned to look at him.

He should say no. Make an excuse that he had too much work to do, or tell his mother to drive the boat herself, but he looked back at Ruby, her eyes large and expectant, and found himself saying, 'Okay, but later in the week. And as long as we're not out too long. I have work to do.' And then he returned to attacking his vegetables.

The women went back to chatting again but a while later Ruby piped up, 'Oh! I almost forgot. Before Sofia went to bed, she insisted I give this to you.' She pushed a piece of paper in his direction. 'I was going to let her do it herself, but you seemed to be so busy, so I just…didn't.' She shrugged. 'Well, here it is, anyway.'

He reached out and pulled the scrap towards him, careful not to brush her fingers. From the thick, riotous turquoise crayon that graced the sheet of paper, he could tell the colouring was Sofia's, but the drawing, that was all Ruby's. He smiled as he looked at it.

She'd drawn one of the crabs they'd caught that afternoon in dark ink. The little crab hanging on the end of the fishing line looked full of personality, feisty and ready to take on the world if anyone dared try to catch him and tame him. It really was rather good.

'I think you caught him perfectly,' he said, and made the mistake of looking up at her. 'You've got that devilish expression down pat.'

She didn't say anything. Just smiled. And her eyes warmed further.

Max returned his attention to his plate.

He forced himself to remember the conversation that had taken place round this dinner table only a few evenings ago. It didn't matter how nice her eyes were, or how relaxed he felt around her, it would be foolishness in the highest degree to be bewitched by that.

Ruby Lange was a drifter. She'd said so herself. She didn't finish what she started, always tempted to run after something better and brighter and shinier.

He didn't need a woman like that in his life. He'd seen what his mother had done to his father, hadn't he?

He returned his gaze to his plate.

Pork. They were eating pork.

He'd do well to keep his mind on concrete things like that. On his work. On his commission, his final gift to the parent who'd stuck around to raise him.

No more distractions, no matter how tempting.

* * *

The following evening Ruby approached dinner with a plan. Max was going home in just under forty-eight hours and still he was treating his mother like the enemy.

However, he'd softened up with Sofia nicely. He no longer held her as if she were an unexploded bomb, and interacted quite easily with her now. Sofia, who maybe had been lacking a positive male role model in her life, simply adored him. It was clear a bond was forming between them.

Surely the potential was there with Fina, too? All he needed was to be thrown in the deep end a bit, as he had been with Sofia.

So Ruby deliberately decided not to natter on at dinner time this evening, hoping it would encourage mother and son to converse. But as they waded their way through the main course, the only sound in the cavernous dining room was the clinking of cutlery and the dull thud of glasses being picked up and set down again.

Fina kept looking at him, willing him to glance her way, but mostly, unless he was reaching for the salt or refilling his glass, Max refused. As the meal wore on Ruby could sense more and more nervous energy in the woman sitting beside her. Fina must sense her chance for reconciliation ticking away with the hours and seconds until Max's flight back to London. It didn't seem as if he'd be in a hurry to return any time soon, either.

Eventually, Fina cracked. She put down her knife and fork and stared at him for a few seconds before opening her mouth. 'Massimo. You've been having such a wonderful time here with Sofia these last few days.'

Max glanced up so briefly Ruby doubted he'd even had time to focus on Fina. He grunted then turned his attention to his plate.

Fina shot a nervous look at Ruby and Ruby nodded her encouragement.

'Ruby's been telling me all about your crabbing expeditions.'

Another grunt. This time without eye contact.

Fina swallowed. 'I was thinking that maybe I'd invite the whole family to visit for the festival of San Martino in November. You used to love decorated biscuits of Martino on his horse, remember?' She laughed. 'You once asked me if we were cousins of the saint, because our last names were so similar.'

Max carried on cutting his chicken, and only when he'd precisely severed a chunk, put it in his mouth and chewed and swallowed it thoroughly, did he answer his mother. 'I don't think I'm going to be able to spare the time from work. If this commission goes through it'll be full steam ahead until the new year.' And then he went back to dissecting his meal.

Fina nodded, even though her son wasn't watching, and hung her head over her plate.

Ruby glared at him. She wanted to fish that little crab they'd met the other day out of the canal and attach it to his nose! He was being so stubborn.

Didn't he know what a gift this was? Maybe Fina hadn't been the perfect mother, but she was trying to make up for it now. Surely that had to mean something? And there had to be good reasons why a woman as warm and caring as Fina had walked away from her marriage. She might try and act blasé, but Ruby couldn't believe she'd done it on a whim, whatever Max might think.

Fina rose from her seat. 'I promised Renata upstairs that I would look in on her. She's not been feeling very well,' she said, and walked stiffly from the room.

Max pushed his plate away. Ruby glared at him. 'Couldn't you just even give her a chance?'

He lifted his head and looked at her. His eyes were empty, blank like the statues topping so many of the palazzos nearby. 'It's not your business, Ruby. What happens in my family is my concern.'

She stared back at him, words flying round her head. But she released none of them, knowing he was speaking the truth and hating him for it. So much for the bond she'd thought they'd forged over the last few days.

She rose and followed Fina out of the room. 'Thank you,' she said as she reached the doorway, 'for putting me firmly in my place.'

At least an hour passed before Max emerged from the library. The apartment was totally quiet. Sofia must be fast asleep and he hadn't heard his mother return from visiting her neighbour.

Everything was dark—well, almost. A few of the wall sconces were lit at the far end of the corridor near the salon. His footsteps seemed loud as he walked down it and entered the large room. In here it was dark, too, with just one lamp turned on near the sofas, making the cavernous space seem smaller and more intimate. He looked for Ruby's dark head against the cushions, for a hint of a purple streak, but there was no one there.

He was about to turn and leave the room, but then he heard a shuffling noise and noticed the doors to the balcony were open. He could just make out her petite form, leaning on the stone ledge, staring out across the water. Taking in a deep breath, he walked over to the open door and stood in the threshold.

'I can hear voices,' she said, her tone bland, 'and I think it must be someone close by, but there are no windows open upstairs and no boats going by.'

'It's just another quirk of this city,' he said. 'Sounds seem oddly hushed at some times and magnified at others. Even a whisper can travel round corners.'

She nodded. Whoever had been talking had stopped now and silence grew around them.

What a pity it wasn't silent inside Max's head. He could hear another whispering voice now, one telling him to apologise. It wasn't the first time he'd heard that voice, but he usually managed to outrun it when it prompted him to do anything as dangerous as letting down his guard, admitting he was wrong, but Venice was amplifying this sound, too, making it impossible to ignore.

Or maybe it was Ruby who did that to him.

Sometimes she looked at him and he felt as if all the things he'd held together for so long were slowly being unlaced.

He should go, retreat back to the library, to the safety of his plans and emails. That was where he'd built the fortress of his life, after all—in his work. Just like his father before him.

Ruby didn't ask anything of him. Didn't demand as his mother would have done. Instead she kept staring out into the night, a faint breeze lifting her feathery fringe.

Max stepped forward. 'I was rude earlier on,' he said. 'I'm sorry.'

She kept her elbows resting on the stone balustrade and turned just her head, studied him. 'I accept your apology, but you spoke the truth.'

She was right, he realised. That was something they always did with each other, whether they wanted to or not. 'Even if it was, I shouldn't have said it the way I did.'

Ruby's cheeks softened and her smile grew. 'Thank you.' She straightened and looked back inside. 'Sofia's appetite for things to colour in is insatiable. I was going to get some outlines done to give me a head start in the morning, but I couldn't resist slipping out here for a moment.'

She moved to go back inside, and his arm shot out across the doorway, blocking her. He didn't know why he'd done that. He should have let her go. Ruby tipped her head and frowned at him, her delicate features full of puzzlement, her eyes asking a question. A question he didn't know the answer to.

But other words found his lips, words he hadn't even realised were his. 'I find it hard to be here... This is the first time I've seen her since my father died.'

She looked back at him, understanding brimming in her eyes.

'She broke him, you know, when she left. Everyone always said he was the same old Geoffrey, hard as steel, never letting anything get to him, but they didn't know him the way I did.'

She moved a little closer, placed a hand on the arm that wasn't blocking her exit, the one that was braced against the rough stone of the balustrade. 'You're angry with her,' she said in a low voice. It wasn't a question.

He nodded. He'd been angry with her for years. It had started as a raging fire that only the indignation and passion of a teenage boy knew how to fan, and had solidified into something darker and deeper. 'Since the day of his funeral I haven't been able to ignore it any longer. I want to but I can't.'

He broke away from her and walked a few steps down the balcony, away from the doors. Ruby, of course, followed him. He heard the soft pad of her ballet pumps on the stone. 'You have to know that it's illogical, that his death wasn't her fault. They've been separated for years.'

He twisted to face her abruptly, his face contorting. 'But that's just it. It *is* her fault. You should have heard some of the things she used to scream at him.' He shook his head. 'And he never once lost his temper. It was the effort of living with her, then living without her, that brought on his high blood pressure.'

Ruby stepped closer. 'Is that how he died?'

He nodded. 'He had a stroke—a little one at first, but while he was in the hospital a bigger one struck, finishing him off.'

He felt the rage boiling inside him now. It was all so perilously close to the surface that he was scared he would punch straight through the five-hundred-year-old wall into the salon.

'She's hurting, too,' Ruby said.

He forced himself to focus on her. For a moment the red haze behind his eyes had blurred his vision.

'Can't you forgive her?'

He shook his head, unable to articulate his answer. No, he didn't think he could. He didn't even know if he'd be able to contain it again, let alone quench it.

She must have seen the tension in his expression, because she stepped even closer, this time so he could smell that maddening elusive perfume. 'You've got to let it go, Max. You can't bury it all inside.' Her eyes pleaded with him. 'If you do it might damage you the same way it damaged him.'

He knew she was right. He just didn't know if he knew how. Or even wanted to.

There was the tiniest noise in the back of his head, something snapping. But instead of releasing his anger he'd unleashed something else. It was also something he couldn't keep buried any longer, and it had nothing at all to do with his mother and everything to do with the firecracker of a woman standing in front of him.

Slowly he leaned forward, and watched Ruby's eyes widen. Darken. He slid his hand behind her neck, relishing the feel of her bare skin, the soft wisps of her hair, until he cupped her head and drew her to him. And then he unleashed the full force of all he was too weary to hold back any longer in one scorching kiss.

Ruby knew she should have frozen, knew she should have slipped out of his arms and retained some degree of decorum. Unfortunately, she wasn't that sensible. Instead of reminding him of the barrier between them, the one that no proper nanny would cross, she let him sledgehammer through it as he ran hot kisses down the side of her neck.

She'd never been one for holding back and she certainly didn't do so now. She ran her hands up his chest, grabbed his shirt collar and lifted herself closer, abandoning herself to the feel of his skin upon hers, his body pressed so tight against her own she felt breathless.

He slid his hands down the curve of her back to her waist, emphasising her femininity against his hard, straight masculinity. He kissed her again and she felt them both teeter on the edge of something, threatening to topple headlong into goodness knew what.

Oh, sweet heaven. She'd been right. When Max Martin let loose there was sizzle and passion and consuming fire, and all of that force was concentrated on her now, at the point where his lips were urgently seeking hers again. It was glorious.

It was also very stupid.

Max must have had an identical revelation at the same time, because he froze, his hands circling her waist, and then he stepped back, effectively dropping her back from her tiptoes onto her flat feet. She swayed, the sudden lack of solid, Max-shaped support and the cold air rushing between their bodies putting her off balance.

'I'm so sorry,' he almost stuttered, a look of complete horror on his face. 'That was totally inappropriate.'

Ruby's lips were still throbbing and her hormones still singing the 'Hallelujah Chorus'. She blinked and stared back at him. *Inappropriate?* That was not a word a girl wanted to hear after the hottest kiss of her life.

He shook his head and strode past her and back into the salon. She watched him go, a gnawing feeling growing in her stomach. She couldn't let him leave like this. This wasn't his fault. She had to let him know that she'd been just as much a part of it as he had been. She heaved in a much-needed lungful of night air and ran after him. 'Max!'

He turned as he passed through the double doors into the corridor.

'You don't have to… I mean, it wasn't just…' She trailed off, unable to find the words. He looked so thoroughly wretched. Part of her sank, but another part wanted to reach out to him, to soothe that crumpled expression from his face.

She'd pushed him too far, when he'd been feeling too raw, and he'd lost control. She got that. But maybe it was a good thing. Maybe loosening up in one area of his life would have a knock-on effect?

But it wasn't just that. The way he'd kissed her, hard and hungry, verging on desperate. He had to feel it, too, this weird attraction, crush…whatever. She wasn't alone in this.

She opened her mouth to speak, hardly knowing how to form the question, but at that moment Fina appeared at the top of the stairs and spotted them farther down the corridor. The atmosphere had been thick around her and Max anyway, but now it became so dense it turned brittle.

Fina walked up to them and looked at her son. Any hint of the distress she'd shown earlier was gone, replaced by a brisk and prickly demeanour. 'It's your last night tomorrow, Massimo.'

With what looked like supreme effort, Max dragged his gaze from Ruby and turned it to Fina. 'I know that,' he replied.

Ruby looked between mother and son. In an earlier century, an atmosphere like this would have been dispersed by cocking pistols and marching twenty paces in opposite directions. She hoped that Fina would say something conciliatory, forgiving her son his outburst instead of nursing her own pain into hardness.

Tell him you love him, Ruby wanted to yell. *Tell him he's everything in the world to you.* Max might not see it, but she did. It was evident in every breath Fina took.

But Fina stared back at her son. It seemed she'd learned a thing or two from her buttoned-up husband about staying granite-like in the face of pain. She nodded. 'Good. Just don't forget you promised to take Ruby out to see the city at sunset. It's her last chance.'

And then she turned and walked down the corridor to her bedroom.

CHAPTER EIGHT

Ruby waited in the salon in her carefully chosen outfit. She'd changed three times, veering between 'boating casual', which made her look as if she were going out for a country walk with her grandparents, and *Roman Holiday*, which made her look as if she was trying a little bit too hard. Maybe it had been the thick liquid liner and the red lipstick.

In the end she'd settled for a boat-necked navy cotton dress with a full enough skirt for clambering, her ballet pumps and a little black cardigan. The eyeliner stayed, but the lipstick was replaced by something in a more natural colour. Something that didn't scream 'Come and get me!', because she had a feeling there was no way Max was going to, even if it did.

While he hadn't answered the question she'd wanted to ask last night in words, his actions had done a pretty effective job for him. He wasn't in the grip of the same fairy-tale crush she had been, that was for sure.

If he had been, he wouldn't have avoided her all day. He certainly wouldn't have taken Sofia out for ice cream on his own that morning, saying that even trainee travelling nannies needed some time off. She knew a brush-off when she heard one. She'd been getting them from her father all her life.

She checked the ornate gold clock on the marble mantelpiece. Ten to seven. Fina had decreed they should leave here on the hour to catch the whole glory of the sunset, which was supposed to be closer to eight.

She wandered over to the long windows and took in the golden light hitting the front of a pink and white palazzo on the other side of the canal. Max had been right. This city spun a spell, making you believe things that weren't real, making you hope for things that could never be. She understood why so many people loved it now. And why he hated it.

She stayed there, watching the light play on the water, for what seemed like only a few minutes, and Fina startled her when she swept into the room and turned on the light. Ruby hadn't realised it had got that dark yet.

'Where's Max?' Fina asked, looking round, her brows drawn together.

Ruby shrugged. 'I don't know. We're supposed to be leaving at—'

The clock on the mantelpiece caught her eye. It was five past seven. He'd be here soon, though, she didn't doubt that. Whatever else Max was, he was a man of his word.

She almost wished he weren't. It was going to be awkward. She'd back out if she could, but she sensed Fina would blame Max somehow if she did, and the last thing Ruby wanted was to cause more trouble between mother and son.

Fina tutted and swept from the room before Ruby could say anything else.

Ruby walked over to an armchair at the edge of the seating area and dropped into it. It was one of those old seats that accepted her weight with a 'poof' then slowly sank until her bottom rested fully against the cushion.

She stared into the empty fireplace and waited. A few moments later she heard Fina clip-clopping back up the corridor. She entered the room and sighed dramatically. 'He has a very important phone call, apparently. The whole of London will fall down if he doesn't speak to this man at this precise minute.' She shook her head. 'I shall go and read to Sofia, but he says he will be out in only a few minutes.'

Ruby nodded, and placed her hands in her lap. She rested back against the armchair instead of sitting up poker straight. No point in getting a stiff back waiting for him.

There was a squeal and the sound of two pairs of footsteps—one small and slippered, the other bigger and harder—and a moment later Sofia ran into the room in her pyjamas, her grandmother in hot pursuit. She launched herself at Ruby and landed on her lap.

Fina pressed a hand to her chest, and said breathlessly, 'She's full of beans tonight, and she wanted to come and see you.'

'That's okay.' Then she turned to Sofia. 'Perhaps doing something quiet together for a few minutes will help you get ready for bed. What do you say, young lady?'

'Daw!' said Sofia loudly and pointed to the crayons and scrap paper that had been left out after their earlier colouring session.

Ruby chuckled and let Sofia slip off her lap before she joined her kneeling by the coffee table. 'And what would you like to draw this evening?'

Sofia thought for a moment. 'Naughty fish!'

Of course.

Ruby couldn't remember how many mischievous crabs she'd sketched since that first one: on the bottom of the lagoon, in a carnival mask, and Sofia's favourite—clinging determinedly to her uncle's big toe with a pair of razor-sharp pincers. She quickly did an outline in black pen, a gentler scene this time, something more in keeping with bedtime. She drew the cheeky crab in the back of a gondola with his equally cheeky crustacean girlfriend, being punted along by a singing gondolier in the moonlight.

When she realised what she'd done, how romantic she'd made the scene, she sighed and pushed it her charge's way.

There Venice went again…messing with her head.

'Here you go. And make sure you colour nicely. I don't want it all scribbled over in two seconds flat.'

Sofia nodded seriously, then set to work giving the lady crab a shock of purple hair, which Ruby approved of most heartily.

The sun was down behind the buildings now. Ruby stood and walked to the window, drawn closer by a patchwork sky of yellows and pinks and tangerines, sparsely smeared with silvery blue clouds. Venice, which often had an oddly monochrome feel to its palette, was bathed in golden light.

She walked back over to where Sofia was colouring and complimented her on her hard work, even though the cartoonish drawing she'd provided her with was almost entirely obliterated with heavy strokes of multicoloured crayon. She pulled out a piece of paper for herself. Most of the sheets had writing on the back. They'd gone through Fina's meagre stash of drawing paper and now were wading through documents Max had discarded, using them as scrap. Ruby flipped it over and looked at what was on the printed side.

It was a detail for an interior arch in one of the galleries of the National Institute of Fine Art. The shape was square with no adornment, and Ruby could see where the metal and studs of a supporting girder were left unhidden, giving it a textured, yet industrial air. She thought of the buildings Max had shown her up and down the canal, how he'd explained the Venetians had taken styles from the countries they visited with their own to make something unique, and, instead of turning the sheet back over again and drawing another princess, she picked up a pen and began to embellish.

She sighed, her heart heavy inside her chest. She might as well occupy herself while she waited.

'You need to get back here right away,' Alex, Max's second-in-command at Martin & Martin insisted, more than a hint of urgency in his tone.

Max closed his eyes to block out the dancing cherubs above his head. He'd been pacing to and fro in his mother's library and he was starting to get the uncanny feeling they were watching him. 'I know.'

'Vince McDermot wants the institute commission and he wants it bad.'

Max opened his eyes and stared at the screen on his laptop. 'I know. But the institute board have committed to giving me this extra few weeks to tweak our designs. They won't go back on that.'

Alex sighed. 'True, but McDermot has been out and about wining and dining key members of the board behind our backs. Either you need to come back to London and start schmoozing this instant or we need to come up with a design that'll blow that slimy little poser out of the water.'

Max knew this. He also knew he wasn't good at schmoozing. 'You're better at buttering clients up than I am.'

Alex let out a low, gruff laugh. 'Damn right, but it's you they want, Max. It's time to stop playing happy families and get your butt back here.'

Now it was Max's turn to laugh. *Happy families? Yeah, right.*

'I've been doing what needs to be done to focus on the work, Al. You know that.'

Alex grunted. 'All I'm saying is that there's no point in

us burying our heads in the sand about this. Otherwise, the month will be up, we'll submit new designs and, even if they do have the "wow factor", the board will be more inclined to go with that flash-in-the-pan pretty boy.'

One of the reasons Max liked Alex, both as a colleague and a friend, was that he didn't mince his words. Alex had a point, though. Vince McDermot was London's new architectural wunderkind. Personally, Max thought his designs impractical and crowd-pleasing. They'd never stand the test of time.

'I'm flying back to London tomorrow afternoon, so that's that sorted,' he told Alex. 'The other stuff? Well, that's another story, but if we can keep them sweet for the next fortnight, it'll give us time to come up with what they're looking for.'

It had to come at some point, didn't it? He'd been hailed for his 'ground-breaking minimalist and elegant style', won awards for it. But that had been before. Now he couldn't come up with anything fresh and exciting. It was as if his talent had been buried with his father.

Alex made a conciliatory noise. 'Listen, I should have more of an idea of who exactly he's been sliming up to in the next fifteen minutes. Do you want me to call back, or are you going to hold?'

Max looked at the clock. It was half past seven.

He hadn't forgotten what that meant.

He was late. Really late.

'I'll hold,' he said.

His conscience grumbled. He let the relief flooding through him drown it out.

It was better this way. It was getting harder and harder to remember Ruby was his employee. Harder and harder to stop himself relaxing so much in her presence that he kept letting his guard down. He couldn't afford to do that. Not here. Not with his mother so close.

Better to put a stop to it now.

So Max made himself sit down. He made himself tinker with the designs for the institute's atrium. He made himself ignore the clawing feeling deep inside that told him he was being a heel, that he was hurting her for no reason.

Unfortunately, he didn't do a very good job of it. Probably because the lines and angles in front of him on the screen kept going out of focus, and he kept imagining what it would be like to be out in the boat with Ruby, the dark wrapping around them, enclosing them in their own little bubble while the lights of the city danced on the lagoon.

That only made him crosser.

Damn her. It was all her fault, waltzing into his neatly ordered life, turning it upside down.

You asked her. Hell, you practically commanded her to come with you.

Yeah? Well, everybody made mistakes. Even him. Occasionally.

It was only when he stood up to pace around the room again that he realised he'd put the phone down on Alex at some point in the last five minutes and hadn't even noticed. He said a word that should have made the cherubs on the ceiling put their fingers in their ears.

And all that messing around he'd done on the atrium plans was a load of rubbish! In fact, all the work he'd done on them in the last couple of days had been tired and uninspiring. What had he been thinking?

He shook his head, perfectly aware of what had been filling it. That was why it would be so much better when he was back in London. He'd be able to get his brain round it then, removed from any distractions. Any strawberry-clad, purple-streaked distractions.

Now, where was the earlier atrium design? The one where he'd pared it all back to the basics? He might as well get rid of all these silly changes and start from scratch.

He rummaged through the papers on his mother's antique desk. He'd had a printout of it. It had to be around here somewhere.

Ruby sat back on her heels and surveyed her handiwork. Not bad, even if she did say so herself. Maybe Max was right about her having some real artistic flair. Maybe she could do something with it, rather than just 'messing around', as her father called it.

There was such beauty and simplicity in Max's designs, but this one had just needed a little something—a curve here, a twirl there. By the time she'd finished, the arch on Max's discarded plan was a strange hybrid between twenty-first-century industrial and Venetian Gothic, with a little bit of Ruby thrown in for fun.

Perhaps she should be an architect?

The fact she didn't burst out laughing then roll on the floor at that thought was all thanks to Max. He'd believed in her ability to draw, seen something no one else saw, and she was starting to think she could even see it herself. She wanted to tell him that when they went out later, to thank him, but she didn't really know how to put it into words without betraying everything else she was starting to feel.

'More fish!' Sofia demanded, grinning at Ruby so appealingly that Ruby didn't have the heart to make her say please.

'I think maybe it's time Grandma tucked you into bed,' she told Sofia, smiling. Fina rose from where she'd been reading a magazine in an armchair, and held her hand out for her granddaughter. After running and giving Ruby a hug, Sofia allowed herself to be led away and Ruby was once again alone in the salon.

She tried not to look, but the gold clock on the mantelpiece drew her gaze like a magnet.

Eight o'clock.

A quick glance outside confirmed her suspicions. Compared to the brightly lit salon, the sky outside was bottomless and dark. Not helped by the heavy clouds that had started to gather over the city in the last half hour.

Max had stood her up.

She let her eyelids rest gently closed and inhaled. It didn't matter.

The heaviness in her heart called her a liar.

But it shouldn't be there. She was a paid employee. He owed her nothing more than her wages.

It was just...

She shook her head and opened her eyes again, then she got off up the floor and started piling the scattered bits of drawing up, putting the crayons back in their tub.

Just nothing.

She'd been fooling herself again, thinking this was something when it wasn't. Max hadn't seen inside her, he hadn't spotted the potential that no one else had. He'd just paid her a compliment or two, that was all. And that kiss? Heat-of-the-moment stuff that produced nothing but regrets. She'd doled out a few of those herself in her time. Nothing to sweat about.

Then why did she feel like going to her room, shutting the door behind her and bawling her eyes out?

She gathered the sheets of paper in various sizes up in her arms and headed towards the door. She wasn't quite sure where she was going to put these, but she suspected Fina wouldn't want them scattered around her most formal living space. Maybe they could find a home for one or two of the best ones on the fridge door?

She couldn't have been looking where she'd been going, because when the salon door burst open and Max came barrelling through she didn't have time for evasive manoeuvres. She stumbled sideways, the stack of paper went flying into the air and then fluttered noisily down like over-sized confetti.

Max just stood in the doorway, looking somewhat stunned.

He didn't say anything, but he shook himself slightly then bent to help her pick up the scattered drawings.

Damn him for being such a gentleman. She wanted to hate him right now.

'Here,' he said, when they'd finished gathering up the last of them, and held a sheaf of papers in her direction.

'Thanks,' she mumbled, chickening out of looking him in the eye.

Max must have been doing the same, because suddenly he got very interested in the top sheet of paper.

'What the hell?' he started to say, and then his expression grew thunderous. 'What's this?'

Ruby rolled her eyes. 'Sorry,' she said, feeling her cheeks heat. 'I didn't intend to make the cartoon of you being bitten by the crab at first, but Sofia thought it looked like you, because it was a man, probably, and then it just became a kind of joke and we—'

'I'm not talking about a silly drawing!' Max said, his voice getter louder.

His words were like a punch to Ruby's gut. 'But I—'

'I'm talking about *this*!' And he thrust a sheet of paper so close to her face that she had to step back to focus on it. It was the doodle she'd just finished: Max's arch with her little bit of decorative nonsense superimposed.

Artist? Hah! Don't kid yourself, Ruby.

'It was just… I mean, I just…' She let out a frustrated sigh and spiked her fingers through her neatly combed fringe. 'It's just a doodle, Max.'

'A *doodle*?'

Ruby's heart thudded and her stomach dived into her ballet pumps. If the heat of Max's anger hadn't been scald-

ing her face, his expression would have been kind of funny.
She nodded, feeling all the while that she was walking into
an ambush that she didn't know how to avoid.

'These are my plans!' Max bellowed. 'What on earth
makes you think you have the right to *doodle* on them?
Are you out of your mind?'

Ruby's mouth moved and she backed away. 'But, it was
there…' her gaze flicked to the coffee table, where the pile
of unmolested scrap paper still sat. '…with the stuff you
tossed out the other day…on the top of the pile.'

'This wasn't *scrap*!' he yelled. 'These are my original
plans. You had no right to use them for Sofia. No right at
all.'

Ruby was so puzzled that she couldn't even react to
Max's anger at that moment. How had Max's plans got
there? How? He'd given them the sheaf of papers himself
yesterday and, okay, she hadn't noticed that one sitting
on top then, but neither she nor Sofia had been anywhere
near the library. The plans couldn't have walked here on
their own.

'I don't understand,' she said, shaking her head.

Max began to laugh. But it wasn't the warm, rich sound
she remembered from the the day they'd gone crabbing. It
was a dark, rasping sound that made the hair on her arms
stand up on end.

'Of course,' he said, shaking his head. 'I knew I shouldn't
have hired you. Why I didn't listen to my gut I'll never
know. What was I thinking? You have no qualifications,
no experience—'

Now was the moment that the furnace of Ruby's anger
decided to *whomph* into life. She went from shivery and
cold to raging inferno in the space of a heartbeat.

'You're right!' she yelled back at him. 'You want to
know if I'm cut out to be a nanny? Well, I can answer that

right now—I'm not! Not if it means I have to like work-ing for closed-off, emotionally constipated jerks like you.'

Max went very still and his expression was completely neutral. If anything, that was more worrying than all the bluff and fluster had been. Ruby felt herself start to shake. She knew she'd gone too far, that she shouldn't have said that. But, as the sensible side of her brain tried to tell her that, the impulsive, emotional side blocked its ears and sang *la la la*.

'I should fire you for this,' he said, and his voice was as cold as the marble floor beneath their feet.

'Don't bother,' she shot back, making enough heat and anger for both of them. 'I quit. I'm not cut out for this and I don't want to be.' And she dumped the pile of paper she'd been holding onto Max's pile and stomped off towards the door. Thank goodness she only had that one rucksack to pack. She could be out of here within the hour.

'That's right,' Max said, his voice low and infuriatingly even as she reached the door. 'Run out on another job.'

She spun round to face him. 'You know nothing about me. So don't you dare judge me.'

He stared her down. The fire from a few moments ear-lier was gone, doused by a healthy dollop of concrete, if his expression was anything to go by.

'I know that you bail when the going gets tough, that you've never seen a single job through to the end.'

'So? That's my business, not yours. You've made that abundantly clear.'

He stepped forward. 'I'm afraid it is my business when you're leaving before the end of your contract.'

That was when Ruby smiled. She really shouldn't, but it started somewhere deep down inside and bubbled up until it reached her lips. 'And there's your problem, Mr Hot Shot. I don't have a contract, remember?'

And, leaving him to chew on that, she stalked down the

corridor. Pity she was wearing ballet slippers, because it would have been so much more effective in heels.

'We had a verbal agreement!' he yelled after her.

Ruby's response was to keep walking but use some non-verbal communication she was pretty sure was offensive in just about any language you cared to mention.

An angry shudder ripped through her as she headed for her room, already mentally packing her rucksack. And she'd thought she was attracted to this man? She really was insane. The sooner she got out of Venice, the better.

CHAPTER NINE

MAX WAS SO FURIOUS he couldn't speak, could hardly even breathe. How dare she act as if he were in the wrong? And how dare she bail on him after only one week? What was he going to do now? Knowing his mother, she'd make an impulsive decision and say she couldn't possibly keep Sofia here on her own, and then he'd be stuck here, right when it was more urgent than ever that he leave this tangled family mess behind and concentrate even harder on his work.

He wanted to march after Ruby, to give her a piece of his mind, but he suspected she was in no mood to listen. She was stubborn as hell, that woman, and bound to dig her heels in if he went in with all guns blazing.

He'd give her half an hour. Then he'd go and find her, make her see sense.

He looked down at the stack of papers in his hands. His scribbled-on plans were on top. Just the sight of them made his temperature rise a couple of notches. He turned and headed for the library. At least he'd be able to distract himself for a short while trying to see if anything was salvageable. Once he was there, he dropped the stack of papers on the desk and sank into the chair.

It had to have been her fault. She must have come and got more paper from his makeshift office at some point, despite what she'd said, because how else could his pristine plans have ended up on Sofia's drawing-paper pile? They hadn't been outside the library all week.

A cold feeling washed through him from head to toe.

Except...

Last night, when he'd taken some papers into the salon as a cure for insomnia, and the plans had been amongst them. It had worked, too. After an hour and a half of poring over them, going over every detail, he'd woken himself up, his head lolling against his chest, and then he'd stumbled back to bed.

Oh, hell.

And he had no idea if he'd stumbled back into the library first and replaced the plans.

He stared at the clean, narrow printed-out lines of his plans, with Ruby's thicker doodlings over the top. It was his fault, wasn't it? Not hers. While he hadn't exactly put them on Sofia's paper stack by leaving them lying around in the salon he'd opened up the way for them to get muddled into it during the course of the day.

Max exhaled heavily and let his forehead drop so it rested on the pile of papers.

Damn.

And he'd lost his temper. Something he never did. He'd always hated losing control like that. Not just because when his really long fuse went, it tended to verge on apocalyptic, but because of how he was feeling right now. Raw. Open. Weak.

If it had been Sofia that had done the drawing he knew he wouldn't have reacted the same way. Oh, he'd have been cross, but he wouldn't have exploded like that, and not just because she was only two and he would have scared the living daylights out of her.

There was something about Ruby that just got under his skin.

He sat up, ran his hand through his hair and stared at the dark green wallpaper.

He should let her leave, shouldn't he?

She wanted to. It would certainly be better for him.

But he needed her.

He shook his head. No. He didn't need anyone. Especially not a woman who ran at the first sniff of trouble, which was exactly what Ruby had done, proving his point very nicely for him.

He needed a nanny. That was all.

The choice was up to her. If she still wanted to go he wouldn't stop her, but there was one thing he needed to do first—apologise.

In a bit, though. Ruby was probably still spitting fire, and if he tried to knock on her door now, he'd probably get a few more of those wonderfully eloquent hand gestures.

A smile crept across his face, even though he knew it wasn't really funny at all.

She was a pill, that one.

He sighed and turned his attention back to the plans in front of him, unfolding the paper and having a good look. It was interesting what she'd drawn. She'd taken his plain, square arch and added some traditional Venetian style to it. She really had been paying attention to the shapes and patterns of the buildings, hadn't she? Here was an ogee arch, and here a lobed one. She'd reproduced them perfectly, even when she'd only been doodling.

That was when something smacked him straight between the eyebrows.

The shapes.

Ruby had been talking about the geometric shapes, the other day, the way simple ones interlocked to make more complicated ones. All he'd been able to see when he came to Venice was the fuss, the frilliness. He'd forgotten that even the most of ornate fasciae were constructed of much simpler, cleaner elements.

If he took Ruby's idea and pared it back, using simpler shapes, overlapping and juxtaposing them to create something, not exactly elaborate, because that wasn't his style, but something more intricate that still kept that essence of simple elegance.

He grabbed one of Sofia's scrap-paper sheets and a pen and began to scribble. Semicircular arches here and here, intersecting to create a more pointed version, with slender pillar for support. His hand flew over the paper, sketching shapes and lines, at first for the arches in the atrium, but then taking the same idea and applying it to other aspects of the space, giving it all a cohesive feel.

He could see it so clearly. Just a hint of gothic style, built in glass and steel. Modern materials that echoed back to classic design. It was just what he needed to tie the new wing and the existing institute building together and make them feel like one space.

He kept going, filling sheet after sheet, until he suddenly realised he'd been at this for ages.

Ruby!

He still hadn't gone and apologised.

He shoved away from the desk, sending a stack of Sofia's colourful drawings flying, and then sprinted down the corridor in the direction of her and Ruby's rooms. He didn't bother knocking when he got there, just flung the door open and raced inside, expecting to find her shoving clothes into her rucksack, a scowl on her face.

Wrong again, Max.

She can pack in under ten minutes, remember? Sometimes five.

Where Max had expected to find Ruby stewing and

muttering insults under her breath, there was nothing but empty space.

Ruby Lange was gone.

Ruby shivered as she waited on the little creaky dock outside Ca' Damiani. The clouds had sunk closer to the water and coloured everything a murky grey. A drop of rain splashed on her forehead. Great.

Her rucksack was at her feet, leaning against her lower legs, and she craned to see if the light bobbing towards her, accompanied by the sound of a motor, was the taxi she'd ordered. She needed to get out of here and she needed to do it right now.

This was so *not* how she'd imagined seeing Venice by water this evening.

More raindrops, one after the other. She could hear them plopping into the canal near her feet.

The approaching craft turned out to be a private boat that puttered past and stopped outside one of the buildings opposite. Ruby felt her whole body sag.

Stupid, stupid girl. You take on a job you know nothing about—just because some random guy says he needs you—and you think he's going to see past all of your inexperience and believe you're something special? Get real. The only thing Max Martin believed about her was that she was a flaky screw-up, just like everyone else on this planet.

She hugged her arms tighter around her, wishing she hadn't packed her jacket in the very bottom of the rucksack.

Not everyone believes you're a screw-up.

Okay, maybe she was being a little dramatic. A number of her bosses over the years had begged her to stay when she'd realised the job wasn't for her and had given in her notice. They'd said she was competent and organised and they'd love to promote her, but she hadn't been able to ignore that itchy feeling once it started. The only way to stop the intense restlessness, the only way to scratch it enough so it went away, was to move on. But Max was wrong. She didn't run away. She ran *to* the next thing. There was a whole world of difference.

The rain began to fall harder now. She pushed her fringe out of her eyes. It was already damp. Where *was* that taxi?

There was a creaking behind her as the boat door that led to the dock opened. Ruby's blood solidified in her veins. She refused to turn round.

She expected another angry tirade, braced herself against it, but when his voice came it was soft and low. 'Ruby?'

'That's my name,' she said, and then grimaced, glad he couldn't see her face. What was this? High school?

'Don't go.'

She spun round to face him, arms still clutched around her middle, as if she was afraid she'd fall apart if she didn't hold herself together. 'What?'

The anger was gone. She could see none of its vestiges on his features. Part of her breathed a sigh of relief, but another, deeper part, sighed with disappointment. The anger had been horrible, but it had been a little wonderful, too.

He walked forwards. Ruby was tempted to back away, but that would mean taking a dip in the canal, so she had to stay where she was. Cold drops peppered her skin and she shivered. Off in the distance there was a muffled rumble of thunder.

'I want to apologise,' he said, looking so earnest her heart grew warm and achy inside her chest. 'I should never have let off at you like that. It was totally uncalled for.'

'Thank you,' she said in a wobbly voice. 'And I should probably apologise for the verbal—and non-verbal—assault. That wasn't very professional.'

A wry smile lifted one corner of his mouth. 'I deserved it.'

Her stony blood started to warm and melt. It danced and

shimmered and sang. *Stop it*, she told it. *You're making it very hard to leave.*

And so was he, looking at her like that.

The itchy feeling returned, stronger this time. Unable to stand still, she walked in a small circle. The falling rain multiplied the lights of the city, but a cold breeze wrapped around her, stealing her breath.

'It was my fault the plans got mixed up with Sofia's drawing paper,' he said, not breaking eye contact. 'I left them in the salon the night before. I'm sorry I accused you of that.'

She nodded, not trusting herself to say anything.

He looked down at his feet briefly before meeting her eyes again. 'Forgive me.'

Revenge, passion and utter, utter devotion. The words spun through Ruby's head.

'Okay,' she croaked.

He nodded, his expression still slightly grim. 'Then stay…please?'

Ruby blinked. Up until now, she hadn't been sure that word was part of Max Martin's vocabulary.

She looked away, even closed her eyes for good measure. She'd wanted to go so badly. So badly… It was a surprise to discover the tug to stay was just as strong. Not to stay and be Sofia's nanny, although she was sure she would enjoy another week of that, but to stay here. In Venice. With Max.

She sucked a breath in and held it. Thank goodness he had no idea about the silly things she'd been feeling. Thank goodness he probably thought she was acting out of hurt pride. And fear, yes. He'd been right about that. She did run when things got too hard. Always had. How could you save yourself the crushing pain of disappointment otherwise?

She opened her eyes and looked out across the water. The moon was rising farther away, where the clouds had not yet blotted it out. It cast a silvery glow on the far-off bell towers and roofs, spilling glitter on the still waters of this back canal, where it undulated softly. It looked like a fairy tale.

And if this were a fairy tale, she'd stay. Max would fall madly in love with her and make her his princess. In their happy-ever-after she'd soothe his pain, teach him to let it go, and they'd be gloriously happy together.

Only real life didn't work that way. It hadn't for her and her father, and it hadn't for Fina. Only a fool wouldn't escape when they had the chance rather than sentence themselves to that kind of misery.

If she stayed, she might fall for him properly, not just teeter on the brink of an *inappropriate* crush.

She pulled her rucksack up from the floor of the dock and hugged it to her before turning to face him. 'I don't know, Max. I don't think it's a good idea I stay...for anybody.'

The water taxi chose that moment to turn up. The driver, oblivious to the tense scene occurring on the little wooden dock, looped a rope round a post and called out in Italian.

Ruby wiped the rain off her face and waved to show she'd heard him, then she slipped the straps of her rucksack over her shoulders. She pressed her lips together and tried not to let her eyes shimmer. 'Goodbye. Tell Fina and Sofia I'm sorry.' And then she turned and steadied herself before stepping into the boat.

As she lifted her foot he called out again. 'Don't go.'

She turned to look over her shoulder. 'Why, Max? Why shouldn't I go?'

For a moment he didn't say anything, but then he looked her straight in the eye. 'Because I need you.'

CHAPTER TEN

IF RUBY HAD THOUGHT she'd felt a little breathless before, now she really struggled to pull oxygen into her body. Max needed her?

He doesn't mean it that way. Don't be stupid.

'No, you just need a proper nanny. It isn't me *specifically* that you need.'

No words left Max's mouth, but she discovered his eyes contradicted her quite beautifully. Her heart literally stopped beating inside her chest, just for a second. When it started up again, her pulse thundered in her ears.

She let her rucksack slip off her shoulders and it landed behind her on the dock with a thud. The rain began to fall in earnest, soaking the thin wool of her cardigan, but she didn't seem to feel the damp and cold seeping into her skin.

Him, too? It hadn't just been a physical, knee-jerk kind of thing?

That made her feel as if the world had just done a somersault around her and she needed to find solid ground again. Pity she was stranded in a city where that was in short supply.

That didn't mean she was about to commit emotional suicide by staying, though. She cleared her throat. 'I meant what I said earlier, Max. I don't think I'm cut out to be a nanny in the long term.'

He nodded. 'I agree. But I'm not asking you to be a

nanny for the rest of your life. I'm just asking you to be one for the next week or so. After that it's up to you.'

She nodded. That all sounded very sensible.

'If you don't think I'm cut out to be a nanny, why on earth do you want me to stay and look after Sofia?'

Max gave her a weary look. 'I didn't say I didn't think you could do the job.' He smiled gently. 'I said it because I didn't think you should commit yourself to something when your talent clearly lies elsewhere.'

Ruby's eyes widened. 'You think I have talent?'

He frowned. 'Don't *you*? Your drawings are fabulous, and that doodle you did on my plans set ideas firing off in my head so fast I could hardly keep up with them.' The smile grew into a grin. 'I have my "wow factor" for the Institute now, Ruby, and it's all because of you.'

She closed her eyes and opened them again, not quite able to believe what she was hearing. 'Do you... Do you think I should be an architect?'

His eyes warmed, making her forget the salty lagoon breeze that kept lifting the shorter bits of her hair now and then. 'I think you could do that if you wanted to, but there's something about your sketches that's so full of life and personality. I think you've got something there. They're quirky and original and full of...'

You. His eyes must have said that bit, because his mouth had stopped moving.

'They're captivating.'

Ruby felt the echo of his words rumble deep down inside her. Or maybe it was the crack of thunder that shook the sky over their heads.

Oh, heck. She really was in trouble, wasn't she? How could she leave now?

And maybe Max was right. Maybe it was time to stop running. She might not have to see being a nanny through to the bitter end, but she could see this job through. How could she leave them all in the lurch like this? Sofia wouldn't understand where she'd gone and feel abandoned all over again, Fina would be saddled with looking after a toddler full time, and Max wouldn't have time to work on his plans, and she really wanted him to do that.

She still didn't believe there was much in the future for them, even if some bizarre chemistry was popping between them, but she'd like to visit the National Institute of Fine Art on a rainy afternoon in a few years' time and sit under Max's atrium and feel happy—and maybe a little sad—to know that she'd had something to do with it, that in some lasting way she had a tiny connection to him.

She looked down at the rucksack threatening to pitch off the dock and into the canal. The taxi driver, whom she'd forgotten all about, coughed and mumbled something grumpily about being made to hang about in this kind of weather. She shot him a look of desperation.

He shrugged in that fatalistic Italian way, his expression saying, *Are you coming or not?*

Ruby looked back at Max. He was waiting. Not shouting. Not bulldozering. It was totally her choice and she knew he would hold no grudges if she got on this boat and told the driver to take her to the Piazzale Roma to catch a train.

She swallowed and twisted to face the driver and rummaged in her pocket and gave him a tip for his trouble. *'Mi dispiace, signore.'*

Ruby woke up to sunshine pouring into her bedroom the next morning. She stumbled over to the window, which overlooked a narrow little canal that ran down the side of the palazzo. It almost felt as if the night before had never happened. There was no hint of the storm. The sky was the clear pale blue of a baby's blanket, hardly a cloud to mar it, and where the sun hit the canal it was a fierce and glittering emerald.

Things were just as surreal at breakfast, with Fina bustling around and fussing over Sofia, never once mentioning that Ruby had packed her bags and tried to leave last night.

Max had been in the library since before she'd got up, and that had been pretty early. She half expected him to bury himself away all day, working on his plans until it was time to pack up and leave for the airport. She didn't know what would be worse: not seeing him most of the day or spending a bittersweet last few hours with him before he returned to London. She'd forgotten all about that last night when she'd agreed to stay. So when the salon door opened at ten o'clock and Max walked in, Ruby's heart leapt and cowered at the same time.

'What do you want to do this morning?' he asked his niece, glancing briefly at Ruby and giving a nod of greeting.

'Fishing!' Sofia yelled and ran off in the direction of the cupboard where the crabbing gear was kept.

Both Ruby and Max charged after her, knowing just how tightly that cupboard was packed and just how much mischief an unattended two-year-old could get up to inside it. They managed to beat Sofia to the lines and hooks, but Max gave her a bucket and a small net to carry to keep her happy. And then they bustled around, getting into the boat, coaxing Sofia into a life jacket, making sure she didn't let go of her bucket and leave it floating down a canal somewhere.

She and Max worked as a team, exchanging words when needed, passing equipment to each other, but it wasn't until they were standing at Max's favourite crabbing spot, the little boat moored up and bobbing about a short distance away, that they slowed down enough for Ruby to get a sense of his mood.

She watched him gently helping Sofia wind an empty

line back up without getting it tangled. He'd been polite this morning, almost friendly.

Had she imagined it? Had it all been some weird dream, a spell cast by this contrary city?

She let out a long sigh. Maybe it was better if that was the case. It was sheer craziness. Even if she'd seen what she'd thought she'd seen in his eyes last night, what did she think was going to happen? A wild fling in his mother's house, with a toddler running around?

Once again, get real, Ruby.

She knelt down and took interest in what Sofia was doing. She'd plopped the crab line into the water for the fourth or fifth time, but so far no luck. The little girl heaved out a sigh. 'Fish go 'way,' she said slightly despondently.

Ruby couldn't help but smile. Despite her self-contained manner, Sofia had a little bit of her grandmother's flair for drama in her. She forgot herself, looked up at Max to share the joke. He was crouching the other side of Sofia, who was sitting on the edge of the *fondamenta* where the railings parted, her little legs swinging above the water, and their eyes met across the top of her head.

Ruby almost fell in the canal.

It was all there, everything he hadn't said last night and everything he had.

Oh, heck. Just when she'd almost managed to talk some sense into herself.

And it still all did make sense. He was her boss. He was going back to London in a matter of hours. He was her total polar opposite. In what world was that anything but a recipe for disaster?

Everywhere but Venice, she discovered as a slow smile spread across her lips. She felt she must be glowing. Actually radiating something. It would probably scare the fish away.

She wanted to lean across, press her lips to his, wind

her arms around his neck and just taste him. Feel him. Dive into him.

'Fish!' Sofia yelled, and it was almost her who did the diving. She got so excited she almost toppled off the edge into the canal. It was only Max's quick reflexes that saved her.

After that they made sure they had their eyes on Sofia instead of each other at all times. It didn't matter, though. It was pulsing in the air around them, like a wonderful secret, a song carried on a radio wave that only they could tune into.

She felt it as they ended their crabbing expedition, a weary Sofia rubbing her eyes and complaining about being hungry. She felt it as they stood mere inches apart at the front of the boat, Max steering, her holding Sofia so she could see over the top of the little motorboat's windscreen. Felt it as they passed buckets and nets and bags to each other from boat to dry land.

As they pulled the last of the luggage from the boat and headed into the large downstairs hall of the palazzo Ruby turned to Max, made proper eye contact in what seemed the first time in decades. 'What time's your flight?' she asked, plainly and simply.

It was all very well dreaming on the canals, but their feet were back on solid ground now. It was time to anchor herself back in reality, remind herself of what really was happening here.

'Five o'clock,' he said.

She nodded towards the first floor. 'You'd better get going if you're going to get any work done before you have to stop and pack.' She held out her hand to take the nets from him.

Max looked at her for a long while, and an ache started low down in her belly. 'Yes,' he said, and then handed her the nets and set off up the staircase, taking the steps two at a time.

* * *

Ruby jiggled her leg while she waited for Sofia to finish brushing her teeth. Once she'd had a try herself, Ruby dived in and gave them another going-over. As mundane as the task was, she was glad of something to do. Sofia had had an extra-long sleep that afternoon. Ruby had gone into her room again and again, expecting to find her jumping on the bed, but each time Sofia had been sprawled on the mattress, her pink rabbit tucked in the crook of her arm and her thumb in her mouth.

She'd heard Max leave the palazzo around three. His plane was probably somewhere over the English Channel now.

He hadn't even said goodbye.

A stab of something hit her in the stomach, but she forced it away. She bundled Sofia from the bathroom and back to her bedroom, where she found Fina sitting on the bed, waiting for them.

'You are looking tired, *piccola.*'

Ruby ruffled Sofia's hair. 'I don't know why, after that mammoth sleep she had.'

Fina smiled and tipped her head on one side. 'I was talking about you, my darling.'

Ruby tried not to react. Was it really that obvious?

Fina waved her hand in a regal manner. 'Well, it is all for the good. I came to say I would read Sofia her story and put her to bed tonight, so you go and relax in the salon.'

Ruby shook her head. More sitting around with nothing to do—the last thing she needed. 'It's my job, Fina—'

Fina stopped her with an imperious eyebrow lift. 'But I wish to. So…off you go.' And she dismissed Ruby with a gracious smile.

There wasn't much Ruby could say to that, so she sloped off in the direction of the salon to do as she was told. The setting sun was streaming in through the windows when she entered the room, almost blinding her, and at first she didn't see the dark shape by the window, but after a moment or two the dark smudge morphed into something more solid.

Ruby's mouth dropped open. 'B-but I thought you were going back to London!'

Max turned round. He was silhouetted against the ornate arches, and she couldn't see his face, let alone read his features.

'So did I.'

She shook her head. 'What changed?'

'Nothing…and everything.'

He stepped forward out of the light and Ruby could see he wasn't wearing his suit, just dark casual trousers and a light sweater. Her heart began to beat faster.

'But this afternoon, when I carried on using the ideas from your doodle and incorporating a pared-down Venetian style into my plans for the institute, I realised I need to be here, not in London. I need to get my inspiration from the source, not just inaccurate and misleading memories. I've spent all afternoon wandering around looking at buildings I've known all my life and seeing them with completely fresh eyes.' He shook his head.

Ruby glanced over her shoulder towards the corridor, and Sofia's bedroom. She could just about hear the warm tones of Fina's voice as she read her granddaughter a fairy story. 'There's something to be said for stripping the preconceptions and prejudices of the past away and looking at things with fresh eyes.'

'Did my mother put you up to saying that?'

She turned back, expecting him to be scowling, but his face was almost neutral, save for the barest hint of a smile.

One corner of Ruby's mouth lifted. 'No. I think I'm quite capable of irritating you without outside help.'

Max laughed, and it made something rise like a balloon inside Ruby and bump against the ceiling of her ribs.

He walked towards the door in the path of a long, golden shadow. 'Come on,' he said.

Ruby frowned, but she turned to follow anyway. 'Where?'

He stopped and looked back at her. 'You missed seeing Venice at sunset last night because I had an attack of stupid. It's only right I should make it up to you tonight.'

CHAPTER ELEVEN

AS THEY WALKED along the little wooden dock in front of his mother's palazzo, Max couldn't help but remember being there with Ruby the night before. He jumped down into the little speedboat, and Ruby followed him. Without even asking, she helped with the ropes and fenders.

She'd only been here a week, and no one had shown her what to do. She'd just picked it up, that quick mind of hers soaking up all the information and putting it effortlessly to use.

She sat in the stern as he drove the boat away, silent. The outfit tonight was the plainest one yet. No hippies. No rock chicks. No damn strawberries. All she wore was a cream blouse with soft ruffles, a pair of capris and a light cardigan thrown over her shoulders. He watched her drink in the way the setting sun made every façade richer and more glorious, harking back to the days when some had actually been covered entirely in gold leaf.

In fact, he found it hard to *stop* watching her.

But he needed to.

Ruby Lange seemed bright and sunny and harmless, but she was a dangerous substance. She dissolved through his carefully constructed walls without even trying. He really should keep her at a distance.

Then why did you invite her to come out with you this evening?

Because it was the right thing to do. He'd acted like a total idiot the previous evening and so he was making it up to her. And he'd given his word. He'd said he'd show her Venice at sunset and so he was going to show her Venice at sunset.

Yeah, right. You keep telling yourself that. It has nothing to do with wanting to be alone with her, with wanting her to melt those walls that have left you claustrophobic and breathless for too long.

Max steered the boat down the canal and busied himself doing what he'd come here to do—no, not spend time alone with Ruby, but offer his services as tour guide and boat driver. He beckoned for her to come up and stand beside him, pointed out a few landmarks, and they talked easily about history and architecture for at least ten minutes.

It wasn't working.

Inside there was a timer counting down, ticking away the seconds until the sun slipped below the horizon and he and Ruby would be cocooned in the dark. He couldn't stop thinking about it.

He needed to remember why this was a bad idea, remember why Ruby wasn't right for him. As alluring as she might be, last night's uproar had proved one thing quite firmly: Ruby Lange ran when things got too close, when things got too serious. And these days he was nothing but serious.

He slowed the engine a little and looked over at her. 'Why do you move from job to job?'

She tore her gaze off the city and looked at him. 'I told you the other night. I want to find my perfect fit, like my father has. Like you have.'

He took his eyes off her for a moment to steer past a boat going a little slower than they were. 'Does it have to be perfect?'

Ruby gave him a puzzled smile. 'Well, I'd like it to be.

Who wants to do a job their whole life if they have no passion for it?'

'Millions of people do.'

She shook her head. 'I want more out of life. I'm tired with settling for crumbs. I want the whole banquet.'

He nodded. That part he understood only too well, but there was something else she hadn't considered.

'Whatever my mother says, I wasn't sure about architecture, at least not when it came time to choose a profession,' he told her, returning his gaze to the canal, as they'd turned into a busier, wider stretch and he needed to pay attention, but every now and then he glanced over at her. 'I liked it. It fascinated me, but, like you, I wasn't sure it was what I wanted to do with my life. I often wondered if I'd picked it because I wanted to impress my father.'

On his next glance across her eyes were wide. 'It's not your passion?' she almost whispered. 'Because if it isn't, I'd be fascinated to see what you're like when you really get into something!'

He smiled. 'No. It is my passion, or at least it is now. What I'm trying to say is that what if there is no perfect job, not at the start? What if it's the learning, the discipline of immersing yourself in it and scaling the learning curves that makes it a perfect fit?'

She frowned and her eyes made tiny, rapid side-to-side movements as she worked that one out in her head. She frowned harder. He guessed she hadn't been able to neatly file that thought and shove it away out of sight.

'But how do you do that and not lose your heart and soul to something that might not be the right choice?' Her voice dropped to the scratchiest of whispers. 'What do you do if you choose something and it doesn't choose you back?'

He shrugged. Maybe he'd been lucky. 'But there's the irony—you may never know unless you try.'

She folded her arms, scowled and turned away to look at

the buildings as he turned the boat onto the Grand Canal. 'That's a very Italian thing to say,' she muttered darkly.

'I *am* half Italian,' he reminded her.

She shot him a saucy look. 'And there was me, thinking you'd forgotten.'

Then she turned and just absorbed the scenery. They'd come from the relative quiet and muted tones of the smaller canals onto the wide strip of water that snaked through the centre of the city. Suddenly it was all light and colour.

Sunset seemed further away here, out of the shadows of the tall buildings, where the remaining light reflected off the water onto the palazzos and back into the sky. Awnings were pulled down over restaurants that lined the water's edge, and the spaces inside were bustling, full of warm light and moving people.

She looked across at him. 'Talking of trying, your mother is very pleased you're staying on.'

He gave her a resigned look. 'I know.'

'So why won't you let *her* try, Max?'

There she went again, tapping at his walls with her little pickaxe, testing them for weak spots.

'Have you ever listened to her side of the story?' she continued. 'Or have you always gone on what your father told you?'

Ouch.

She'd found one. A chink in his perception of his life that he hadn't even realised had been there. He tried to plug it up. 'I saw enough with my own eyes,' he replied gruffly. 'And my father rarely spoke of her.'

But the damage had been done. Memories started spilling into his brain, scenes of his parents' marriage. He'd always thought he'd understood what was going on so clearly, but it was as if this was another version of the same film, and different details sprang to life, tiny things that tipped everything on its head—the look of desperation in his mother's eyes, the way she'd sobbed late into the night, the way she'd looked at his father, with such adoration, in both good times and bad.

He drowned them out by taking another, busier route with the boat, so he had to give driving it his full concentration. He steered the boat down the canal and out towards St Mark's Square. It was full of gondolas of sighing tourists here, and he felt his irritation with the city, with its over-the-topness returning. Maybe Ruby had something in her idea of not wanting to give your heart and soul to something, only to be disappointed.

'Can *you* try?' she asked softly.

As always, she took what he was prepared to give and pushed him to cough up more. The sensation was one rather akin to having a particularly sticky plaster ripped off a tender patch of skin.

'And that's what happens in your family, is it?' He glanced skyward, noticing neither the pink drifting clouds nor the orange sky behind them. 'Last I heard, you were all for keeping parents at a safe distance.'

Ruby looked at her shoes. He couldn't see her cheeks, but he'd bet they were warmer than they'd been a few seconds ago. 'I didn't think you'd remember that,' she mumbled.

'Well, I did.' She could have been right, though. He managed to tune out most people most of the time, but there was something about Ruby that made him listen, even when he'd dearly like to switch everything off and sink into blessed silence. 'So maybe you should practise what you preach before you start lecturing me.'

She shuffled her feet and looked up at him, arms still hugging herself. 'Okay, maybe I should. But I've tried over the years with my father, Max, and he always keeps me at arm's length, no matter what.'

That was hard to believe. Look at her, with her large, expressive eyes, her zest for life, which still seemed to be threatening to burst out of her, despite her slightly sub-dued mood. He was having trouble *maintaining* a distance of arm's length.

'Why?' he asked, glad for a chance to swing the inter-rogation light her way.

Ruby sat down on one of the cushioned benches. Max slowed the motor and brought the craft to a halt, letting it bob on the canal as the pleasure boats, *vaporetti* and gon-dolas drifted past. He turned to lean against the steering wheel and looked back at her.

She shook her head, staring out across the dark green canal, now flecked with pink and gold from the setting sun. 'It took me years to even come close to forming a the-ory on that one. It's partly because he's so absorbed in his work, and it's got worse the older he gets. There are only so many weeks and hours left to educate the world about the unique habitats the human race is ripping through, the species we're forcing into extinction. How can one "flighty" child compete against all of that?'

'What's the other part?'

Ruby looked up at him. 'He has plenty of friends and colleagues who have wild children—celebrity offspring syndrome, I've heard him call it. Over-indulged, privileged, reckless. I think he wanted to save me from that.'

That was understandable, but surely anyone who knew Ruby knew she wasn't that sort. She might be impulsive, but that came from her creativity, not out of selfishness or arrogant stupidity.

She sighed and stood up, walked to the back of the boat, even though it was only a few steps. 'I came to understand his logic eventually. I think he thinks that if he rations out the attention and approval then he won't spoil me.' She sighed again. 'It's so sad, especially as I know he wasn't like that with my mother. He'd have given her anything.'

Max didn't say anything, mainly because he was rubbish at saying the right thing at the right time, but he also suspected she just needed room to talk.

'I can't live on the scraps he hands out,' she said sadly. 'He doesn't understand it, but women, be they wives or daughters or sisters, need more than that.'

They both fell into silence. Max thought of his mother, and wondered if Ruby was thinking of her too. He'd never wanted for approval from his father—not that the old man had ever said anything out loud—but they'd been so alike. It had been easy to see the things beneath the surface, hear the words his father had never been able to say. For the first time ever it struck him that maybe not everyone had that ability.

They'd been so different, Geoffrey and Serafina Martin. His mother emotional and demonstrative, his father stoic and silent. He'd always thought their extreme personality types should make them the perfect complement for each other, but maybe he'd been wrong. Maybe that had been the reason for his mother's midnight tears; she'd desperately needed to reap some of the tangible demonstrations of love she'd so generously sowed.

He nodded slowly. 'I'm starting to understand that.' He caught her eye. 'And it makes sense why it's easier to run away, rather than stay.'

He didn't like to say that. It went against everything in him, but he couldn't ignore the sense in it.

Ruby read him like a book. She laughed a soft little dry laugh. 'And you think you don't?'

Max stood up, his brows bunching together. No, he didn't run. He was the one that was solid, stuck things out.

She walked towards him, until she was standing right in front of him. 'You can't be fully committed to something if you keep part of yourself back. It's cheating—a bit like this lagoon.' She stretched her arm out to encompass the water, including the tiniest glimpse of the open sea in the distance. 'It looks like the deep blue sea, smells like it, tastes like it, but when you try and jump all the way in you find out how shallow it is. Commitment is easy when it's only ankle deep.'

Max wanted to be angry with her. He wanted to tell her she was so very wrong, but he couldn't. Instead he exhaled long and hard and met Ruby's enquiring gaze. 'That makes us two very similar creatures, then.'

She stared back at him, more than a hint of defiance in her expression. 'Yes.'

On the surface he and Ruby were chalk and cheese. She was quirky and outspoken, where he was taciturn and strait-laced. She was emotional and effusive, where he...wasn't. But underneath? Well, that was a whole different story.

Her eyes softened a little, but the hard-hitting honesty in them remained. 'Okay, I admit it. I'm a coward when it comes to my family. And maybe I do flit from thing to thing because I'm nervous about committing to anything fully, but you have to face it, Max, despite all your fine words, the only thing you're truly committed to when it comes to your family is your prejudice and lack of forgiveness.'

He turned and started up the engine again. The canals—even this wide, spacious one—we're closing in on him, and the sun would slip below the horizon soon. He headed out of the end of the Grand Canal and into the lagoon, so they could see the painfully bright orange smudge settling behind the monastery on Isola di San Giorgio. Out here the salty wind soothed him. He felt as if he could breathe properly again.

Ruby hadn't said anything since they'd set off again. She'd just sat down on the bench and crossed her arms. He slowed the motor and checked on her. She didn't look happy. He had a feeling he'd have no trouble keeping her at arm's length now. He might as well dig himself in further.

'Have you forgiven *your* father?'

She chewed her lip for a while. 'I hadn't realised I needed to, but maybe I do.' She looked up and noticed the sunset for the first time. 'Oh,' she said, her face lighting up, and Max couldn't bear to tear his eyes from her and turn around.

After staring for a moment, her focus changed and he could tell she was now studying him instead. 'I'm not sure it'll change anything. He'll probably still treat me the same way, but with you and Fina… It could change everything.'

'Maybe,' he said. And then he turned to watch the sun descend into the blue-grey water. They didn't say anything as it went down, just watched in silence, the only sound the gentle waves of the lagoon slapping against the hull of the little painted boat, then he started up the engine again. 'Do you want to go round the island?'

A twinkle of mischief appeared in her eyes, totally blindsiding him. 'You know what I'd really like?'

He shook his head.

'We're always being so safe when Sofia is in the boat, puttering around, going slow down the canals. I'd like to go out onto the open water and build up some speed, see what this little vintage baby can do.'

Max set off again at a moderate speed, at least until they'd rounded the large island in front of them and faced the open lagoon. Out here there was only the occasional ferry, plenty of room to let off some steam, and he discovered he was yearning for it as much as she was.

'Ready?' he asked, and shoved the throttle forward before she had time to answer.

Ruby squealed and hung on to the woodwork in front of her as the bow of the little boat lifted, skimming through the moonlit waves, and the wind rushed through their hair. At first she was silent, her breath taken by the change in speed, but as he circled around and the boat tilted she began to laugh, then she let out a loud whoop.

Max found himself laughing too, which was insane, seeing as how serious he'd been feeling only minutes earlier. He kept the speed up, took a few unexpected turns, raced the waves out towards Lido Island and then back again until they were both windswept and breathless.

As they circled the Isola di San Giorgio again, he reluctantly slowed the engine. The sky was a velvety midnight blue above them and the lights and reflections of Venice were threatening to outnumber the stars in their brilliance and beauty.

Ruby sighed. 'Can we stop here for a moment, before we head back home? I won't get a chance to see this again.'

He didn't answer, just circled one last time then flipped the key in the ignition and cut the engine. Ruby got up and walked shakily towards him as they got caught up in their own wake. She stopped before she got too close, though. Still out of reach. Just.

Another surge hit them. Max hardly noticed it, being used to boats as he was, but Ruby lost her footing, wobbled slightly.

Her arms, which had still been loosely hugged round herself, flew out for balance. At the same time he reacted on reflex and his hand shot out and curled round her elbow, steadying her.

Not at arm's length now. Not at all.

He looked down at where they were joined and wondered how hard it would be to let go. He looked up again to find Ruby's eyes large, but her expression calm and open. Very hard, he decided. Even after the boat had rocked itself back into equilibrium he found he hadn't been able to do it.

But maybe he didn't need to.

He slipped his hand down her arm, over her wrist, until his fingers met hers, and he laced them together, reminding himself of those intersecting arches he'd stolen for his design. How simple the shapes were on their own, but how much better they were when they were joined with something similar.

He reached for her other hand, meshed it to his in the same way. She looked down at their intertwined fingers, so tangled up with each other that he couldn't tell whether he was holding her or she was holding him, and then she looked back up at him, her breathing shallow, her cheeks flushed.

This was *way* more than ankle deep.

Gently he tugged, and she came. Their hands remained joined, and he bent his head to brush his lips against hers. It wasn't enough. He kissed her again, lingering this time. Ruby sighed and leaned against him. Gently she slid her fingers from his and ran her hands up his arms, onto his neck. He could feel her fingertips on the bare skin above his collar, her thumbs along his jaw.

She pulled away and opened her eyes. He looked back at her. Her fingers continued to roam, exploring his jaw and temple, tracing his cheekbones, and then they kissed again, sinking into it.

It wasn't like their first meeting of lips. It wasn't hot and urgent, fuelled by simple physical need, but neither was it hesitant and testing. It was slow and intimate, as if they'd been lovers for years, nothing but truth flowing between them, even if he was a little fuzzy on what exactly that truth was.

As the bells of the far away *campanili* rang out across the lagoon, and Venice glittered like a jewel in the distance, Max wrapped his arms around Ruby, pulled her as close as he could get. He might be rubbish with words, but he spoke to her in the poetry every Italian knew so well.

CHAPTER TWELVE

THEY DIDN'T GET BACK to the palazzo until well after nine. Max cut the engine and stared at the hulking exterior of his mother's house. Here, his and Ruby's roles were defined for them, clearly marked out. Out there on the lagoon, there had been nothing but a delicious blurring of all the reasons they shouldn't be together.

Ruby jumped out of the boat, took the rope from him and secured it to a post. Max stayed where he was in the boat.

He didn't want to go back inside.

For the last hour he'd felt alive again, free. The grief that had been the wallpaper of his life since his father's death had evaporated briefly, but now it was back again, slamming into his chest with such force he had to draw in a breath.

Ruby smiled at him, a sweet, beguiling smile, but he found he couldn't return it. Shutters were clanging up fast inside him, like those in a bank when the panic button had been pressed, and by the time he climbed out of the boat and headed inside no chink remained.

Each step up the staircase made him feel heavier, as if gravity were increasing.

'Max?' Ruby said as they reached the top, her eyes clouded with worry. He wanted to tell her it wasn't anything to do with her, that she was the only bright spot in his life at the moment, but the words didn't even make it up his throat, let alone out of his mouth.

He did what he could: he reached for her hand, caught it in his and wove his fingers into hers the way he'd done back on the boat just before he'd kissed her.

He saw relief flood her features and the smile came back. Sweeter this time, softer. What he wouldn't give to just lose himself in that smile.

'You have returned?' His mother's voice came from inside the salon.

Ruby jumped and slid her fingers from his before his mother appeared in the doorway. His skin felt cold where hers had just been.

'Why don't you come and have a coffee with me and tell me all about it?'

His mother looked hopefully at him, and Ruby joined her.

His head started to swirl—with the memories that had assaulted him earlier, with the conversation he'd had with Ruby out on the lagoon. He knew he should try with his mother, knew he should at least let her share her side of the story, that going in for coffee now would be a tiny and harmless step in that direction, but he couldn't seem to make his feet move.

'Max?' Ruby said, her smile disappearing, her brow creasing.

He felt as if he were made of concrete. 'I'm sorry,' he said, his voice a little hoarse, 'but I need to make up the time I took away from my work.'

Ruby's face fell. His mother just stared at him.

'I'm sorry,' he said again, and strode off in the direction of the library.

Ruby and Fina watched Max go. When the library door had shut behind him, Fina sighed and turned back into the salon.

'I don't blame him, you know,' she said as she walked to the coffee table and poured espresso into delicate cups. 'When things were at their worst between me and Geoffrey, I didn't behave well. He probably has many memories that make it easy for him to hate me.'

Ruby wanted to reach out to her, put a hand on her arm. 'I'm sure that's not true,' she said softly.

Fina shook her head. 'I loved that man, even though he was just as pig-headed as his son.' Fina sighed. 'I could have handled that. It was the fact he locked himself away…here.' She thumped her chest with her palm then looked Ruby right in the eye. 'I grew tired of hungering for something I thought he wouldn't—or couldn't—give me.'

Fina didn't pick up her coffee cup, but walked over to the windows and stared out. Ruby couldn't tell if she was focusing on the moon beyond or her reflection in the glass.

'I had glimpses of the man underneath,' she said. 'Foolishly, I thought that once we were married the process of slowly unravelling all that bound him would start. I tugged, pulled at threads, but I could never find the right place to begin.'

Ruby swallowed. She knew all about glimpses. Knew all about how tantalising they could be.

'In the end I used to do anything I could to provoke emotion from him. Anger was the easiest. I told myself that if I could make him feel *something* it proved he still cared.' She shook her head and looked at Ruby. 'I pushed him and pushed him. Doing things, saying things, I shouldn't have. And each time I had to try harder, do more. I must have seemed like a monster to my son, but really I was just…' She paused, struggling for the right word.

'Desperate?' Ruby finished for her.

Fina gave her a grateful look. 'Yes.' She looked back at

her reflection in the window. 'And in the end I succeeded. I pushed him to the ultimate limit.'

Ruby held her breath for a moment. 'What did you do?'

Fina blinked. 'I left him.'

Ruby stepped closer.

'It broke him,' Fina continued, her tone taking on a ragged quality. 'I finally had my proof. But I could never go back. I'd done too much damage.'

Ruby didn't know what to say, which was just as well, because if she'd tried to speak, tears would have coursed down her face. She just nodded, letting Fina know she was listening.

'It's my fault Massimo is the way he is,' Fina added softly, 'so I cannot be angry with him. I just don't want him to harden himself further, end up like his father.' She paused a moment and heaved in a breath. Ruby sensed she was trying not to lose composure completely. 'I shouldn't have left him behind, but I thought I was doing the right thing. He had his school...and Geoffrey adored him. I couldn't rob him of his son, too.'

'Of course you couldn't,' Ruby said.

Fina suddenly turned to face her, grabbed her hands and leaned in. 'Be careful when you fall in love,' she said hoarsely. 'It is a curse to love something so much, believe it is in easy reach, and then discover it will always be kept beneath lock and key.' Fina sighed dramatically and dropped her hands.

Ruby nodded and then stepped away, walked back to the table and picked up her espresso. She finished it quickly, even though it felt like gravel going down.

'I'd better check on Sofia,' she mumbled, then fled from the room.

Fina knew. Ruby didn't know how. Maybe she'd worked out that Ruby's dishevelled appearance after the boat ride had been down to more than a brisk twilight wind, but she knew. And she was warning Ruby off.

The morning was clear and bright. A light mist hovered over the lagoon and the Damiani family boat carved through it at speed as it headed away from the city and out into the open water. Max stood at the wheel, breeze lifting his hair, and concentrated on pinpointing their location. It had been a long time since he'd visited this place and he knew if he didn't pay attention that he'd miss it altogether.

'Where go?' Sofia piped up from the back of the boat.

He glanced over his shoulder and gave her a smile. Sofia was snuggled up between Ruby and his mother and all three of them were surrounded by a jumble of beach equipment—an umbrella, a picnic basket, various bags containing sunscreen and towels and changes of clothes.

He deliberately didn't catch Ruby's eye. Mainly because he was only just hanging on to the last bit of his control. The urge to touch her every time he saw her was quickly becoming overpowering—and had led to a few interesting stolen moments over the few days since their sunset trip. She was like a drug. The more he had, the more he wanted. Needed.

He took a deep breath and forced himself to behave. His mother and his not quite three-year-old niece were also in the boat; that should help somewhat. And it did. Just about.

'We're going to the beach,' he told Sofia and turned back round to concentrate on where he was going. A few moments later he slowed the motor and peered around, first at the water directly in front of the boat and then at the horizon, checking the location of various landmarks on the coast.

This was it. He was sure it was. He cut the motor and let down the small anchor.

'Want beach,' Sofia said, most determinedly, and Max threw her another smile.

'We're here.'

Ruby frowned at him. 'Don't tease her. She doesn't understand.'

'I'm not teasing,' he said. She was even adorable when she was cross with him, which was just as well, really, seeing as he was rather good at getting her in that state. He turned his attention to Sofia.

'This is a magic beach. You just wait and see.' And he stuck his thumb and forefinger in his mouth and whistled loudly. 'That's what gets the magic started,' he explained.

His mother just patted the child's hand and looked back at him with soulful eyes. This place had always been special to him, a highlight of their family holidays each year, and he knew she was experiencing the same rush of memories that he was. He'd thought it would help, bring them a sense of connection, but he managed to return her gaze for a second or so before he looked away.

He didn't have many memories of his father in Venice, especially as he'd often worked through the long summer holidays and had only joined them for snatched days and weekends, but this had been one of his favourite places. He'd been charmed by the sheer contrariness of it.

The tide had caused the boat to swing on its anchor slightly, just as he'd planned, and now he gave Sofia a salute, kicked off his shoes and jumped overboard.

'No!' screamed Ruby and stood up, but then she sat back down again with a plop when she realised he was standing and the water was only lapping round his calves. Sofia ran over to the edge of the boat and peered over the edge.

Ruby gave him an exasperated look and mouthed an insult that wasn't fit for Sofia's ears. He grinned back at her. Some primal part of him was stupidly pleased she'd been worried for him. She shook her head and smiled, rolling her eyes.

He didn't want to move, didn't want to do anything but

stand here, the water turning his toes pruney, and look at her. It was the kind of thing he'd mocked his friends for doing when they'd met someone special, and had never, ever expected to fall prey to himself. He had to force himself to look away.

'Told you it was magic,' he said, and lifted Sofia out of the boat, lifejacket and all, and put her down beside him, careful to keep a grip on her hand. Sofia squealed, at first from the surprise of the cold water, but then from delight. He walked along a short length of the hidden sandbank just under the water then back to the boat.

'It's all very well having a magic beach,' Ruby said, trying to maintain an air of superiority and failing, 'but what good is it if it stays underwater?'

'You just wait and see. Coming in?'

Ruby nodded, and began stripping off her skirt to reveal shapely legs and the bottom half of her swimming costume. His mouth dried. He turned to his mother and raised an eyebrow.

'Don't be an idiot, Massimo. I'm far too old to be wading about in the lagoon. You just carry on and I'll enjoy the sun in the boat for a while.'

He nodded and held out his hand to Ruby so she could steady herself getting out of the boat. Once she was in the shallow water, they placed themselves either side of Sofia and went exploring. The remains of what once might have been an island was tiny, maybe only thirty metres by ten, but as they splashed around in the shallows, swinging Sofia between them, the tide crept away and revealed a perfect golden sandbank.

Sofia stood on the damp sand and stared at the grains beneath her feet. 'Magic,' she whispered. 'How do, Unc Max?'

He crouched down beside her. 'I whistled and it came.'

Sofia jammed all five fingers of her left hand in her

mouth and puffed. 'No work,' she said, after she'd pulled them out again.

'That's because learning to whistle takes practice,' he told her. 'You have to do it again and again until you're good at it. When you're older, you'll be able to call the is-land, too. Everyone in our family can.' In the meantime, he showed her the basics—how to pucker her lips, how to blow gently. Sofia didn't manage to produce more than a raspy sound, but she seemed quite happy trying.

He looked up at Ruby. 'Can you whistle?'

She smiled and rolled her eyes. 'Not like you. In com-parison my efforts seem pathetic.'

Max stood up, still holding Sofia's hand. The patch of sand was growing now, the almost imperceptible tilt of the land helping the tide to recede rapidly. 'Let's all whistle to-gether, and perhaps the rest of the island will come.'

So they stood solemnly in a row, faced the lagoon, and blew, his whistle loud and long, Ruby's slightly throaty, with a unique little trill at the end, and Sofia's determined puffing filling out their little orchestra.

It was strange. He'd found it hard to be at the island again at first, but bringing Ruby here was changing that. Some-how she soothed the dark voices in his head away, made him believe he could be free of them one day.

When they'd finished they headed back to the boat and began unloading their beach stuff. He set up the umbrella and spread the blanket while Ruby held on to Sofia. Fina directed from the bow of the boat, and only when it was all set up to her liking did she consent to let him pull the boat closer so she could step onto dry sand.

They ate their lunch under the umbrella, a simple affair of meats and cheeses, bread and olives, and when they'd finished Ruby grabbed a towel, headed out from under the shade of the umbrella and laid it on the sand. She unbuttoned her white, Fifties-style blouse and shrugged it off, to reveal a matching swimsuit.

Not matching in colour, because it was a deep ruby red with large black roses all over it, but matching in style. It was one of those weird things he'd seen in old-fashion photos, with a wide halter-neck strap, a ruched front and a leg line that was low, completely covering her bottom and reaching to the tops of her thighs. It should have been un-flattering, and on many women it would have looked like a Halloween costume, but on Ruby it looked sensational. She reminded him of those sirens with the rosy cheeks, red lips and long legs that he'd seen painted on the side of wartime planes.

'I didn't think you'd remember the whistle,' his mother muttered beside him, her eyes a little misty.

His first reaction was to bristle, to bat the comment away and pretend he hadn't heard it. Of course he'd remembered. It had been his father's trick to call the island that way. For a man who'd had a hard time expressing his emotions, he'd been unusually imaginative. It had made him a good architect, but it had made him an even better father, softening the gruff edges.

He turned and watched Ruby as she finished getting her towel just so, then lay down on top of it to face the sun.

He thought about her willingness to try and try again, even when things didn't go according to plan. She never gave up, never locked herself away from new experiences. Never locked herself away from hope that it would all turn out right one day. She wasn't weak and flaky, as he'd thought her. She was strong. Resilient.

And she was right. He needed to try with his mother. Not just for the sake of his family, but because he wanted to be the kind of man who was worthy of Ruby Lange. The kind of man who knew how to do more than just 'ankle deep'. That was what she needed, and that was what he wanted to give her.

His mother was staring out to sea, and had obviously given up on him giving her an answer. For the first time he saw it—what Ruby had been trying to tell him about—the deep pain behind her eyes. The same kind of desolation he'd seen his father wear in unguarded moments, the same one that had eaten away at him, until it had sucked the life right out of him.

Something warm flooded his chest. Something that wasn't bitterness or rage or judgement, something that made him remember how warm and kind she'd been when he'd been younger, how she'd have given anything for her children, and even more for her husband.

Words rushed around inside his head, the beginnings of sentences. The beginnings of a truce.

But none of them left his mouth. It felt as if he were looking at his mother from behind a large sheet of bulletproof glass. There was so much he wanted to say, so many questions he wanted to ask, but he found he could release none of them. It wouldn't come, even though, for the first time in almost two decades, he wanted it to. He wanted to *try*.

Eventually his mother picked up a book and began to read. Max sat there, adrenaline making his blood surge and his skin prickle, but anyone looking at him would have thought he was resting his hands on his knees, relaxing in the sun. He twisted his head and searched for a flowery red and black costume.

For most of his life he'd been proud when people had called him his father's son, when they'd remarked on the likeness, not just in looks but in temperament, but for the first time that pride chilled into fear. If he was the cookie-cutter offspring everyone always said he was, there was a real chance that he would never deserve a woman like Ruby Lange.

CHAPTER THIRTEEN

RUBY RETURNED TO THE SALON that evening after dinner to tidy some of Sofia's things away. She sorted through a stack of drawing papers, thinking she'd find one or two to present to Fina as a memento of Sofia's visit.

She reached a shortlist of seven. Some drawings that she'd done and Sofia had coloured in, and a few of her charge's own creations. They needed skilful interpretation, but the intent was there. Ruby stopped as she stared at a page that was filled with different-coloured crayon blobs, all lined up. The shocking pink blob was Fina, apparently. The smaller one next to her, a vibrant, bright yellow, was Sofia herself. The dark blue one off to the side, looking a bit like a navy, vertical thundercloud, was Max. Ruby had giggled at that when Sofia had pointed it out.

That only left the purple blob.

The purple blob so close to the blue one they practically merged at the edges, creating an indigo smudge.

It was understandable, Ruby supposed, that Sofia should put her and Max next to each other. She spent a lot of time with the pair of them, after all. Ruby had smiled when Sofia had told her the scribble of purple was her, honoured to have been included, but now she looked at it she realised just how much artistic licence Sofia had taken.

But Max didn't do that, did he? He didn't let his edges blur like that. And maybe he never would.

That was what Fina had been trying to tell her.

Was she just fooling herself?

Ruby sighed and sank onto the rug. The pieces of paper she'd collected fluttered out of her hand and fell onto the floor unseen. She was so confused.

They'd spent a lot of time together over the last five days. Not just the morning outings with Sofia, but in the evenings Fina often disappeared to visit her friend Renata after they'd eaten dinner, then Ruby would creep into the library and she'd have a glorious hour or two alone with Max.

When she was with him, everything was amazing and she couldn't think about anything else. When he kissed her, she felt as if she were touching something deep inside him. More and more he was giving her 'glimpses' of the real Max, and each time she dived deeper in she got lost a little more. One day soon there'd be no going back.

But then she'd leave him and the little doubts would start to creep in, nibbling away at her.

He had to feel the same way, didn't he? The truth of it rang between them every time they were in the same room together, and she really wanted to believe it, but…

Never once had he mentioned where this was going—or even *if* it was going—once their stay in Venice ended. Never once had he put words to how he felt about her, given her any hint about the future. Their days here were numbered; she knew that. Gia had phoned saying she needed a little longer in L.A., but the original fortnight was up in just two days' time.

She sighed and collected the pieces of paper together and put them away in the sideboard with the other drawing things, forgetting that she'd sorted out the masterpieces and jumbling them back in with the others again.

Once she was finished putting them away she headed for the library. Max was poring over his laptop, as usual, but when he saw her he got up from his chair and crossed the room to where she was standing just near the doorway. He stood close, far too close for a boss approaching his employee, then gave her an impish smile as he closed the door behind her, pressed her up against it and kissed her until her head was spinning and her lungs were convinced oxygen was just a deep and distant memory.

When he pulled back to look at her, she saw a flash of something in his eyes. Something deep. Something true. It sent her heart spinning like the waltzer at the fairground. She so wanted to forget about tomorrow and just do what felt right for now, but that was how she'd spent her whole life so far, and it was time to step back and take a more mature approach. Where Max was concerned, she really needed to pay attention to the big picture.

She wanted him to say something.

Exactly what, she didn't know. Just something. Something that she didn't have to prise out of him. Something to let her know what was happening between them, if he was as confused as she was, but Max just leaned in and stole another kiss. It made her blood dance right down to her toes.

She pulled away, looked him in the eyes. 'What are we doing?' she whispered.

Just one of Max's eyebrows hitched up a little. 'I thought we'd covered enough ground for you to be sure, but if you want a little more demonstration?'

He leaned close again, but Ruby stopped him with her hands on his chest. Hands that dearly craved a little more 'demonstration', but she forced them to stay put instead of using them to explore him further.

'I mean *us*. Is this just a holiday fling, or what?'

He frowned. She'd upset him, she could tell, but she had to know. She'd spent her whole life straining for the crumbs one man doled out to her. She'd had no choice but to accept what her father gave her, but with Max she did, and she'd be insane to follow that pattern with him. *Glimpses* were all well and good for now, but for the long term? That was like trying to nourish yourself with only a diet of canapés for the rest of your life.

'Ruby? Don't you know?'

She shook her head. All she knew was that she had a choice: dive in and hope that one day Max would shed the same chains that had bound his father, or run now before things got even more serious.

More serious? Hah. She was kidding herself. She was already half in love with him. It wouldn't take much more to push her over the precipice.

Max's hands moved to circle her waist, to pull her as close as she could possibly get without their physical boundaries blurring just as they had done in Sofia's drawing. *'Lascia che ti mostri.'*

Let me show you.

When he touched her lips with his again she just about melted clean away. She'd thought she'd experienced passion from Max before. She now realised they'd just been paddling in the shallows. But even as he unleashed the force of it on her, as the kiss continued, she got the sense that Max was a like a dam, holding back the pressure of a million gallons of water. There was still more beneath, so much more.

She wanted him to tear that last barrier down, to unleash the torrent and let it sweep her away, but the structure was solid, impenetrable. Nothing she could do could get it to crack. A tiny part of her cried out in pain as she realised that, even in this, Max was holding himself back.

He picked her up and carried her to the small love seat in the corner of the room, and they both fell onto it in a tangle of arms and legs, hot breath and pounding hearts, and as his lips found the curve of her neck and his hands smoothed down her body she discovered something did crumble after all. But it was all her good resolves, not him.

* * *

Ruby lay in bed that evening and reached for her mobile phone, which had lain untouched most of the last fortnight. Partly because it was too expensive to turn data roaming on, but also because she was avoiding communication from her father about The Job.

However, she'd started fantasising about carrying on back in London with Max, about being the kind of woman he'd consider sharing his life with. That clearly meant that the world was upside down and back-to-front, and she obviously needed a sharp dose of reality to counteract that and help her think straight. And a *What have you done now?* lecture and an exorbitant phone bill would do nicely on that front.

Just as she feared, an email from dear old dad was lurking in her inbox. She shifted position, took a deep breath and opened it.

FAO: Ruby Lange.

That was typical Dad. Other people started emails with *Hi!* or *Hey!* or just launched into the subject at hand as quickly as possible. Only Patrick Lange could make an informal communication sound like a court summons.

Dear Ruby,
I had hoped to hear from you by now on your current employment situation. I understand from your flatmate that you are in Europe somewhere, doing something, but she could not enlighten me any further. Would you care to? I'm holding the job open for you, and I'd greatly appreciate it if you could let me know if you're going to take it. There are plenty of other people who would kill for this kind of opportunity, you know.

Yes, she knew. He'd told her often enough.

You need to approach life with a more adult attitude, Ruby. You can't flit around for ever 'finding yourself'. At your age it's time you stopped running away from responsibility and started embracing it.

I need to know about the production assistant position before next Monday. Please get in contact and let me know.
Dad x

Ruby scowled at her mobile screen. No *I know I've been incommunicado for a month, but how are you doing, Ruby?* No *Great you've found yourself a new job, Ruby!* Just judgement and how much she was disappointing him, as always.

She knew she really shouldn't message angry, but she couldn't help herself.

Thanks for the vote of confidence, Dad.

Much to her surprise, her message alert went off a few minutes later.

Ruby, understand that I don't say the things I do to hurt you. You have so much potential and it's a crime to waste it drifting from thing to thing. The job offer stands. I think you might enjoy it, and I expect you will be good at it. You have just the right kind of energy the team needs. D x

Ruby flipped her phone case closed and put her mobile back on the bedside table. She didn't know whether to be angry that she'd finally forced him into giving her a back-handed compliment or just stupidly happy he thought she could be good at something. She folded her arms across her chest on top of the quilt and stared at the ceiling.

Well, she'd wanted reality, and her father had dished up some five-star fare.

But there was a difference between not being able to stick with something and not wanting to. Why didn't he understand that?

Because it looks the same, smells the same, tastes the same...

No. It wasn't the same. It was always her choice. Always her decision.

You choose to get that itchy feeling, want to feel it torment you until you have no other option but to outrun it?

She scowled at the pretty looping baroque designs on the ceiling. Now even her subconscious was ganging up on her. That wasn't true, was it? That feeling of being pinned down, of getting so close to something to feel its heat, to feel how much it could scorch and burn, that wasn't what made her seek out new and exciting things. It couldn't be.

But as she followed the patterns and shapes on the ceiling with her eyes she catalogued all the jobs she'd had over the last five years, all the people and places she'd thought she'd become attached to, and she discovered there wasn't one time that she hadn't left because, not only had her feet got itchy, but her whole being had got itchy. She used to think it was the yearning for fresh pastures that made her feel that way, but now she was staring it in the face, dissecting it and pulling it apart, she saw it for what it really was.

Fear.

Plain and simple.

You're not a free spirit, Ruby Lange. You're a coward.

There wasn't one time she hadn't succumbed to that itch, except...

Except that night almost a week ago on the dock, when it had been itching so hard she'd almost jumped into the canal to stop the burning. When Max had asked her to stay. And she had.

Ruby let out a long and shuddering breath.

She wanted to stick with Max. No matter what. She wanted that with all her heart.

The realisation shocked her. It should have made her heart race and her breathing shallow, but all she felt instead of blind panic was a strange but not unwelcome sense of peace creeping up on her.

Ruby threw the covers back, jumped out of bed and walked over to stare out of the window. For some reason, the gently lapping water soothed her, helped her think.

She had to be sure about this.

Not just about Max's feelings for her, but about her feelings for Max. If they went forward with this, and he held back from her, she knew she wouldn't be able to stay around and let her heart endlessly beg for more. Look at what that had done for Fina.

But she also knew that if she dived into this relationship, and then bailed, it might seal his fate. He would shut down completely. And that would lead to consequences, not just for her, but possibly for Fina and Sofia and the rest of his family. Max had so much to give, if he would only let himself, and she didn't want to be the reason he didn't.

She started to pace. Back and forth, back and forth she went. She finally fell into bed and tossed back and forth there too. At 3:00 a.m. she punched her pillow hard and let out a low moan of frustration.

The only thing solid she could come up with was that she'd rather be with Max than without him. And she could do it, she knew she could, but it was one thing for her to be sure of it, and another entirely to convince Max of the same.

Another realisation hit her straight between the eyebrows. Maybe that was why he was holding back! Maybe it was nothing to do with him and everything to do with her.

She wouldn't blame him if he didn't trust her not to run when things got sticky. Her track record was all hundred-metre dashes: exciting and adrenaline-inducing while they lasted, but over quickly and leaving everyone feeling burnt out and exhausted. She needed to convince him she was capable of a marathon; that she'd changed in the space of two short weeks and was ready to do more. Be more. That she was a safe pair of hands for his heart.

But how?

Words wouldn't be enough. Max was all about the concrete, the tangible evidence. She'd have to prove it to him in no uncertain terms. She went back to staring at the ceiling, familiar with its intricate patterns and leafy trails now, and after only a few moments the solution dropped into her brain with a thud.

Of course! It was perfect.

She rolled over, picked up her phone and began typing in an email with her thumbs.

CHAPTER FOURTEEN

THE PLANS FOR the institute were almost finished. It was just as well, because, although he had got up at four the last few days to put in the hours needed, the whole time he worked away at his desk there was an internal timer that clicked away within him, counting down the seconds to ten o'clock, when he could rise from his desk, shove the papers away and go and see her.

Every day was a surprise, something new. And he didn't just mean her wardrobe, although it was an endless source of fascination to him that the handful of clothes she'd stuffed into that rucksack could be combined in so many different ways to create so many different looks.

No, he meant Ruby. Every day she brought him something fresh, something exciting. When he'd first met her, he'd thought she needed to grow up and settle down, but now he realised how fearless, how magnificent she was. He didn't want her to change a thing about herself.

The timer on his watch beeped at him and he looked up from his desk. Two minutes to ten. It was time. He'd done his duty, done his hours, and now he could spend time with Ruby. He didn't even mind that Sofia was always thrown into the mix.

To be honest, he was glad to have a reason to take things slowly. Otherwise he wasn't sure he'd be able to help himself. She wanted new experiences? She wanted romance?

He wanted to show her just how amazing Venice could be, just how it could imprint itself on a soul. He wanted to talk about dreams and plans and for ever. And he would have done, if not for one thing: he didn't want to scare her off. It was only a supreme act of will that prevented him spilling it all out to her and laying it at her feet.

Breathe, Max. Give the girl time. Don't spook her.

He just needed to get the groundwork in before Gia arrived back to claim Sofia.

He slowed in the corridor that led to the salon, took a moment to inhale and exhale, and then he turned the corner and walked through the door.

As he often found them when he arrived for his morning session with his niece, she and Ruby were drawing. Sofia was colouring-in a princess in a flowing robe, having got over her 'naughty fish' obsession, and Ruby was bent over her sketchbook. He crept up behind her while she was absorbed and sneaked a look.

She was working on a drawing of a gondola floating in front of a palazzo. Her style was interesting. She often drew in black pen, but the lines were always fluid and emotive. It should have given a messy look to the sketch, but somehow she managed to get the shape and structures perfectly without making it look staid and formal, something he could never have done. And he could see she was growing, developing. There was a new confidence in her work that hadn't been there when she'd arrived.

That was the elusive 'niche' she'd been looking for, he was sure of it, but he sensed she lacked confidence to pursue it. He wondered what he could do to encourage her. She'd helped him rediscover the real excitement and passion that had been missing from his work for months now, and he'd like to return the favour.

She started, suddenly realising he was close, jumped up and turned round, smiling. 'Nosey,' she said.

The air crackled between them, and he bent down and stole a kiss. 'Guilty as charged.' He nodded at his niece, who'd almost finished obliterating her princess in a cloud of bright orange crayon so thick one could hardly see the black lines of Ruby's pen underneath.

Ruby chuckled. 'She's nothing if not thorough. I have no idea where she gets that from.'

'Shut up,' he said. 'Are you ready to go?'

She nodded. 'We're off to feed the pigeons in St Mark's Square, right?'

He didn't answer. When he'd mentioned pigeons, it wasn't necessarily feeding them he'd been thinking about, seeing as the city was trying to actively discourage it. Chasing them had been a much preferred boyhood pastime, one he thought Sofia would enjoy with equal relish, and almost verged on the side of civic duty these days, as the birds caused so much damage to the delicate buildings and statues.

When Ruby stood back, he frowned. Something was different. Something was not quite right....

And then he realised what it was. He'd seen that outfit before. It was the plain T-shirt and jeans she'd worn a couple of times before, but today it was unadorned. No loops of beaded necklaces, no vintage waistcoat, no floaty scarves. It was most odd. But since Ruby had always been one to defy expectation where her wardrobe was concerned, he supposed she was following true to form.

It should have only taken ten minutes to walk to St Mark's from Ca' Damiani, but it took Max, Ruby and Sofia closer to twenty. Mostly because they didn't bother with the buggy and had to accommodate Sofia's tiny little legs. When they were there, Sofia delighted in chasing the pigeons, which flew up in clouds as she cut a path through them, but settled back down nearby only seconds later.

He and Ruby watched on from the sidelines, smiling.

He reached over and took her hand, relished the feel of her warm skin in his. She always felt that way, never cold, always soft and inviting.

'That drawing you were doing this morning was very good,' he told her. 'I really think you should do something with it.' He thought about the overpriced prints and postcards for the tourists, the sickly, sentimental paintings in some of the shops that sold carnival masks by the bucketload. 'Your drawings of Venice are better than a lot of what's out there.'

He thought she'd be pleased at some encouraging words, but she pressed her lips together and stared out across the vast square with its arcades and hundreds of pillars. 'Nah,' she said, lifting just one shoulder in a little shrug. 'I think it's better if I keep it as a hobby for now.'

His brows drew together as he waited for her to carry on, say something more cheery and upbeat, but she just let out a huge sigh. Something really was different, and it wasn't just the wardrobe.

'Come on,' he said, 'let's walk a bit more.'

She nodded and called for Sofia, who wasn't that enthralled at the idea of leaving the pigeons alone, but she came without too much grizzling.

It wasn't just today, was it? This strange behaviour. There had been little things for the past few days. Tiny things he'd hardly noticed when they'd been random, individual occurrences, but now they were building to make something bigger, forming themselves into a pattern. She'd been quieter, more restrained. She'd laughed less. And there was something else, too, about the way she looked that was different. Something other than the lack of accessories. He just couldn't put his finger on what it was.

Was this connected to the drawing thing?

She talked about passion, about wanting to find it. It was clear to him that drawing was what she really loved to do. She couldn't *not* do it. He couldn't count the number of scraps of paper, backs of receipts, paper napkins he'd seen her sketches on in the last couple of weeks. So why did she resist it? Why did she avoid it when the thing that tugged her heart most was under her nose?

They walked out towards the Doge's Palace. He'd been going to tell her some interesting facts about it, things linked to conversations they'd had earlier in the week, but now it just felt like the wrong thing to do, so they strolled in silence to the water's edge and stared over to Isola di San Giorgio. Out on the lagoon, he could see the exact spot he'd cut the motor on their sunset trip, but there was no moonlight now, no gently flickering stars, just bright sun, beating down on them and bleaching all the shadows away.

'I've got something to tell you,' she said, after they'd been staring at the water for a couple of minutes. 'It's really great news.'

She twisted to look at him, but the smile she wore seemed hollow, like the trompe l'oeil in his mother's salon. It had the appearance of reality, but there was no depth to it.

'I've decided to take the job with my father's production company.' She looked at him, waiting for a response.

Max froze as the vague feeling that had plagued him all morning solidified into something hard and nasty, turning his insides cold. This wasn't her dream, her passion. In fact, it was the very opposite of what she'd said she'd wanted out of life.

He shook his head. 'Why?'

Her smile disappeared. '*Why?* Not "well done, Ruby. Good on you for choosing something you're going to stick to"?'

His mouth moved. He had *not* seen that coming. 'I thought it was the last thing you wanted.'

She shrugged and bent to retie Sofia's shoelace, which had come undone, then stood up again. 'I thought about what you said about finding the perfect thing by doing the hard stuff. Maybe you're right. And since my parents were both nuts about television and nature, maybe it's in my genes. Who knows?'

'Don't do it,' he said, and she turned to face him, shocked.

'Max, you are making no sense. I thought you'd be overjoyed at this. I thought you'd understand.'

He could tell she was hurt by the way she folded her arms across her middle, by the way she rubbed the toe of her shoe against the flagstones.

'It's too late, anyway' she said quietly. 'I've already formally accepted the offer.'

'When?'

The toe ground harder into the floor. 'Two days ago.'

He wanted to grab hold of her, to tell her not to turn her back on her dreams, to run with them and to hell with the consequences. He wanted to tell her to try every damn job in the universe if she liked, not to care what anybody else said, as long as she didn't give up. This was worse. This was way worse than not finishing something. For some reason he sensed Ruby was waving the white flag of defeat.

He wanted to tell her all of that and more. That he loved her. That he wanted her to brighten his day every day for the rest of his life. But he didn't. Couldn't. What if he got too intense too soon and scared her away? He didn't think he could bear it.

He opened his mouth, got ready to say something. Anything. He had to tell her something of how he felt, even if he only let a fraction of it slip, but then he realised what he'd been trying to put his finger on, what else had changed about her. He closed his mouth again and stared.

As she looked at her feet the sun glinted off her dark hair. It looked beautiful, shiny and thick, but not one hint of purple remained.

* * *

Ruby knocked softly on the library door. It was ten past ten and Max hadn't turned up for their usual session with Sofia. The day was grey and drizzly, the mist hanging so low over the whole city that the tops of the buildings seemed to melt into the white sky. A castle-building session was much needed.

'Yes?' came his reply from behind the door.

Ruby hesitated for a second. He didn't sound angry exactly, but there was a definite edge to his voice. She pushed the door and leaned in, keeping her feet on the threshold. 'It's past ten.'

He didn't turn round for a moment, just kept making deft, straight lines on a piece of paper with a pencil. When he turned round a faint scowl marred his features. It was just the concentration of working on his plans, right? As far as she was aware she hadn't done anything wrong in the last few days. In fact, she was doing her level best to do everything right, to prove to Max that she could be the kind of woman he could rely on.

'I don't think I'm going to be able to join you today,' he said, his voice neutral.

'Oh.' It took Ruby a moment to adjust to that information. They'd got into such a rhythm that it felt as if they'd missed a step and everything had jarred. And then there was the fact that he hadn't taken the opportunity to grab her, press her up against the wall and kiss her until she was breathless, a ritual she'd come to look forward to.

'But you promised your mother—'

'I promised my mother I'd stick to her terms for a week. I did that—and more. My agreement with her has ended, Ruby.'

She frowned, then nodded. She hadn't thought about it that way, but she supposed he was right. He hadn't needed to come out with her and Sofia for the last week. It should have made her happy that he'd possibly done so in order to spend time with her, but the expression on his face stopped that. It was like glass. Hard, solid, reflecting everything back at her.

He also hadn't softened one iota with his mother. That scared her. And not just for Fina's sake. Were those walls of his ever going to come fully down?

'The deadline for getting the final plans into the National Institute of Fine Art is next week,' he explained calmly. 'I have to focus on that for a while.'

'Okay,' she said slowly. For some reason she felt she was missing something here. Something big. Or was she just being paranoid? 'We'll miss you.'

Max just nodded. His body shifted, and she could tell he was itching to get back to his plans. She did her best not to take it personally, not to take it as a rejection.

'Will we see you at dinner this evening?'

A bit of the familiar, world-weary Max she'd met at the beginning of their trip returned. 'My mother has insisted I take you out to eat. She told me in no uncertain terms that it's a travesty that you've spent more than a fortnight in a city full of fabulous restaurants and haven't sampled their food yet.'

'Oh,' Ruby said again. 'That's lovely.'

Maybe Fina had decided she'd been wrong about what she'd said to her. Ruby had grown more and more suspicious that Fina's evenings out visiting Renata had quickly become an excuse to give them time alone together. Maybe she thought there was hope for her and Max after all.

Then why wasn't Ruby happy about that? Why did her stomach feel as heavy as a bowling ball?

Max just gave her a single nod.

Silence filled the space between them.

'Well…I'll just go and…' Ruby gestured in the direction of the salon. 'I'll see you this evening.'

'This evening,' Max echoed, but he'd already turned and started making swift lines on his plans.

Ruby slid her body from the space between door and frame and closed it softly behind her.

CHAPTER FIFTEEN

WHEN IT WAS TIME to leave that evening, instead of jumping in the launch via the boat door Max lead Ruby out of Ca' Damiani's tiny, almost dowdy street entrance, through a little, high-walled courtyard and out of a nondescript wooden door. There, the narrow *calle* opened onto a wider one, and within five minutes they had entered a secluded little square with a few restaurants and shops that were closed for the night.

They headed for an unremarkable-looking restaurant almost in the corner of the *campo*, with a dull, cappuccino-coloured awning and a few tables and chairs outside. The inside, however, was always a surprise after the mundane exterior. There were whitewashed brick walls and dark wood panelling. A counter stretched down one side, full of doors and drawers, reminiscent of an old-fashioned haberdashery shop. A gramophone perched on a table in the corner and glasses and bottles of wine filled what looked like a bookshelf at the far end of the space.

Ruby turned to him and grinned. He'd guessed she'd like this place. It was quirky and unique, as she was. And it didn't hurt that it served some of the best seafood in Venice.

They sat at a small table in the corner, overlooking the square, decked out in thick white linen and spotlessly shiny silverware.

It should have been romantic.

It was.

Well, it would have been, but for the conversation he knew had to come. One neither of them would like, but was totally, totally necessary. His plan to work on his designs that morning had been shot to pieces after Ruby's visit, and he'd spent the couple of hours until lunchtime mulling their situation over and over.

Ruby was changing herself. For him. He'd finally realised that when he'd noticed she'd dyed her hair. The clothes, the more sedate version of Ruby who'd appeared over the last couple of days...it all made sense now. And he hated himself for it.

He *needed* her to be the Ruby he'd fallen in love with, couldn't settle for anything less. Drastic action was needed.

He wanted to tell her that over dinner, as they ate their marinated raw fish starters, but it was as if there were a glass wall between them. Not a thin sliver, either, that could have been shattered with a ball or a fist, but one ten inches thick that repelled his words, weighed him down.

Was this what his father had felt when he'd looked at his mother? Everything swirling inside so hard and so fast he thought it might consume him with no way to let it out? He feared it was.

Geoffrey Martin had loved his vibrant Italian wife so much. Max had always known that, always respected it. But now he saw that maybe his father had grasped too hard and given too little back. Serafina had been what he'd needed to bring him out of his shell, balance him out, but he hadn't been what she'd needed. Or had chosen not to be. For the first time in his life, Max realised his father had been selfish, and that had created an imbalance in the relationship that had ultimately doomed it to failure.

The same kind of imbalance he was aware of when he thought about himself and the petite, vibrant woman sitting opposite him, eating her blackened sea bass.

He would not make the same mistake. He would not be a coward and make Ruby pay for his weakness. He wouldn't let her crush her spirit for him, deny everything she was and wanted to be. It was too high a price to pay. But there was only one way he could think of preventing that, even if it meant a colourless, bleak future ahead for himself. But he'd do it—for her.

He took a deep breath, hoping she'd answer differently this time, hoping she'd spare them both. 'Are you still determined to take that job with your father?'

Ruby looked up from her fish and met Max's gaze. When he'd mentioned going out to dinner this evening, she'd thought the conversation might have been a little more... intimate. This was a wonderful chance for them to be away from the palazzo, to be romantic with each other, and yet he wanted to talk about her father? Talk about a passion killer.

'Yes.' She was determined to show him she could stick at something, think about the big picture rather than just the details of the here and now.

He sighed. 'I wish you wouldn't.'

She put her knife and fork down and looked at him helplessly. 'Why?'

'Because it's not your passion.'

She reached for her wine glass. 'It could be my passion. Like you said, how do I know if I don't try?'

To be honest, she didn't care about the job. It was just a means to an end. What she was really passionate about was being with Max. But in his current strange mood, she wasn't sure he was ready to hear that. She'd do anything it took. Anything. Even taking that job with her father.

'And I can't say anything to change your mind?'

She shook her head. 'No.' Max wanted to see if she could stick to something? Well, she wasn't budging on this, even if it killed her.

He went back to eating his food, his expression grim. What had she said now?

They finished their meals, only punctuating the silence with odd snatches of meaningless conversation, until their espressos came, then Max sat up straighter and looked her in the eye. 'I need to talk to you about something…something important.'

His expression was so serious, but instead of making her jittery, it melted her heart. He was so earnest, so full of wanting to do the right thing, and she loved him for it. When Max's heart was in something, it was all-in, and she could allow him a little severity in return for that. She reached out and covered his hand with hers across the table. His skin felt cool and smooth.

'I told you when I hired you that this was going to be a two-week job at most and we've exceeded that now.'

This was it. This was the conversation. About where they were going when they got back to London, her stupid secret fantasies on the verge of coming true. Ruby forced herself to sit still and listen, which was hard with her heart fluttering about madly inside her ribcage like a trapped bird. She nodded, encouraging him to keep going.

'Well, I think it's time your contract came to an end.'

Ruby blinked. That wasn't what she'd expected him to say at all. Was this a particularly 'Max' way of saying their relationship was moving fully from professional to personal? 'Okay. So when are we heading back to London?'

He swallowed. 'I'm not, but you are.'

Ruby removed her hand from on top of his and sat back. 'I don't understand.'

'I can't begin to thank you for the way you've helped me change,' he said, and while his expression remained granite-like his eyes warmed. She could feel her heart reaching out to him, even as all her other instincts told her to back away. 'But it's time for me to fly solo.'

'What does that mean?'

He broke eye contact. 'I need to learn to interact with my family without having you there as both catalyst and buffer. I need to learn to do it on my own, Ruby.'

She shook her head, not really sure which bit of information she was rejecting, or why. 'But I can just keep out of the way... I can...'

He shook his head. 'You've been amazing, but now it's time for you to go home.' A gruff laugh followed. 'I'd say it was time for you to travel, to explore, to find whatever it is you're looking for in life, but you're determined to take that damn job with your father.'

She frowned. 'Yes, I am. But what has that got to do with anything?'

He just looked at her, as if he was trying to send a message with his eyes, but she got nothing. Those walls were back up, weren't they? He was shutting her out. Her stomach dropped as she realised that was what this had all been about. He'd been pulling away slowly for the last couple of days, hadn't he? She'd just been too stupidly in love with him to notice.

You've finally done it, Ruby. Brava. You've jumped in with your heart, given it wholly and completely, and the man you've given it to doesn't want it. He's handing it back to you on a plate. Thanks, but no, thanks.

Part of her couldn't quite believe it.

'But when you get back to London, will we...?'

Now the message from his eyes got through. Loud and clear.

No.

There would be no London.

There would be no Max for her. All they would ever have was what had happened here in Venice.

'Max?' she croaked.

He shook his head. 'I'm sorry, Ruby. Professionally speaking, I don't need you any longer.'

She swallowed. 'And personally?'

Max didn't say anything, just sat ramrod straight in his chair, jaw tense, eyes empty.

That was when the bird inside stopped fluttering madly. In fact, Ruby wasn't sure there was any movement at all any more.

She'd never been fired from a job—mainly because she always left before that kind of eventuality arose—but Max had managed to make her first experience of it a real doozy.

I don't need you.

Professional and personal rejection in one go. Nice shot.

She got up, threw her napkin down and walked out of the restaurant.

Thankfully, the fact they'd walked here meant she could find her way back to the palazzo on her own, and once there she'd pack. In *three* minutes. And then she'd be out of here, and there was no way Max Martin would stop her this time.

He caught up with her not long afterwards, as she was leaving a wider street and turning into a narrow, cobbled one.

'Ruby!'

Heavy footsteps pounded behind her, getting closer. She kept walking.

'Where are you going?' He didn't sound flustered or bothered at all, just slightly out of breath from the running. It made her want to scream.

Home, she almost said, but then she realised just how stupidly inaccurate that was. 'Back to the palazzo,' she said. 'I thought that was obvious.'

He fell into step beside her, and the narrowness of the *calle* meant he was far too close. 'You don't have to leave straight away. Wait until the morning.'

That sounded so generous, so reasonable. She regretted not having that contract now, because maybe, just maybe, she could have found something in it so she could sue his sorry hide for breaching it, for false advertising...*something*. There was no way she was staying here overnight. What did he want her to do? Lie in bed and cry over him? She wasn't that girl. It was time to move on. Onwards and upwards, remember?

She stomped down the street, glad she was wearing her ballet flats. They might not produce a satisfying echo, but they did make for a quick getaway. How could she have read him so wrong?

A series of images flashed through her head: kissing on the boat as the sun set over the lagoon, watching him building castles with Sofia the very first time, the moment that stupid little crab had bit her on the finger, and, last, the way he'd whistled for an island to appear out of the sea.

She stopped walking.

That was the real Max. She was sure of it.

He froze beside her, but she kept staring straight ahead.

She'd lived in the same house as this man for two weeks, and one thing she knew: he wasn't that good of a liar. He might keep things locked away, but he wasn't a man to kiss and run, to promise one thing with his eyes and smiles and lips and then deliver another. Was he?

She turned to face him. His features gave nothing away.

That should have made her angry, but it didn't. Instead, the fire she'd been ready to unleash on him flickered out. This was the façade, wasn't it? The face he showed when he wanted to pretend to the world that nothing got to him. The face he was showing to her to let her know the same. If there was a lie Max Martin told, this was it. The only one.

She searched his face, desperately looking for some hint she was right. His expression remained blank, but his jaw tightened. She started walking again, until they reached the little wooden door that led to the palazzo's tiny courtyard. Once there, she pushed the gate open and walked inside. She waited while he closed it behind him.

Nothing about this evening made sense, except the one truth she kept coming back to. Max Martin did the right thing, even if it killed him, even if it cost all that he had. So what about sending her away was 'right', and how on earth did she go about changing his mind?

Something drastic. Something shocking. Something he couldn't ignore. She was usually good at that. She dug down inside herself, poking in the dark corners of her imagination, to see if she could find anything to help, and came away empty, save for one thing—the only thing she'd been able to think about for the last few days.

'I love you,' she blurted out, and waited for his reaction.

He seemed to grow another layer of cement. 'I know.'

'Is that why you're sending me away?' she asked, a small wobble in her voice betraying her.

He nodded.

No breaking ranks and pulling her into his arms as he had done countless times since that evening on the lagoon. No echoed protestations of love. The silence grew around them. Here in the tiny courtyard with its high wall, it was complete.

So I tried to make him angry...

Fina's words floated through her head. It wasn't a great plan, but telling him she loved him had been a worse one. If at least she could get him to show *some* emotion, those walls might start to crack; she might be able to tell if he really felt anything for her at all, or whether it had just been another mirage this city had thrown up. Her heart was telling her one thing and her brain another and she had to stop the Ping-Pong match between them and just *know*.

It shouldn't be too hard. She seemed to have a special talent for lighting Max's fuse.

'You paint yourself as this big, strong man, who can rule the universe and isn't scared of anything, but underneath it you're nothing but a coward.'

He blinked. Very slowly.

Ruby felt the air pulse around her head. It had felt good to say those words. She hadn't anticipated how much.

'No wonder you can't get that design for the institute right, no wonder they had reservations about going with you. Because to create something stupendous, first you'd have to *feel*, to dream, but you don't have the courage.'

This time he didn't move at all. Now the air in the whole courtyard throbbed.

She was running out of things to say, things she thought might wound him, provoke some kind of a reaction. He might seem to be made of stone, but her blood was rushing round her veins, her cheeks heating. Feigned anger was quickly becoming the real deal.

He had to feel something for her—he had to. She drew in a deep breath, then gave it her best shot. 'Your father dug his own grave, you know. He finally imploded with the effort of keeping himself under lock and key, and you're going to end up the same way. He didn't deserve your mother, who's more patient and loving and forgiving than you will ever realise, and you're going to turn out just the same if you're not careful.'

She was on a roll now, couldn't stop herself if she wanted to. Hot tears began to stream down her face and her throat grew tight, making her voice scratchy. 'And you know what? Maybe it is better if I go, if I get as far away from you as I can, because I don't think I could stand being with a man like you anyway. I need someone who actually knows how to live and breathe, who knows how to love and be loved. Who, when he feels something for a woman, comes out and says so—not just stands there like a lump of stone doing nothing!'

And he was like stone. Still.

She had no volume left now, only a hoarse whisper that only just made it past her lips. She started walking backwards towards the door. 'Well, you've got your wish. I'm leaving. And not because you're telling me to, but because I want to. I know you feel something for me!' She thumped her chest with her closed fist. 'I know it! But you can't—or won't—bring yourself to show it. And that means you don't deserve me, Max Martin, and you never will.'

Max stood in the courtyard long after Ruby had left him. It had taken all his effort to take what she'd thrown at him, every last ounce of his strength, and he had none left to open the door and follow. He'd wanted to kiss her fiercely, deeply, as if his very life depended on it—which it well might—and tell her just how much he cared, but he couldn't. Wouldn't.

He wondered if he was actually dripping blood, because that was what it felt like. Her words had stabbed him in the heart. This was what he'd always tried to avoid, what he'd always protected himself against. Did she think he didn't know that he didn't deserve her, that *he* wasn't what *she* needed? That was why he hadn't answered her question, had just let her assume the worst. He was letting her go, setting her free.

It felt as if he hadn't taken a breath in minutes, and he dragged one in now, the cool night air burning his lungs. He could see the lights on in the *piano nobile* of Ca' Damiani, could imagine her shoving clothes into her scruffy little rucksack, calling him every name under the sun.

A foolish part of him hoped that this wasn't it. That one day they'd meet again, and it would be the right time, that they'd both be ready, but he knew it was probably impossible. He didn't think she'd ever forgive him. And she had every reason not to.

But he'd had to do it this way. Otherwise she wouldn't have left, she'd have just kept trying, killing herself off piece by piece in the process. Damn her resilience.

He closed his eyes and swore out loud. In Italian. And then he walked through the ground floor of the palazzo, the space that used to be the merchants' warehouse when the Damiani family had been part of the city's elite, and out of the boat door.

He needed to get out of this place, out of this glittering city that promised with one hand then took away with another.

He knew of somewhere much more appropriate. There were a number of deserted islands scattered across the lagoon that had once been quarantine islands, places where those with the plague had been imprisoned to stop them infecting the city, places where forgotten souls were still supposed to howl on a moonless night like this.

As the mist descended across the lagoon he started up the launch and headed away from the deceptive lights of the city, fully intending to join the dead in their howling.

Ruby flung all her belongings in her rucksack, but it took her considerably longer than three minutes. More like twenty. Maybe because she had to keep stopping to either wipe her eyes so she could see what she was doing or shout at the painting of the old man in a large black hat on the wall about what a pig-headed idiot his descendant was being.

When she was finally finished she crept next door to Sofia's room and watched the little girl sleeping, legs and arms flung carelessly over the covers. She pressed the gentlest of kisses to her temple, then quickly left, before she dripped tears on her and woke her up.

She met Fina in the hallway. 'You're back early!' she said, smiling, and then she stopped smiling. 'What has that fool of a son of mine done now?'

Ruby shrugged. 'He fired me.'

Fina went pale. *'What?'*

'Maybe "fired" is a little dramatic.' She sighed. 'It's the end of my contract. I knew it was only going to be a couple of weeks, but—' The tears clogging her throat prevented her from saying more.

Fina just walked forward and drew her into a hug. The kind of hug Ruby's mother used to give her when she was small and she hadn't realised she'd missed quite so badly. Ruby's torso shuddered and she clung on to Fina for a few long minutes before pulling away, putting the pieces of herself back together.

'You must come again,' Fina said, her eyes shining and her voice husky.

Ruby looked at her helplessly. She didn't know if she could return to this place. Somehow it had burrowed under her skin and she feared she'd always be reminded of what she'd almost had, of what it had snatched away from her on a fickle whim.

Fina must have understood that look, because she smiled softly. 'Well, when I come to London, then… You must take me out for tea and scones.'

A watery giggle escaped Ruby's lips. 'It's a deal.' She could just imagine Fina at the Ritz tea room, holding court and charming all the waiters, while the pianist played and the china clinked.

She checked her watch. 'I've ordered a taxi, so I really should go and get my things.'

'So soon?' Fina asked, looking a little forlorn.

Ruby nodded, and then Fina did, too. She was a woman who understood that when the time came a swift exit was the cleanest, if not the least painful, method of departure. Ruby was grateful for that.

She went and fetched her rucksack, hugged Fina once more, then descended the stone staircase for the last time

and pushed the boat door open to walk onto the dock.
The water taxi arrived only a few minutes later and Ruby
climbed inside and looked steadfastly at the buildings on
the other side of the canal as it turned around and pulled
away.

She kept staring like that, stiff and unseeing, all the
way to the train station. She didn't want to see any more
of Venice. Not the details, anyway. Not the shapes of the
arches or the patterns in the lace-like gothic façades. She
was happier if it all just blurred into one big pool of light
before her eyes.

CHAPTER SIXTEEN

'No, I'M AFRAID the four o'clock flight won't do. The crew need to catch another connection out of Paris to Antananarivo at five. We need them on the two forty-five.'

The travel agent on the other end of Ruby's phone huffed.

She lowered her voice, made it softer. 'Mr Lange would be ever so grateful if you could swing it. I'd even arrange to have a box set of his last series sent round as a thank-you.'

She could tell he'd just opened his mouth to give her an excuse, but he paused. 'My mum really does love his programmes. Have you got the one with the penguins in it?'

The Ice World of Antarctica?' Ruby asked, drawing a little black-and-white penguin with a bobble hat on in the corner of her office pad. Now, they'd make a great subject for a series of drawings. What was not to like? They were cute and walked funny.

'That's the one,' the man said, then chortled most unappealingly. 'And I'd have one less Christmas present to buy come December.'

Ruby pulled a face at the phone. Cheapskate. 'So can you help me?' she asked, almost purring down the line.

'Leave it with me,' he said, sounding a bit chirpier than when she'd first started talking to him. 'What did you say your name was again?'

'Ruby,' she said with a sigh in her voice. 'Ruby Lange.'

'Wow! You related?'

She resisted the urge to say *I'm his grandmother.*

'Yep. He's my dad.'

Ruby wilted a little further towards her desk. Just about every conversation she had these days ended up like this one. And she made hundreds of calls a week.

'It must be really cool to be Patrick Lange's daughter!' he said. 'What's it like working for him?'

Okay, *now* he wanted to be friendly and chatty, after making the last twenty minutes trying to get the flights for the next filming trip booked like squeezing blood from a stone.

'It's a blast,' she said as she drew a jagged crevice that her cartoon penguin was about to fall into. Still, she said her thank-yous and goodbyes politely and sweetly. No point zinging him until after the flights were booked.

The phone on her desk rang. She picked it up, half expecting it to be the travel guy again, and prepared herself to tell him, yes, she could send an autographed photograph to go with the DVDs, he just needed to let her know who her dad should make it out to, but it turned out to be Lucinda, her father's secretary.

'Mr Lange would like to see you in his office,' she said, then hung up.

Ruby stuck her tongue out at the phone. Lucinda always called Dad 'Mr Lange' in her presence; it was most weird. She was laced up as tight as the man in question was, so no wonder they'd been working well together for the last ten years.

Ruby shoved her chair away from her desk and picked up her pad and pencil. She ripped off the top sheet and hid it in her letter tray. Dad didn't really 'get' the doodling. Drawing while she was on the phone always helped her think, but if he saw it he'd only think she'd been slacking off, which she so hadn't.

She walked through the open-plan office and knocked on her father's door.

'Come!' he shouted.

Ruby obeyed.

'You wanted to see me?' she asked, choosing not to sit down. She had rather a lot to do today, what with the trip coming up. One of the crew wasn't British and needed an extra visa, and the paperwork was a nightmare.

Her father looked up from his desk. He was approaching sixty, but he was still fit and healthy, if a little weathered round the edges from all his travelling. 'Have you managed to source that special lens Cameron was after?' he asked.

She nodded. Their top cameraman had a brochure sitting on his desk and an appointment at one of the best video equipment suppliers to test it out in a few days' time.

'And how are we on getting that actress to do some of the voiceovers?'

Ruby hid a smile. 'That actress' was a multi-Oscar winner, who'd gone all fangirly when Ruby had called her people and asked if she'd like to work on the next series of Patrick Lange documentaries. 'Her office has just confirmed, but she won't be available for recording during September and October because she's shooting in Bulgaria.'

'Great.' Her father steepled his fingers and looked at her. 'And what about the tea?'

'In the kitchen,' she answered. Seriously, you'd have thought that finding a tin of his fresh leaf lapsang souchong when it had run out had been a national emergency. Thankfully, there was a little tea shop round the corner in Wardour Street that stocked just what she'd wanted.

'Do you want a cup?'

'Yes,' he said, and Ruby turned to go. 'But in a minute.'

She turned back again.

'Why don't you sit down?'

Uh-oh. He wasn't going to fire her, was he? She thought

she'd been doing okay for the two months she'd been working here, and that incident with the delivery guy and the ten-thousand-pound camera really hadn't been her fault.

She sidled round the chair sitting opposite his desk and slid into it.

'I think we need to talk about your future here, Ruby.'

Oh, Lord. Here it came.

'Lucinda has let me know that she's going to have to take maternity leave in the autumn, and I wondered if you'd be interested in filling in for her.'

Ruby's mouth dropped open. Whether it was because her father was offering her what was, in fact, a temporary promotion, or the idea of someone actually knocking frosty old Lucinda up, she didn't know.

'You've made quite an impression since you've been here,' he continued. 'I think it could be a nice step up for you.'

Ruby closed her eyes and opened them again. She'd obviously been transported into a parallel universe. 'I beg your pardon?'

Her father smiled at her, actually smiled! 'You've been doing a great job. Everyone thinks so.'

Ruby couldn't help the next words that fell out of her mouth. They just popped out before she had a chance to edit herself. 'Do *you*?'

He gave her a bemused smile, as if what she was asking was confusing or funny in some way. 'Of course I do. I always knew you could be good at something if you just settled to it.'

Yes, she was definitely in a parallel universe. It must have happened when she'd crossed the threshold into his office, because before then everyone and everything had been behaving as normal.

She looked back at him, searching his face. Was he really being serious?

What she saw shocked her.

Well, at least her time with Max had given her something more than bittersweet memories of a city she could probably never bear to visit again, because, just as she'd been able to look at Max, see the shell, know of its existence, but still catch glimpses of what was underneath, suddenly she could do the same with her father.

What she saw was different, of course. A little bit of paternal pride, more than a smidge of affection. Why had she never seen this before?

To be honest, she didn't know and she didn't care.

'What do you think?' her father said.

'I don't know,' she said truthfully. 'I've enjoyed the challenge of working here, and I'm not about to quit any time soon, but I'm just not sure it's…'

'You're not sure it's for you,' he finished for her softly.

She shook her head, afraid words would make the 'glimpses' disappear.

'Neither am I,' he said, standing up. 'But I thought I should offer you the opportunity.'

Ruby stood up, too. On a burst of emotion she ran over to her father and flung her arms around his neck. 'Thanks, Dad.'

He hugged her back, but muttered something about not making a fuss and nonsense at work.

Ruby pulled back and grinned at him. 'Sorry, I forgot. Lucinda would flay me alive if she heard me talking that way. I meant to say, "Thanks, Mr Lange".'

Real humour sparkled in his eyes, but he shooed her away. 'Go and get me that tea,' he said. 'And then it's probably about time you took your lunch break.'

Ruby looked at the clock. It was quarter to three already. No wonder her stomach was gurgling. She'd just been so busy that she'd forgotten to even think about lunch.

Ten minutes later she emerged from the Soho offices of

One Planet Productions and turned left, her large slouchy patchwork bag tucked under her arm. She hadn't used it since that day she'd tried to blag a job in Thalia Benson's office, and she'd made herself bring it out today. One couldn't spend all one's life hiding from half the contents of one's wardrobe because of the memories they conjured up. Sometimes one had to suck it up and keep moving. Onwards and upwards. Her motto was still keeping her strong.

First stop was her favourite coffee shop for a latte and a wrap, and then she headed for the little park on Golden Square. She sat on her favourite bench on the south-west corner, under a tree, and ate her lunch. Once that was disposed of, she opened her bag and pulled out a large A4 sketchpad. She flipped the cover open and turned to the first blank page and began to draw.

Not a cheeky crab. She'd given up on those. Instead a grumpy pigeon.

Her whole sketchbook was filled with Grumpy Pigeon drawings. Pigeon on Nelson's Column, Pigeon at the palace with the Queen, Pigeon on the Tube...

Max had been right. This was her passion. She drew when she got up in the mornings now. She drew during her lunch break and she drew when she got home from work. Her flatmate was threatening to use the accumulated stack of papers in their flat to wallpaper the toilet.

Drawing also had another benefit. While she was throwing herself into it, she didn't think of Max.

Well, okay, she did, but the memories got pushed to the back instead of jostling themselves to the front, where they were sharp and painful.

She hadn't heard anything from him since her return to London or, presumably, at some point, his. At first she'd hoped it had all been some Venice-induced hysteria, that everything would right itself and he'd come and see her, make contact somehow. She should have remembered that Max wasn't big on communication.

But she had other things to concentrate on now. She was finally laying the path for her own future, rather than wandering around in the dark. Not only did she know her next step, she knew where she wanted to be in six months' time, and five years' time.

She had a big picture.

How sad there was a dark hole in it that should have been filled by someone, but he'd decided it wasn't his perfect fit.

She sighed and carried on drawing. She had a meeting with a young, funky greetings-card firm that had offices in Shoreditch. They loved the grumpy little pigeon and she was talking to them about trialling a series of cards. And the owner of the vintage fashion shop she'd worked at wanted her to do some drawings for their new publicity drive—too fabulous to be true fifties divas in sunglasses and headscarves. Then there was a friend of a friend who said he might be able to put her in touch with people who did book jackets. All in all, things were looking promising.

Oh, she knew she'd have to keep working at One Planet for at least another year or two, maybe more. But she enjoyed it and it was a way to pay the bills. That was what grown-ups did, didn't they? They dug in and worked hard for what they wanted instead of drifting around and waiting for the universe to drop it into their laps.

When her hour was up, she packed her stuff away and headed back to the office. When she walked up to her desk, Jax, one of the other production assistants, leaned over the partition between their desks.

'You had a telephone call while you were out,' he said.

'Oh?' Her heart did a little flip. *Stop it*, she told it. *You can't keep doing this every time the darn thing rings. It's pointless... Hopeless... Give it up, already.*

'Yeah. It was some guy from a travel company.'

Ruby sank into her chair and laid her head on her desk.

'He wants to know if you can get a set of DVDs for his nan, too.'

Serafina Martin glided into the high-rise offices of Martin & Martin, her sunglasses on and a scarf tied round her neck. Her son resisted the urge to roll his eyes as he watched her from the confines of his glass office. She wafted through the main floor in his direction, bestowing regal smiles on his employees.

He'd finally gone to his mother at the end of his stay in Venice, had given her the space and time to tell her side of the story. It hadn't been easy to hear it, but he'd done it. And upon his return to London he'd remembered what she'd said about never having seen his flat, so he'd invited her over.

Not that she'd consented to actually stay with him, but she'd very kindly let him foot the bill for a room at the Dorchester. It was probably worth it, anyway. If they were under each other's feet twenty-four-seven, they'd probably drive each other crazy and undo all the progress that they'd made.

They'd had a long heart-to-heart the night before over dinner. He'd been aware that he'd listened to her side of the story in Venice, but he'd finally managed to release the things he'd needed to say, too. Like how he was sorry that he'd pushed her away for most of his life. He should have been loyal to both parents, not barricaded the doors against her as if she were the enemy. And he'd done it without Ruby there to egg him on, prod him when he was being stubborn. She would have been proud of him.

He ignored the stab of pain in his chest at the thought of her. That particular wound still hadn't closed, still dripped and weeped every day.

Neither he nor his mother were exactly sure what was going to happen from here on, but at least they were willing to try. He'd attempted to explain it to her. In actual words. The best he'd been able to do was tell her he wasn't sure how to deconstruct a relationship back to where it had been almost twenty years ago and start again, build it up in a different shape, with a different foundation.

Yes, he'd used a lot of building metaphors. He couldn't help it. He was new at this talking stuff, and it was the only way the words would come.

Fina had just leaned across the table and patted his hand. 'You're the best architect I know, Massimo. You'll work it out.'

His mother finally reached his office door and entered without knocking, then collapsed gracefully into a leather chair and smiled. 'Shopping is so tiring, don't you think?'

Max frowned. If it was that tiring, you'd think she'd do less of it.

'I thought you said you'd be back at two. It's past four.'

She waved a hand, as if minutes and seconds were of no consequence. 'I was otherwise engaged.'

'Oh, yes?'

She fidgeted with her handbag. 'I met Ruby for afternoon tea at the Ritz.'

It was a warm August day outside, and the sun was glinting off the skyscrapers in the City of London, but Max's skin chilled and his heart lumbered to a stop.

'She showed me this,' she said, and handed him a small rectangular card in a cellophane sleeve. He turned it over to discover it was a greetings card. He hadn't seen the design before—a rather fierce-looking pigeon, who was standing guard at the Tower of London—but he recognised the style instantly.

She'd done it? She'd really done it?

His mother took the card back from him and tucked it in her handbag. 'I told her I thought the pigeon reminded me of someone we both knew, but she said she couldn't see it.'

'I do *not* scowl like that.'

'Darling,' she said sweetly, 'you're doing it now.'

He shook his head and walked back round the other side of his desk. 'How was she?' he asked, keeping his tone light, neutral, and messing with some bits of paper on his desk.

It had been hard knowing he was in the same city as her. He'd have considered moving back to Venice if the institute commission hadn't been ploughing ahead at full steam. They'd loved his new designs. Had eaten them up, and Vince McDermot had scurried off with his tail between his legs.

And it was all because of Ruby. He wished he could see her to tell her that.

Hell, he wished he could see her full stop. He looked up, realising his mother hadn't answered him.

'Honestly, Massimo,' she said, giving him that same look she'd used to give him as a boy when he'd been caught stealing the family launch to go racing with his friends. 'When are you going to give up and admit you're head over heels for that girl?'

He stared back at her. Admitting it wasn't the problem. Forgetting it was.

And now he'd seen her drawings he knew he'd done the right thing. He'd only have weighed her down, held her back.

'Sometimes it's better to walk away. I thought you'd understand that better than anyone.'

His mother threw her hands in the air, indicating she did not know what to do with him. 'For a very intelligent man, my darling son, you can be incredibly stupid.'

'Thanks, Mamma,' he said between gritted teeth.

She stood up and walked over to him, her eyes warm and full of compassion. 'You are not your father, Massimo.'

He opened his mouth, but she held up her hand.

'Yes, you are very like him, but you are not a carbon copy.' She gave him a heartfelt look. 'You have a chance, darling, to make this right, to be happy. You can be what your father could not. I know it.'

It was surprising to discover just how much her faith warmed him. 'How can you be so sure?'

'Because I gave birth to you, because I know you. Because I've seen the way you've changed this summer.'

'I don't know how to tell her.'

She kissed him on the cheek and patted his arm. 'Skills like that are just like muscles. The more you use them, the stronger they get, and you've already made a start.'

Max thought of all the things he'd said to Ruby that last night in Venice. The way he'd seen her crumble in front of him. He wasn't sure words would ever be enough to repair that damage.

'Anyway,' she said, regaining some of her usual breezy air and heading for the door, 'I've got a taxi waiting downstairs and I need someone to carry my bags.'

Max raced after her. A taxi? They'd been talking for at least five minutes!

'What bags?' he said, sounding more like his usual self.

'Oh, I paid a little visit to Harrods before the Ritz.'

Four large bags were waiting for him in the back of the cab. He climbed in and passed them to his mother. The cabby smiled. He'd seemed quite happy to wait, with the meter ticking over at the speed of light. When the last one had hit the pavement, his mother gave him a gentle shove so he lost his balance and landed on the back seat.

'Go! Go and see Ruby.'

He looked back at her helplessly. He'd had no time to prepare, no time to think up any building-related images to help him explain. 'What will I say?'

'Just start, Massimo,' she said as she shut the door. 'The rest will come.'

And then she thumped the taxi on the roof and it sped off into the London traffic.

Ruby was supposed to be working, but she'd drifted off, staring out of the window. It wasn't something she usually did, but she'd looked up at the sky between the narrow buildings. It was exactly the same colour as the day they'd taken the speedboat out into the lagoon and found the secret beach, and for some reason she'd just ground to a halt.

She supposed she could call it a coffee break, but she usually filled her breaks with sketching, because when they were filled with sketching it blocked out other things she didn't want to think about.

A large, heavy sigh deflated her ribcage.

She hadn't let herself look back much, but some of the memories were so lovely, even if it hurt like hell to think about them.

If only whistles were really magic…

Then she could put her lips together and let out that breathy little sound and everything she wanted would just rise from the London street to meet her.

She pursed her lips, and the noise that came out was both pathetic and forlorn.

Nothing happened. But why would it? This was London, not *La Serenissima*.

She shook herself. This was no way to live. *Come on, Ruby. Find yourself something to do, something to keep yourself occupied.* In this madhouse, it shouldn't be hard enough.

And, right on cue, a commotion erupted near the foyer. It was probably that clumsy motorbike delivery guy again. Thank goodness she was nowhere nearby to get blamed for his mishaps again.

The noise got louder. It was coming closer.

The One Planet office was large, but full of clutter and equipment, and the desks were separated by low screens to make cubicles. Ruby half stood and peered round the edge of hers to see what was going on.

There was a man walking down the central aisle, looking terribly grim, terribly stern. Everyone else cleared out of the way, but Ruby found she couldn't do anything but freeze as her pulse went crazy. If it got any faster, she was either going to have a stroke or shoot straight through the ceiling.

That was Max. Here in the office.

He spotted her—half crouching, half leaning out of her cubicle—and his trajectory changed.

Jax, who fancied himself a bit as the office bouncer, was on his heels. 'Hey, mate! Where d'you think you're going?'

'I'm going to see Ruby Lange,' Max replied, not taking his eyes off her.

Ruby stood up, and the folds of the skirt of her strawberry dress fell around her knees.

He stopped when he was about ten feet away. 'Wh-what do you want?' she stammered.

Faces appeared above partitions and some of those who worked down the other end of the office drew closer to see what was going on.

Max just stared at her.

My, he looked amazing. All tall and gruff and…Max. She wanted to smile, to run to him, but she held back. Wasn't he going to say anything?

He stopped looking quite so stern. She saw him swallow.

He wasn't going to be able to do it, was he? He found saying what needed to be said impossible at the best of times. That was why she'd left him in Venice. Not because he hadn't cared, but because he'd been too much of a coward to show it. How was he going to do it with all these people looking on, all these strangers?

But then he straightened, grew even taller and smiled at her.

'I need you.'

The words hit her heart like an arrow, but this time she would not be wooed by them so easily. She needed to test them, to know their strength.

'I'm not a nanny any more,' she answered softly.

The heads of the onlookers swivelled back to look at Max.

The smile disappeared. 'I don't need a blasted nanny,' he told her. 'I need *you*, Ruby.'

'Why?' she almost whispered. Her heart thudded madly inside her chest, blood rushed in her ears. The seconds ticked by.

Details, Max. I need details.

He took a step forward. He was so close now that she could have reached out and touched him if she'd wanted to. The crowd shuffled closer. Someone walked in the door, back from a meeting and talking loudly on their mobile phone, and was shushed by at least five others.

'Because,' Max said, 'you are bright and beautiful and talented.'

She let out a shaky breath.

But he wasn't finished yet. 'Because you brought joy back into my dull, structured life.'

She felt a lump rise in her throat. She started to speak anyway, but he stopped her with a look.

'Because you challenge me, contradict me and generally drive me crazy.'

There was a rough laugh from behind her. 'Yes, but isn't she wonderful?'

Ruby turned to see her father standing at the end of the room. He was smiling. She looked back at Max, hardly knowing whether to laugh or cry.

'I wouldn't have it any other way.'

And then he was reaching for her, pulling her to him and his lips were on hers and his arms crushed her to him.

'And because I love you,' he whispered in her ear, but she didn't mind that. These words were hers and hers alone. 'More than anything in this world, more than designing or building or even breathing. I promise you I am no longer ankle deep. I am in way, way, way over my head.'

She pulled back to look at him. 'Good answer,' she said, grinning. 'Because so am I.'

Max just laughed and kissed her again.

* * * * *

MEET THE FORTUNES!

Fortune of the Month:
Amelia Fortune Chesterfield

Age: 23

Vital Statistics: Doelike eyes, ivory complexion. As fragile as a china doll—and in the family way.

Claim to Fame: Did we mention that she's English royalty?

Romantic Prospects: Many men have pursued her for her title, but will anybody love her for just herself ?

"My whole life I've been a good girl, following the rules, being a proper princess. But everything changed when I met Quinn in Horseback Hollow. He made me realize what was really important. In his strong cowboy arms I finally felt safe. I never should have gone back to London. Everything went so wrong so fast! Now Quinn is acting like he hates me. How can I possibly tell him I'm carrying his child?"

* * *

The Fortunes of Texas:
Welcome to Horseback Hollow!

FORTUNE'S PRINCE

BY
ALLISON LEIGH

Published in Great Britain 2014
by Mills & Boon, an imprint of Harlequin (UK) Limited,
Eton House, 18-24 Paradise Road, Richmond, Surrey, TW9 1SR

© 2014 Harlequin Books S.A.

Special thanks and acknowledgement are given to Allison Leigh for her contribution to the FORTUNES OF TEXAS: WELCOME TO HORSEBACK HOLLOW continuity.

ISBN: 978-0-263-91290-6

23-0614

Harlequin (UK) Limited's policy is to use papers that are natural, renewable and recyclable products and made from wood grown in sustainable forests. The logging and manufacturing processes conform to the legal environmental regulations of the country of origin.

Printed and bound in Spain
by Blackprint CPI, Barcelona

There is a saying that you can never be too rich or too thin. **Allison Leigh** doesn't believe that, but she does believe that you can *never* have enough books! When her stories find a way into the hearts—and bookshelves—of others, Allison says she feels she's done something right. Making her home in Arizona with her husband, she enjoys hearing from her readers at Allison@allisonleigh.com or PO Box 40772, Mesa, AZ 85274-0772, USA.

For all the Fortune Women.
As always, it is an honor to be among you.

Chapter One

He stopped cold when he heard a faint rustle. The only light there was came from the moonlight sneaking through the barn door that he'd left open behind him.

Standing stock-still, Quinn Drummond listened intently, his eyes searching the black shadows around him. He'd built the barn. He knew it like the back of his hand. He knew the sounds that belonged, and the ones that didn't. Animal or human, it didn't matter. He knew.

He reached out his right hand, unerringly grabbing onto a long wooden handle. He'd prefer his shotgun, but it was up in the house. So the pitchfork would have to do.

This wasn't some damn possum rooting around.

This was some*one*. Someone hiding out in his barn.

He knew everyone who lived in his Texas hometown. Horseback Hollow was the polar opposite of a metropolis. If someone there wanted something, they'd have

come to his face, not skulk around in the middle of the
night inside his barn.

His hand tightened around the sturdy handle. His
focus followed the rustling sound and he took a silent
step closer to it. "Come on out now, because if you don't,
I promise you won't like what's gonna happen."

The faint rustle became a scuffling sound, then the
darkness in front of him gathered into a small form.

His wariness drained away. His tight grip relaxed.
Just a kid.

He made a face and set aside the pitchfork. "What'd
you do? Run away from home?" He'd tried that once,
when he was seven. Hadn't gotten far. His dad had
hauled him home and would have tanned his butt if his
mother hadn't stepped in. "Never works, kid," he advised. "Whatever you think you're running from will
always follow."

The form shuffled closer; small, booted feet sliding
into the faint moonlight, barely visible below the too-
long hem of baggy pants. "That's what I'm afraid of,"
the shadow said.

Forget wariness. The voice didn't belong to a child.
It was feminine. Very British. And so damn familiar his
guts twisted and his nerves frizzed like they wanted to
bust out of his skin. A runaway would have been preferable to this. To *her.*

Amelia.

Her name blasted through his head, but he didn't say a
word and after a moment, she took another hesitant step
closer. Moonlight crept from the dark boots up baggy
pants, an untucked, oversize shirt that dwarfed her delicate figure, until finally, *finally,* illuminating the long
neck, the pointed chin.

The first time that he'd seen her had been six months ago on New Year's Eve, at a wedding for one of her newly discovered cousins, right there in Horseback Hollow. Her long dark hair had been twisted into a knot, reminding him vaguely of the dancers at the ballet that his mom had once dragged him and his sister to. The second time that he'd seen her months later at the end of April, had been at another wedding. Another cousin. And her hair had been tied up then, too.

But that second time, after dreaming about her since New Year's, Quinn hadn't just watched Amelia from a distance.

No.

He'd approached her. And through some miracle of fate—or so he'd thought at the time—later that night, he'd taken the pins from her hair and it had spilled down past her shoulders, gleaming and silky against her ivory skin.

He blocked off the memory. He'd had enough practice at it over the past two months that it should have been easy.

It wasn't. It was the very reason he was prowling restlessly around in the middle of the night at all when he should have been sleeping.

"What the hell'd you do to your hair?"

She made a soft sound and lifted her hand to the side of the roughly chopped short hair sticking out from her head. She'd have looked like a boy if her delicate features weren't so distinctively feminine. "It's lovely to see you, too." She moved her hand again, and it came away with the hair.

A wig. It was stupid to feel relieved, but he did.

She scrubbed the fingers of her other hand across

her scalp, and her hair, the real stuff, slid down in a coil over one shoulder, as dark as the night sky. "It's a wig," she said, stating the obvious. Her voice was unsteady. "The second one, actually. The first was blond, but there were reporters at the airport, and—" She shook her head, breaking off.

That night—the night he'd twisted his hands in her hair and thought he'd tasted perfection on her lips—she'd talked about the reporters who had dogged her family's footsteps for as long as she could remember. How she hated being in a fishbowl. How her life felt claustrophobic. How she envied his life on a ranch; the wide-open spaces, the wind at his back when he rode his horse.

Again, he pushed away the thoughts. He shoved his fingertips into the pockets of his jeans, wishing he could wipe away the memory of her silky hair sliding over his chest as they'd made love. "What are you doing here?"

"In your barn? Proving I'm better at remembering a Google Map than I thought." She let out a nervous sound that was maybe supposed to be a laugh but could have been a sob.

"Not my barn," he said tightly. *"Here."*

She took a quick, audible breath. She was young. Seven years younger than his own thirty. Practically a girl. Except she wasn't a girl. She was full-grown. Self-possessed. Aristocratic.

And now, she was hiding in his barn, stumbling around for words.

"Amelia," he prompted sharply. He couldn't pretend her unexpected appearance didn't make him tense. Any more than she could hide the fact that she was clearly nervous. The way she kept shifting from one foot to the other, almost swaying, told him that.

"Yes. Right. The, um, the last time we spoke—"

"*What* are you doing here?" He didn't want to rehash that phone conversation. It had been nearly two months ago. He didn't want to think about what had precipitated it. Didn't want to think about it and damn sure didn't want to feel anything about it. Not that conversation, or whatever was making her so skittish now.

Her lips moved again but no sound came out. She lifted her hand to the side of her head again. Swayed almost imperceptibly.

And pitched forward.

He let out an oath, his heart nearly jumping out of his chest, and barely caught her limp body before it hit the ground at his feet.

He crouched beside her, carefully holding her. He caught her chin in his hand. She felt cold. And was out cold. "Amelia!"

Dim light or not, he could see that her lashes, so dark against her pale, pale cheeks, didn't so much as flicker.

He rose, lifting her in his arms. It was easy. He routinely tossed around hay bales that weighed more than she did, and she seemed even thinner now than the night he'd replaced her fancy gown with his hands. She was neither short, nor tall. Pretty average height. But that was the only thing average about Amelia Fortune Chesterfield.

Everything else—

He shook his head, blowing out a breath and carried her out of the barn, not even bothering to pull the door closed though he'd likely come back in the morning to find that possum taking up residence there again. He aimed for his truck parked up by the house, about a hundred yards away, his stride fast and gaining speed as he went. The moonlight shone down on her, painting her face an even whiter hue, and her gleaming head bounced against his arm as he ran.

He could hardly breathe by the time he made it to his truck, and it wasn't because he was out of shape. It was because the nearest hospital was in Lubbock, a good hour away.

He could deal with a lot of minor medical emergencies.

He couldn't deal with an unconscious Amelia Fortune Chesterfield.

Adjusting his grip beneath her, he managed to get the door open with one hand and settled her on the seat.

Her head lolled limply to the side, quickly followed by her lax shoulders.

"Come on, princess," he whispered, gently situating her again, holding her up long enough to get the safety belt clipped in place. The chest strap held her back against the seat and he started to draw his hands away from her waist and her shoulders so he could close the door, but her arm shifted slightly. Then her hand. Sliding over his, lighter than a breath but still enough to make the world seem to stop spinning.

"I'm not a princess," she whispered almost inaudibly.

He exhaled roughly. She'd said the same thing *that* night, too.

Only then she'd been looking up at him through her lashes; a combination of innocence and sexiness that had gone to his head quicker than the finest whiskey.

Maybe she wasn't a princess. But she was still the youngest daughter of Lady Josephine Fortune Chesterfield and the late Sir Simon John Chesterfield. And since it had come out last year that Horseback Hollow's own resident Jeanne Marie Jones was a long-lost sister of Lady Josephine, the Chesterfield family was officially one of the town's hottest topics. Even Quinn's own sister, Jess, usually practical and definitely down-to-earth, had been struck royal-crazy. It had gotten so bad lately that he'd pretty much avoided her whenever he could, just so he wouldn't have to listen to her jabber on about the latest news from across the pond.

And for the past few months, particularly, he couldn't even visit the Superette in town to pick up his weekly milk and bread without seeing a magazine on the racks that mentioned Amelia in some way.

He took her hand and set it away from him, backing away to slam the truck door closed. He strode around the front and got in behind the wheel, not wanting to look at her, yet not being able to stop himself from doing so. The dome light shining on her face was more relentless than the moonlight, showing the dark circles under her eyes.

She looked ill.

He swiftly turned the key and started the engine. "I'm taking you to the hospital in Lubbock," he said flatly.

She shifted, her hand reaching for his arm again. Her fingertips dug into his forearm with surprising strength for someone who'd nearly face-planted in the dirt. "I don't need a hospital," she said quickly. "Please." Her voice broke.

"You need something." He shrugged off her touch and steered the truck away from the house. "And you won't find it here."

She sucked in an audible breath again and even though he knew he was in the right, he still felt like a bastard.

"You fainted. You need a doctor."

"No. I just… It's just been a long trip. I haven't eaten since, well since Heathrow, I guess."

He wasn't going to ask why. Wasn't going to let himself care. She was just another faithless woman. He'd already graduated from that school and didn't need another course. "First-class fare not up to your standards?"

She ignored his sarcasm. "I was in economy." She plucked the collar of her shirt that was mud-colored in the truck's light. "I was trying not to be noticed." She turned away, looking out the side window. "For all the good that did. I managed to lose Ophelia Malone before I left London, but there were still two more photographers to take her place the second I landed." She sighed. "I lost them in Dallas, but only because I changed my disguise and caught a bus."

He nearly choked. "You rode a bus? From Dallas to Horseback Hollow?" It had to have taken hours. On top of the flight, she'd probably been traveling for nearly twenty-four hours. "You have no business riding around on a bus!"

She didn't look at him, but even beneath the rough clothes that dwarfed her slender figure, he could tell she stiffened. "It's a perfectly convenient mode of transportation," she defended.

Sure. For people like him. He was a small-town rancher. She was *the* Amelia Fortune Chesterfield. And since the day she'd returned to England after her night dabbling with Quinn—after making him believe that she was going back to London only to attend to some royal duties and would quickly return to Horseback Hollow— she'd become one half of the engaged couple dubbed "Jamelia" by the media that dogged her steps.

Amelia Fortune Chesterfield was to marry James

Banning in the most popular royal romance since the Duke and Duchess of Cambridge. *Lord* James Banning. A viscount, whatever the hell that was. A man who was her equal in wealth and family connections. A man who was slated for an even higher title, evidently, once Amelia was his wife. Earl something of something or other.

His sister had talked about it so many times, the facts ought to be tattooed on his brain.

His fingers strangled the steering wheel. "Wedding plans becoming so taxing that you had to run away from them?" He didn't wait for an answer. "Never mind. I don't want to know." He turned through the overhead arch bearing the iron Rocking-U sign and pressed harder on the gas. The highway was still a fair piece away, but once he hit that, it'd be smooth sailing. He'd leave her in capable medical hands and wash his hands of her, once and for all.

Somewhere inside his head, laughter mocked the notion. He'd been doing that so-called washing for the past two months and hadn't gotten anywhere. There had to be something wrong with him that he couldn't just file her away as a one-night stand where she belonged and be done with it.

"*Please* don't take me to Lubbock," she said huskily. "I don't need a doctor. I just need some sleep. And some food." She reached across as if she were going to touch his arm again, but curled her fingers into a fist instead, resting it on the console between their seats. "Drop me on the side of the road if you must. I'm begging you. Please, Quinn."

He ground his molars together. Would he have had more resistance if she hadn't said his name? "I'm not gonna drop you on the side of the damn road."

He should take her to Jeanne's. Recently discovered family or not, the woman was Amelia's aunt. Jeanne would take her in. Even if it *was* the middle of the night.

He muttered an oath and pulled a U-turn there on the empty highway.

Maybe Amelia wouldn't mind Jeanne's questions, asked or unasked, but Quinn would. Particularly when he had unanswered questions of his own.

He didn't look at her. "I'll take you back to the Rocking-U. And then you can start talking."

His voice was so hard.

His face so expressionless.

Amelia wrapped her arms around herself and tried to quell her trembling. She was so, so tired.

She'd foolishly thought that once she got back to Horseback Hollow, once she saw Quinn in person, everything would be all right.

She could explain. And he would understand.

He would take her in his arms, and everything would be perfect and as wonderful as it had been the night of her cousin Toby's wedding. Quinn would know that there was only him. That there had only ever been him.

It had been the single thing keeping her going throughout the dreadful ordeal of getting to Horseback Hollow.

"You can start—" Quinn's deep voice cut through her "—with explaining why you came to the Rocking-U at all."

"I wanted to talk," she whispered.

He gave her a long look. Animosity rolled off him in waves, a stark contrast to the tender warmth he'd shown her just six weeks earlier. "Yet so far you haven't said anything new."

She wanted to wring her hands. Such a silly, naive girl to think that her presence would be enough to make up for everything she hadn't said that she should have. For everything she hadn't done that she should have.

"What did Banning do? Disagree over china patterns? So you run away again to the States to bring him to heel? Your last trip here was pretty effective. Ended up with a royal engagement the second you got back home. Or maybe you're just in the mood for one more final fling before the 'I do's' get said."

"I told you weeks ago that there's no engagement," she reminded carefully. After a week of the frantic telephone messages she'd left for him once she'd arrived in London, he'd finally returned her call. She'd tried to explain to him then about the media frenzy that had greeted her at the airport when she'd returned from Toby's wedding.

Reporters shouting their congratulations on her engagement to James. Cameras flashing in her eyes. She'd been blindsided by the unwanted attention as much as she'd been blindsided by news of an engagement she and James had discussed, but had never agreed to.

He grunted derisively. "And I don't believe you any more now than I did when you said it the first time. You came to Horseback Hollow two months ago and you had sex with the poor dumb cowboy who didn't know enough to recognize things for what they were. Your little walk on the wild side, I guess, before settling down all nice and proper with the English earl."

"James isn't an earl yet." Which was the furthest thing from what she wanted to say.

"I don't give a damn what he is or isn't." He slowed to make the turn through the iron archway, but the tires still kicked out an angry, arching spit of gravel. "He's your fiancé. That's the only thing I have to know. And as good as you were in the sack, princess, I'm not interested in a repeat performance."

She bit down on her tongue to keep from gasping and stared hard out the side window until the tears pushing behind her eyes subsided. They hadn't ever made it to a "sack," as he so crudely put it. They'd made love under the moonlight in a field of green, surrounded by trees, singing crickets and croaking frogs. She'd slept in his arms under the stars and wakened at dawn to chirping birds and his kisses.

It had been magical.

"It was six weeks ago," she whispered.

He still managed to hear. "Six. Eight. Whatever it was, it no longer matters to me. You want to screw around with a cowboy, do it on someone else's ranch."

She snapped her head around, looking at him. Even though it was dark as pitch, and the only light came from the glow of his pickup truck's instrument panel, she still knew every inch of his face. Every detail. From the dark brown hair springing thickly back from his sun-bronzed forehead to the spiky lashes surrounding his hazel eyes to his angular jaw. She knew his quiet smile. The easy way he held his tall, muscular body.

"Don't do that," she said sharply. "Don't cheapen what we had."

"What we had, prin*cess*—" he drew out the word in a mocking British accent "—was a one-night stand. And the next day, you returned to the loving arms of your intended. Poor bastard. Does he know what he's getting?" He pulled to a stop in front of a modestly sized two-storied house and turned off the engine. "Or maybe he doesn't care. Maybe he's just happy to merge one highfalutin' family with another and fidelity doesn't matter one little bit."

"He's not my fiancé!"

"And that's what you came all the way here to talk about," he said skeptically. "To claim that he's not your fiancé? While every newspaper and trashy tabloid in print, every gossipy website that exists, is dissecting the great 'Jamelia' romance. If he's not your fiancé, why the hell aren't there any quotes from you saying *that?* Everything else about the two of you has been chronicled across the world. Seems to me there have been plenty of opportunities for you to state otherwise." He stared into her face for a long moment, then shook his head and shoved open his truck door. "We had this same conversation two months ago on the phone." His voice was flat. "Should have saved yourself a ten-hour flight in coach." He slammed the door shut and started walking toward the house.

"Six weeks ago," she whispered again

But of course he didn't hear her this time.

Chapter Two

Amelia finally got out of the truck and headed slowly toward him. Quinn watched only long enough to assure himself that she wasn't going to collapse again, before he turned toward the house once more. He wanted her in his home about as much as he wanted holes drilled into his head.

It was hard enough to forget about her when she'd never stepped foot in his place. Now she was going to do just that. And his need to keep her out of his thoughts was going to become even more impossible.

He shoved open the front door and waited for her to finish crossing the gravel drive. Her dark hair gleamed in the moonlight, reminding him of the last time. Only then the long strands had been fanned out around her head, and her face bathed in ecstasy.

He clenched his teeth and looked at the scuffed toes of

his leather boots. The second she crossed the threshold, he moved away. "Close the door behind you."

His steps sounded hollow on the wood floor as he headed through the house to the kitchen at the back and he heard the soft latch of the front door closing behind him.

He slapped his palm against the wall switch, flooding the kitchen with unforgiving light, and grabbed the plastic-wrapped loaf of bread from where he'd last tossed it on the counter. He yanked open a drawer, grabbed a knife, slammed the drawer shut and yanked open the fridge. Pulled a few things out and slammed that door shut, too.

None of it helped.

She was still in his damned house.

Another woman he'd let himself believe in.

Didn't matter that he knew he was to blame for that particular situation. He'd barely known Amelia. And he'd known his ex-wife, Carrie, for years. Yet he'd made the same mistake with them both.

Trusting that he was the one.

The only one.

He carelessly swiped mayonnaise on the two slices of bread, slapped a slice of cheese on top, followed by a jumble of deli-sliced turkey.

Every cell he possessed knew the minute Amelia stepped into the kitchen behind him, though she didn't make a sound. She was as ghostly quiet as she was ghostly pale.

He dropped the other slice of bread on top of the turkey and managed not to smash it down out of sheer frustration. He tossed the knife in the sink next to his elbow and it clattered noisily.

He turned and faced her, choking down the urge to take her shoulders and urge her into a chair.

She looked worse than ill.

The shadows under her eyes were nearly purple. The oversize shirt—an uglier color than the contents of his youngest nephew's diaper the last time he'd been stuck changing it—had slipped down one of her shoulders and her collarbone stuck out too sharp against her pale skin.

It wasn't just a day of traveling—by means he damn sure knew she wasn't used to—taking its toll.

"What the hell have you done to yourself?"

Her colorless lips parted slightly. She stared up at him and her eyes—dark, dark brown and enormous in her small triangular face—shimmered wetly. "You're so angry," she whispered.

Angry didn't begin to cover it. He was pissed as hell. Frustrated beyond belief. And completely disillusioned with his judgment where women were concerned.

Especially this woman, because dammit all to hell, there was still a part of him that wanted to believe in her. Believe the things she'd said that night. Believe the things she'd made him feel that night.

And he knew better.

"I should have taken you to the hospital," he said flatly. "Have you had the flu or something?" God forbid she was suffering anything worse.

Her lashes lowered and she reached out a visibly unsteady hand for one of the wood chairs situated around his small, square table. But she only braced herself; she didn't sit. "I haven't been sick. I told you, I just need food and a little rest."

"A little?" He snorted and nudged her down onto the chair seat. A nudge is all it took, too, because her legs folded way too easily. He would have termed it collapsing, except she did even that with grace.

As soon as she was sitting, he took his hand away, curling his fingers against his palm.

Whether to squeeze away the feel of her fragile shoulder, or to hold on to it, he wasn't sure.

And that just pissed him off even more.

He grabbed the sandwich, and ignoring every bit of manners his mom had ever tried to teach him, plopped it on the bare table surface in front of her. No napkin. No plate.

If she wanted to toy around with a cowboy, she'd better learn there weren't going to be any niceties. He almost wished he chewed, because the notion of spitting tobacco juice out just then was stupidly appealing.

She, of course, not-a-princess that she was, ignored his cavalier behavior and turned her knees beneath the table, sitting with a straight back despite her obvious exhaustion. Then she picked up the sandwich with as much care as if it were crustless, cut into fancy shapes and served up on priceless silver. "Thank you," she said quietly.

He wanted to slam his head against a wall.

Every curse he knew filled his head, all of them directed right at his own miserable hide. He grimly pulled a sturdy white plate from the cupboard and set it on the table. He didn't have napkins, but he tore a paper towel off the roll, folded it in half and set it next to the plate. Then, feeling her big brown eyes following him, he grabbed a clean glass and filled it with cold tap water. She was surely used to the stuff that came in fancy tall bottles, but there was no better water around than what came from the Rocking-U well. Aside from water, he had milk and beer. He wasn't sure the milk wasn't sour by now, and she definitely wasn't the type to drink beer.

"Thank you," she said again, after taking a long sip of the water. "I don't mean to put you to any trouble."

He folded his arms across his chest and dragged his gaze away from the soft glisten of moisture lingering on her full, lower lip. "Shouldn't have gotten on the airplane, then." Much less a bus.

She looked away.

For about the tenth time since he'd found her hiding in his barn, he felt like he'd kicked a kitten. Then ground his boot heel down on top of it for good measure.

"Eat." He sounded abrupt and didn't care. "I'll get a bed ready for you."

She nodded, still not looking at him. "Thank—" Her voice broke off for a moment. "You," she finished faintly.

That politeness of hers would be the end of him.

He left the kitchen with embarrassing haste and stomped up the stairs to the room at the end of the hall. He stopped in the doorway and stared at the bed.

It was the only one in the house.

It was his.

"You're a freaking idiot," he muttered to himself as he crossed the room and yanked the white sheets that were twisted and tangled and as much off the bed as they were on into some semblance of order. He'd have changed the sheets if he owned more than one set.

Once she was gone, he'd have to burn the damn things and buy different ones. For that matter, he might as well replace the whole bed. He hadn't had a decent night's sleep since learning she'd gotten engaged to that other guy within hours of leaving his arms. He was pretty sure that sleeping was only going to get harder from here on out.

He realized he was strangling his pillow between his fists, and slapped it down on the bed.

It was summertime, so he hadn't personally been bothering with much more than a sheet, but he unearthed the quilt that his mother had made for him years earlier from where he'd hidden it away in the closet after Carrie left him, and spread it out on top of the sheets. It smelled vaguely of mothballs, but it was better than nothing.

Then he shoved the ragged paperback book he'd been reading from the top of the nightstand into the drawer, effectively removing the only personal item in sight, and left the room.

He went back downstairs.

She was still sitting at the table in his kitchen, her back straight as a ruler, her elbows nowhere near the table. She'd finished the sandwich, though, and was folding the paper towel into intricate shapes. Not for the first time, he eyed her slender fingers, bare of rings, and reminded himself that the absence of a diamond ring didn't mean anything.

When she heard him, she stood. "I should go to Aunt Jeanne's."

"Yes." He wasn't going to lie. She'd already done enough of that for them both. "But it's after midnight. No point in ruining someone else's night's sleep, too. And since Horseback Hollow isn't blessed with any motels, much less an establishment up to your standards," he added even though she was too cultured to say so, "you're stuck with what I have." He eyed her. "Bedroom's upstairs. Do you have enough stuffing left in you to make it up them, or do I need to put you over my shoulder?"

Her ghostly pale face took on a little color at that. "I'm not a sack of feed," she said, almost crisply, and headed past him through the doorway.

His house wasn't large. The staircase was right there to the left of the front door and his grandmother's piano. She headed straight to it, closed her slender fingers over the wood banister and started up. The ugly shirt she wore hung over her hips, midway down the thighs of her baggy jeans.

He still had to look away from the sway of her hips as she took the steps. "Room's at the end of the hall," he said after her. "Bathroom's next to it."

Manners might have had him escorting her up there.

Self-preservation kept him standing right where he was.

"Yell if you need something," he added gruffly.

She stopped, nearly at the top of the stairs, and looked back at him. Her hair slid over her shoulder.

Purple shadows, ghostly pale and badly fitting clothes or not, she was still the most beautiful thing he'd ever seen and looking at her was a physical pain.

"I need you not to hate me," she said softly.

His jaw tightened right along with the band across his chest that made it hard to breathe. "I don't hate you, Amelia."

Her huge eyes stared at him. They were haunting, those eyes.

"I don't feel anything," he finished.

It was the biggest lie he'd ever told in his life.

Amelia's knees wobbled and she tightened her grip on the smooth, warm wooden banister. Quinn could say what he wanted, but the expression on his face told another story.

And she had only herself to blame.

No words came to mind that were appropriate for the situation. Even if there *were* words, she wasn't sure her tight throat would have allowed her to voice them. So she just gave him an awkward nod and headed up the remaining stairs. Because what else was there to do but go forward?

There was no going back.

He'd made that painfully clear more than once and her coming to Horseback Hollow to see him face-to-face hadn't changed a single thing.

At the landing, the room he spoke of was obvious. Straight at the end of the hall.

The door was open and through it she could see the foot of a quilt-covered bed.

She pushed back her shoulders despite her weariness, and headed toward it. If she weren't feeling devastated to her core, she would have gobbled up every detail of his home as she walked along the wooden-floored hallway. Would have struggled not to let her intense curiosity where he was concerned overtake her. Would have wondered how each nook and cranny reflected Quinn. The man she'd fallen head over heels in love with on the foolish basis of a few dances at a wedding reception.

And a night of lovemaking after.

The thought was unbearable and she pushed it away. She'd deal with that later.

She stopped at the bathroom briefly and shuddered over her pallid reflection in the oval mirror that hung over a classic pedestal sink when she washed her hands. It was no wonder he'd stared at her with such horror.

She looked hideous.

Not at all the way she'd looked the night he'd stopped next to her at Toby's wedding reception, smiled quietly and asked if she cared to dance. She'd looked as good that day as her gawky self was capable of looking.

But when Quinn took her in his arms and slowly circled around the outdoor dance floor with her to the croon of Etta James, for the first time, she'd felt beautiful. All because of the way he'd looked at her.

Tears burned behind her eyes again and she quickly left the bathroom behind, hurrying the remaining few feet into the bedroom. She shut the door soundlessly, leaned back against it and slid down it until her bottom hit the floor.

Then she drew up her knees and pressed her forehead to them.

He believed their lovemaking had been some sort of last fling for her, before settling down with Jimmy, whom she'd been seeing during the months before she'd spontaneously attended Toby's wedding. Quinn had accused her of that during that dreadful phone conversation. In the weeks since, he'd obviously not changed his opinion.

So how was she ever going to be able to tell him that she was pregnant?

With *his* child?

If he accused her of lying about that, too, she wasn't sure she could survive it.

She sat there, her sorrow too deep for tears, until her bottom felt numb. Then feeling ancient, she shifted onto her knees and pushed herself to her aching feet. The boots she'd borrowed from Molly, one of her mother's junior secretaries whom Amelia trusted, were too wide and too short. They, along with the ill-fitting jeans and the shirt, belonged to Molly's teenage brother as had the other set of clothes she'd started out in. They'd been left, shoved deep in the rubbish, at the airport in Dallas alongside the blond wig and the knapsack in which she'd carried their replacements.

She dragged her passport out of the back pocket and set it on the rustic wooden nightstand. Even though Molly had helped with the disguises, neither one of them had been able to think of a way around traveling under Amelia's own name. Not with security standards being what they were. All she'd come with had been the passport, her credit card and a small wad of American currency tucked among the well-stamped pages of her passport. Molly had insisted on the credit card, though Amelia had wanted to leave it behind. She knew cash was untraceable, while a credit card wasn't, and she'd stuck to it. The only thing she'd purchased had been the bus fare from Dallas. Once she'd reached Lubbock, she'd hitched a ride with a trucker as far as the outskirts of Horseback Hollow. Then, using the directions she'd memorized from Molly, she'd walked the rest of the way to what she'd hoped was Quinn's ranch. But in her exhaustion and the darkness she hadn't been certain. So she'd hidden in the barn, intending to rest until daylight.

Her head swam dizzily and she quickly sat at the foot of the bed, the mattress springs giving the faintest of creaks. She closed her eyes, breathing evenly. She didn't know whether to blame the light-headedness on pregnancy or exhaustion. Aside from her missed period, she hadn't experienced any other signs that she was carrying a baby. And if it hadn't been for Molly who'd suggested that her irregularity might *not* be a result of stress as Amelia had believed at first, she probably wouldn't know even now that she was carrying Quinn's baby. She'd still be thinking she was just stressed over the whole engagement fiasco.

Why, oh, why hadn't she spoken up when those reporters greeted her at the airport six weeks ago, clamoring for details about her engagement to James? Why had she just put up her hand to shield her face and raced alongside her driver until reaching the relative sanctuary of the Town Car? She hadn't even dared to phone James until she'd gotten home because she feared having her cell phone hacked again. Even though it had happened well over a year ago, the sense of invasion still lived on.

If she'd only have spoken up, denied the engagement to the press right then and there, she wouldn't be in this situation now. After the initial embarrassment, James's situation with his family would have ironed itself out in time.

Most important, though, Quinn wouldn't have any reason to hate her.

She would have returned to him weeks ago exactly as they'd planned while lying together atop a horse blanket with an endless expanse of stars twinkling over them. Then, learning she was pregnant would have been something for them to discover together.

If only.

Her light-headedness was easing, though she really felt no better. But she opened her eyes and slowly pulled off the boots and socks and dropped them on the floor next to the bed. She wiggled her toes until some feeling returned and flopped back on the mattress.

The springs gave a faint squeak again.

It was a comforting sound and, too tired to even finish undressing, she dragged one of the two pillows at the head of the bed to her cheek and closed her eyes once more.

Things would be better in the morning.

They had to be.

When there were no more sounds, faint though they were, coming from his room upstairs, Quinn finally left the kitchen where he'd been hiding out. He left the house and walked back down to the barn with only the moonlight for company. He closed the door and even though there'd be endless chores to be done before the sun came up and he ought to be trying to sleep the last few hours before then, his aimless footsteps carried him even farther from the house.

But he kept glancing back over his shoulder. Looking at the dark windows on the upper story that belonged to his bedroom. Amelia had eaten the sandwich. But did that really mean anything?

If she fainted again how would he even know?

She'd been raised in the lap of luxury. First-class flights and luxury limousines driven by guys wearing suits and caps. Not economy class and bus tickets and God knew what.

Clawing his fingers through his hair, he turned back to the house. It wasn't the house that he and Jess had grown up in. That had burned nearly to the ground when Quinn was fifteen, destroying almost everything they'd owned. The same year his dad had already succeeded in literally working to death on the Rocking-U, trying to prove himself as good a rancher as the father who'd never acknowledged him. Jess, five years older, was already off and married to Mac with a baby on the way.

Ursula, his mom, would have sold off the ranch then if she'd have been able to find an interested buyer other than her dead husband's hated father. But she'd only been able to find takers for the livestock.

Despite Quinn's noisy protests, she'd moved the two of them into a two-bedroom trailer on the outskirts of town and there they'd lived until Quinn graduated from high school. Then she'd packed him off to college, packed up her clothes and moved away from the town that had only ever seemed to bring her unhappiness. Now she lived in Dallas in one of those "active adult" neighborhoods where she played bridge and tennis. She had a circle of friends she liked, and she was happy.

Not Quinn. The moment he could, he'd headed back to Horseback Hollow and the fallen-down, barren Rocking-U. He'd had a few years of college under his belt—gained only through scholarships and part-time jobs doing anything and everything he could pick up—and a new bride on his arm.

He was going to do what his father had never been able to do. Make the Rocking-U a real success.

At least one goal had been achieved.

He'd built the small house, though it had cost him two years and a wife along the way. He'd had his grandmother's piano restored and the dregs of the old, burned house hauled away. He'd shored up broken down fences and a decrepit barn. He'd built a herd. It was small, but it was prime Texas Longhorn.

He'd made something he could be proud of. Something his father had never achieved but still would have been proud of and something his father's father could choke on every time he thought about the people he liked to pretend never existed.

And when Quinn had danced with Amelia at a wedding reception six weeks ago, he'd let himself believe that there *was* a woman who could love his life the same way that he did.

All he'd succeeded in doing, though, was proving that he was Judd Drummond's son, through and through. A damn stupid dreamer.

He went back into the silent house. He had a couch in the living room. Too short and too hard to make much of a bed, but it was that or the floor. He turned off the light and sat down and worked off his boots, dropping them on the floor.

He couldn't hear anything from upstairs.

He stretched out as well as he could. Dropped his forearm over his eyes.

Listened to the rhythmic tick of the antique clock sitting on the fireplace mantel across the room.

What if she really was sick?

"Dammit," he muttered, and jackknifed to his feet. Moving comfortably in the darkness, he went to the stairs and started up. At the top, he headed to the end of the hall and closed his hand around the doorknob leading into his bedroom.

But he hesitated.

Called himself a damned fool. He ought to go back downstairs and try to redeem what little he could of the night in sleep.

Only sleeping was a laughable notion.

He'd just glance inside the room. Make sure she was sleeping okay.

He turned the knob. Nudged open the door.

He could see the dark bump of her lying, unmoving, on his bed. He stepped closer and his stockinged toes knocked into something on the floor. They bumped and thumped.

Her shoes.

It was a good thing he'd never aspired to a life of crime when he couldn't even sneak into his own bedroom without making a commotion. He'd probably been quieter when he'd found her in his damn barn.

Despite the seemingly loud noise, though, the form on the bed didn't move. He ignored the sound of his pulse throbbing in his ears until he was able to hear her soft breathing.

Fine. All good.

He had no excuse to linger. Not in a dark room in the middle of the night with another man's fiancée. There were lines a man didn't cross, and that was one of them.

It should have been easy to leave the room. And because it wasn't, he grimaced and turned.

Avoiding her shoes on the floor, he left the room more quietly than he'd entered. He returned to the couch. Threw himself down on it again.

He'd take her to her aunt's in the morning. After she woke.

And what Amelia did after that wasn't anything he was going to let himself care about.

Chapter Three

Quinn stared at the empty bed.

Amelia was gone.

It was only nine in the morning, and sometime between when he'd left the house at dawn and when he'd returned again just now, she'd disappeared.

If not for the wig that he'd found on the ground inside his barn door, he might have wondered if he'd hallucinated the entire thing.

It didn't take a genius to figure out she'd beat him to the punch in calling her aunt. One phone call to Jeanne, or to any one of the newfound cousins, and rescue would have easily arrived within an hour.

He walked into the bedroom.

The bed looked exactly the way it had when he'd tossed the quilt on top of it, before she'd gone to bed. Maybe a little neater. Maybe a lot neater.

He'd also thought her presence would linger after she was gone. But it didn't.

The room—hell, the entire house—felt deathly still. Empty.

That was the legacy she'd left that he'd have to live with.

He tossed the wig on the foot of the bed and rubbed the back of his neck. He had a crick in it from sleeping—or pretending to—on the too-short couch.

It shouldn't matter that she'd left without a word. Snuck out while his back was essentially turned. He hadn't wanted her there in the first place. And obviously, her need to "talk" hadn't been so strong, after all.

"Gone and good riddance," he muttered.

Then, because he smelled more like cow than man and Jess would give him a rash of crap about it when he showed up at his nephew's baseball game in Vicker's Corners that afternoon, he grabbed a shower and changed into clean jeans and T-shirt.

In the kitchen, the paper towel that he'd given Amelia was still sitting on the table where she'd left it, all folded up. He grabbed it to toss it in the trash, but hesitated.

She hadn't just folded the paper into a bunch of complicated triangles. She'd fashioned it into a sort of bird. As if the cheap paper towel was some fancy origami.

I have lots of useless talents.

The memory of her words swam in his head.

She'd told him that, and more, when they'd lain under the stars. How she had a degree in literature that she didn't think she'd ever use. How she spoke several languages even though she didn't much care for traveling. How she could play the piano and the harp well enough to play at some of the family's royal functions, but suffered stage fright badly enough that having to do so was agonizing.

He pinched the bridge of his nose where a pain was forming in his head and dropped the paper bird on the table again, before grabbing his Resistol hat off the peg by the back door and heading out.

He paid Tanya Fremont, one of the students where Jess and Mac taught high school, to clean his house once a week and she'd be there that weekend.

She could take care of the trash.

"Aunt Jeanne, *really?*" Amelia lifted a glossy tabloid magazine off the coffee table where it was sitting and held it up. "I can't believe you purchase these things."

Her aunt's blue eyes were wry as she sat down beside Amelia on the couch. She set the two mugs of herbal tea she was carrying on the coffee table and plucked the glossy out of Amelia's hands. She spread it over the knees of her faded blue jeans and tapped the small picture on the upper corner of the cover. "It had a picture of you and Lucie," she defended. "You and your sister looked so pretty. I thought I'd clip it out and put it in my scrapbook."

Amelia was touched by the thought even though she deplored being on the magazine cover. The photo was from the dedication of one of the orphanages her mother helped establish. Amelia recognized the dress she'd worn to the ceremony. "I don't even want to know what the article said." Undoubtedly, it had not focused on the good works of Lady Josephine or Lucie's latest accomplishments, but the pending nuptials of Amelia and Lord James Banning, the Viscount St. Allen and heir apparent to the Earl of Estingwood.

"No article," Jeanne Marie corrected. "Not really. Just a small paragraph from *close friends*—" she sketched quotes in the air "—of 'Jamelia' that the wedding date had been set, but was being kept under wraps for now to preserve your and James's privacy."

"There *is* no wedding date," Amelia blurted. She slumped back on the couch.

"Oh?" Jeanne Marie leaned forward and set the magazine on the coffee table. She picked up her tea and studied Amelia over the rim of the sturdy mug with eyes that were eerily similar to Amelia's mother.

That was to be expected, she supposed, since Josephine and Jeanne Marie were two thirds of a set of triplets. What wasn't the norm, was the fact that the siblings had only recently discovered one another. Amelia's mother hadn't even known that she'd been adopted until she'd met Jeanne Marie Fortune Jones and their triplet brother, James Marshall Fortune. He was the only reason the trio had found one another after having been separated as young children. There was even another older brother, John Fortune, to add to the new family tree.

Amelia realized her aunt wasn't gaping at her over the news there was to be no wedding. "You don't seem very surprised."

Jeanne Marie lifted one shoulder. "Well, honey. You *are* here." And again, even though her words were full of Texas drawl, her mild, somewhat ironic lilt was exactly the same as Josephine's entirely proper Brit would have been.

It was still startling to Amelia, even after meeting her aunt nearly a year ago.

"I'm assuming you have a good reason for not announcing you broke things off with your young man in England?"

"It's complicated," she murmured, even as she felt guilty for leaving her aunt under the impression that there had ever been something to break off in the first place. James had been as much a victim of their supposed engagement as she, since the presumptuous announcement had been issued by his father. But once it had been, and Amelia hadn't denied it, James had been doing his level best to convince her to make it a reality. Under immense family pressure to make a suitable marriage, he'd given up hope of a match with the girl he really loved—Astrid, who sold coffee at the stand in his building—and tried giving Amelia a family ring in hopes that she'd come around, though she'd refused to take it. "Jimmy and I have known each other a long time."

While she really only knew Quinn in the biblical sense. The irony of it all was heartbreaking.

"Sometimes a little distance has a way of uncomplicating things," Jeanne said. "And as delighted as I am to have you here, it does tend to raise a few questions. Particularly havin' to get you from Quinn Drummond's place practically before sunup. And havin' you dressed like you are."

Amelia's fingers pleated the hem of the oversize shirt. "I was trying to avoid paparazzi."

"So you said while we were driving here." Jeanne Marie finally set down the mug. She was obviously as disinterested in her tea as Amelia was. "What's going on between you and Quinn?"

"Nothing." She felt heat rise up her throat.

"And that's why you called me from his house at seven in the morning. Because nothing is going on between

you two." Jeanne Marie's lips curved. "In my day, that
sort of *nothing* usually led to a shotgun and a stand-up
in front of a preacher whether there was another suitor
in the wings or not."

Amelia winced.

Her aunt tsked, her expression going from wry to concerned in the blink of an eye. "Oh, honey." She closed her
warm hands around Amelia's fidgeting fingers. "Whatever's upsetting you can be worked out. I promise you
that."

Amelia managed a weak smile. "I appreciate the
thought, Aunt Jeanne. But I grew up with my father always telling us not to make promises we couldn't keep."

Jeanne Marie squeezed her hand. "I wish I'd have had
a chance to meet your daddy. Your mama says he was
the love of her life."

Amelia nodded. Her father had died several years ago,
but his loss was still sharp. "He was." She couldn't contain a yawn and covered it with her hand. Despite having slept several hours at Quinn's, she still could hardly
keep her eyes open. "I'm so sorry."

"I'm the sorry one," Jeanne Marie said. She patted
Amelia's hand and pushed to her feet. "You're exhausted,
honey. You need to be in bed, not sitting here answering questions."

It took all the energy Amelia possessed to stand, also.
"Are you certain I'm not imposing?"

Jeanne Marie laughed. "There's no such thing as imposing among family, honey. Deke and I raised seven
kids in this house. Now they're all off and living their
own lives. So it's nice to have one of those empty rooms
filled again."

"You're very kind." She followed her aunt along the

hall and up the stairs to a corner bedroom with windows on two walls. Amelia remembered the room from her first visit to Horseback Hollow six months ago, though it had been her mother who'd been assigned to it then. It was obviously a guest room. Simply but comfortably furnished with a bed covered in a quilt with fading pastel stitching that was all the lovelier for its graceful aging, a side table with dried cat's tails sticking out of an old-fashioned milk bottle, and a sturdy oak wardrobe. White curtains, nearly translucent, hung open at the square windows and moved gently in the warm morning breeze.

"This used to be Galen's room," Jeanne Marie said. "Being the oldest, there was a time he liked lording it over the others that he had the largest room." She crossed to the windows to begin lowering the shades. "Would have put you in here back when you came for Toby's wedding in April, but James Marshall and Clara were using it."

"Leave the windows open," Amelia begged quickly. "Please."

"The sunlight won't keep you awake?"

She self-consciously tugged at her ugly shirt. Light was the least disturbing thing she could think of at the moment. And better to have sunlight than darkness while the memories of the last time she'd been at her aunt's home were caving in on her. "The breeze is too lovely to shut out."

Jeanne Marie dropped her hands. She opened the wardrobe and pulled out two bed pillows from the shelf inside and set them on the bed. "Bathroom is next door," she reminded. "I'll make sure you have fresh towels. And I'm sure that Delaney or Stacey left behind some clothes that should fit you. They might be boxed up by now, but I'll try to scare up something for you to wear once you're rested."

Her welcome was so very different than Quinn's, deserved or not, and Amelia's eyes stung.

She cried much too easily these days. "Thank you." She sat on the foot of the bed and tried not to think about sitting on the bed at Quinn's.

She'd thought that had been a guest room, too. Until she'd awakened early that morning and had gone looking for him. She'd done what she hadn't had the energy for the night before. The rooms upstairs were spacious and full of windows and nothing else. Almost like they were stuck in time. Waiting for a reason to be filled with furniture. With family. Downstairs, he had a den with a plain wooden desk and an older style computer on it. The living room had a couch, a television that looked older than the computer, and a gleaming black upright piano. She'd drawn her fingers lightly over the keys, finding it perfectly tuned.

What she hadn't found was Quinn. Not only had he been nowhere to be found inside the two-story house, but she'd seen for herself that his home possessed only a single bed.

Which, regardless of his feelings, he'd given up for her.

Jeanne Marie watched the tangled expressions crossing her new niece's delicate features and controlled the urge to take the girl into her arms and rock her just as she would have her own daughters. "We've got most of the crew coming for supper tonight. But you just come on down whenever you're ready," she said comfortingly. "And don't you worry about me spilling your personal beans to your cousins. You can do that when you're good and ready." Then she kissed Amelia's forehead and left the room, closing the door behind her.

She set out fresh towels in the bathroom, then headed downstairs to the kitchen again and stopped in surprise at the sight of her husband just coming in from the back. "I thought you'd be out all morning."

"Thought I could get the engine on that old Deere going, but I need a couple more parts." He tossed his sweat-stained cowboy hat aside and rubbed his fingers through his thick, iron-gray hair before reaching out a long arm and hooking her around the waist. "Which leaves me the chance for some morning delight with my wife before I drive over to Vicker's Corners."

Jeanne Marie laughed softly, rubbing her arms over his broad shoulders. How she loved this man who'd owned her heart from the moment they'd met. "We're not alone in the house," she warned.

His eyebrow lifted. "I didn't notice any cars out front. Who's come this early for supper? Can't be Toby and his brood." He grinned faintly. "Those kids've been coming out of their shells real nice lately."

"And they'll continue to do so," Jeanne agreed, slightly distracted by the way Deke's wide palms were drifting from her waist down over the seat of her jeans. "As long as no more hitches come up to stop Toby and Angie adopting them." Their middle son and his new wife were trying to adopt three kids he'd been fostering for the past eight months and the process hadn't exactly been smooth so far.

Her blood was turning warm and she grabbed his wide wrists, redirecting his hands to less distracting territory. "Amelia's here."

His brows pulled together for a second. "Amelia? Josephine's youngest girl?"

"We don't know another Amelia," Jeanne Marie said dryly.

His hands fell away. He leaned back against the counter and folded his arms over his chest. "Fortunes are everywhere," he murmured.

She knew his face as well as she knew her own. She had happily been Jeanne Marie Jones for forty years. But learning that she had siblings out there, learning that she had a blood connection to others in this world besides the children of his that she'd borne, had filled a void inside her that Deke had never quite been able to understand. Even though her adoptive parents had loved her, and she them, not knowing where she'd come from had always pulled at her.

And now she knew.

And though Deke hadn't protested when she'd added Fortune to her own name, she knew also that it hadn't been entirely easy for him. When their kids followed suit, it had gotten even harder for him to swallow.

No. The advent of the Fortunes to the Jones's lives hadn't been easy. And maybe it would have been easier if James had gone about things differently when he'd tracked her down. Her newfound brother was a self-made business tycoon used to having the world fall into place exactly the way he planned and he'd not only upset his own family in the process, he'd sent Jeanne Marie's family reeling, too, when he'd tried to give her part of his significant fortune.

She'd turned down the money, of course. It didn't matter to her that all of her siblings turned out to be ridiculously wealthy while she was not. She and Deke had a good life. A happy life. One blessed with invaluable wealth for the very reason that it had nothing to do with any amount of dollars and cents.

Convincing her pridefully suspicious husband that the only fortune that mattered to her was the *name* Fortune, however, had been a long process.

One that was still obviously in the works, judging by Deke's stoic expression.

"How long's she staying?" he asked.

"I have no idea. The girl came here to figure some things out, I believe." Because she always felt better being busy, she pulled a few peaches out of the basket on the counter and grabbed a knife. She'd already made a chocolate cake for dessert for that evening, but Deke always loved a fresh peach pie. And even after forty years of marriage, a man still needed to know he was in the forefront of his wife's thoughts. "Do you think she should stay somewhere else?"

He frowned quickly. "No. She's family." His eyes met hers. "I get it, Jeanne Marie."

Her faint tension eased. He might not exactly understand the way she'd taken on the Fortune name, but he did get "it" when it came to family. Nothing was more important to him, even if he didn't always have an easy time showing it.

"She'd been at Quinn Drummond's," she added. Then told him everything that had happened since Amelia had called. She pointed the tip of the paring knife she was using to peel the peaches at Deke. "I don't care what everyone's saying about her and that Banning fella." She deftly removed the peach pit and sliced the ripe fruit into a bowl. "There's definitely something going on between her and Quinn."

"I'd think Quinn's too set in his ways to be interested in a highbred filly like Amelia." Deke reached past her to filch a juicy slice. "'Specially after the merry chase that ex-wife of his led him on. She was a piece of work, remember?"

She did and she made a face. "That was years ago."

"Yup. Having your wife leave you for her old boyfriend leaves a stain, though. Least I think it would. Now he's interested in a girl the world thinks is engaged?" He stole another slice, avoiding the hand she batted at him.

"You keep eating the slices, I won't have enough left to make a pie for you," she warned.

His teeth flashed, his good humor evidently restored. He popped the morsel in his mouth and gave her a smacking kiss that tasted of him and sweet, sweet summer. It melted her heart as surely now as it had the first time he'd kissed her when they were little more than kids.

Then he grabbed his hat and plopped it on his head again. "I'll stop at the fruit stand on my way back from Vicker's Corners," he said, giving her a quick wink. "Replenish the stock." He started to push open the back screen door.

"Deke—"

He hesitated.

"You're the love of my life, you know."

His smile was slow and sweeter than the peaches. "And you're mine. That's what gets me up in the morning every day, darlin'."

Then he pushed through the screen door. It squeaked slightly, and shut with a soft slap.

Jeanne Marie pressed her hand to her chest for a moment. "Oh, my." She blew out a breath and laughed slightly at the silliness of a woman who ought to be too old for such romantic swooning.

Then she looked up at the ceiling, thinking about her young niece. Amelia was running away from something, or running to something. And she needed to figure out which it was.

Jeanne Marie was just glad that she was there to provide a resting place. And that she had a man of her own who could understand why.

Quinn had no intention of going by Jeanne Marie and Deke's place later that evening. But he ran into Deke at the tractor supply in Vicker's Corners before the baseball game and the man—typically short on words and long on hard work and honor—asked after Quinn's mom. That brief exchange of pleasantries had somehow led to Deke casually tossing out an invitation to come by for supper.

"Havin' a cookout," Deke had said. "All the kids're coming. And you know how Jeanne Marie always cooks more'n we need."

Quinn had wondered then if it was possible that Deke didn't know his wife's new niece was there. And then he had wondered if it was possible that Jeanne's new niece *wasn't* there.

Which had led to him poking at that thought all through the ball game, same way a tongue poked at a sore tooth, even though it hurt.

He ought to have just asked Deke.

Instead, here he was at six o'clock in the evening, standing there staring at the front of Jeanne and Deke's place.

He could smell grilling beef on the air and hear the high-pitched squeal of a baby laughing. Ordinarily, the smell of a steak getting seared really well would have been enough to get his boots moving. He didn't even mind the babies or the kids much. He'd had plenty of practice with Jess's batch, since she popped one out every couple of years.

His reluctance to join them now annoyed him. He'd had plenty of meals at the Jones's place over the years. He'd been in school with the older ones and counted them as friends. He'd danced at Toby's wedding. *With Amelia.* Right here, in fact, because Toby and Angie had been married out in back of the house.

Quinn hadn't been back since.

Muttering an oath, he grabbed the short-haired wig, slammed the truck door and headed around the side of the house. He knew they'd all be out back again and he was right.

This time, though, instead of rows of chairs lined up like white soldiers across the green grass and a bunch of cloth-covered tables with pretty flowers sitting on top arranged around the space, there were a couple of picnic tables covered with plastic checked tablecloths, a bunch of lawn chairs and a game of croquet in the works.

He spotted Amelia immediately and even though he wanted to pretend he hadn't been concerned about whether she had or had not sought haven with her aunt, the knot inside him eased.

She was off to one side of the grassy backyard where Toby's three kids were playing croquet, and talking with Stacey, Jeanne's and Deke's second youngest. The two females were about the same age and the same height, but Stacey was as sunny and blonde as Amelia was moonlight and brunette.

Both women were engaged, too, he thought darkly,

though only one of those engagements caused him any amount of pleasure. He was just a little surprised that Colton Foster, who was Stacey's fiancé, hadn't gotten her to the altar already. As he watched, Amelia leaned over and rubbed her nose against Piper's, Stacey's year-old daughter, who was propped on her mama's hip.

He looked away and aimed toward Deke where he and Liam were manning the grill. "Smells good," he greeted. "Would only smell better if that was Rocking-U beef."

Liam snorted good-naturedly. Horseback Hollow was dotted with small cattle ranches and all of them were more supportive than competitive with each other. "You got yourself a new pet there? Looks like a rat."

Quinn wished he'd have left the wig in the truck. He'd only thought as far as returning it to its owner so he wouldn't have the reminder around. He hadn't thought about the questions that doing so would invite. "It's a wig. Thought maybe one of Toby's kids might want to keep it around for Halloween or something." The excuse was thin and he knew it. "My sister's kids outgrew it, I guess," he improvised and felt stupid even as he did. He'd never developed a taste for lying. Anyone who knew Jess's brood would also know the five boys were hellions who wouldn't be caught dead wearing a wig.

Liam was eying him oddly, too. "Whatever, man." He grabbed a beer from an ice-filled barrel and tossed it to him. "Crack that open and get started. Maybe it'll soften you up before we get to dickering over that bull of yours I want to buy."

Despite everything, Quinn smiled. He tossed the wig on one of the picnic benches nearby. "Rocky's not for sale, my friend."

"Even if I paid you twice what he's worth?"

They'd had this debate many times. Quinn knew Liam wouldn't overpay and Liam knew Quinn wasn't selling, anyway. "That bull's semen's worth gold to me."

"Oh." The word was faint, brief and still filled with some shock.

The knots tightened inside him again and Quinn turned to see Amelia standing beside him.

Chapter Four

Her fragility struck Quinn all over again, like a fist in his gut.

The red dress that she was wearing was pretty enough, he guessed. But it was loose. And the straps over her shoulders couldn't hide the way her collarbones were too prominent.

She looked like she needed to sit at a table and stuff herself for a month of Sundays.

As if she read his disapproving thoughts, her cheeks were nearly as red as the dress.

The day of Toby's wedding, she'd worn a strapless ice-blue dress that ended just above her perfect knees, and a weird little puff of some feathery thing on her head. When they'd ended up sneaking off for a drive in his truck, he'd teased her about it. She'd promptly tugged it off, and plopped his cowboy hat on her head, where it had slipped down over her eyes, and said she was in the market for a new look, anyway.

His lips twisted, his eyes meeting hers. "You're going to hear words like *bull's semen* if you're going to play around cowboys, princess."

Stacey, standing beside Amelia, rolled her eyes. "Good grief, Quinn. Manners much?"

"It's quite all right," Amelia said quickly. She lifted her chin a little. "This is Texas, for goodness' sake. Cattle ranch country. I certainly don't imagine anyone stands around discussing tea and biscuits. Or, cookies, I guess you call them."

He nearly choked. Because they'd laughed together about that, too. Only she'd been naked at the time, and throatily telling him that she'd bet he'd enjoy teatime perfectly well if she served it up for him after making love.

"Depends on whose cookies you're talking about," Deke said. "Jeanne Marie makes some oatmeal peanut-butter deals that are the talk of three counties." His dry humor broke the faint tension. "Stacey girl, you wanna grab a tray for these steaks? They're 'bout ready."

"Sure."

"I'll take her," Amelia offered quickly, reaching out her hands for Piper, and Stacey handed her over. She settled the wide-eyed toddler on her hip and tickled her cheek, making Piper squeal and wriggle. "Who is the prettiest baby girl here, hmm?"

For some reason, Quinn's neck prickled.

He twisted the cap off his beer and focused on Liam. "Where's your better half, anyway?" There was no sign of his friend's red-haired fiancée.

"Julia's meeting with one of the suppliers over at the Cantina. She'll be here as soon as she finishes up."

"Is the restaurant still going to open on schedule?" Amelia asked.

Liam nodded. "Two weeks from now, right on track."

The Hollows Cantina was a big deal for their little town. It was owned and to be operated by Marcos Mendoza and his wife, Wendy Fortune Mendoza, who'd relocated all the way from Red Rock, a good four hundred Texas miles away. They'd hired Julia as an assistant manager and the establishment promised upscale dining that was intended to draw not only the locals from Horseback Hollow and nearby Vicker's Corners, but as far away as Lubbock. Considering the Mendozas' success with Red, a fancy Mexican food restaurant in Red Rock that was famous even beyond the state lines, Quinn figured they had a decent shot of success at it.

He was reserving judgment on whether that all would be a good thing for Horseback Hollow or not. He wasn't vocally opposed to it like some folks, nor was he riding around on the bandwagon of supporters, though he was glad enough for Julia. She'd always been a hard worker and deserved her shot as much as anyone did.

He, personally, would probably still choose the Horseback Hollow Grill over the Cantina. Even on a good day, he wasn't what he would call "upscale" material.

"My mother has the grand opening on her calendar," Amelia said. "I know she's looking forward to it. Not only is Uncle James going to be there, but Uncle John, as well. It should be quite a family reunion."

Quinn stopped pretending an interest in his beer and looked at her. Ironically, the British Fortunes seemed too upscale for the Cantina. "And you? Is it on your calendar, too, princess? Maybe you'll drag your fiancé along for the trip."

Amelia's chocolate-brown eyes went from her cousin's face to Quinn's and for the first time since he'd met her, they contained no emotion whatsoever. "I'm not sure what I'll be doing by the end of the month." Her voice was smoothly pleasant and revealed as little as her eyes did.

Her "royal face," he realized.

She'd talked about having one. Having had to develop as a little girl the ability to give nothing away by expression, deed or word.

He'd just never seen it in person before. And not directed at him.

Piper was wriggling on her hip and Amelia leaned over to set the little girl on her feet. She kept hold of Piper's tiny hands as the girl made a beeline toddle for the wig sitting on the picnic bench next to them.

"Keekee," she chortled, and reached for the wig.

Amelia laughed lightly and scooped up the wig before Piper could reach it and brushed the short thick strands against the baby's face. "That's not a kitty, darling. It's a wig."

She'd crouched next to Piper and while the child chortled over the hairy thing, she glanced up at Quinn. "There was no need to return the wig to me, Quinn," she told him. "You could have tossed it in the trash bin."

He really wished he would have.

Liam tilted his beer to his lips but not quickly enough to hide his faint grin. "Thought the rat belonged to your sis's kids."

"Here's the tray," Stacey announced, striding up with a metal cookie sheet in her hand that she set on the side of the grill.

She was also carrying a big bowl of coleslaw under

her other arm, and, glad of an escape route, Quinn slid his hand beneath it. "I'll put it on the table before you drop it." He turned away from the lot of them and carried it over to a folding table that had obviously been set out to hold the food.

Trying not to watch Quinn too openly, Amelia continued entertaining the sweet baby with the wig while everyone else seemed to suddenly spring into action organizing the food onto plates and the people onto picnic benches.

Though she tried to avoid it, she somehow found herself sitting directly across from Quinn. He was hemmed in on one side by Delaney, Jeanne Marie and Deke's youngest daughter, and Liam on the other. Amelia was caught between Jeanne Marie and Deke.

If she didn't know better, she almost would have suspected her aunt and uncle of planning it.

Judging by the way Quinn noticeably ignored her, he was no more comfortable with the seating plan than she was. Fortunately, his friendship with Liam was evident as the two men dickered over the issue of Rocky's studding abilities and whether or not the summer season would be wetter or drier than usual.

"Have some more corn bread," Jeanne Marie said, nudging a basket of the fragrant squares into her hands.

Amelia obediently put another piece on her plate, and managed a light laugh when Deke tried to talk her into another steak, though she'd only eaten a fraction of the one on her plate. "If I ate all this, I'd pop," she protested.

"So, Amelia," Delaney drew her attention. "What are you doing in Horseback Hollow, anyway?" Her eyes were bright with curiosity as she grinned. "Are you planning some secret meeting with your wedding gown designer? Texas has our very own Charlene Dalton. She's based in Red Rock and I hear she did Emily Fortune's gown."

"Delaney," Jeanne Marie tsked, handing the corn bread across to her daughter. "You're sounding like one of those nosy reporters."

Delaney made a protesting sound. "That's not fair. None of us expected to find ourselves family with *The* Fortunes. If you can't share some secrets among your own family, who can you share 'em with? It's not like I'll go tattling to the newspapers. And besides. I didn't get to see Emily's gown outside of pictures, 'cause she got married before we even knew we all were cousins!"

"It's all right," Amelia said quickly. Not only could she sense her aunt's sudden discomfort, but she was painfully aware of Quinn across from her. "I'm not...not planning any designer sessions." She was loath to discuss her personal business in front of everyone, even if they *were* family. That just wasn't the way she'd been raised. Even among her four brothers and sister, she didn't get into whys and wherefores and the most personal of emotions. She hadn't even divulged all the facts to her own mother about her "engagement," though she knew Josephine had her suspicions.

She tried not looking at Quinn, but couldn't help herself. "I'm not planning anything." It wasn't exactly a public admission, but since she'd discovered she was pregnant with his child, it was entirely truthful.

"'Scuse me." He suddenly rose and extricated himself from the picnic bench and the human bookends holding him there.

Amelia's fingernails dug into her palms as she

watched him carry his plate over to the table of food and make a point of studying the display.

"Getting a microphone stuck in your face or a camera flash blinding you every time you go out in public would be a pain in the butt," Deke said, as if nothing had happened. Then he looked around at the silence his unexpected input drew. His eyebrows rose. "Well. Would be," he drawled in conclusion.

And that seemed to be that.

Nobody else broached the subject about Amelia's unplanned appearance. Nor did the topic of the wedding come up again.

And Quinn never returned to their picnic table.

He stuck around long enough to have a piece of the three-layer chocolate cake when Jeanne Marie presented it, along with a peach pie that was so picturesque it might have come out of the kitchens at the Chesterfield estate. But whenever Amelia entered his vicinity, he exited hers.

It was so plainly obvious that he was avoiding her that she felt herself receiving looks of sympathy from Stacey, Delaney *and* Liam's fiancée, Julia, who'd arrived in time for dessert.

She didn't want sympathy.

She wanted Quinn's love.

In the absence of that, at least his understanding.

But clearly he wasn't going to offer that, either.

She saw him shake Deke's hand, drop a kiss on her aunt's cheek and exchange easily a half-dozen goodbyes with some of the others, without a single glance her way. And then he was walking away, heading out of sight around the corner of her aunt's house.

She swallowed and sucked all of her feelings inward until she felt reasonably confident that her expression was calm. She listened in on Toby and Angie's conversation as they talked about the difficulties they kept encountering trying to adopt the three Hemings children Toby had been fostering ever since she'd first met him, and knew she made the appropriate nods and sounds when she should have. But a portion of her mind was wondering if she could get back home again without drawing undue media attention.

Which was rather laughable to worry about now.

The attention she'd draw once word of her pregnancy got out would thoroughly eclipse what she'd already garnered.

And poor James. Instead of dealing with the embarrassment of a broken engagement, he would have to endure speculation over being the baby's father. It wouldn't matter that he wasn't. It wouldn't matter what statements were issued or what proof was given.

Forever on, people would whisper. Every time either one of them did something to draw the attention of the media, the scandal would be dug up all over again, regurgitated on the internet or on gossip networks.

They'd all pay the price and none more dearly than her and Quinn's innocent baby.

Her head swam dizzily and she excused herself, walking blindly. She instinctively followed the path that Quinn had taken, heading around the side of the house and away from all of the noisy gaiety.

Going home was as impossible as staying in Horseback Hollow would be.

The thought came over her in a wave and her knees went weak. She stopped, bracing herself with one hand against the side of the house.

"Are you going to pass out again?"

She nearly jumped out of her skin at the sound of Quinn's voice. He was standing a few feet away, his hazel eyes alert, as though he was ready to leap forward if he had to.

At least he didn't hate her badly enough to allow her to collapse flat on her face.

She let out a choking laugh at the thought, which only had him closing the distance between them, his expression even warier as he clasped her bare arms.

She shivered, looking up into his face. The night they'd danced, she'd felt as if they'd known one another for all their lives. "I think I'm losing my mind, Quinn." Even her voice sounded unhinged, shaking and pitched too high.

He made a rough sound. "You're not losing your mind."

Where was her dignity? Her self-control? Her throat tightened even more, her voice almost a squeak. "But you don't know—"

"Shh." His big warm hand slid around the back of her neck and he pulled her against his chest in a motion that felt both reluctant and desperate. "You're going to make yourself collapse again. Is that what you want?"

Her forehead rubbed against the front of his soft plaid shirt as she shook her head. She could feel the heat of his hard chest burning through the cotton. Could hear the rhythmic beat of his heart when she turned her cheek against him.

He was holding her, though not cradling her. But her ragged emotions didn't care. They only wanted her to burrow against him while he safely held everything that didn't matter at bay.

She'd never felt even a fraction of this need when she

was with James. If only she had, things wouldn't be in such a mess.

Her fingers twisted into Quinn's shirt lapel. "There's something I need to tell you."

"Well it's gonna have to wait." His hands tightened around her arms as he forcibly set her back a foot. "I only came back to warn you that there's an SUV parked maybe a hundred yards down the road that's not from around here. Has a rental car sticker on the bumper." His fingertips pressed into her flesh and his gaze, as it roved over her face, was shuttered once more. "It's probably nothing, but the strangers that've been coming around the Hollow these days usually stick to town. They don't traipse out onto private property and park off the side of the road half-hidden behind the bushes."

She grasped at the shreds of her composure and came up with threads. His thumbs were rubbing back and forth over her upper arms and she wondered if he even realized it. "You think it's a reporter." Maybe even that dreadful Ophelia Malone had managed to catch up to her. The young paparazzo had sprung from nowhere after Amelia's "engagement" and seemed determined to earn her stripes on Amelia ever since.

"All I'm thinking is that the car doesn't belong." His thumbs stopped moving. He still held her arms to steady her, yet managed to put another few inches between them. "But I don't figure any of the Joneses—*Fortune* Joneses," he corrected himself, "deserve their lives intruded upon."

"Whereas this Fortune Chesterfield does?"

His lips twisted and his brows lowered. "Don't make me feel sorry for you, princess."

"I'm not trying to!" Despair congealed inside her

chest and she lifted her palms to his face. She felt his sudden stillness and mindlessly stepped closer. "Please give me a chance to make things right, Quinn." Feeling as powerless as a moth flying into a flame, she stretched up on the toes of her borrowed sandals and pressed her mouth to his jaw. The hard angle felt bristly against her lips. "That's all I want. A chance." She stretched even farther, pulling on his shoulders, until her lips could reach his.

And for a moment, a sweet moment that sent her hopes spinning, he kissed her back.

But then he jerked away.

His hands felt like iron as he held her in place and took another step back, putting distance between them yet again. "Finish making one bed before you try getting in another." His voice was low. Rough.

"I was never in James's bed," she whispered. Her lips still tingled. "I'm not in it now. What can I do to make you believe me?"

A muscle worked in his jaw. "Walk out to that SUV and see if it's a reporter, and if it is, tell 'em what you told me. That the two of you aren't engaged. Never were."

She swallowed. "And that would make everything all right? Between you and me?"

He didn't answer and her stomach sank right back to her toes.

Of course it wouldn't.

He'd made up his mind where she was concerned and that was the end of it.

It didn't matter who was to blame for what as far as the "engagement" was concerned. James's father had precipitated everything by announcing they were engaged.

And she'd compounded the problem by not denying it when she could have.

By talking to the paparazzi now, all she would succeed in doing would be hurting James, embarrassing his family, and by extension, her own.

And in the process, she wouldn't gain a thing where Quinn was concerned.

She drew herself up. Lifted her chin. She was a Chesterfield. A Fortune Chesterfield. Even if her world was disintegrating around her, she needed to remember that fact. "That would be throwing James to the wolves."

His eyes flattened even more. "So?"

She exhaled, praying for strength. It was obvious that he wouldn't welcome hearing any defense of the other man. "An announcement like that needs to come through official channels, not some random gossipmonger on the side of the road. *Don't!*" She stared him down. "Don't look at me like that. Whether you want to believe me or not, it's true. Otherwise it would be just one more rumor tossing around among the flotsam."

"Even though it came from you."

She nodded. "Even though." This time, she was the one to put more space between them, though she had to force herself to do it. But it was enough to make his hands finally fall away from her arms. It took every speck of self-control she possessed not to clasp her arms around herself to hold in the feel of his touch. "James and I had been dating nearly a year when you and I—" She drew in a shuddering breath. "When I came here for Toby's wedding," she amended. "The…advantages of us marrying had come up a few times. I never lied to you about that."

"No, princess. Your lie was in pretending you weren't

going to bring those advantages to reality. You said you weren't in love with him. And that I did believe. Or there's no way we'd have ended up out in that field that night." His lips thinned. "Wouldn't have happened."

"Are you trying to convince me of that or yourself?"

The muscle in his jaw flexed. Once. Twice. Then it went still. His expression turned stoic and he didn't speak.

She realized she'd pressed her hands to her stomach and made herself stop. "And…and after I went back home to all that—" she waved her hand, trying to encompass the indescribable media storm that had greeted her "—and you made it plain once you finally deigned to speak with me that there was no…no hope for us—" Her voice broke and she stopped again, gathering herself. "James suggested we go on with the illusion. His father is in very poor health. For an assortment of reasons, he wants to see James married and pass on his title to him while he's still alive. We weren't the great romance everyone wants to make us out to be, but we *were* friends and, given time, he hoped we might be more." Her vision glazed with tears as she stared at him. "I didn't have you. So, yes. I made no public contradictions. I'd had one night of magic and I let it slip through my fingers. Maybe a life with him was the best I could expect after that. But then I—"

"Enough!" He slashed his hand through the air between them. "Enough of the fairy-tale bull, princess. I've been down this road before. I already know how it goes." His smile was cold and cutting. "I made the mistake of marrying the last woman who was selling a story like this. I am not in the market to buy it again."

Then, while she was frozen in speechless shock, he turned on his boot heel and strode back to his truck parked nearby.

Chapter Five

The next morning it was Quinn's sister, Jess, who saw the photograph first.

It was grainy. It had obviously been taken from a considerable distance and the subjects' faces weren't entirely visible, or even entirely clear.

But it was enough for Jess.

She slapped the piece of paper on Quinn's kitchen table in front of him and jabbed her finger at the image. "That's you." She jabbed again. "That's Amelia." Then she propped her hands on her hips and stuck her face close to his, wholly, righteously in big-sister mode. "What the *hell*, Quinn? They've already coined a nickname for you!"

Annoyed, because even though she was five years his senior, he was a grown man and not in the least interested in being called on her metaphorical carpet, he pushed her aside and picked up the sheet of paper that she'd obviously printed off her computer. "They who?"

Her arms flapped as she gaped at him. "It doesn't matter who! You've got eyes. You can read reasonably well, last time I checked. The caption is right there!"

Is this the end for Jamelia? Who is the tall, dark Horseback Hollow Homewrecker caught in a passionate clinch with England's own runaway bride?

He let out a disgusted sound and crumpled the thin paper in his fist. "You have five kids, a husband and a full-time job at the high school. When the hell do you have time for hunting up this sort of crap on the internet?"

"Summer vacation," she returned. "And obviously you've never acquainted yourself with internet alerts." She waved her cell phone that she seemed perpetually attached to under his nose, then shoved it back in her pocket.

He wasn't sure if she was more disgusted with the photograph itself or with his seeming ineptitude where technology was concerned. The only thing he kept a computer for was ranch records and he detested using it even for that. He'd rather be out in the open air than sitting in the office pecking at computer keys.

"That picture is everywhere," she added. "All this time and you never said *anything* about her to me! How long has this been going on?"

"There's no *this*." He opened the cupboard door beneath the sink and pushed the wad of paper deep into the trash can stored there.

"Please. Don't try saying that isn't you and Amelia in the picture. Where were you, anyway?"

Standing to one side of the Joneses' house, not as hidden from view as he'd thought.

He didn't voice the words. Just eyed his sister. "It's Saturday morning," he said instead. "Shouldn't you be at a soccer game or something instead of cornering me in my own kitchen?"

She pointed her finger at him, giving him the stink eye that she'd had perfected since she was a superior eight years old and didn't like him coming uninvited into her room anymore. "She's an engaged woman, Quinn."

It wasn't anything he didn't know and hadn't been tarring himself for. But that didn't mean he welcomed his sister's censure, too. And, he justified to himself, the photograph hadn't caught him kissing Amelia; it had caught *her* kissing *him*. "Engaged isn't married."

He scooped up a Texas Rangers ball cap and tugged it down over his eyes before shoving through the wood-framed screen door leading outside. For her, Saturdays were chock-full of squiring one kid or another hither and yon.

For him, Saturdays meant the same chores that every other day meant and he fully intended on getting to them. If he kept acting normal, sooner or later, things would be normal. It had worked that way when Carrie left. He had to believe it would work again now, or he might as well order up a straightjacket, size extra-large-tall, right now.

Amelia woke early the next day after yet another fitful night of sleep. She could smell the heady aroma of coffee wending its way from downstairs and she rolled out of bed, donning the robe that Jeanne Marie had loaned her. Downstairs, she found her aunt sitting at the kitchen table. Her silver hair—usually pinned up—was hanging in a long braid down her back and she had a pair of reading glasses perched on her nose as she perused a newspaper.

When Amelia walked into the room, she looked over the top of her eyeglasses and smiled. "Aren't you the early bird this morning," she greeted. "Would you like coffee?"

Amelia waved her aunt back into her seat when she started to rise. "Don't get up." She wanted coffee in the worst way, but had read that caffeine was something pregnant women were supposed to avoid. "Water's all I want." To prove it, she pulled a clean glass out of the dish rack where several had been turned upside down after being washed, and filled it from the tap. Then she sat down across from her aunt. She was determined not to think about Quinn for the moment.

She'd spent enough time doing that when she'd been unable to sleep. She'd thought about him. And the fact that he'd once been married. Something he hadn't shared before at all.

"I need some clothes of my own," she said. "I can't keep borrowing." It was something she'd never done in her entire life. And she needed underwear. She'd been washing her silk knickers every night, but enough was enough.

"Well." Jeanne Marie looked amused. "You can, you know. But a pretty girl like you doesn't want to keep walking around in things two sizes too large." She adjusted her glasses and glanced at her newspaper again. "Guess you already know you won't find much in the way of clothes shopping here in Horseback Hollow."

"I know." Much as she loved the area, Horseback Hollow only consisted of a few small businesses. "I thought perhaps Vicker's Corners." She hadn't been to the nearby town, but she'd heard mention of it often enough and knew it was only twenty miles away. "When I was talking to Stacey yesterday, she mentioned that there are a few shops there."

"Yes," Jeanne Marie agreed. "You'll find more of a selection in Lubbock, though."

She didn't want to go to Lubbock. She wanted to avoid all towns of any real size. Vicker's Corners was probably pushing it as it was. "I just need a few basics," she said. "I'm sure Vicker's Corners will suit." She chewed the inside of her lip for a moment. "I also ought to purchase a cell phone." Molly had called it "a burner." One that nobody—namely Ophelia Malone and her ilk—would know to track. "Do you think I'd be able to find one there, as well?"

"Imagine so. There's a hardware store that carries everything from A to Z." Jeanne Marie turned the last page of the newspaper and folded it in half. "I'd drive you myself, but I have to go to a baby shower my friend Lillian is giving her niece this afternoon. I can call one of the kids or Deke to drive you."

"I don't want to put anyone out." She'd sprung her "visit" on them uninvited. She certainly didn't expect them to rearrange their plans because of her. "I don't suppose I could hire a car around here? I have some experience driving in other countries."

Jeanne Marie's smile widened. "We're not exactly blessed with car rental companies," she said mildly. "But if you want to drive yourself, there's no problem. You can use my car and drop me off at Lillian's. Her place is on the way to Vicker's Corners."

Amelia hesitated. "I don't know, Aunt Jeanne. It's one thing to rent a car, but to impose—"

Her aunt waved her hand. "Oh, hush up on that imposition nonsense, would you please? Would you think your cousins were imposing if they came over to England to visit y'all there?"

"Of course not."

"This is about money, then."

Dismayed, Amelia quickly shook her head. "No," she lied. Because it was exactly about money. Her aunt and uncle had an undeniably modest lifestyle in comparison to the Chesterfields. The whole lot of Jeanne and Deke's family could visit their estate and they'd still have room to spare.

Jeanne Marie just eyed her.

Amelia's shoulders drooped. "Mum'll want to put me in chains if I've offended you."

Her aunt's lips twitched. "I'm not offended, Amelia," she assured. She propped her elbows on the table and folded her hands together, leaning toward her. "There are all kinds of wealth, honey. I have no problem whatsoever with the type of wealth I've been blessed with. I love my life exactly the way it is. A husband who loves me, kids we both adore and the opportunity to see them starting on families of their own. Just because we're not millionaires like my brothers and sister, doesn't mean we don't have all that we need." She tapped her fingertip on the table and her eyes crinkled. "And if I want to lend my niece my car, I will."

Amelia studied her for a moment. "Did you always know that this was the life you wanted?"

"Pretty much. I was only twenty-two, but I knew I wanted to marry Deke almost as soon as I met him." She chuckled. "Depending on the day, he might not necessarily admit to the same thing."

Her chest squeezed. She'd felt the same way about Quinn. "I'm a year older than you were then, and I don't feel half the confidence you must have felt."

Jeanne Marie rose and began puttering around the kitchen. She was wearing an oversize plaid shirt that looked like it was probably Deke's and a pair of jeans cut off at the knees. "Comparing us is as silly as comparing apples and oranges, sweetheart. I was learning how to be a good rancher's wife. You're out there establishing orphanages and dedicating hospital wings and such."

"Mummy's the one who gets those things done. I just—" She broke off and sighed. "I don't know what I just do." She made a face. "Maybe the media's right and the only thing I was perfectly suited for was being a proper wife for the future Earl of Estingwood."

"Which you've already admitted you're not planning to do," Jeanne reminded. "So *you* know you're not suited."

Her aunt had no idea just how unsuited.

She rose and restlessly tightened the belt of her borrowed flannel robe. "You really don't mind lending me your vehicle?"

Jeanne Marie smiled. "Just make sure you drive on the right side of the road."

Unfortunately, after Amelia had let off her aunt later that afternoon at her friend's home, she discovered driving on the right side was a task easier said than done.

Her aunt had told her that it was a straight shot down the roadway to Vicker's Corners. What she hadn't said was that the roadway wasn't, well, *straight*.

It was full of curves and bumps and dips and even

though there was hardly any other traffic to speak of, more than once Amelia found herself wanting to drift to the other side of the road.

By the time she made it to the quaintly picturesque little town of Vicker's Corners, her hands ached from clenching the steering wheel so tightly, and she heartily wished she'd just have waited until her aunt was available to bring her into town.

Which was such a pathetic, spoiled thought that she was immediately disgusted with herself. Back home, more often than not, she used the services of a driver. It was simpler. And as Jimmy had so often told her, it was safer.

But that privilege also came as part and parcel along with public eyes following her activities. And that was something she'd always hated. Growing up was difficult enough without having an entire country witnessing your missteps.

She didn't care what the supposed advantages were of being raised a Chesterfield. No matter what happened with Quinn, she was not going to raise their child in that sort of environment. It was fine for some.

But not for her. Not for her baby.

When she saw the way several cars were parked, nose in to the curb between slanted lines, she pulled into the first empty space she spotted and breathed out a sigh of relief. She locked up the car and tucked the keys inside the pocket of her borrowed sundress. It was the same red one from the day before because the other clothes from Stacey and Delaney that Jeanne Marie had found had been from their earlier years. It was either wear the slightly oversize sundress once more, or skintight jeans and T-shirts with the names of rock bands splashed in glitter across her breasts.

Even though she was the only one who cared about what she wore, the sundress was preferable.

Looking up and down the street, Amelia mentally oriented herself with the descriptions that Jeanne Marie had given her of the town. Her impetuously chosen parking spot was directly in front of the post office. Across the street and down a bit was the three-story bed and breakfast, identifiable by the green-and-white-striped awnings her aunt had described. Which meant that around the corner and down the block, she would find the hardware store her aunt recommended.

She waited for two cars to pass, then headed across the street. Her first task would be to secure a phone and then she'd check in with her mother. Amelia had instructed Molly to let Josephine know her plans once she'd left the country.

It wasn't that she'd been afraid her mum would talk her out of going. It was that Amelia didn't entirely trust everyone on her mother's staff to have the same discretion that Molly did. Someone had been feeding that Malone woman details concerning Amelia's schedule and the only ones who kept a copy were her mother's staff and James's assistant.

She reached the hardware store and went inside. There was a girl manning a cash register near the front door and she barely gave Amelia a look as she continued helping a customer, so Amelia set off to find what she needed.

The aisles were narrow; the shelves congested with everything from hammers and industrial-sized paint thinners to cookware. But she didn't see any electronics. She returned to the clerk who'd finished with the customer. "Do you offer cell phones?"

The girl chewed her gum and looked up from the magazine lying open on the counter. "Yeah." She jerked her chin. "Over on aisle—" She broke off, her eyes suddenly widening. "Hey, aren't you that fancy chick related to Jeanne Jones who's marrying this guy?" She lifted the magazine and tapped a photo of James Banning astride one of his polo ponies, his mallet midswing. "He is *so* hot."

"Jeanne Marie is my aunt." She managed a calm smile. "The phones?"

"Oh, yeah. Right." The girl slid off her stool and came around the counter. "I'll show you." She headed toward the rear of the store. "Keep alla that stuff on this aisle over here 'cause the only way out is back past the counter. Cuts down on shoplifting." She gave Amelia a quick look. "Not saying *you* would—"

"I know you're not." Amelia spotted several older-style cell phones hanging from hooks. They were generations away from the fancy device she was used to using. But then that fancy thing had been hacked.

She grabbed the closest phone. It was packaged in the kind of tough, clear plastic that always seemed impossible to open.

The girl snapped her gum. "Are you gonna want a phone card, too?" She gestured at the rack next to the small phone selection. It held an array of colorful credit-card-sized cards. "You pay for the minutes up front," she added at Amelia's blank look. "You know. Otherwise you gotta get a contract and all that."

Feeling foolish, Amelia studied the cards for a moment. Contracts were certainly something to avoid. "Do they cover international calls?"

"Yeah." The girl looked over her head when a jangling bell announced the arrival of another customer. Then she tapped one of the cards. "That one's the best value for your money," she provided as she backed away. "I've gotta get back to the register," she excused herself.

"Thank you." Amelia looked at the display. She wasn't going to use her credit card. Just the cash. Which meant, for now at any rate, she needed to use it wisely. She chose the card the girl suggested and flipped it over, reading the tiny print on the back. Not once in her life had she ever needed to concern herself with such details.

She carried the phone and the card back to the register, but stopped short at the sight of the young blonde woman standing there with the clerk.

Ophelia Malone.

Amelia ducked back in the aisle with the cell phones where she couldn't be seen. There was country music playing over a speaker and she couldn't hear what they were saying, but she didn't need to. There was only one reason why Ophelia would be in that store at that moment and Amelia was it.

She quickly returned the phone and the card to their places on the racks and scurried around the opposite end of the aisle, looking for an escape even though the girl had said there wasn't another way out. She discovered the reason quickly enough. There *was* another exit. But it was a fire exit and she knew from regrettable experience in similar situations that going through it would set off an alarm. Gnawing on her lip, she edged to the end of the aisle again and peeked around the racks toward the front.

Ophelia wasn't there. But the door hadn't jangled, meaning she was still in the store somewhere.

She felt like the fox in a hunt and that never ended well for the fox. She continued sneaking her way around the aisles, keeping to the ends because there was less chance of getting caught, hearing the door jangling periodically. When the urge to look grew too great, she held her breath, darting up the empty row next to her where she could see the entrance just as another customer came in.

She quickly backed out of sight again, then nearly jumped out of her skin when the clerk appeared.

"There you are," she said. "Your friend's looking for you."

"She's not my friend," she corrected, keeping her voice low. Feeling increasingly hemmed in, she grabbed the clerk's hands and the girl's eyes widened. "She can't find me. Is there another way out or an office where I can wait until she's gone?"

"Too late, Lady Chesterfield." Ophelia stepped into sight. Her green eyes were as sharp as her smile, and in a move she'd probably practiced from the womb, she deftly lifted her camera out of her purse.

Chapter Six

Amelia could hear the clicking whirr of the shutter even before the lens aimed her way and she wanted to scream in frustration.

"Any comments on Mr. Tall, Dark and Nameless you were kissing yester—" Ophelia broke off when a shrieking alarm blasted through the store, making all three of them jump. "What the bloody hell is *that?*"

"The fire alarm." The salesclerk waved her hands, looking panicked. "You have to leave the store."

"Oh, come on," Ophelia said impatiently.

"There are flammable items everywhere, ma'am. We don't take chances." The clerk pushed the reporter toward the aisle where a half-dozen other customers were jostling around the displays in the narrow aisle toward the front door.

Seizing the opportunity, Amelia dashed instead for

the fire exit in the rear. The alarm was going off already so what did it matter?

She hit the bar on the door and it flew open, banging against the wall behind it, and she darted out into an alleyway. Her heart pounding, she shoved the door closed behind her. The fire alarm was noisy even through the door, pulsing in the air and making it difficult to think straight. Could she make it back to Aunt Jeanne's car without Ophelia seeing her?

"Hey. Over here." A tall, dark-haired woman dressed in cutoffs and a tank top beckoned from one side near a large, metal trash bin. "They won't see you over here."

Amelia's didn't stop to question the assistance and her sandals slipped on the rough pavement as she took off toward her. She caught herself from landing on her bottom and hurried, half jogging, half skipping after her rescuer who set off briskly away from the hardware store. "*You* set off the alarm?"

"Yes, but if they try to fine me for it, I'm denying it. Already had to pay a few of them thanks to my oldest boy." They reached the end of the alley and the woman held up a warning hand as she cautiously checked the street. A fire truck, siren blaring and lights flashing, roared past. She waited a moment, then beckoned. "Come on. You need to get off the street before more people see you."

"How'd you—"

"Never mind." The woman grabbed her arm and tugged her out into the open. Amelia could see her aunt's car still parked in front of the post office down the street, but they didn't head that way. Instead, the woman pulled Amelia through the propped-open door of the bed-and-breakfast.

A teenager wielding a dust cloth across a fake Chippendale desk looked at them, clearly surprised. "Mrs. O'Malley. What're you doing—" her eyes landed on Amelia and widened with recognition "—here," she finished faintly. She pointed her dust rag at Amelia. "You're…you—"

"Yes, yes. She's her." The brunette—Mrs. O'Malley, obviously—nudged the teen's shoulder to gain her attention again. "You have any guests today, Shayla?"

Shayla shook her head and her wildly curling orangey-red ponytail bounced. "Not yet, but Ma's expecting some newlyweds t'night."

Mrs. O'Malley boldly stepped around the desk and grabbed an old-fashioned hotel key off a hook. "Gonna use number three for a while, then. Keep quiet about that, though, if anyone comes asking, all right?"

Shayla's lips moved, but no words came.

"All right?"

The ponytail bounced again, this time with Shayla's jerky nod. "Yes, ma'am."

"Good girl. Now come on." Mrs. O'Malley tugged Amelia toward a lovely staircase with a white painted banister and dark stained wood treads and started up. "Shayla's a student of mine," she said over her shoulder. "Her mother owns this place."

Thoroughly discomfited, Amelia followed. "You're a teacher?"

"High school English." The other woman turned on the landing and headed up another flight, her pace never slowing. "Better hurry your tush, hon," she advised.

Amelia grasped the banister and quickened her pace. Her head was pounding from the adrenaline rush. "Why did you set off the alarm?"

"Figured somebody needed to do something." She glanced over her shoulder. "I went in to buy paint for my youngest's room—the sweetest shade of pink you ever saw—and I saw that woman showing Katie your picture and asking about you."

"I should have tried Lubbock," Amelia muttered. "You didn't get your paint and I didn't get my phone." They'd reached the top of the stairs and Mrs. O'Malley unlocked the only door there, pushing it open to reveal a cozy-looking guest suite.

They went inside and Mrs. O'Malley immediately crossed to the mullioned window and looked out. "Talk about the nick of time," she said.

Amelia shut the door before joining her, and keeping to one side of the window, looked down. She could see Ophelia marching up the street, her stride determined as she systematically went in and out the doors of each business until she disappeared beneath the striped awning over the B and B's front door.

Hoping she hadn't jumped from the pot into the fire, Amelia sank down on a white wicker rocking chair situated near the window and eyed the other woman. "What do you want out of this? If it's money, you'll be sorely disappointed. My family's dealt with more embarrassing situations than shopping for a discount cell phone."

Mrs. O'Malley didn't look calculating, though. If anything, her light brown eyes turned pitying. "Never heard of a Good Samaritan?"

Amelia's lips twisted. "I apologize for my suspicions, but lately helpful strangers have been in rather short supply."

The woman sat on the corner of the bed that was covered in a fluffy white duvet. "Not as much a stranger as you think. Doesn't seem fair for me to know who you are when you don't know me." She held out her hand. "I'm Jess O'Malley," she said.

Amelia shook her hand. "It's nice to make your acquaintance, Mrs. O'Malley."

"Jess'll do." The woman's lips quirked. "I'm Quinn's sister," she added meaningfully.

Amelia's mouth went dry. "Oh."

Jess shifted and pulled a fancy phone from her back pocket, tapped on the screen a few times then held it out.

Amelia warily took the phone.

The sight of herself in Quinn's arms on the display didn't come as a shock. Since her supposed engagement, she'd become almost numb to the existence of such photographs. The fact that she'd drawn Quinn into the mess, though, caused a wave of grief. "Where'd you find this?"

"It's all over the internet."

She scrolled through the image then handed back the phone. Her mouth felt dry. "Has he seen it?"

"My brother? Or your fiancé?"

Amelia tucked her tongue behind her teeth, gathering her wits. Jess pulled as few punches as her brother. "Quinn."

"He's seen it." Jess sat forward, her arms on her knees. Her eyes—hazel, just like Quinn's, Amelia realized—were assessing. "He doesn't need his heart broken again, Lady Chesterfield. Once was bad enough."

"Amelia," she said faintly. She loathed the courtesy title of "Lady" when she hadn't done a single thing to earn it. "I'm not trying to break anyone's heart. Quinn—" She swallowed and looked away from his sister's eyes. "Your brother hates me, anyway."

"Hate and love are two sides of the same coin, hon."

"Not this time." One corner of her mind wondered if she'd have been better off facing Ophelia than Quinn's sister. And another corner of her mind argued that she would probably get her chance momentarily, because she had significant doubts that any teenager would be able to hold up under the determined paparazzo, no matter how devoted she was to her high school English teacher.

The rest of her mind was consumed with Quinn.

It didn't take a genius to know it was Quinn's ex-wife who'd caused his heartbreak. She pressed her numb lips together for a moment but her need overcame discretion. "What exactly did his ex-wife do to him?"

"Cheated on him with her ex-boyfriend." Jess's voice was flat and immediate. She clearly had no reservations about sharing the details. "Got pregnant and left him for her ex-boyfriend."

Amelia felt the blood drain out of her head. She sat very still, listening as Jess went on, oblivious to Amelia's shock.

"They're still married, living right here in Vicker's Corners. Didn't even have the decency to get out of Horseback Hollow's backyard." Her tone made it plain what she thought of that.

"I haven't cheated on anyone," Amelia said. Her voice sounded faraway. "Least of all Quinn." No matter what he believed right now, six weeks ago, she had been nothing but honest with him. As for James, she'd never made any promises to him either before or after her night with Quinn. And when she'd returned to all the engagement commotion, she'd told him about the man she'd met in Horseback Hollow. The man she'd intended on returning to.

Only that man had said in no uncertain terms that her return was no longer wanted at all.

How would Quinn react once she informed him of her pregnancy?

Trying not to cry, she stood and looked out the window again. There were a few vehicles driving up and down the street. A young family pushing a stroller was walking along the sidewalk, looking in the shop windows. The cars on either side of her aunt's in front of the post office had been replaced by different ones. The fire engine siren had gone quiet.

Ophelia hadn't come pounding up the stairs, her camera whirring away.

"D'you mind if I ask what you're doing in Texas?"

Amelia laughed silently and without humor. Learning she was pregnant had changed everything. She could no longer remain in England actually considering marriage to a man she didn't love. Regardless of what Jess had revealed about Quinn's ex-wife, he still needed to know he was going to be a father. And she had to learn how to become a mother.

She blinked hard several times before looking at Jess, more or less dry-eyed. "Yes." Even that one word sounded thick.

Jess's eyes narrowed for a moment. Then she smiled faintly. "Well, at least that's honest."

Amelia's eyes stung all over again. She looked away. "I'm not a Jezebel."

"No." Jess sighed audibly. "I want to say you're a twenty-three-year-old kid. But that'd be ironic coming from me since Mac and I already had two babies by the time I was your age." She rose also. "Stay here. I'll see if your nosy gal-pal is still snooping around downstairs."

Amelia waited tensely until Quinn's sister returned. "Shayla says she doesn't know you're up here, but she checked in to the room downstairs anyway," she said. "Unfortunately, that room opens right onto the lobby. And there's no convenient fire exit this time."

Dismayed, Amelia could do nothing but stare.

"Yeah." Jess rubbed her hands down the sides of her cutoff denims. "I didn't expect her to check in, either," she grumbled.

"What am I going to do?" Amelia stared at the room around them. "I can't stay here! I have to get my aunt's car back to her."

Jess patted her hands in the air, obviously trying to calm her. "I'll figure something out." She made a face. "Shayla couldn't very well turn down a paying customer. There are only three rooms here. But she said she'd try to let you know if your fan heads out to look for you. If not, just be glad there's an entire floor between you with a newlywed couple expected to occupy it." She gave her a wry smile. "Maybe they'll make enough noise you can sneak out without anyone noticing."

Try as she might, Amelia couldn't prevent heat from rising in her cheeks.

"Wow." Jess eyed her flush openly. "Just how sheltered *were* you growing up?"

Amelia blushed even harder. She thought of the private schools. The tutors. The chaperones. There were days when she and Lucie had felt like the only thing they were being raised for was to become a pristinely suitable choice for a noble marriage. Something their mother had vehemently denied since *her* first marriage had been just that type. Arranged. And terribly unhappy despite the production of Amelia's half brothers, Oliver and Brodie.

Jess looked at the sturdy watch on her wrist and made a face. "I'm going to have to leave you here. Just for a bit," she assured quickly. "I've got to pick up my two oldest from baseball and drop off my middle at karate class. But I'll be back in an hour, tops. And, I'll, uh, I'll make sure Shayla keeps quiet in the meantime. At least the room's comfortable and it has its own bathroom, right?"

Amelia wanted to chew off her tongue. "The room's comfortable," she allowed. But a prison was still a prison. "My aunt's car—"

"I promise. It's my fault you're stuck up here and I'll figure something out," Jess said again. "Just hang tight for a little bit. Here." She handed Amelia her cell phone. "I'll leave that with you to prove I'll be back quickly. Everyone knows I don't go far without my cell. Quinn's always complaining about it."

"Fine." Amelia took the phone only because Jess seemed so intent on it and once the other woman left, she set it on the narrow dresser against the wall across from the bed and went back to the window. She saw Jess hurry out from beneath the striped awning a few minutes later and heartily wished that it was Ophelia Malone who was the one departing.

It was warm in the room and she figured out how to open the window to let in some fresh air. Then she sat back down on the wicker rocker.

She didn't even realize she'd dozed off until the buzzing of Jess's phone startled her awake. She had no intentions of answering the other woman's phone, and she ignored the ringing until it stopped. She used the bathroom and turned on the small television sitting on one corner of the dresser and flipped through the meager selection. Black-and-white movies, a sitcom repeat and an obviously local talk show. She smiled a little when the hostess with a helmet of gray hair talked about the buzz surrounding the Horseback Hollow Cantina slated to open in two weeks, and switched the telly off again just as Jess's phone began ringing again.

She picked it up, hoping to find some way of silencing it. But the sight of Quinn's name bobbing on the phone's display stopped her. Her thumb hovered over the screen almost, *almost,* touching it.

But she sighed and turned the phone facedown on the dresser instead. The ringing immediately stopped and she went back to stare out the open window. The street outside was undeniably picturesque with its street-lights shaped like old-fashioned gas lamps and big pots of summer flowers hanging from them. Her aunt's car was now the only one in front of the post office. Everything looked peaceful and lovely and on any other day, she'd be perfectly charmed by the town.

When there was a bold knock on the door, she went rigid, feeling panicked all over again.

She wouldn't put it past Ophelia Malone to go door-to-door looking for her. She looked out the window. There was plenty of space for her to climb out, but nothing to climb onto. No terrace. No fire escape ladder. Just the awning below her window that hung over the front entrance.

She'd never jumped out of a window onto an awning but she'd jumped out of plenty of trees. Now she was pregnant, though, so that option was out no matter *how* badly she wanted to avoid the reporter.

The knock came again. Followed by a deep voice that she would recognize anywhere. "Open up, princess."

Not Ophelia.

Shaking more than ever, she ran to the door and pulled it open, looking up at Quinn for only a second before dragging him inside. "Are you *crazy?* What if someone saw you?"

He was wearing faded blue jeans that hugged his powerful thighs, a plain white T-shirt stretched over his broad shoulders and he needed a shave. Badly. And even though his lips were thin as he looked down at her, he still made her knees feel weak. "If answering a phone wasn't beneath your dignity, you wouldn't have missed an opportunity to get out of here."

"What?"

"Your camera-toting friend went to the sandwich shop next door."

"How do you even know what she looks like? I didn't see her leave." She reached around him for the door. "If we're quick—"

"She's already back," he cut her hopefulness short. "And there aren't a lot of people browsing around Vicker's Corners with that sort of camera clenched in their hands."

"Shayla was supposed to let me know if Ophelia left!"

"Yeah, well, Shayla's a seventeen-year-old kid and her mom sent her out on an errand."

"How do you know that?"

His expression turned even darker. He crossed to the window and glanced out. "Because I heard them when I came in to see why the hell you weren't answering the damn phone."

Her head swam and she leaned back against the door for support.

He crossed to the window and glanced out. "Jess called me from the park where her boys play baseball. She got tied up there with the coach trying to keep the

guy from kicking Jason off the team for fighting. For
some unfathomable reason she was worried about you."

She winced. "You can return her phone to her, then."
She'd have to take her chances with Ophelia whether the
prospect nauseated her or not.

She was a grown woman carrying a baby. She
shouldn't need rescuing. Maybe that was one of the ways
she was supposed to start acting like one. "You might
have gotten up here without Ophelia seeing you, but try
not to be caught on camera when you leave again." She
reached behind her and closed her hand over the doorknob. "I appreciate your…efforts…but I need to get my
aunt's car back to her. I'm sure the baby shower she's
attending is over by now."

He looked impatient. "Jess told me about the car. I already got hold of Deke. He's got Jeanne covered."

Amelia exhaled. At least that was something, though
it didn't alleviate her anxiety over Ophelia, much less
Quinn. "That was—" *unexpected* "—very good of you."

"Jess also told me she's the reason you're stuck here."

"*Ophelia*'s the reason. I never imagined that woman
would go to these lengths for a few pictures to sell." Her
stomach churned and her palm grew sweaty on the doorknob. "Regardless, you shouldn't have come."

"Afraid your fiancé'll find out?"

She strongly considered opening the door and walking
out. Only the fact that she'd brought this on herself by not
addressing the press—the legitimate press—straight-on
from the beginning kept her from doing so.

She took her hand away from the doorknob and wiped
it down the side of her borrowed sundress. "Insult me all
you want. I still don't want Ophelia taking after you, too.
Right now—" her lips twisted "—assuming she doesn't

find us here *together,* all you are is a faceless man with dark hair. She's still focusing on me, and it's best to keep it that way."

"You'd prefer hiding out here on your own until she gives up and goes away?"

"If I confront her, she'll somehow use that for her own gain. I know how these people work, Quinn. She's not breaking any laws—"

"Yet. Or have you forgotten already about the ones who did when they hacked into your phone calls?"

She sighed. She would never forget. "Ophelia doesn't know for certain that I'm here. And she can't stay cooped up in this B and B forever. She's not gaining anything unless she has photos to sell."

Or a story.

And Amelia's pregnancy would be a whale of a tale. It would put the detestable woman's career on the map, at least until the next scandal came along.

"I'm just grateful your sister happened to be in the hardware store at the right time to provide a distraction." It was at least one thing that had gone her way.

His lips curled derisively. "Don't kid yourself, princess. My sister never *happens* to do anything."

"She was there to buy pink paint for her daughter's room!"

"Jess doesn't *have* a daughter. And I can promise you that none of my nephews would be caught dead in a pink room."

"But—"

"Don't try to figure it out," he suggested darkly. He paced around the room as if he found it as cagelike as she. "Jess is a law unto herself. She's just as infected with royal-fever as the rest of the people around here."

Except for him. He'd been fully vaccinated, courtesy of an engagement that didn't exist.

"I don't care why she was there," Amelia said abruptly. "Facing your sister, whatever her reasons, is always going to be preferable to Ophelia Malone. At least she's—" She broke off.

"At least she's what?"

Family. Amelia stared at him, the word she'd been about to blurt still alarmingly close to her lips.

Just tell him.

She'd wanted a chance to speak with him alone, and now she had it.

Just tell him!

Her mouth ran dry. She started to speak. "O-only trying to protect you," she finished, instead.

His eyes narrowed, studying her face so closely she had to work hard not to squirm.

"I wish I had another disguise," she said. "We could just get out of here. Even if Ophelia doesn't discover us, Shayla's mother probably will."

"We don't have to worry about her." He pulled something from his pocket and tossed it on the bed.

She eyed the old-fashioned key.

"I rented the room for the night," he added flatly.

Amelia's stomach hollowed out. "We're *both* stuck here?"

Chapter Seven

Quinn paced across the room, putting as much distance as he could between them. "I'm not the one who's stuck," he corrected.

The bed with the puffy white comforter loomed large between them. Particularly when she sank down on the corner of the mattress.

With the red dress and her dark, dark hair, she looked like she might have been posed there for an advertisement. If not for the fact that her face was nearly as white as the bedding.

He ruthlessly squashed down his concern.

"I can come and go any time I want," he continued. "You're the one who isn't supposed to be here."

"Right. Silly of me to forget," she murmured.

He exhaled roughly. "Maybe she'll want to go out for dinner later and we'll be able to get out of here."

Before morning.

Before they spent an entire night together in a room with only one freaking bed.

He pinched the bridge of his nose and sat on the rocking chair. The wicker creaked a little under his weight, sounding loud in the quiet room.

He cleared his throat. "How many times have you had to do this?"

"Hide out from paparazzi?" She pushed her hair behind her ear. "I have no idea. Lucie and I've been doing it since we were teenagers, I guess."

Lucie, he knew, was her older sister. "She doesn't seem to be in the news as much as you."

"That's just because nobody thinks she's marrying a future earl right now. We've always been in a fishbowl, but never as bad as the last several weeks have been." She rubbed her hands nervously over the bed beside her hips.

He looked away. Whether she looked terrifyingly fragile or not, imagining her hair spread out over all that white was way too easy and the effect it was having on him wasn't one he needed just then. "It's a first for me," he muttered.

She spread her hands, smiling without any real amusement. "Welcome to my world." Then even the fake smile died. "You didn't tell me before—" Her lashes swept down. "In April I mean, that you were married."

It was the last thing he expected to hear and as a cold shower, it was pretty effective.

"It was a long time ago," he finally said.

"How long?"

"Why does it matter?"

"Because you're painting me to be just like her."

His jaw tightened. Knowing she was right didn't mean that he was wrong. "History tends to repeat itself."

Her long throat worked. "You have no idea," she murmured.

The hairs on the back of his neck stood up and he sat forward. The chair creaked ominously. "What's *that* supposed to mean?"

She pushed off the bed and pressed her hands together. "Look, despite you trying to help me here, I understand that things are...are over between us. You've been more than clear about that. And no matter what I say I don't expect that to change. You are not under any obligation—"

His jaw tightened. "Amelia—"

She moistened her lips. Her dark brown eyes met his, then flicked away again. Her tension was palpable.

"I'm pregnant," she said in a low voice. "I came back to Horseback Hollow to tell you."

He stared at her. There was a strange, hollow ringing inside his head. "You're...pregnant."

She chewed her lip. "Keep your voice down. Who knows how thin the walls are."

"You're *pregnant*," he repeated, a little more softly, but no less incredulously.

"And saying it a third time won't change that fact." She went into the adjoining bathroom and returned with a glass of water. She pushed it into his hand. "Drink."

The kind of drink he felt in sudden need of came out of a bottle and was strong enough to put down a horse. He set the glass on the windowsill. "How do you know?"

She paced across the room again. "The usual way."

"You missed your period?"

A tinge of color finally lit her cheeks. She didn't look at him. "Yes."

"And you're saying its mine."

"Yes." The word grew clipped.

"Even though you're engaged to someone else."

She thrust her fingers through her hair and tugged. "I am *not* engaged!" She dropped her hands and sank onto the foot of the bed again. "And before you accuse me, I know this baby is yours because you're the only man I've ever slept with," she added in a flat voice.

He shook his head once, sharp enough to clear it of the fog that had filled it. "You expect me to believe you were a virgin? And I didn't happen to notice?"

Her cheeks turned bright. "I don't care what you noticed or not. That night with you was the only time I—" She broke off. "This baby is not James's," she said crisply. "What earthly reason would I have for being here—" she lifted her arms "—if it were? You think I like facing you and, and telling you—" her voice grew choked "—knowing how you feel about me?"

"Calm down."

"Easy for you to say." She rushed into the bathroom and slammed the door behind her.

He sat there, hearing his pulse pounding in his head. Remembering that April night. The dawn following.

She'd been shy, yes. At first. But he'd never suspected—

He shoved to his feet, crossed the room and pushed open the door.

She was sitting on the closed lid of the commode, tears sliding down her cheeks. And her jaw dropped at his intrusion. "What—"

"It's only been six weeks." He bit out the fact that

she'd been so careful to point out to him. "How can you be certain? Do you have any other symptoms? Have you seen a doctor?"

Her expression went smooth, her eyes remote. "I did a home pregnancy test."

"Sometimes they come back false." He grimaced when she just looked at him. "Another experience from my regrettable marriage." Before the "I do's" Carrie's test had been positive. After, the test was negative. But he couldn't even accuse her of lying about it, because at that point, he'd still believed she loved him and he'd been right beside her when they'd looked at those test results.

Carrie had been relieved.

He hadn't been. Not at that point, anyway. He'd built their house with a family in mind. A family that had never come. Not for him.

"Two years later she got pregnant for real," he added abruptly.

"With her ex-boyfriend's child."

He studied her for a long moment but could see nothing in her expressionless eyes. "Either you've been listening to really old gossip or my sister's got a big mouth."

She didn't respond to that. "I'll agree to whatever tests you want." Her tone was still cool.

He really, really hated that "royal" face of hers. "Another pregnancy test will do for starters."

Her brows lifted, surprise evidently overcoming remoteness. "I meant paternity tests."

"I know." He could only deal with so much at once. "When you arrived in my barn, you were worn out. Exhausted and full of stress. You collapsed, for God's sake. Let's just make certain there's a pregnancy to begin with."

She sucked in her lower lip for a moment. "I don't think now's a good time for me to stroll into a pharmacy to buy a test kit."

He stifled an oath. For a moment there, he'd managed to forget the very reason they were in the guest room at all. "After we get back to the Hollow," he said. "My sister's pregnant so often she's probably got a stockpile of tests."

As far as humor went, it fell flatter than a pancake.

Turning slightly, she swiped her hand over her cheek. As if he couldn't see perfectly well that she was crying.

"First things first," he said gruffly. "Sooner or later, your stalker downstairs will have to eat. Or sleep. And then we'll get the hell out of this place."

"Here." Several hours later, Shayla handed Quinn a set of keys on a key chain with a plastic heart hanging from it. "Mrs. O'Malley said to give these to you, too."

It was finally dark and Ophelia had left the B and B, presumably for dinner, though Shayla reported that she'd had her camera with her when she'd gone.

The teenager—who clearly thought she was taking part in an exciting adventure—had also delivered a knapsack much like the one Amelia had ditched in the airport restroom, filled with clothing and a long blond wig.

"Those are the keys to Mrs. O'Malley's van?"

The girl nodded, looking conspiratorial. "It's parked at the end of the block in front of the bar. You could see it from your window if you looked out."

The bar, Amelia knew, was O'Malley's and it belonged to Jess's father-in-law. She looked at Quinn. Aside from working out their escape plan with his sister and Shayla, he hadn't said much in the past few hours.

He hadn't done much except watch Amelia, leaving her to imagine all manner of dark thoughts he was having about her.

"I can just as easily drive my aunt's car," she argued not for the first time.

"Ophelia probably already knows it belongs to your aunt," he returned, also not for the first time. "It's been sitting there all day even though the post office closed at noon."

As long as Ophelia didn't spot them together, there was no reason for him not to drive his own pickup truck back to Horseback Hollow.

Her stomach was churning. The longer they'd waited in the pretty guest suite, the crazier she'd felt. The news that Ophelia had left the B and B on foot had been a relief, but it didn't mean the end of her problems.

Not by any stretch of the imagination.

"I'll change into the clothes then." It wasn't as if she had many options. She looked at Shayla. "You've been a big help, Shayla."

The girl bounced on her toes. "Are you kidding? Nothing interesting ever happens here! I'm just glad my ma's out on a date tonight. I love her, but if she knew *you* were here, so would the rest of the town. She can't keep anything a secret." Holding her finger to her lips, she slipped out the door and closed it behind her.

Amelia exhaled and, avoiding Quinn's gaze, took the clothing into the bathroom. She changed into the diminutive bandage of a skirt that was as bright an orange as Shayla's hair and the white V-neck shirt that came with it. Amelia wasn't wearing a bra and when she pulled the thin cotton over her head, she cringed at her reflection. The neckline reached midway down her chest and the shadow from her nipples showed clearly through the fabric.

If she asked for another blouse, though, they'd be delayed even longer. And they had no idea how long a window Ophelia was unwittingly allowing them. So she swallowed her misgivings and wound her hair into a knot on her head before pulling on the cheap wig that Shayla had provided. The hair was synthetic and an obviously false platinum blond. But it covered Amelia's dark hair and reached down to her waist.

As a disguise, she decided she far preferred the boy look she and Molly had attempted.

She kept the sandals on that she was already wearing. There was nothing distinctive about them and the platform wedges that Shayla had stuck in the knapsack were too small anyway. Then she zipped the discarded dress inside the pack and, hauling in a steadying breath, opened the door to face Quinn.

"Jesus," he muttered.

"I look like a tart," she said before he could.

"You look like jail bait." His gaze was focused on her chest.

Flushing, she dragged the cheap blond hair over her shoulders so it covered her breasts. "Are you ready to leave or not?"

In answer, he opened the door and handed her the heart-shaped key ring. "Like we agreed. You first. I'll follow in a few minutes. We'll meet up at the Rocking-U. You remember how to get there?"

"I got there on foot. I imagine I can get there by van." Squeezing the hard metal heart in her fist, she left the room.

This wasn't her first rodeo, as they said, when it came

to avoiding the paparazzi, but it was the first time she'd done so as a scantily clad teenage girl. Even when she'd *been* a teen, she'd never dressed like this. Her parents wouldn't have allowed it.

She encountered no one on the stairs between the third and second floors. On the second, she could hear music coming from behind the door of the honeymooners who had arrived a short while ago. On the last flight, she descended more gingerly.

But Shayla, dusting again though there was surely no need for it, caught her eye and quickly nodded. "All clear, Lady Amelia," she whispered loudly.

Resisting the urge to look back up the staircase to see if Quinn was watching, Amelia skipped down the rest of the stairs and sailed across the small lobby and out into the night air. She turned left, walking briskly to the end of the block, waiting with every footstep to hear a camera shutter clicking or see a camera flash lighting the night.

But there was nothing.

And soon she was jogging. Then running flat out, the knapsack bouncing wildly against her backside, until she reached the green van right where it was supposed to be. Her heart was pounding in her chest as she fumbled with the keys, nearly dropping them, before managing to unlock the door and climb inside. Once there, she worked the knapsack free and tossed it behind the seat before fitting the key into the ignition.

The engine started immediately and she cautiously drove away from the curb. She hadn't been accustomed to her aunt's car and the van—considerably larger—felt even more unwieldy to her.

She drove around the corner, then the next and the next until she was right back where she'd begun the day, near the post office. She waited for a car to pass, then turned again and headed out of town. Back to Horseback Hollow.

Going from one fire into the next.

Amelia was sitting at Quinn's piano, rubbing her fingers over the keys but not really playing anything, when he arrived. He walked over to the piano and deliberately closed the lid on the keys as if he couldn't stand the idea of her touching it.

"Here." He tossed her a small white sack. "I stopped at the drugstore on the way back."

She dumped out the contents on her lap.

A three-pack of pregnancy test kits.

Evidently, he *really* wanted to be certain.

"Decide you didn't want to let your sister know?"

His smile was thin. "Something like that."

She dropped the paper sack on top of the discarded blond wig sitting on top of the piano and turned the box over, pretending to read the instructions on the back, but not seeing any of the words.

She'd been waiting nearly an hour alone at his home before he got there. He'd told her the door wouldn't be locked, and it hadn't been. Only the fact that she needed the loo had made her go in, though.

Otherwise, she would have just sat in his sister's van and waited.

It wasn't as if he truly wanted her in his home, after all.

"You weren't followed?"

He shook his head once.

She pressed her lips together and rose. "I suppose you want me to do this now?" She waved the box slightly.

"You want to wait until morning?"

She wanted to turn back the calendar six weeks and do things right. She wanted the warm, tender man back that he'd been the night they'd made love.

Her eyes burned. Not answering, she walked past him and down the hall to the bathroom there. When she was finished, she put the cap back on the stick and left it sitting on the bathroom counter.

She opened the door to find him standing on the other side and heat ran up under her cheeks. "Two minutes."

He lifted his hand and she realized he was holding a pocket watch.

"My father used to carry a pocket watch," she murmured.

He crossed his arms and leaned back against the bathroom door, his hooded gaze on the test stick. "So did mine. This one." He dangled the watch from the chain. "One of the few things the fire didn't take. This and the piano." He could have been discussing the weather for all the emotion in his voice.

She chewed the inside of her lip.

Never had two minutes passed so slowly.

When finally it had, he picked up the stick and studied it silently. Then he flipped it into the little trash can next to the cabinet.

"It's late," he said, walking past her. "You need to eat."

Amelia's throat tightened.

Even though she knew, she *knew* what the test would show, she plucked the plastic stick out of the empty can and looked at the bright blue plus sign.

Tears slid out of her eyes and she dropped it in the trash once more.

She turned on the cold water and splashed it over her

face until her cheeks felt frozen. Then she dried her face
and followed him.

He was in the kitchen. Just as he had been the night
he'd found her in his barn.

Only this time the sandwich was sitting on a plate,
and a glass of milk sat next to that.

Her stomach lurched. Whether from a sudden attack
of morning sickness-at-night or from the horrible day it
had been she didn't know. But the thought of choking
down any kind of food just then made her want to retch.

She forced herself to sit down, though, in front of the
plate. He, however, remained standing by the window,
looking out into the night. "Aren't you going to eat?" He
had spent nearly as much time cooped up in the B and B
as she had.

"We'll go to the justice of the peace on Monday." He
didn't look at her. "Unless you want a minister. It'll be
more complicated that way, but—"

"A *minister*." She pushed aside the plate and stared at
his back. "What are you suggesting?"

He turned, giving her a narrow look. "What do you
think? My kid's not going to be born without my name."

Her jaw went loose. "So," she said with false cheer,
"now you magically believe it's yours?"

His lips twisted. "Don't push me, princess."

She shoved back from the table so abruptly the chair
tipped over and crashed to the tiled floor. "Don't push
you? I can't believe I ever thought I—" She broke off,
grasping for some semblance of self-control even though
she wanted to launch herself at him, kicking and screaming. Which was altogether shocking, because she never
lost her temper like that. "If I wanted a marriage with-

out love, I could have stayed in England and married Jimmy! It certainly would have been easier than this!"

"That—" he pointed toward her midsection "—changes things."

She lifted her chin, channeling her mother at her most regal. "It doesn't change the fact that I won't be arranged into a convenient marriage. I've done a lot of things in my life purely for propriety's sake, but not this."

He swore and planted his boot on one leg of the up-turned chair and kicked it away from her.

She gasped as it slammed against the wall.

"Next time you give me that royal face, I'll put you over my knee." He leaned over her, tall and furious. "And I won't let you take *my kid* back there to be raised by another man!"

Shocked to her very core, she stood there frozen. "I wouldn't do that."

A muscle ticked angrily in his jaw and his eyes raked over her face.

"I swear to you, Quinn." She stared into his eyes, wishing with all of her heart that he'd just take her in his arms the way he had six weeks ago. "I would never do that," she finished hoarsely.

"Then you can prove it on Monday in front of the JP."

She hauled in an unsteady breath. Marriage to Quinn Drummond was something she'd dreamed about since they'd made love. Since they'd unknowingly created the baby inside her.

But not this way.

Not ever this way.

"No."

Then she retrieved the chair, turned it upright and tucked it under the table and walked out of the kitchen.

Chapter Eight

When he heard the front door open and close, Quinn bolted after her, catching her at the bottom of the porch steps. "Where the *hell* do you think you're going?"

She yanked her arm out of his grasp and gave him a glacial look. "Where I go is not *up* to you."

"You wanna strut out to the highway and hitch a ride, princess?" His lips twisted as he looked her over. "Imagine a trucker will go by eventually. Depending on what sort of guy he is, he might or might not stop for someone looking like you."

She gave a futile yank down on the hem of the skirt that showed nearly every inch of her gloriously God-given stems. "You are *not* the man I thought you were," she said through her teeth.

"And you aren't the woman I thought, either," he returned.

She turned on the heel of her little sandals, her hair flying around her shoulders and started walking away, her sweet hips swaying.

He cussed like he hadn't cussed since he was fifteen and his mom had washed out his mouth with soap. "You're not going anywhere, princess." In two long steps, he reached her and hooked her around the waist, swinging her off her feet before she had a chance to stop him.

Her legs scissored and he slid her over his shoulder, clamping his arm over the back of her legs before she could do either one of them physical damage. "Cut it out."

She drummed her fists against his backside, trying to wriggle out of his hold. "Put me *down* this instant," she ordered imperiously.

"I warned you," he said and swatted her butt.

She pounded his back even harder. "You...cretin."

"Yeah, yeah. Sweet nothings won't get you anywhere, princess." He stomped back into the house and into the living room. He lifted her off his shoulder and dumped her on the sofa.

She bounced and tried scrambling away, but he leaned over her, pinning her on either side with his hands. "Stay," he bit out.

She glared at him through the hair hanging in her face. "I. Don't. Take. Orders." Her chest heaved.

He didn't move.

Didn't do a damn thing even though he should have, because she was there, in his house and she was pregnant with his kid and he didn't want to ask for a polite dance or gentle, moonlit kisses.

He just *wanted*.

With a need that was blinding.

She suddenly went still.

A swallow worked down her long, long throat and the glint in her eyes shifted to something else entirely.

She moistened her lips. "Quinn," she whispered.

And then her hands weren't pushing at him, they were pulling.

At his shirt that he ripped off over his head.

At his belt that slid out of his belt loops with a loud slither.

"Hurry," she gasped, squirming beneath him as she yanked his fly apart and dragged at his jeans, nearly sending his nerves out the top of his skull.

He reached under that excuse of a skirt and tore her panties aside. She was wet and hot and she gasped when he dragged her closer and drove into her.

He let out a harsh breath, trying to slow down, get some control, get some sanity, but she wrapped her lithe legs around his hips, greedily rocking. And then she was shuddering deep, deep inside, her body clutching at him and her lips crying out his name.

And he was lost.

Every cell Amelia possessed was still vibrating when Quinn silently rolled away. She felt like they'd just been tossed out of a tornado.

The night they'd made love had been magical. Tender. Sweet.

This was…raw. Most assuredly not sweet.

And every bit as powerful.

She let out a shuddering breath, knowing that if he touched her again, she'd welcome him just as wantonly. "Quinn—"

"This shouldn't have happened." He sat up and slid

off the sofa. He didn't look at her as he fastened his jeans and his voice was low. "Did I hurt you?"

She caught her breath, aching inside. "No," she whispered honestly. "Did…did I hurt you?" She dimly recalled her nails sinking into his flesh while pleasure exploded inside her.

He looked over his shoulder at that, genuinely surprised. His gaze raked over her and she trembled, muscles deep inside her still clenching. The thin cotton shirt felt rough against her agonizingly tight nipples and she tugged the skirt down where it belonged. She had no idea what had become of her underpants.

"No," he said gruffly. "You didn't hurt me." He leaned over and picked up his T-shirt. The neckline was nearly torn right out of it. He looked at it for a moment, then bunched it in his fist. "I'll get you something to put on."

She sat up, curling her legs to the side. "Thank you."

The roping muscles defining his strong shoulders seemed to tighten when she spoke. He went up the stairs and returned in minutes with a button-down shirt. "You still need to eat," he said evenly, handing it to her. "And decide if you want a minister or not."

Then he turned and went into the kitchen. Through the doorway she could see him readjusting the chair.

Her eyes stung.

She didn't know what she was going to do.

But she knew she was not going to marry Quinn Drummond without his love.

Swiping her cheeks, she stood on legs that felt as insubstantial as candy floss. The shirt he'd given her was clearly a dress shirt but it definitely wasn't the one he'd worn to Toby's wedding. That one had been stark white while this one was a pale gray with an even paler pinstripe. When she unbuttoned it and found a tag still attached to the collar inside, she realized it was new. Never been worn.

She'd have preferred something he'd worn. At least she'd have been able to take a little comfort from it. And she wouldn't be wondering who'd bought the shirt for him because it looked too fancy for anything he'd have chosen for himself.

She removed the tag and pulled the shirt over the one she already had on. New or not, there was something very intimate about wearing his shirt. She needed all the barriers against that feeling that she could get.

She buttoned it up, then folded the long sleeves over several times until they didn't hang past her wrists. She spotted her panties and picked them up. The thin silk was torn in two.

Thank goodness the shirttails reached her knees, though just thinking why that was a good thing made her cheeks hot and her stomach hollow out.

She toed off the one sandal that she was still wearing, blushed some more over that as well, then hurried down the hall to the bathroom, the ruined silk bunched in her fist.

She washed up, dropped the panties in the trash next to the test stick, and tried to restore some order to her tangled hair with her fingers. Finally, with no other excuses remaining, she returned to the kitchen.

The sandwich was still there on the plate.

He was sitting in the chair opposite it, his long legs stretched out across the floor, a dark brown bottle propped on his hard, tanned abdomen.

She ignored the curling sensation inside her belly at the sight and sat down. Unlike earlier, she was suddenly

famished, but she cringed a little when she picked up the
sandwich, because the bread hadn't even had an opportunity to grow stale while they'd been…:been—

"Don't think about it," he said abruptly and she
jumped a little.

"I beg your pardon?"

"You're thinking about what we just did on the couch."
His hazel eyes were hooded and unreadable. "My suggestion is don't." He lifted the bottle to his lips and took
a long drink. "Safer that way," he added when he set
the bottle down again. The glass clinked a little when it
hit the metal tab still unfastened at the top of his jeans.

She dragged her eyes away and took a bite of the
sandwich. For something that had transpired in a span
of minutes, she was quite certain *not* thinking about it
wasn't going to be as easy as he made it out to be.

"I didn't have anything but peanut butter and jelly,"
he said.

She chewed and swallowed. "I like peanut butter."

His lips twisted a little. "So do my nephews. They go
through a jar every time they're here."

She gingerly took a sip of milk. On a good day, she
didn't much care for it, and now was no exception. She
slid out of the chair and saw his eyes narrow. "I prefer
water," she said quickly, lifting the glass. She dumped
the milk down the drain, rinsed the glass and refilled it
from the tap then sat down again to the sandwich. "Your
sister really doesn't have a daughter?"

"She really doesn't," he said evenly.

"How old are her boys?"

"Fifteen, thirteen, nine, six and two."

"Goodness." She toyed with the water glass. He might
not have told her before about an ex-wife, but he had

talked about his family. The death of his father. The fact
that he had only one older sister.

"Who else knows you're pregnant?"

She looked at him quickly, then back at the sandwich.
"Just, um, just Molly." She tore off a tiny piece of crust.
"She's one of my mother's secretaries."

He bent his knees and shifted forward, setting the
bottle on the table. "You told a *secretary?* Not a friend
or your sister?"

"Molly is a friend. And Lucie—" She shook her head.
"Lucie's busy with her own issues. Besides, we've never
exactly shared secrets."

"Thought you were close in age?"

"We are. She's only two years ahead. But—" She
shrugged. "We've all had our responsibilities growing
up. Some more than others." She smashed the tidbit of
crust between her thumbs. "Mostly, mine has been to
provide window dressing at my mother's events."

"You pulled together the companies who funded that
last orphanage. That's a little more than window dressing."

She looked at him and it was his turn to glance away
and shrug. "I can read," he muttered. "And Jess was
yammering on about it not too long ago."

In other words, don't get excited thinking he'd been
following her activities. She wondered how impressed
he'd be if he knew the companies she'd been able to pull
together for the funding were all controlled by the Earl
of Estingwood, and took another bite of the sandwich.

The peanut butter and jelly stuck to the roof of her
mouth, reminding her of the sandwiches she used to
beg off their cook when she was a little girl. "Well—"
she swallowed it down with another drink of water
"—speaking of reading. We might have avoided Oph-

elia Malone for now, but I doubt she'll go quietly into the night."

"She got lucky with one photo," he dismissed.

"Sometimes one photo is all it takes to set off a firestorm."

"Afraid your—" he hesitated for a moment "—future earl is going to see it?"

She was certain he'd been going to say *fiancé*. Undoubtedly, James and his staff had already seen the photo and were organizing the appropriate damage control. But she didn't share that fact because Quinn wouldn't want to hear about it. "May I use your phone?" she asked instead.

He looked at the pocket watch he'd left earlier on the table. "Nearly eleven. Your aunt figures we're still in Vicker's Corners."

"I'm not calling my aunt." It would be early in London, but James always rose early. "I'm calling James."

His hazel eyes went flat. "Missing Lord Banning already?"

"If I didn't know better, I'd think you were jealous," she said sweetly. Of course he wasn't. He'd have to feel something other than reluctant lust and duty for him to be jealous. "May I use your phone or not?"

He picked up his bottle and gestured with the bottom of it. "It's right there on the wall, princess."

And he wasn't inclined to give her any privacy. That was more than apparent.

She went over to the phone that was, indeed, hanging on the wall just inside the doorway. Even though she knew Quinn had built the house within the past ten years, the phone was an old-fashioned thing with a long coiled cord tethering the receiver to the base. She plucked the receiver off the hook and punched out the numbers she knew by heart. After a number of clicks and burps, the line finally connected and James answered.

"It's Amelia," she greeted. She could feel Quinn's eyes boring holes in her backside. "How's your father?"

"Amelia! Where the bloody hell have you been? The media here is going mad. Not even your mother knew you were leaving. Are you all right?"

"I know. And I...I'm fine." She absently worked her finger into the center of the coiling phone cord. "You've got to issue a statement that we're not being married."

Even across the continents, she could hear his sigh. "You're back with that fellow, then."

She didn't know how she'd describe the situation with Quinn, but "back with" wouldn't be it. "I know what you'd hoped, Jimmy, but you've got to trust me. It's better to come from you. And the sooner the better." She looked over her shoulder when she heard a scrape on the floor.

Quinn had pushed back his chair and he walked past her, leaving the room.

"Ophelia's been hunting me around," she said into the phone, wanting to laugh a little hysterically because there was a gun rack containing several rifles attached to the wall above the doorway.

"If you hadn't given her something to find, she'd have had to give up," James returned. "You let her catch you kissing that man."

She exhaled, pressing her forehead to the cream-colored wall for a moment. "Just tell your father the truth," she said. "Tell him you're not in love with me. You never were!"

"Father doesn't care about love. He cares about bloodlines and he decided a year ago that yours was the right one."

"A marriage between us would be a disaster." She said the same thing she'd been telling him for months, ever since the whole idea of a union between them had come up. "You're in love with Astrid and I'm—"

"In love with your Horseback Hollow rancher," he finished and sighed again. "Father's condition is worse. He's home still. Refuses to go to hospital. Says there's no point alerting the vultures and he wants to die in his own bed."

She exhaled. "I'm so sorry, Jimmy." For all the earl's faults, he thought he knew what was best for his son. "How's your mum?"

"A rock, like always. Can you just hold on a few more days, Amelia? That's what the doctors have told us he has left. Days." He cleared his throat. "Once father is… gone…I'll issue a statement. You won't come out looking badly. I'll blame it on my increased duties or something. Mutual decision and all that."

She knew his request wasn't because of the Earldom he'd inherit. It was because, despite the problems between them, he wanted his father to die in peace, believing his son was on the track he'd laid.

"A few days," she agreed huskily.

"Thank you. You've been a good friend, Amelia." She heard him speaking to someone in muffled tones, then he came back. "I have to go. Take care of yourself. And look out for Ophelia Malone."

"I will." The line clicked, going dead and she unwound her fingers from the cord and replaced the receiver. She left the kitchen, thinking that Quinn would be in the living area. But he wasn't. Nor was he upstairs.

She went to the window and pulled up the blinds, looking out. She could see a light on inside the barn and she pushed her feet back into the sandals and went outside. The night air was balmy and quite a bit warmer than it had been six weeks earlier, and it smelled earthy and green.

He'd parked his pickup truck next to where she'd left his sister's van and she walked around them as she headed toward the barn. Unlike the house, which he'd built not so long ago, the barn looked like it had stood there for generations and in the dark now, with gold light spewing out the opened doorway, it looked almost medieval. She stepped inside.

Quinn, still shirtless, was stacking bales of hay against one wall.

She pulled in a soundless breath at the sight of him, entirely too aware of her lack of undergarments beneath the shirttails.

Her sandals scuffed the hard packed ground and he looked at her.

"I, um, I would have been much less nervous the other night had I known there were lights in here," she said, gesturing with her hand toward the row of industrial looking fixtures hanging high overhead.

He turned his back and tossed another bale into place. She wasn't sure why. To her, it looked as if he were just moving the stack from one spot to another.

She rubbed her damp palms down her thighs. "James will issue a statement in a few days."

He just kept working. "Why the wait?"

She hesitated and saw the way his lips twisted as if she'd done exactly what he expected.

Annoyed, she walked across the barn, feeling bits of straw and grit crunching beneath her shoes. "I told you James's father is in poor health. He's also been hiding

that fact because, in addition to being the Earl of Estingwood, he is head of Estingwood Mills."

"The textiles."

She wondered if he'd learned that courtesy of his sister, or if he'd found out on his own. "James has been running the company in his father's stead and fending off
a takeover bid by one of their competitors. If the earl's
health was made public it would endanger their hold.
Once James succeeds his father, that will no longer be
the case. The mill will be safe, as will the hundreds of
people it employs."

"Again, why the wait?" His tone was hard.

"The title is passed on at the earl's discretion during
his lifetime, or to his son upon his death which, according to James, sadly is fairly imminent. Before now, he's
insisted that James be married to an appropriate mate
before receiving the title and had been doing his best to
see that happened."

He tossed another hay bale and turned to her. "So the
old man was yanking Banning's strings."

"I suppose it might look that way." Sweat gleamed
across his broad chest and she looked away, shocked at
how badly she wanted to press her mouth against that
salty sheen. "Lord Banning's not a bad man. He just has
very traditional expectations where his family is concerned. You behave suitably. You marry suitably."

"Fine. The old man kicks the bucket in a few days. So
which is it going to be? Justice of the peace or a minister?"

Stymied, she just stared. "Your callousness aside, regardless of what announcements James makes, I'm still
not marrying you like this!"

He tugged off the worn leather gloves he'd been wearing and grabbed the shotgun she hadn't even noticed leaning against the wall.

"I've heard of shotgun weddings," she said, smiling weakly, "but this is taking it too literally."

"I've got a possum."

She blinked. "Excuse me?"

"A possum," he repeated with exaggerated care. "It's raiding my feed."

She grimaced. "And you want to shoot it?"

"I don't want to make it a pet," he drawled. "Ranching, princess." He dragged the leather gloves beneath her chin and flicked her hair behind her shoulder. "It's not fine linens and sidesaddles."

Fine linens had their place, but she was just as happy sitting in the kitchen with a peanut butter and jelly sandwich. "I've never once sat sidesaddle," she said with a cool smile. "Some of the Chesterfields are champion riders. I do know what manure smells like."

"You'll get even more familiar with it." He smiled, too, but it was fierce-looking and dangerous. "Along with the stench of branding and the mess of castrating. JP or minister?"

Her smile wilted. Her stomach lurched more alarmingly than ever before and she suddenly knew it wasn't going to go away so easily this time.

She whirled on her heel and barely made it outside of the barn before she leaned over and vomited right onto the dirt.

Quinn came up beside her.

"This is the most humiliating moment of my life," she managed miserably. "Please, *please* just leave me alone."

He carefully gathered her hair behind her shoulders. "Not a chance in hell, princess."

Chapter Nine

"There you are!" Jeanne Marie waved her hand from the window of her car and pulled up alongside Quinn's pickup truck. She got out quickly and strode across the gravel, a wide smile on her face.

Even though Amelia had gotten a few hours of actual sleep after tossing her cookies the night before, her stomach still felt rocky half a day later. She gingerly pushed out of the porch chair where she'd been sitting, soaking up the fresh afternoon air while Tanya, the teenager Quinn paid to clean his house, worked inside, and went down the three steps to greet her aunt. "I'm so sorry about the car."

"Oh." Jeanne Marie waved her hand. "These things happen." Then she laughed. "Well, not exactly *these* things. Nobody around here has ever had to hide out from the paparazzi before. But it turned out perfectly convenient for me. After church, Deke dropped me off in Vicker's Corners and was able to go back home rather than waiting around while I browsed the shops for you. Which made him a very happy camper." She gave Amelia a quick, squeezing hug. "And I'm glad that you didn't go to church this morning. That woman with the camera was there asking questions about you." She sniffed. "Not that *anyone* gave her the time of day."

"A fine churchlike attitude," Amelia said wryly, though she was glad the citizens of Horseback Hollow were showing some discretion, even if it was only because of loyalty to her aunt.

Jeanne Marie laughed again. "Now. Shall we discuss this *nothing* going on between you and Quinn?" She looked over Amelia's head at the ranch house behind her.

Amelia assumed her aunt didn't know about the internet photograph or she would have mentioned it. And she was glad for that. "Something is going on. I'm just—" she tugged at the red sundress that she'd pulled on yet again that morning "—not ready to say exactly what that is."

Her aunt's eyes narrowed a little, studying her. "At least you don't look quite like the whipped puppy that you did last week, so I'll give you a pass for now. Have you spoken with your mother?"

Amelia nodded. She'd called Josephine that morning and told her that the false engagement was over, though not the entire reason why. She wasn't ready to share her pregnancy with anyone other than Quinn, though she knew she'd need to sooner rather than later. She couldn't very well wait until she was round as a house. Her mum had been glad to hear about the pretense coming to an end, but Amelia wasn't so sure how she'd react to having another grandchild. Her brother Oliver had little Ollie already, but at least he'd been born *before* Oliver and his wife divorced.

Amelia could be married before her baby arrived, too, if she were willing to marry a man who didn't love her.

"She's really looking forward to coming for the Cantina's grand opening," Amelia told Jeanne Marie. "She hinted that she might be able to stay a few days longer than she expected."

"That would be marvelous." Jeanne turned back to her car and opened the back door. She pulled out a plastic shopping bag and handed it to Amelia. "Whatever doesn't fit can be returned," she said. "I made sure of that."

Amelia peeked inside the bag, seeing a couple T-shirts, a skirt and a package of white cotton underpants. "Perfect," she breathed. "Thank you so much, Aunt Jeanne." She carried the bag up onto the porch and set it on the wooden rocking chair and her aunt followed.

"Where's Quinn?"

"Off doing chores," she said vaguely. She wasn't entirely sure, because she'd been giving the man a wide berth since he'd insisted she take his bed the night before.

She'd been as wary of instigating another episode that led to torn panties as she was finding herself weakly admitting that she preferred a minister over a justice of the peace.

And her cheeks heated just thinking of panties and a minister in the same thought.

She realized her aunt was watching her thoughtfully, and quickly plucked the receipt for the purchases out of the bag. She drew a couple folded bills to cover the amount out of her sundress pocket and handed them to her aunt.

"All right now," Jeanne Marie said, tucking the cash in her own pocket. "Can you and Quinn come for dinner later? Christopher and his gal, Kinsley, will be there. You know he's opening a branch of the Fortune Foundation here."

Amelia smiled. "I know you're excited about that, but I suspect it's more because Christopher's moving back here from Red Rock."

"It was hard when he was gone," Jeanne Marie admitted. "When he left, there was such turmoil between him and Deke. All came to a head because of that darned money James Marshall wanted to give me." She let out a huge sigh as if she were dismissing all her bad thoughts and smiled again. "The important thing is our boy is coming home. Kinsley will be a beautiful wife for him and he's happier than he's ever been. He's finally found his niche with the Foundation."

"Tell me again how we're all connected to it?"

Jeanne Marie leaned against the porch rail, her expression bright. "Chris could tell you far more than I ever could since he works there, but it was founded in memory of Ryan Fortune who was a distant cousin of ours. They have all sorts of community programs and they help fund clinics and—oh, just bunches of good things for people. Having a branch in Horseback Hollow is going to mean so much. It'll be jobs, it'll be aid for those who need it—" Her eyes sparkled as she focused on Amelia's face. "Where was I? Oh, yes. Ryan's cousin William Fortune—he used to have a business in California—is married now to Lily, who was Ryan's widow and they're in Red Rock. I know it sounds scandalous, but it really wasn't. And then there are the Atlanta Fortunes—John Michael is our oldest brother, then James Marshall and your mama and me."

Amelia chuckled. "I need a map."

"I know." Jeanne Marie laughed merrily. "And they all have grown children and some of them are starting families, and it's just… Well, I hit the mother lode in family when I grew up with none except my adoptive parents."

Amelia smiled. It was hard not to let her aunt's delight infect her as well. "And to answer your question, yes, I'd love to join you all for dinner." She wasn't going to speak for Quinn.

Jeanne Marie glanced at her watch and tsked. "Speaking of, I've got to get the roasts in the oven or we'll be stuck eating at the Horseback Hollow Grill. Come by anytime. Food'll be on around six." She kissed Amelia's forehead and went back down the steps, briskly returning to her car.

Amelia watched her drive away, then jumped a little when Quinn appeared around the side of the house.

He was wearing a white T-shirt covered in sweat and dirt, multi-pocketed cargo shorts, heavy work boots and had a tool belt slung around his lean hips.

And he still needed a shave.

She felt heat gather inside her and dug her fingernails into her palms as a distraction.

It failed miserably, particularly when he spotted her hovering there on the front porch. It felt as if his gaze saw right through her dress to the sum total of nothing that she wore beneath it.

She pulled the strap that kept slipping off her shoulder back into place and snatched up the bag of clothes that Jeanne had delivered. "My aunt played personal shopper," she said.

The top rail surrounding the porch was chest high to him and he dropped his arm over it before tipping back the bill of the ball cap he wore. Throwing up in front of him may have been excruciatingly embarrassing, but it had served to break *some* of the tension.

At least he didn't have accusation clouding his eyes every time he looked at her.

"Guess you're wishing you'd have had her do that in the first place," he said

The bag crinkled in her fingers. "It would have been easier," she allowed. The memory of the way his T-shirt had torn the night before taunted her, and she focused instead on the dirt covering the one he was wearing now. "What, um, what have you been doing?"

He lifted his arm off the rail again and tilted his head. "Come on. I'll show you."

Surprised by the invitation, she squeezed the bag again. "I should, uh, probably change."

His lips quirked and he plucked his dirty shirt. "What for?"

She dragged her eyes away from his chest. "Aunt Jeanne invited us for dinner later."

"Nice of her. S'pose you want to go."

"Christopher will be there. I haven't seen him since Sawyer's wedding over New Year's. He's engaged now."

"I heard."

It wasn't an answer of whether *he* wanted to go. "So?"

He smiled faintly. "I generally don't turn down a meal cooked by someone else."

She didn't know if she was relieved or not. But she left the porch anyway.

He waited until she reached him before turning and heading away from the house and the barn and the antique-looking windmill beside it that stood motionless in the still summer air. They passed several pens, all empty and fenced in by round metal rails, following a path that was more dirt than gravel with a strip of grass growing down the center.

He kept to the dirt part and puffs of dust rose around his sturdy boots as he went and he eyed her when she moved to the grassier strip and shook one foot then the other to get out the grit that had worked its way into her sandals.

"These boots aren't made for walking," she said wryly.

"I could toss you over my shoulder," he deadpanned.

She flushed and continued walking. "I don't think so," she said primly.

He laughed softly.

Something in her stomach curled, and it was not morning sickness.

She stared ahead at the land. It seemed more covered in scrubby bushes and wild grasses than anything. And the horizon seemed to stretch forever. "Don't you have fences to pen in your cattle?"

"There's fence. Just can't see it from here."

"What about your horses?"

"We're getting there."

She moistened her lips. "It's, uh, it's very warm today, isn't it?"

He shot her an amused look. "Probably close to ninety. 'Bout average for this time of year. Be glad there's air-conditioning in the house. The one I grew up in didn't have it. Probably just as well that shack burned down. Made tearing down what was left easy."

"You told me back in April you were very young when it happened."

He shrugged. "Fifteen." The hammer hanging from his tool belt made a soft brushing sound against his khaki-colored cargos with each step he took and she realized her steps had slowed, intentionally or not, allowing her an excellent view of his backside.

She picked up her pace again, skipping a few times until she was level with him once more.

He didn't seem to notice.

"Same year my dad died," he added.

She studied his profile. The night of Toby's wedding, they'd talked about everything under the sun. But he hadn't told her that he'd been married. Or that the fire had happened the very same year he'd also lost his father. "That must have been devastating."

"You lost your dad, too."

"And it was horrible," she murmured, "but we still had a home."

"The Chesterfield estate," he drawled.

Her nerves prickled at his tone. "Yes."

He stopped. Propped his hands on his hips and stared out. "Lot different than this place, no doubt."

She continued forward a few steps and turned until she was facing him. "Yes," she agreed. "But, like the Rocking-U, it has been in the Chesterfield family for generations. I understand ancestral ties to one's land."

His lips twitched again.

"What?"

"Just listening to you talk, darlin'." He shook his head. "Kills me."

She huffed. "There is nothing wrong with the way I speak. *You* are the one who's all…all…drawly." Had he really called her *darlin'?*

"Drawly." His smile stretched. "That some grammatical term they taught you in those fancy schools you attended?" He shook his head again, then started walking once more, brushing past her since she was standing right in his path.

Wholly bemused, she turned and followed and shortly, the road began descending and she realized his house and his barn were positioned on the top of a ridge. "There's a river!"

"That's like calling a mosquito an eagle. It ain't a river, but it's a decent creek. The Rocking-U always had water and thank God it still does since Texas has been drying up around our ears for too damn long." He headed for the trees and the grass growing lush and thick alongside the glittering water.

She hurried after him. Several horses were grazing contentedly, barely even giving a flick of their tails at their approach. "It's beautiful down here."

He pointed at an enormous oak tree. "That is what I've been doing."

Confused, she walked toward the tree, feeling the coolness its shade provided. She had no idea how tall it was, but it was *huge,* with a trunk so wide not even Quinn could have circled it with his arms. "Pruning the tree?"

"Nah. Nature prunes that beast. Even lost a couple limbs during a lightning storm when I was a kid." He closed his hand around her upper arm and moved her around to one side, pointing up into the canopy above them. "You can still see the scar there."

She couldn't see anything because her entire being seemed focused on the feel of his fingers. "Right," she said faintly.

"Figured I'd build it back up."

"Hmm?"

He was still pointing and she mentally shook herself, looking. She saw the healed over slash on the trunk, nearly hidden among the leaves. And then she saw the pieces of lumber a few feet above that, forming the frame for a floor. "You're building a *tree house?*"

"Rebuilding." He let go of her, circling the base of the tree where she realized he'd fastened fresh boards for a ladder. "The one my dad put up was about like everything he put up." He looked wry. "Half-assed and half-done," he murmured. "But the guy never stopped trying."

Quinn's efforts were half-done, too, but that was the only comparison she could see. "I used to love climbing trees. I'd go as high as I could and feel like I was flying. My mother didn't agree. She used to send me to the nursery as punishment. Since I considered myself much too mature as a teen for that, it seemed a fate worse than death." She eagerly placed her foot on the first foothold.

"No way, princess. You're not climbing up there."

She huffed. "I'm perfectly capable!"

"You were perfectly capable of riding a bus all the way from Dallas, too, and look what state you were in once you got here."

He closed his hands around her hips and she went breathless, her nerves vibrating. But all he did was lift her away from the tree and set her feet on the thick grass. "You're pregnant," he added. "You're not going up there. The floor isn't close to being finished. What if you fell?"

Her lips parted. Why hadn't she realized that herself?

"But I want to go up there." She craned her head back and studied the tree house. It wasn't complete, of course, but when it was, she could tell it would be magnificent. "I think you have a bit of Peter Pan in you."

His expression sobered. "I grew up a long time ago."

"Why are you build—*re*building this now?"

He looked back up into the branches. "It was a good place to be when I was a kid."

She chewed the inside of her cheek, watching him. "And you think it'll be a good place for—"

"Our kid." His hazel gaze slid over her. "Yeah."

She was melting inside. There simply was no other description for it. "It'll be years before he—"

"Or she—"

"—is ready for that," she finished huskily.

"Yeah, well, it's also a good way to burn off some energy. And lately, I have a lot of—" He suddenly tugged the strap that had slipped from her shoulder back into place. "Energy."

Her mouth went dry and breathing became an effort. She stared up at him, feeling the warmth of him sliding around her, through her.

"What's this?" He dragged his finger along her collarbone where her skin was faintly irritated.

Her heart lurched. "I think it's, um—" She moistened her lips. "From your beard."

Something came and went in his eyes. He abruptly turned away and slapped his palm against the tree as he walked around it, heading toward the stream. "It'll be a good tree house," he said briskly.

She actually felt herself sway and was glad he was looking elsewhere. She hauled in a soundless breath and pressed her hand to her heart, willing it to calm. She'd blame the effect he had on her on pregnancy hormones if she could, but he'd had the same effect on her from the very beginning.

It's the reason she was pregnant in the first place.

"You coming?" He'd taken off his tool belt and sat down on the grass and was unlacing his boots. "Might as well cool off in the water for a few minutes."

She knew the water wasn't deep enough to swim; she could see right through the crystal clear water to the rocky bottom.

No skinny-dipping here.

She held back a nervous giggle at the shockingly disappointing thought and started toward him, only to trip a little when he tossed his cap aside and pulled his T-shirt over his head.

He glanced her way. "You all right?"

She balled her fists in the folds of the dress at her sides and smiled brightly. "Just shoe… Just caught my, uh, my shoe. In the grass."

He looked away but not before she saw his smile and she knew she was turning as red as the borrowed, too-oft-worn dress.

Pressing her lips together, she crossed the grass purposefully and sat down beside him. "Would serve you right if I whipped *my* dress over my head," she said crossly.

He laughed outright, tossing his T-shirt behind him. "Darlin', if you're expecting a protest from me, you're dreaming. Unless you took to stealing boxers from my drawer, I know what all you *don't* have on under there so feel free to get naked as a jaybird. No telephoto lens in the world strong enough to spot you out here."

Flushing even harder, she slid her feet out of the sandals and stuck them in the water. "Whoa!" She just as rapidly jerked them back. "Cold."

"Refreshing," he countered, and tugged off his boots and socks. Then he stood and stepped into the creek. The water swirled around his strong calves, only a few inches below the bottom of his long shorts. "Come on." He held out his hand and beckoned.

"What if I slip and *fall?*"

He smiled faintly. "I'm getting the sense you were pretty spoiled growing up. You're the baby of the lot, right?"

"Yes. And I was not spoiled," she grumbled and pushed to her feet, stepping gingerly into the water, bunching the dress in one hand above her knees.

After the initial shock, the water was possibly more refreshing than frigid, though she wasn't going to admit it. She was glad for his hand, though, because the rocks littering the bottom of the creek were smooth and slick.

"If you start to fall *here,*" he said calmly, "I would catch you." He squeezed her free hand.

And her heart squeezed right along with it.

They walked quite a distance and he kept to the center of the creek which she quickly discovered was far less rocky and far more sandy and she was able to let go of his hand and walk unaided.

When he finally stopped, he swept his arm from one side to the other. "All Rocking-U land right up to there." He pointed. "That water tower over there is the eastern border."

She could see the structure well off in the distance across an expanse of unyielding looking red earth peppered with stubby trees, wild grasses in every shade from olive to straw, and lazy-looking cattle in just as many hues from yellow to black with horns that looked deadly even from a distance. And the blue sky overhead went on and on, without a single cloud in sight.

In her mind's eye, she pictured him on horseback, riding out there. Open and free. "It's no wonder you came back," she breathed. "Built your house. Built your herd." She looked up to find him watching her.

"This life isn't for everyone."

She wasn't sure if he was warning her, or remembering. In April he'd told her how his mother had been happy to leave this place. "Maybe your mum couldn't bear staying after losing your dad."

"She wasn't the only one who didn't like it here." He touched her elbow but she didn't want to take the hint that it was time to turn back.

"You mean your ex-wife," she said instead. "She didn't go far," Amelia added boldly. "Jess told me she lives in Vicker's Corners."

His eyes were narrowed against the bright sun. "Might not seem like it to you, but there's a big difference between Horseback Hollow and Vicker's Corners."

Yes. Horseback Hollow possessed a single main street with a handful of businesses, though that was already changing with the coming Hollows Cantina and Fortune Foundation office. For now, Vicker's Corners, while still small and quaint, was considerably more developed.

"I like Horseback Hollow," she said evenly and sloshed her feet through the water, her toes squeezing into the sandy bottom as she started back the way they'd come.

For how long?

The question stuck in Quinn's head though he didn't

voice it. He watched her walking in front of him. She was holding up the dress, but the back of it had still dragged in the water below her knees, and it trailed behind her, dark and wet. Her hair was tangled around her shoulders that were turning pink from too much sun.

Right now, she might want to be there.

But she didn't know how hard his life could be. Didn't know that sometimes there could be as many bad years as good. That's what had driven his dad to his early grave.

Ahead of him, Amelia leaned down and swiped her hand through the water, then splashed it over her head.

She looked young. And carefree and ungodly sexy.

He blew out a harsh breath and leaned over, cupping water to throw over his own face. It was cold.

But it wasn't enough to douse the heat.

It wasn't ever going to be enough to do that.

Chapter Ten

"I was getting used to the red dress."

Amelia smiled ruefully as she entered the kitchen. Once they'd returned from their walk, Tanya was finished, so while Quinn paid the teenager, Amelia had gone upstairs to shower and change into the clothes that her aunt had procured for her while Quinn headed into the barn.

"This isn't going to fit me for long," she told him now and twitched the skirt that reached her ankles. The light gray knit hugging her hips before flaring out loosely had wide black stripes angled across it and was much livelier than her usual taste, but she'd toned it down with a white T-shirt with a deep scooped neck and snug cap sleeves. She knew the second she developed a bump, it would show. "The sundress was roomy enough to last awhile."

He was sprawled at the kitchen table wearing jeans

and a black T-shirt. He'd obviously used the downstairs bathroom to shower as well; his hair was wet and darker than ever. He'd also shaved.

She nearly told him she'd been getting used to the ridiculously sexy stubble.

"Not that it matters," she blathered on. "I'll have my own wardrobe soon enough."

He didn't move, but his gaze sharpened. "Is it being shipped here?"

She had the sense to realize she'd just stepped right into a minefield. All because she obviously couldn't think sensibly when she was near him.

"No," she said cautiously. "But I can't stay here forever."

"Here." His jaw canted slightly to one side for a moment. "Rocking-U here? Horseback Hollow here?" His eyes narrowed and he rose. It was like watching a cobra uncoil. "*United States* here?"

She stood her ground though the desire to back up was strong. "I do have responsibilities at home. I can't avoid them forever."

"I told you, I'm not letting you take my child away from here."

"Actually, to be specific," her tone cooled, "you said you weren't going to let another man raise your child."

He slowly pushed the chair back into the table. "What did I tell you about pulling that royal face with me?"

A jolt shot through her from her head to her toes.

She wisely took that step back after all, only to find her spine against the countertop. "I'm not pulling anything," she attempted reasonably. "I'm not saying I intend to return to the UK permanently."

"You want to go back, you can go. After we visit the justice of the peace."

"I don't have the choice of a minister anymore?" Her smart question fell flat and she exhaled. "At least you seem to believe me about James," she muttered.

He snorted. "Honey, I don't give a goddamn anymore if you were engaged to the man for real." He stepped up to her and pressed his palm flat against her abdomen. "The second you told me you're pregnant with *my* kid, that no longer mattered."

She braced herself against the shudder that rippled through her.

He angled his head toward hers. But all he did was speak softly next to her ear. "I may not be some fancy-pants future earl with money and connections, but there is no way on this earth I will let my child grow up without me." He suddenly straightened and dragged his palm upward until it was pressed flat between her breasts. Then he spread his fingers, rubbing them pointedly over the stab of her nipple through the white fabric. "I'll use every advantage I've got."

She couldn't very well deny the fact that she was weak where he was concerned. She'd slept with the man after only a few dances, something she'd never once been remotely tempted to do even though she'd been squired around by suitable matches since she was sixteen.

But neither could he hide the fact that he was equally aroused by her.

"Is that a threat?" she asked evenly. "Or a promise?"

His eyes darkened. "Don't pull an animal's tail, princess. Even the most patient one'll eventually turn on you."

The man who'd counted stars on a magical April

night with her was the same one who was building a tree house, and the same one who was standing here now, she reminded herself, and she lifted her chin.

"You already turned on me," she reminded boldly. "When I didn't immediately deny the engagement stories." Her heart was thundering so hard in her chest he couldn't fail to notice. "And whether that was wrong or not, you obviously didn't care about me as much as I'd believed, or you wouldn't have mistrusted me as easily as you did. And you *still* don't trust me, only this time it's because you think I'll take your child away from you."

Instead of trying to pull away, she leaned into him until her breasts were pressed against his chest, his hand caught between them. "I am not your ex-wife," she said evenly. "No matter what you thought, or still think for that matter, I didn't betray you with anyone. And I have no intention of keeping you from being this baby's father." She went onto her toes until her mouth was only inches from his. "Using sex," she whispered slowly, "still isn't going to make me agree to a loveless marriage."

Then, taking advantage of the fact that he'd gone still as a statue, she shimmied out from between him and the cabinet and deliberately lowered her gaze to the hard length of him clearly evident behind his zipper. "Now, are we going to my aunt's for dinner, or do you have something else in mind?"

His eyes narrowed until only a greenish-brown sliver showed. His jaw flexed. And for a breathless moment that seemed to last an eternity, she was afraid he would call her bluff.

But he finally moved and the sound of his boot against the tile floor seemed loud. "Be glad there's hardly any food in the fridge," he said, and pulled open the kitchen door, stomping outside.

Her shoulders sank and she brushed her hair behind her shoulders with shaking fingers.

"You waiting for a pumpkin carriage or something?" he called from outside.

She pressed her lips together, lifted her chin and joined him.

Deke and Jeanne Marie's place was so packed inside with people when Quinn and Amelia arrived that, at first, their entrance wasn't even noticed.

But then Piper, half crawling and half walking, latched on to Amelia's leg and she chuckled, picking up the little girl and stepping into the crowd of family, leaving Quinn behind.

He couldn't seem to drag his eyes away from her. The shirt she was wearing hugged her lithe torso like a lover, and the skirt was just as guilty around her narrow waist and slender hips. It hardly seemed possible that she was sheltering a baby inside her.

"You going to stand there and drool or do you want a beer?" Liam stood beside him looking amused.

Quinn took the beer bottle and twisted it open. He nodded toward Liam's younger brother, Christopher, who seemed to be holding court in the middle of the parlor, his arm around a pretty blonde. "Guess your family's going to be having a lot of weddings in the near future."

Julia, Liam's fiancée, tucked herself under Liam's arm. "We might have to draw dates out of a hat," she said humorously. But then she looked stricken, looking from Quinn's face to Amelia and back again.

He pretended not to notice.

All of Jeanne Marie and Deke's offspring were engaged except for Galen and Delaney. The oldest and the youngest. And Toby, as well. He and Angie had already gotten hitched.

He finally managed to pull his gaze away from the swell of Amelia's hips where she'd pulled the hem of her snug T-shirt over the long, flowing skirt. As a teenager, he'd always been more preoccupied with the front of a woman.

But the perfect sweep of Amelia's back, nipping into her waist then flaring out again was enough to bring him to his knees.

He chugged a little more beer. The front door was open, but the room was still too warm thanks to all the bodies. He asked the first thing he could think of. "Toby and Angie get their adoption approved yet?"

"Not yet." Almost absently, Liam brushed his lips against Julia's forehead as he looked over at his middle brother. He was sitting on the couch with Kylie on his knee, watching over the checker game that Brian and Justin were playing.

Quinn hadn't been around the Hemings kids all that much, but it was the quietest he'd ever seen them. "Never thought adoption proceedings took this long. Toby was already taking care of them for months before he filed."

"I don't think all adoptions have the challenges that Toby and Angie have had," Julia murmured.

"You'd think learning we're Fortune-connected would have made it easier," Liam added, even though Quinn could remember a time when his buddy hadn't been remotely thrilled about that particular connection. He'd been suspicious the Fortunes were invading Horseback Hollow, throwing their moneyed weight around and making too many changes. "Instead, the social worker's got some bug about the kids' safety *because* of it."

Christopher joined them, holding Kinsley's hand. "Yeah, well, there've been times over the years when being a Fortune was sort of like having a target painted on your chest. The stories I learned while I was in Red Rock—" He pursed his lips and blew. "Lot of history there. Some serious stuff."

"That was years ago," Liam dismissed.

"Tell that to Gabriella," Julia reminded. "She only came to Horseback Hollow to take care of her dad after his plane accident. And those anonymous letters to the post office, saying it wasn't an accident? That it was sabotage and the *Fortunes* were the target and not Mr. Mendoza at all?" She made a face. "You'd think people around here would be grateful your cousin Sawyer and his wife opened their flight school and charter service in Horseback Hollow instead of somewhere else. I'm sure the investigators will get to the bottom of things, but what a horrible business."

"You gonna let that scare you off of marrying me? My mama's a Fortune, too," Liam goaded lightly, clearly not afraid of any such thing.

Julia's eyebrows rose. "Oh, no," she assured. "You're not getting off the matrimonial hook, mister, any more than Jude is with Gabi."

Quinn sucked down half the beer. Everyone around him seemed as happy as pigs wallowing in mud. He wished he found it revolting.

Instead he just found it…enviable.

His gaze strayed back to Amelia. She was perched on the arm of her aunt's chair, still holding Piper on her lap and trying to untangle the kid's fingers from her long hair.

She couldn't be accustomed to gatherings like this. Nearly twenty people jammed into the front parlor of an old ranch house. The night they'd spent together she'd told him about the huge house where she'd grown up. The servants. The carefully orchestrated public functions.

What reason would be strong enough to keep her in Texas when she had *ancestral lands* and a family estate and God knew what else waiting for her back home?

It wasn't love.

She'd already said as much. No loveless marriages for her.

One small sliver of his mind kept listening to the conversation around him.

"Has Toby been able to find out who made that donation to him yet?" someone asked.

"Don't think he cares. That anonymous money'll go a long way to raising those kids. There's enough for college funds even."

"Must be nice," Quinn murmured. Generally speaking, there weren't too many packed into that parlor who'd been able to go to college at all. Or, like him, they'd had to scrimp and save and pray for every scholarship that came their way.

Not Amelia, though.

She'd gone to the finest schools that her family's money and position could buy.

Through no effort of his, her baby—his baby—would never want for anything.

He'd finished his beer and needing escape he excused himself, heading into the kitchen that was nearly as congested as the parlor. Jeanne Marie was at the center of things, giving out orders to her helpers with the precision of a master sergeant. She caught his eye with a smile as he continued right on through until he'd escaped out the back where Deke and Galen were hanging over the opened hood of an old pickup truck.

He joined them. "You still trying to keep this old thing running, eh?"

"Never get rid of something that still works." Deke's hands were covered in grease as he worked.

"*Works* being the operative word here," Galen said wryly. His hands weren't quite as filthy as his dad's but they were close. Quinn still shook the man's hand when he stuck it out, then propped his elbows on the side of the truck to watch them tinker.

"Guess that reporter girl has been making the rounds in town," Galen said. "Has she found her way out to the Rocking-U yet?"

Quinn grimaced. "Don't expect her to. She only knew to find Amelia here because it's no secret Jeanne's her aunt." He absently grabbed a hose that Deke couldn't quite reach and held it in place.

"What's going on between you two?" Deke pinned Quinn with a look. "Jeanne Marie's real fond of that gal. Do I need to ask your intentions?"

Galen laughed silently and lifted his hands up. "Good luck, bro. I'm outta here." He turned on his heel and strode away.

Deke's brows rose. "Well?"

"You don't need to ask," he said flatly.

"Recognize the side of my own house when I see it," the other man said.

He damned the heat rising in his neck. "Jeanne know about the photo, too?"

The other man's eyebrow rose. "Who d'ya think showed it to me?"

Quinn grimaced. "She's not engaged to that other guy."

"Heard that, too. Amelia 'fessed up on that score to Jeanne Marie right off," he added at Quinn's surprised look.

"She comes from a different world," Quinn said after a moment.

"Yup," Deke agreed, drawing out the word. He scratched his cheek, leaving behind a streak of black. "You worried about that?"

Quinn started to deny it but the older man's steady gaze wouldn't let him. "Yes, sir."

"Yeah." Deke's piercing gaze finally flicked past Quinn to look at the house behind them. "Jeanne Marie coulda bought anything her heart desired if she'd kept that money her brother wanted to give her. Clothes. New car. New furniture. Coulda travelled around the world a dozen times and stayed in the fanciest hotels there are. Hard to figure why a woman wouldn't care about those things but she says she doesn't." He pursed his lips for a second and scratched his cheek again.

"Deke Jones!"

They both looked back to see Jeanne Marie hanging out the screen door. "You get your hands outta that rust bucket and wash up for supper!"

Deke straightened and wiped his hands on a thin red rag he pulled from the back pocket of his jeans. He smiled a little at Quinn and tossed the rag to him. "All comes down to trust," he said and headed toward the house.

It was easy for Deke to trust Jeanne, Quinn thought,

wiping his hands and following. They'd been married longer than he'd been alive.

The first time he'd set eyes on Amelia had been six months ago. And he could count on his fingers how many actual days they'd spent together in the time since.

He pulled open the screen door and went inside. Jeanne Marie was smiling up into Deke's face, rubbing a dish towel over the black streak on the man's weathered cheek. "What am I going to do with you?" he heard her murmuring.

"Don't you want to be like them after forty years together?"

Startled, Quinn found Stacey and Colton standing behind him and he realized her words had been for her fiancé. He gave them a dry look.

"Considering the two of you can't look at each other without a besotted expression on your face, I'd say your chances are pretty good," Quinn said.

Colton chuckled and Stacey smirked, jerking her chin toward the doorway opening up to the dining room where Amelia was standing, talking to her cousin Jude and Gabriella. "Get out a mirror whenever you're looking *her* way," Stacey suggested smartly.

"Dishes, dishes," Jeanne Marie called out. "If you are standing in *this* kitchen, and your hands are empty, then grab something and take it into the dining room," she ordered. "Meal's not going to get onto the table by itself!"

Quinn grabbed the closest thing—a basket of fragrant, yeasty rolls—and escaped into the dining room.

They'd had to set up folding card tables on either end of the actual dining room table to accommodate everyone but they were covered with tablecloths. None of them matched. Some had colorful flowers stitched on the corners. Some didn't. But they were all crisply ironed and Quinn had a sudden memory of the way his mom had stood at an ironing board doing just the same thing before every Thanksgiving and every Christmas. The plates weren't all matching, either, nor were the glasses, but they were Jeanne's best.

She had all of her family home and it was obvious that she was celebrating that fact with all the finery she had.

She bustled in to the crowded room, pointing and directing and soon everyone's butt was in their designated chair. Deke at the head of the pushed-together tables. Jeanne Marie at the opposite.

Quinn and Amelia were situated midway down, next to each other. The chairs—another mixture of real dining room chairs, folding chairs and even the picnic table bench from outdoors—made for cozy seating, and there was barely two inches to spare between them and that, only because Amelia was as narrow and slender as she was.

Deke said the blessing and the dishes started passing. Quinn was relieved to see Amelia pile on the food for once. She was too thin as it was, and now she was eating for two. And fortunately, there were so many simultaneous conversations going on that nobody seemed to notice the fact that they were barely participating.

Her arm brushed his when they both reached for the cucumber salad at the same time and she quickly drew back. "Excuse me."

He grabbed the bowl and held it for her. "Go ahead."

Her gaze flicked over his, then away again. She scooped some of the salad onto her plate. "I feel like a glutton," she murmured as she handed him the handle of the serving spoon.

"It's about time you're finally eating more than a few bites." He dumped some of the cucumber and onion mixture on his plate. His mom made the same thing every time he visited her in Dallas. "Were you the one who gave that money to Toby for the kids?" He kept his voice low so only she would hear.

She blinked, looking genuinely surprised. "No." She looked across and down the tables. Toby's brood was surrounding one of the folding tables, with him and Angie on either side.

Supervising referees, he figured.

"Even if I'd wanted, *I* don't personally have that kind of money," she said quietly. "From what Aunt Jeanne told me, it was quite a large sum. It wasn't my mum, either. Aunt Jeanne asked her outright."

"How much money do you have?"

She let out a soft sound and gave him another quick look. "Why are you asking?"

He just eyed her. "Why do you think?"

Her soft lips compressed. "This is hardly the time, Quinn."

"Preacher or justice of the peace?" He waited a beat. "If you can't make up your mind, we could put it out for a vote right here. See what everyone else has to say."

Beneath the edge of the starchy white tablecloth, she dug her fingertips into his thigh. "You wouldn't dare."

He damned the heat collecting in his gut and closed his hand over her wrist, pushing her hand away. "Don't tempt me." The warning worked on all counts. Outing her pregnancy to the entire family all at once. Pulling her hand up to his fly despite sitting in the middle of that very family.

She twisted her wrist free. "I have a personal account

that I control," she said after a moment. "It allows me a comfortable existence."

"Comfortable's a subjective term."

"Comfortable," she repeated evenly. "Not extravagant. Then there are family trusts as well from both my mother's and my father's sides that my brothers and sister and I all come into at various ages. It's all managed and very secure, and frankly I haven't ever much thought about it." She speared a green bean with her fork and smiled tightly. "Does that answer your question?"

Enough to underline the differences between their worlds.

Even if he sold every acre of Rocking-U land, and every hoof that ran on it, he wouldn't be able to match the resources she had at her disposal.

Amelia suddenly grabbed his hand beneath the table and pressed it against her belly. "I am not taking him away," she murmured, sliding him a look. "Now, quit looking shocked and eat your supper."

Chapter Eleven

By the time they returned to the Rocking-U it was late.

Quinn parked where he usually did halfway between the house and the barn and turned off the engine. "Your aunt's a good cook," he said after a moment and felt the look Amelia gave him.

"Maybe she'll give me lessons," she said. "It'd be more useful than most of the other lessons I've had." She pushed open the door herself and got out, heading around the truck toward the house.

His neck prickled, though he didn't really know why and his eyes searched out the shadows of the barn and the windmill.

But there was nothing to see.

That's what came from studying every unfamiliar car he spotted. Every unfamiliar face. He was letting paranoia get the best of him.

He left the keys hanging in the ignition like always and caught up to her. "Let me turn on a light first." He went up the front steps and inside. Turned on the porch light and held the door open for her. His gaze roved over the porch. The two rocking chairs his mom had given him a few Christmases ago were in their usual spot. Nothing out of place.

Amelia slipped past him. "What's wrong?"

He rubbed the back of his neck and closed the door. "Nothing." He hit the wall switch again, turning on the light that hung over the small foyer.

"You should take the bed tonight." She folded her arms around herself. "It's your bed. And the sofa is too short for you."

The simple answer squatted like a fat elephant in the middle of the room.

Share the bed.

"I'll live." Once she was gone—and he was convinced she would be sooner or later—he'd need to get rid of the couch, too. Like the bed, it would be riddled with memories. "I'm gonna take a look around outside."

Amelia studied him for a moment. He was still rubbing the back of his neck. "Seriously, Quinn. What's wrong?"

"Nothing," he said again and went into the kitchen to retrieve the shotgun from the rack over the door. "Just want to check if that possum's rooting around again." He went outside before she could comment.

Sighing, Amelia wrapped her hand around the banister and dragged herself upstairs.

She'd never felt so tired in her life and wanted to blame it entirely on being pregnant. But feeling like she

was on one side of a war with Quinn on the other was
not helping.

She washed her face and cleaned her teeth—blessing
her aunt who'd had the forethought to include some basic
toiletries among the clothes—and pulled on the pinstriped
shirt of Quinn's again for something to sleep in. She bundled up the quilt—it was warm enough that a person didn't
need any covering but a sheet anyway—and carried it
downstairs, along with one of the bed pillows.

She didn't care what Quinn said. He was over six feet
tall and couldn't possibly stretch out comfortably on the
sofa. He needed his own sleep, too.

She spread the quilt out on the brown cushions, then
flopped down on it, bunching the pillow under the back
of her neck. She yawned hugely and pressed her hands
to her belly.

How long would it be before it was no longer flat?

Before her secret—*their* secret—was visible for anyone and everyone to see?

How long would it be before Quinn would trust her?

She flexed her toes against the arm at the end of the
sofa, and yawned again before turning on her side, cradling the pillow to her cheek, and slept.

She didn't even wake when Quinn came in a while
later and spotted her sleeping on the couch.

He hadn't found the possum, though the evidence it
had been there was obvious thanks to the trash can it
had upended and strewn across the ground in back of
the barn.

He'd cleaned up the mess, slammed the lid back on the
can and weighted it down again with a concrete block.
He should've remembered to warn Tanya to do the same
when she was cleaning.

Now, looking at Amelia's defiant possession of the couch, he debated the wisdom of carrying her upstairs and putting her in bed where she belonged.

Some remaining cells of common sense inside his brain laughed at that. There *was* no wisdom in carrying Amelia anywhere. He'd already proven that.

Sleeping in his own bed without her—now that she'd occupied it twice—held zero appeal but it was safer than the alternative.

He returned the shotgun to its rack, turned on the light over the stove so it wouldn't be completely dark if she woke, then turned off the foyer light and went upstairs.

Evidence of her was everywhere.

In the damp hand towel she'd folded neatly over the rack next to the sink

In the inexpensive clothes she'd folded and stacked on the top of his dresser in the bedroom.

For someone who'd grown up with servants at her beck and call, she was a whole lot neater than he was.

He flipped off the light and peeled out of his clothes, pitching them in the general direction of the hamper. It was stupid to be avoiding his own bed, but there was no denying that's what he was doing when he went to the window and fiddled with the blinds. Pulling them up. Letting them down. Tilting them until they were just so and then repeating the whole damn process again.

Finally, he gave up. He pulled on a pair of ancient sweatpants and went back downstairs and scooped Amelia off the couch.

She mumbled unintelligibly, turned her nose into his neck as trusting as a babe and slept on.

He carefully carried her upstairs and settled her on the center of his bed. It let out its faint, familiar squeak.

He started to back away, but she made a protesting sound and caught his arm.

Not asleep after all.

"I wish we could start over," she whispered.

So did he.

But he was afraid he wouldn't know how to do anything differently the second time around.

She pulled slightly on his arm. "Quinn."

He exhaled roughly and nudged her. "Move over."

She quickly wriggled over a few inches.

He lowered himself onto the mattress. "Come here." His voice was gruff.

She scooted back, until she was tucked against his side, her arm sneaking across his chest.

He stared into the dark. "We're getting a marriage license tomorrow." He wasn't sure if he said it to piss her off or to remind himself how adamantly opposed to marrying him she was.

She shifted slightly, but surprised him by not moving away. "Did your parents love each other?"

"What?"

"I always knew my parents loved each other," she whispered. "It was obvious in everything they did. He'd walk in a room and she'd light up. She'd smile at him when he was upset about something and place her hand on his chest, and everything would be all right." Her palm slid over his skin, leaving a trail of heat in its wake.

He steeled himself against it. "Get to the point, Amelia."

"That's what I want," she finished huskily. "The whole package. Can you give me that?"

His jaw was tight. "My father was illegitimate. I know that stuff doesn't matter these days, not like it used to.

But it mattered to his mother. It mattered to my old man. And it matters to me. You're having my kid. He's going to come into this world with my name. Nobody's going to steal that right from me. Not even you."

Pressing her hand against his chest, she levered herself up until she was half sitting. He could feel the weight of her gaze just as clearly as he could feel the long ends of her silky hair drifting over his ribs. "I'm not trying to steal anything, Quinn."

"Then prove it. Minister or justice of the peace?"

Her fingertips flexed against him with frustration, but only succeeded in sending heat through his veins.

"That's all marriage is to you? A means of legitimizing our baby? It has nothing to do with love?"

"Love's never been a friend of mine."

She was silent for so long he hoped she'd drop it.

But she didn't.

"If I said yes, what happens after the baby is born? What then? We live our separate lives? Passing the baby back and forth on what? Alternate weekends and holidays?"

His jaw went so tight it ached. "If that's the way you want it," he said stiffly. "You're used to a life that I won't ever be able to give you. Things I'll never be able to provide."

She was silent again for a long, long while before speaking, and when she did, her voice was husky. Careful. "I told you before that none of those…trappings… mattered to me. Did you…never believe me?"

"It's one thing to talk about it. It's another to actually live it."

Her fingers curled against him, then pulled away. "Be

glad I'm too exhausted to fight." She lay back down on the bed, her back to him.

Fighting was safer than making love.

He threw his arm over his eyes, grimly aware that there was no point in doing either.

And equally aware that it would only take a nudge, and he'd be ready for both.

He didn't expect to sleep, but eventually he did and when he woke it was only because his arm was going to sleep where it was tucked beneath Amelia's cheek and the rest of him was wide-awake thanks to her warm thigh tucked between his.

For a while, he stared at the sunlight streaking through the slats in the window blind. It had been years since he'd slept past dawn.

Then he carefully extricated himself, arms and legs, grabbed a pair of jeans and a shirt and left the room, quietly pulling the door closed after him.

He showered, letting the cold water pour over him, then pulled on his jeans and went downstairs. His mind consumed with the woman upstairs, he went through his usual routine by rote. Started water running through the coffeemaker. Dumped cereal into a bowl and ate it, standing in the back doorway, looking out over his land while it brewed. He had stock to check, horses to feed. Same things as every other day. Day in. Day out.

It was a life he loved. A life he knew he couldn't exchange for anything else, not unless he wanted his soul to shrivel up and die.

He heard a faint noise and looked back to see Amelia shuffling into the room, her eyes soft with sleep, her hair tangled and the shirt Jess had given him for his last birthday wrinkling around her bare thighs.

"Coffee smells so lovely." Her bare feet crossed the kitchen floor and she leaned over the coffeemaker, inhaling deeply.

The shirttails had climbed a few inches as she'd leaned against the counter and he dragged his eyes away from the smooth thighs and the tender spot behind her knees that he knew from experience was ticklish.

He knew his sister didn't drink any caffeine when she was pregnant. She also always gave up the margaritas she loved, and she'd complained often and long about that fact. Particularly since her husband, Mac, hadn't had to give up either.

"Sorry." He crossed the room and yanked the plug out of the outlet. The gurgling continued for only a moment before sputtering to a stop. "I'll quit making it."

She pushed her hair out of her face. Her gaze roved over his face. "You don't have to do that."

"Because you don't plan to be around?"

She tucked her hands behind her, leaning back against the counter. Unplugged and half-brewed or not, the scent of coffee filled the room. Same as her beauty shined through whether she was clothed in designer dresses or a man's wrinkled shirt.

"Because there's no reason for you to give up something you enjoy just because of me." She tucked her hair behind her ear. She wore no earrings. Didn't even have pierced ears at all. He knew, because he'd spent enough time kissing his way around her perfect earlobes to know there were no holes marring them. "There's no—" She broke off when there was a loud knocking on the front door.

He didn't want to answer it. Didn't much care who was out there, because he wasn't expecting anyone.

But she'd pressed her soft lips together and her lashes had swept down and whatever she'd been about to say was obviously going to go unsaid.

Particularly when the knocking continued, intrusively annoying and noisy as hell.

He left the kitchen and strode to the front door. "Cool your jets," he said, yanking it open.

He barely realized there were at least a half dozen people crammed onto his porch because of the cameras suddenly flashing and the microphone that was shoved close to his face.

"Do you have anything to say about your involvement with Amelia Chesterfield when her fiancé is reportedly sitting by his father's deathbed?"

Amelia suddenly raced up behind him and slammed the door shut on the words that just continued shouting through the wood.

Her eyes were huge in her face and she was visibly shaking. "How do they keep *finding* me?"

"I don't—" He broke off, because they were pounding on his door again and one of 'em—a guy with spiky hair and wide-lensed camera—was even peering through the unadorned front window.

Quinn grabbed Amelia's arm and steered her toward the staircase which was out of view from the window. "Stay."

"Don't aggravate them," she insisted, though she backed up several steps before sinking down onto one and hugging her arms around her knees. "It only makes them behave more outrageously." Her teeth were chattering and she'd gone white. "Did you tell anyone I was pregnant? Your sister? *Any*one? If that gets out—"

"I haven't told anyone," he said flatly.

The pounding and questions hadn't ceased and he stomped into the kitchen. He grabbed his shotgun off the rack above the doorway and loaded it with birdshot.

"What are you doing?"

She bolted to her feet and her huge eyes engulfed her entire face. They were the haunted eyes she'd had when she'd fainted in his barn.

And they made him want to string somebody up from the nearest tree.

"Getting rid of the vermin."

She shook her head rapidly. "Don't, Quinn. You have to ignore—"

"They're trespassing. Maybe they should've concerned themselves with aggravating *me*," he finished harshly.

Then he yanked open the door, greeting the intruders with the business end of the shotgun. "Get off my land."

Like cockroaches hit with the light, they scrambled off his porch, but only so far as to shield themselves.

He stepped out onto the wood porch and cocked the gun. It sounded satisfyingly loud and threatening. "Get."

"How long have you been sleeping with her?" some fool called out and Quinn swung the barrel toward the voice, finding the gel-haired guy who'd had the nerve to aim a camera through his front window.

"You're trespassing," he said coldly. "And I'm a real good shot." He met the man's eyes. At least he had the good sense to take a nervous step backward. "You want to test it out?"

"Lord Banning's a powerful man," someone else

yelled in a shrill voice. "You're not afraid of retribution for trying to steal his bride?"

He aimed beyond them where the vehicles they'd arrived in were parked every which way all over his gravel, and planted a load of shot exactly six inches from the front tire of the closest car. The noise was shockingly loud and gravel spewed, pinging against the car.

The roaches scattered even faster.

"Next one goes in the car!"

He had no intention of shooting anyone, but they didn't need to know that. There were seven of them, three men and four women, and he wondered which one, if any, was the Ophelia who'd plagued Amelia.

He eyed them each before cocking the gun again. *"Get off my land."*

They scrambled for the cars, nearly colliding among themselves as they poured into doors, gunned engines and spun tires.

Only when the last of them was nearly out of sight and the clouds of dust were starting to die did his grip on the gun relax.

And it was several minutes after that before the rest of him relaxed enough that he could go back inside the house.

He closed and locked the door, unloaded the rest of the birdshot and left the gun propped against the door.

Amelia was no longer huddled and hiding on the staircase.

She was pacing around the living room, looking agitated. "You couldn't have just *ignored* them? You had to go all...all Texas Ranger on them?" She sank down on the couch and clawed her fingers through her hair. "You may know ranching, Quinn, but I know the paparazzi.

There will be pictures of you on every network by the evening news." Just as fast as she'd sat, she shoved off the couch. "I have to phone my mother. Warn her." She laughed, sounding on the verge of hysteria, and her face was white. "If she hasn't already been treated to the same sorts of questions."

He caught her arms before she made it to the kitchen. "Calm down," he said. "You're going to make yourself sick again."

"Calm down?" She shook off his hands. "Would you feel calm if you knew you were causing nothing but embarrassment to the people you love?"

The words felt like blows.

"That's what involvement with me is. An embarrassment."

She looked stricken. "No! I never said that. I—I—" She broke off hugging her arms tightly around her. Her eyes turned wet. "I don't like being the cause of scandal. That's all."

"I don't believe you."

Her lips parted. She seemed to sway a little.

Then her face smoothed, though her eyes still gleamed, wet and glassy. "Of course you wouldn't," she said expressionlessly. "You haven't believed me about anything I've said yet. You just want to maneuver me into marriage to protect *your* interests. Same thing James wanted to do."

"You're gonna compare our baby to a textile company?"

She just shook her head, looking weary, and walked over to the stairs.

There was no phone upstairs. The only one inside the house hung on the wall in the kitchen.

"Thought you were calling your mother."

She didn't answer him. Just kept going up the stairs.

He was still standing there, rooted in place, when she came down a few minutes later.

She'd twisted her hair into a knot at the nape of her neck and pulled on a black T-shirt with the same striped skirt she'd worn the day before. The clothes were inexpensive. Hardly fancy. Yet she still managed to look untouchably elegant.

Her eyes didn't meet his. "If you'd be kind enough to drive me to Aunt Jeanne's, I would be grateful."

His hands curled into fists. "Aren't you afraid the vultures will be waiting?"

"I'm sure they will be." Her triangular chin lifted. "I'll handle it."

Unlike him.

She didn't say it.

But she didn't need to.

Chapter Twelve

"When is this going to die down?" Jeanne Marie fretted, and turned off the television and yet another gossipy tidbit on the morning news speculating about the most intimate details of Amelia's, Quinn's and James's lives while a silent video ran in the background showing Amelia, dressed only in Quinn's shirt slamming his front door shut on the photographers' cameras. "It's been a week already."

This time, the commentator—Amelia refused to call the vapid woman an actual reporter—had even dug up ancient stories about her mother's first marriage to Rhys Henry Hayes and even more ancient stories about King Edward's abdication of the throne for the woman he'd loved. Trying to manufacture out of thin air similarities where there were none at all.

"It's because of the funeral," Amelia said on a sigh.

James's father's funeral service had been held in London that morning and the timing made it a prime topic for the morning's national news shows. "The story will lose traction eventually, once something more interesting in the world comes along." She made a face. "Horrible of me to wish for a slew of natural disasters somewhere in the world."

Jeanne Marie squeezed her hand and sat down beside her. "Have you spoken with Quinn?"

Just the sound of his name caused a pang inside her and she shook her head.

Since he'd dropped her off at her aunt's home that dreadful morning a week ago, he hadn't tried to reach her once.

To be fair, she hadn't tried to speak with him, either. The only thing she'd been able to do was unleash threats of a lawsuit against the offenders who'd trespassed on the Rocking-U.

Only because her family had won the last suit they'd brought against the phone hackers a year ago had there been enough teeth behind the threat to encourage many of the pests to finally move on. Amelia wished that were true of Ophelia Malone, but the woman was still taking up residence at the B and B in Vicker's Corners. She was a freelancer, according to the sketchy information Molly had been able to unearth. She didn't have publishers keeping her on a leash they could retract when necessary.

"You're going to want to talk to Quinn sooner or later," her aunt said gently.

"I know." Amelia plucked the knee of her jeans. She just didn't know what she was going to say when she did. He'd had an up close and personal taste of the sort of things she'd had to deal with almost daily back in London.

Who would blame him for wanting no part of it?

For the past week, she'd lived in the seclusion of her aunt and uncle's house. Avoiding going outdoors in case there were still remaining telephoto lenses aimed their way. Avoiding all but the most necessary of phone calls. She'd even been careful not to find herself standing or sitting near windows.

It wasn't fair to burden her aunt and uncle with that sort of behavior, but they'd both been adamant that she remain with them. Even Amelia's mother had agreed that Amelia should stay in the States while she and James—now the Earl of Estingwood himself—dealt with the official media back home.

Everyone around her was taking care of her.

And she was heartily tired of it.

"I need a good solicitor," she said abruptly. "An attorney. Is there anyone you recommend? Someone you trust?"

Jeanne Marie looked thoughtful. "We haven't had a lot of need for attorneys, but Christopher once mentioned an attorney in Red Rock he knew through people at the Fortune Foundation. Or I can contact James Marshall. He surely has his own legal department at his company."

Amelia knew that JMF Financial was located in Georgia. Red Rock, though, was only four hundred or so miles away. "Would you mind calling Christopher for me?"

"Of course not." Jeanne Marie hesitated a moment. "Do you want me to call him right away?"

Now that Amelia had brought it up, she did.

In fact, she was suddenly impatient to do *something*.

"If you would. I need an appointment as soon as possible. Preferably before Mum arrives in a few days. I can
call Sawyer Fortune and arrange for a charter flight to
Red Rock." Until her latest escape from London and
subsequent trek making her way to Quinn's, she'd used
the flight service her cousin ran to get from Dallas to
Horseback Hollow the other times she'd visited.

"You're ready to go out in public?"

Amelia made a face. "No," she admitted. "But the longer I hide out, the harder it will get. And I'd rather get
used to it now than wait until the Cantina's grand opening this Friday." She followed her aunt into the kitchen
and found herself looking out one of the windows at the
picnic table and benches sitting on the grass.

But she wasn't really seeing them.

She was remembering dancing with Quinn out there
on a portable dance floor.

He'd put his arms around her, and even though it was
the first time he'd touched her, the first time they'd ever
done anything but see each other from a distance really,
she felt like she'd come home.

Her throat tightened and her nose burned with un-
shed tears.

Now, she feared that home was nothing more than a
fantasy. A silly girl's romantic longing.

"Pour another." Quinn tapped the empty shot glass sitting on the bar in front of him. At seven in the evening,
he hadn't expected the Two Moon Saloon to be entirely
empty, even on a Tuesday. But he'd been the only one
there for a good hour now.

He'd had no particular desire to go out at all, but Jess
had nagged him into meeting up at the Horseback Hol-

low Grill for burgers with her family. He'd been avoiding her, like he'd been avoiding most everyone else in town for the past week. But he'd been sick of his own company, and since the paparazzi that had plagued him for most of the week since the whole shotgun incident had finally gone off for greener pastures, he'd agreed.

And even though, for once, his sister had wisely showed the good sense not to bring up anything to do with Amelia or the fact that his image—shirtless and brandishing a shotgun like some kind of madman—was all over creation thanks to the magic of the worldwide web and nonstop news services, he'd been glad when the meal was over.

While his sister and brother-in-law had corralled their sons out the door to go home, he'd just gone next door to the saloon that was attached to the grill.

He was sick of his own company, true. But he also wasn't in the mood for socializing.

Nor was he in the mood to hide out inside his own damn house because everywhere he looked, he saw Amelia.

One night last week he'd even slept out on the porch.

Damned pathetic.

He eyed the pretty bartender who was pouring him another shot of bourbon. "You're new." She had brown hair and brown eyes, just as dark as Amelia's, and was slender as a reed, also like Amelia.

And he didn't feel the faintest jangle of interest.

"What's your name?"

"Annette."

"Why'd you come to Horseback Hollow, Annette?" He tossed back the drink and clenched his teeth against the burn that worked down his throat. "Nothing going on in this place." He set the shot glass down on the wood bar with a thud.

She swiped her white bar towel over the wood. "Wouldn't say that, Mr. Drummond," she countered.

He narrowed his eyes, studying her while his fingers turned the small glass in circles on the bar. "How'd you know my name?"

She smiled faintly. "How d'ya think? I have a television." She lifted the bottle. "Another?"

He moved his hand away and she filled the glass, then set the bottle on the counter behind her and returned to her polishing.

"It wasn't as bad as it looked," he muttered.

"It looked like a man trying to protect what's his," she said calmly. "What's so bad about that?"

He lifted the glass, studying the amber-colored contents. The deputy sheriff who'd come calling about the matter had agreed with that notion and it'd been plain from the ample video coverage that Quinn hadn't tried shooting at anyone.

But that didn't change things for Quinn.

Amelia *wasn't* his. She'd made it plain she didn't want to be his. The only thing that *was* his was the baby she carried.

His chest tightened and hating the feeling, he put the glass to his lips. The liquor burned again, but brought no relief. No blurring of reality. No softening of the facts.

Amelia came from one world. He came from another.

"Send us over a round of margaritas and a couple a' waters, would you, darlin'?"

He realized that a group of people were coming in through the street-side entrance and glanced over to see Sawyer and Laurel Fortune coming in along with a few of the folks he knew were working for them over at their charter service. He lifted his hand, returning the greeting they sent him, then turned back to his solitude.

He quickly realized, though, that Sawyer and his group weren't cooperating with that notion, insisting that he join them as well.

Quinn had no desire to be among the Fortunes, but Orlando Mendoza was with them, and his daughter Gabriella was marrying Jude Fortune Jones, whom he'd known all his life. The new bartender was noisily scooping ice into margarita glasses with one hand and pouring tequila into a pitcher with the other so he reluctantly left his empty shot glass and moved over to their table.

"Y'all look like you're celebrating," he greeted.

"We are." Sawyer gestured to his companions. "You know everyone here, don't you, Quinn?"

"Some, more 'n others." Quinn gave a general nod, sticking out his hand to Orlando and the older man shook it. "Glad to see you're up on your feet again."

The pilot grinned. "Needed to if I'm going to be able to walk Gabi down the aisle and give her away when she and Jude get married. Glad to get the casts off at last. Things were itching me like crazy."

The bartender delivered the tray of waters and ice-filled, salt-rimmed glasses and set the margarita pitcher in the middle of the table before returning behind the bar.

"Broke my arm once." Quinn shook his head when Laurel started pouring out drinks and offered him one. "Couldn't stand the cast so bad I ended up cutting it off myself a week before the doctor said. Are you cleared for flying again?"

The salt-and-pepper-haired man nodded, looking relieved.

"That's what we're celebrating," Sawyer said. "That and the fact that the investigators have finally closed the case about the accident." He held up one of the glasses and waited while the others did the same. "No sabotage. No pilot error—" he gave a nod toward Orlando at that "—and no maintenance insufficiencies."

"So what happened?"

"Aircraft design," Orlando supplied.

"The plane's been recalled," Laurel added. She clinked her glass against her husband's and the others. "Just wish the manufacturer could have caught their error before people got hurt."

"Manufacturer is wishing the same thing," Sawyer said. "Not saying we're planning to, but it's a given that someone will bring lawsuits against them about it all."

Laurel looked at Quinn. "Speaking of lawsuits, is that what Amelia's planning?"

His skin prickled. "What do you mean?"

Orlando sat forward. He was the only one around the table drinking only water. "I flew Miss Chesterfield to Red Rock this morning. She was meeting with one of my cousin Luis's boys. Rafe's a lawyer over there. Told her she could've just waited until this weekend to talk to him, since he'll be in town for the opening of his brother's restaurant, but she was anxious to go now. I'll be picking her up again tomorrow afternoon."

Was she just adding on another layer of protection against more media invasions like they suspected? Or was she really laying the groundwork to keep his child away from him? "You'd have to ask Amelia what she's planning," he said abruptly and started backing away from the table. "I'll leave y'all to your celebrating. Congratulations." Not leaving them an opportunity to respond, he peeled a few bills off his wallet and dropped them on the bar.

Annette tucked the bills in the cash register. "You want some coffee before you head out, Mr. Drummond?"

He had never felt more stone-cold sober but to keep her satisfied and quiet about it, he told her to give him one to go, and then he went on his way, a foam cup of hot coffee in his hand. He was parked on the other side of the grill, so instead of leaving on the street side, he walked through the doorway separating the bar from the grill.

Only a few people were still sitting at the old-fashioned tables positioned around the ancient tiled floor. The little game room where his nephews always fought over playing the race car game was silent, the light turned off.

The coffee smelled bitter, like it was a day old by now, and his first sip confirmed it tasted that way, too.

The coffee still reminded him of Amelia.

He dumped the cup in the trash can next to the pay phone that hung in one corner of the diner and pulled out the thick phone book that was stuffed on the shelf below the phone. He paged through the yellow pages, finding the section he wanted. He tore out the first page of law firm listings, pushed the book back on the shelf and left.

Amelia paged through the agreement that Rafe Mendoza had sent with her and read through the paragraphs yet again. The attorney had tried talking her out of some of the stipulations that she'd wanted included, but she'd been adamant.

"You may change your mind," he'd argued. "You want to stay in Texas now, but there's no reason to sign away your choice of moving away later on." His dark eyes had been kind. "You're only twenty-three, Amelia. At least think about it."

"I won't change my mind," she'd told him. But she'd agreed to give it a day and had picked up the agreement that afternoon on her way to the Red Rock regional airport for her return charter to Horseback Hollow.

She closed the document and tucked it back inside the folder Rafe's secretary had provided with the custody agreement and then she climbed out of her aunt's car that she'd borrowed and walked past Quinn's truck toward the house.

It was the middle of the afternoon, so she wasn't particularly surprised when he didn't answer her knock. When she tried the knob and found it locked, though, she was.

A lesson learned from the paparazzi, she assumed with a pang of guilt. Once your privacy was invaded, it was hard to trust that it wouldn't happen again.

Carrying the folder with her, she walked down to the barn and found it empty. There were six horses standing around in the corral next to the barn, their long tails swishing against the heat of the day. She held out her palm over the metal rail and the nearest one nuzzled her palm, obviously looking for a tidbit.

"Sorry, girl," she murmured and rubbed her hand down the horse's white blaze. "Next time I'll bring a treat."

If she'd be allowed a next time.

Following the road with the grassy strip in the center, she kept walking until it began to dip and she could see Quinn's tree house tree in the distance. When she drew closer, she heard the distinctive beat of a hammer.

And even though she'd been gearing herself up for

the past twenty-four hours to see him, her mouth still went dry and her chest tightened.

She tucked the folder under her arm and smoothed back a strand of hair that had worked free from the chignon at her nape. She aimed toward the tree while the hammering grew louder and more distinct, and soon she was standing beneath the shady leaves.

She moved around to where the footholds were and tapped the lowest one with the toe of the Castleton cowboy boots she'd purchased while killing time in Red Rock. Since her whereabouts weren't remotely a secret, she'd also visited Charlene's boutique with her credit card, and stocked up on clothing, including a black silk dress for the Cantina's grand opening. She'd also had lunch with her cousin Wyatt and his wife, Sarah-Jane. And even though Amelia had found Red Rock surprisingly sophisticated and quite lovely, she knew she still preferred the rugged, much smaller Horseback Hollow.

"Fancy boots. You buy them before or after meeting up with that Red Rock lawyer?"

She looked from the detailed stitching over her toe up into the leaves and met Quinn's hazel gaze. "As usual, news is traveling at the speed of light." She ran her palm over the rough tree bark. "Can you come down?"

He swung down from the floor he was constructing and climbed down several footholds before jumping the rest of the way to the ground. He straightened and looked down at her, his expression unreadable. "You going to tell me anything I want to know?"

"I don't know," she said huskily and handed him the folder. "Considering everything that happened last week, you might not welcome anything to do with me."

His lips thinned and he made no attempt to open the

folder. "A hundred reporters camped out on my front porch wouldn't change the fact that you're pregnant with my baby."

"They didn't cause you any more problems, did they?" She tucked her hands in the front pockets of the narrow, black trousers she'd bought at the boutique. There'd been a small selection of delightful maternity clothes, though she hadn't had the nerve to purchase any. Not with the other customers there who'd watched her, somewhat agog, as she'd shopped.

"Guess you'd have seen it on the news if they had." His tone was flat. He gestured with the folder. "You bring this here to settle the fact I can't prevent you from going back to England? Already found that out myself from three different attorneys over in Lubbock."

A pang drove through her. "If that's what you think, you really don't know me at all."

"Saw your earl's press conference."

"Evidently not," she countered, "if you still have the impression that James is *my* anything."

"'Amelia Fortune Chesterfield's support during this difficult time has been steadfast,'" Quinn said, quoting almost verbatim the brief statement that James's staff had released. "'And though we are not betrothed,'" his lips twisted, "'we remain loyal friends.' Didn't exactly say you were never engaged to marry him in the first place."

"People in James's positions don't explain," she said. "They don't complain to the media and they never lend credence to speculation by commenting on anything that smacks of scandal. Which is not to say they won't use the media if it serves their purposes. James's father certainly proved that." She exhaled. "I didn't come here to talk about him." She nodded toward the folder. "I came here to give you that."

Looking even more grim, he flipped open the folder.

His eyes narrowed as he read, his frown coming and going as he flipped slowly through the pages.

"It's a shared custody agreement." Of course he could read for himself what it was, but his silence was more than she could bear. "With stipulations that the baby will bear your name and be raised here in Horseback Hollow."

He finally looked at her. "Why would you do this?"

She lifted her chin. "Why wouldn't I? I've told you more than once I don't want that life." She unconsciously pressed her hand to her abdomen. "I didn't want it for myself and I don't want it for our child. I don't know how else to prove it to you."

"You've already signed it."

"Yes. Duly witnessed by the appropriate individuals." She pressed her tongue to the back of her teeth, hunting for strength. "Go back to your Lubbock attorneys and have them review it. They'll tell you it's exceedingly fair. And once you sign it, there'll be no need for a justice of the peace or a minister."

His jaw canted to one side. He closed the folder and tapped it against the side of his jean-clad thigh. "You *really* don't want to marry me."

"No." She suddenly jabbed her forefinger into his unyielding chest. "*You* really don't want to marry *me.* You're stuck in the past with the one who did betray you. The only reason you want to marry me is to ensure the baby has your name." She gestured at the folder. "Well, happy tidings. Sign it and neither one of us need worry about that a moment longer."

"I don't have a pen."

She felt like her heart was turning to dust inside her chest. She looked up into the leaves above their heads.

He'd build a magical place for their child.

But he wouldn't let himself believe in love.

At least not love with *her*.

"I'm sure you'll find one somewhere," she managed. "You can send me a copy of the agreement once you do."

"And then?"

"And then I guess we'll figure out what to do next." She lifted her hands, feeling helpless. "At least things can't possibly get any worse."

Then she turned on her boot heel and walked away.

Chapter Thirteen

But Amelia was wrong.

Things could get worse.

And they did.

"She is *pregnant?*" Jess's screech could have been heard around the world.

It was certainly enough to wake Quinn from his stupor where he was sprawled on his couch, and he bolted upright, rubbing his hands down his face as his sister stormed into his house brandishing a magazine over her head.

"What?"

She slapped the glossy tabloid on top of Amelia's custody papers that were sitting on the coffee table and picked up the bottle of whiskey he'd tried working his way through the day after Amelia had left him. "Oh, my God." She was clearly disgusted. "You're drunk."

"No. I was drunk." He pinched the bridge of his nose. "Now the term would be *hungover.* So if you'd take your hysterics and leave me the hell alone, I'd appreciate it. And give me back your key to my front door while you're at it."

She sat down on the coffee table in front of him and caught his chin in her hand, giving him a look that was unreasonably similar to their mother's. "You're a grown man who's going to be a father," she tsked. "Start acting like it!"

He brushed her hand aside. The fact that she knew about Amelia's pregnancy was seeping into his throbbing brain. "How'd you find out?"

She shifted and tugged the magazine from under her hip and waved it in front of his face. "Same way everyone on the planet did."

He snatched it from her and stared at the cover of the international tabloid. It contained only a single photograph of a positive pregnancy test stick, with a question mark and the words The Real Cause Behind the End of Jamelia? superimposed over the top.

Disgusted, he threw it aside and shoved off the couch. "Why the *hell* won't everyone just leave her alone!"

Jess narrowed her eyes and studied him. "It's true, then. Amelia is pregnant."

"Whatever happened to people's right to privacy?"

"Privacy's an illusion," Jess said. "I think somebody famous said that. Or the government did. Or—" She shook her head. "Doesn't matter. I'm asking you, Quinn. Is that story true?"

He raked his fingers through his hair. "I didn't read the damn story."

She made a face and straightened. She tilted her head slightly, studying him. "Quinn."

"Yes," he said grudgingly.

"Is it yours?" She quickly lifted her hands peaceably when he glared at her. "I'm just asking!"

"It's mine."

"How do you know? I mean, a week and a half ago, she was supposedly engaged to marry Lord Banning."

"She wouldn't lie to me." His head was clanging and he headed blindly into the kitchen. There was still coffee in the pot from the day before and he dumped it in a mug and drank it cold and stale. Amelia wouldn't lie, yet how many times had he accused her of it, anyway?

Jess had followed him into the kitchen. Her eyes were concerned. "What are you going to do?"

"Not much I can do," he said wearily. "She won't marry me."

His sister's eyebrows disappeared up her forehead. "You, Mr. Never-Get-Married-Again, *proposed?*"

"She refused." More than once and the memory of each time felt engraved on his throbbing brain. He turned on the faucet and stuck his head under the cold water.

When he came up for air, Jess stuck a dish towel in his hand. "Did you tell her you loved her?"

He jerked. "This isn't above love."

"Oh, Quinn." Jess shook her head, looking disgusted all over again. "When it comes to a woman, particularly a pregnant woman, everything is *always* about love."

"Maybe for you." He ran the towel over his face and tossed it aside. "And Mac." His brother-in-law had grown up in Vicker's Corners. "You two've been together since high school. You're the same. Hell, you even teach together at the same school!"

"So? Carrie and you had the same backgrounds, too, and that wasn't exactly a stellar success!"

"There's no comparison between Carrie and Amelia." His voice was abrupt. Carrie had never made him feel half the emotion that Amelia did.

She gave him a look. "Well, duh. It's about time you realized it."

He shoved his fingers through his hair, slicking the wet strands back from his face. He hadn't been talking about the other similarities, despite what his sister obviously thought. "Where'd you see the tabloid?"

"It's front and center on the racks in the Superette."

He exhaled. "This'll send her off the rails." He reached for his Resistol and headed for the door, but his sister grabbed the back of his shirt.

"Hold on there, Romeo," she drawled. "Might want to at least brush your teeth before you go after the fair maiden."

He yanked away. "You're a pain in the ass, you know that?"

"Yeah." She patted his cheek like he was ten. "But nobody loves you like I do. And I kinda fancy the idea of getting some blue blood in our family gene pool." Then she shoved his shoulders, pushing him toward the living room. "And clean clothes wouldn't go amiss, either."

The fact that she was right annoyed the life out of him. He headed toward the steps. "I don't know how Mac puts up with you."

"He loves me," she assured blithely and patted her flat belly. "Which is why we're trying for a girl again." Her eyes were revoltingly merry. "According to that tabloid, your baby and mine will be born right around the same time next January."

Quinn squinted. "You're pregnant, too? Again?"

Jess smiled. "Isn't life grand?"

Amelia stared at the cover of the magazine that her mother had presented the second she'd walked into Aunt Jeanne's house.

The pregnancy stick in the picture was not the same brand Amelia had used either time, but some portion of her mind knew that it didn't really matter.

The message was still the same.

"Well?" Josephine propped her hands on her slender hips and raised her eyebrows. She'd arrived a full day earlier than expected because of the dreadful magazine, and her blue eyes were steely. "Is it true?"

Amelia rubbed her palms down the thighs of her cropped slacks and nodded. Then she gestured at the cover. "I don't know how they found out. Were you contacted for a comment?"

Her mother just gave her a look. "As if we would have offered one to such a disreputable publication? My senior social secretary gave me a copy when no one else on my staff seemed to have the nerve to show it to me." She sighed and sat down on the couch next to her. They were alone in the house only because Jeanne Marie and Deke had gone to see Toby and his crew for a while. "We'll have to release something officially at some point, but I wanted to see you for myself, first. Darling, why didn't you *tell* me?"

Amelia's throat tightened. "I was going to. I just wanted to clean up some of the mess I made after the whole Jamelia business exploded."

Her mother closed her cool hands around Amelia's

and squeezed gently. "Are you feeling all right? I hate knowing you've been dealing with this all on your own."

"It's about time I finally dealt with something on my own," she murmured thickly. She met her mother's eyes. "I'm sorry I've done such a poor job of it."

"Amelia." Josephine sighed. "I love you. The only thing I am concerned about is that you're happy. I knew you weren't happy in London even before this ridiculous betrothal business with James came about." She tucked Amelia's hair behind her ear the same way she'd been doing since Amelia was a tot. "Had you confided in me, perhaps we could have prevented some of this outrageous publicity."

Amelia chewed the inside of her cheek. "Molly knew," she whispered. "She's the only one other than Quinn who knew I was pregnant."

Josephine's expression cooled. "*My* Molly?"

Amelia nodded miserably. "I don't want to believe she would have said something, but who else was there?" James hadn't known she was returning to Horseback Hollow, much less that she was pregnant with Quinn's baby, so the information couldn't have come from his quarter.

"And your Quinn," Josephine said gently. "He wouldn't have—"

"No." Amelia shook her head, adamant. He might have threatened that one time to out her pregnancy during Jeanne Marie's and Deke's family dinner, but he never would have gone beyond that. Certainly not to the very type of strangers he'd threatened off the Rocking-U. She reached for the hateful tabloid and flipped it open to the main article that turned out to be only a few paragraphs, accompanied by two pages of photographs obviously meant to chronicle the rise and fall of her and James's supposed romance.

There were also a startling number of images of Quinn that had to have taken some effort to collect. One was even of him as a solemn boy, standing next to an easily recognizable Jess and a woman she could only assume was their mother, given the casket they were looking at. She trailed her fingertip over his young face then made herself look at the text.

"'Sources close to Amelia Fortune Chesterfield and her baby daddy, Horseback Hollow Homewrecker Quinn Drummond, confirm that the stick turned a big, positive blue,'" she read aloud. Then she made a face and flipped the magazine closed, tossing it aside. "Ophelia Malone finally gets her big payday," she muttered. "And Quinn didn't do a thing to deserve her trashy comments."

"I'll have to deal with Molly." Josephine rose and paced around the parlor. Her silver hair was immaculately coiffed and despite her day of travel, she looked impeccable in a black and white pantsuit. "I'll have Jensen look into her finances." She referred to Amelia's third-eldest brother. "If there's proof she was compensated, we can take her to court since it's a violation of her confidentiality agreement. Jensen knows how to be discreet."

"Whereas I don't."

Her mother sent her an exasperated look. "Stop reading between the lines, Amelia. I wasn't implying any such thing."

"I want it all to go away." She twisted her hands together. "You always said if we ignored rumors and gossip, they'll die of starvation."

"Well, that used to be truer than it is nowadays. People don't depend on news to come from reputable newspapers and the nightly news." She sighed. "It's become quite exhausting in the past few years." She brushed her hand down her silk sleeve. "Either that, or I'm just getting too old to want to put up with it."

"You're not old, Mum."

Josephine's lips twisted a little. "I'm sixty-two, darling. I've divorced one husband and buried another. Now I'm going to be a grandmamma again, and maybe I would like to slow down my schedule and enjoy that more this time around than I was able to do with Oliver Junior."

She sat down beside Amelia again and hugged her arm around her shoulders. "I don't want you worrying about Molly. She's my secretary and I'll see that matter is handled appropriately. In the meantime, you can tell me more about your Mr. Drummond."

Amelia's nose burned. "Quinn is anything but *my* Mr. Drummond," she said thickly.

"Do you love him?"

Amelia nodded. "I knew he was special the first time I saw him. When we were here for Sawyer's wedding. Remember?"

"I remember."

"I couldn't get him out of my head. When I came for Toby's wedding, I made the excuse that I just wanted some space from James pressuring me about marrying, but I had to see Quinn again."

Her mother smiled softly. She rested her head against Amelia's. "I felt the same way the first time I saw your father."

Tears collected and squeezed out her eyes. "He'd be so ashamed of me," Amelia whispered.

Josephine tsked. "He'd have been ready to put Quinn's head on a spike," she allowed, gently teasing. "Because you were his baby girl. But then he'd have come to his senses, the way Simon always did, and start campaigning for the baby to be named after him."

Amelia smiled through her tears. "Yes." She wrapped her arms around her mother's neck. "Yes, he would have. I love you, Mum."

"I love you too, darling." Josephine squeezed her back. "And everything is going to be all right. You'll see."

They both heard the crunch of tires from outside and Josephine stood again while Amelia swiped her cheeks. "Sounds like my sister and Deke are back already. I hope they have good news finally about Toby and Angie's adoption."

Only it quickly became apparent that it wasn't Amelia's aunt and uncle, when her mother looked out the window. "Oh, my." She turned and eyed Amelia for a moment, then picked up her suitcase that was still sitting near the front door where she'd left it upon arriving. "I'm going to go upstairs and get settled."

Amelia started to tell her that she was using the room her mother was accustomed to, but broke off when she spotted Quinn crossing in front of the window.

A moment later, he was pounding on the front door. "Open up, Amelia," he said loudly. "I saw you sitting in there."

She nervously tucked her hair behind her ears and moved to the door, waiting until her mother was gone before tugging it open.

His hazel eyes were bloodshot and they raked over her face. "Was that your mother I saw?"

She nodded. "She's a day earlier than I expected," she said inanely.

He brushed past her, entering the house even though she hadn't exactly issued an invitation. "Are you all right?"

He was looking at the magazine lying on the coffee table.

Dismay sank through her belly and her shoulders bowed. "You've seen it." She could tell by the lack of shock on his face.

"Jess brought a copy by."

"I'm sorry," she said huskily. "If I would have just stayed in London, you would never have been dragged into any of this."

"And I wouldn't know you're having my baby." His voice was flat. "Regretting the papers you had drawn up already?"

"No!" She lifted her hands. "I don't know what else to do, Quinn." She waved at the tabloid. "Thanks to that nastiness, every last bit of privacy we might have had is lost."

"I don't give a rip who knows about us," he said impatiently. "But I also don't want you working yourself up into a state over it."

Her lips parted. "You were worried about me?"

His gaze raked over her again. "That's my baby you're carrying. You think I want anything endangering that?"

She pressed her lips together, her hopes sinking yet again. Of course his concern would be for the baby. "As you can see, I'm fine."

"Suppose your mother wants to take you back."

"Actually, no." Her voice cooled even more. "I've

made it more than clear to you that I intend to remain in Horseback Hollow and raise our child here where he—"

"She—"

"—will have both parents in his life." She stepped closer to him, looking up into his face. She'd seen him just the day before when she'd left him the agreement, but he looked like he hadn't slept in weeks. "Why are you so insistent that the baby is a girl?"

He picked up the magazine and flipped it open to the article. "Got enough boys in the family," he muttered. "Little girl would be a change of pace."

Her throat tightened. How easy it was to imagine him holding a baby girl. Their child would succeed in wrapping him around a tiny finger.

He would love the baby. He just wouldn't love her.

She rubbed her damp palms down her thighs again, banishing the image before she started crying like a baby herself. "Did you consult an attorney about the, uh, the agreement?"

He tossed the magazine down again. "I don't need to consult anyone. And I haven't signed it."

"Why not? It gives you everything you wanted!"

His lips twisted. "You'd think."

Her head felt light in a way that it hadn't since she'd first arrived in Horseback Hollow. She thought about how many times he'd seemed stuck on the idea that she'd be happier back in London. "Do you *want* me to go back to London?"

His brows pulled together. "No."

Her hands lifted, palms upward. "Then what, Quinn?"

"I want to know I can protect you from crap like that!" He gestured at the magazine. "And I know I can't."

Her heart squeezed and she had to remind herself that

feeling protective wasn't the same thing as feeling love. "I wanted to protect you, too," she said huskily. "And I didn't do a good job of it, either. I confided in Molly—" She broke off and shook her head. "I shouldn't have trusted anyone but my own family. And you."

"You know for sure it was her?"

"Who else?" She sat down on the arm of the couch and held her arms tightly around her chest. "You said nobody saw you buy the test kit I used here. I know you didn't tell anyone. That just leaves Molly. You think you trust someone and they betray—" She broke off. "I don't want to think about it anymore." She watched him for a moment. "I thought I'd, um, speak with Christopher about volunteering at the Fortune Foundation office once he gets it up and running here. I could offer music lessons or something."

"Thought you didn't like playing in front of people."

"I don't like performing. But one-on-one? I told you once I liked working with children." She wished she wouldn't have brought it up, because it only made her remember that perfect April night when she'd talked about her life and he'd actually seemed to listen. "I…I have to do something to fill my days."

"You'll have a baby to fill your days." He waited a beat. "Or are you planning to hire some nanny to do that? That's what people like you do, right?"

"People like you," she repeated, mimicking his drawl. "I was born into a family that happened to have money," she said crisply. "It doesn't make me a different species than you!"

His jaw flexed. "People with your financial advantage," he refined. "That's what my dad's father's *real* family did. Hired…nannies."

She studied the fresh lines creasing his tanned forehead. He'd said his father was illegitimate but hadn't offered anything else about it. Only had used it as a reason why she ought to marry him. "What do you mean?"

"Baxter Anthony." He practically spit the name. "My grandfather. He had a wife. He had kids. His *real* family. The ones who lived in comfort on a big old ranch in Oklahoma. While my grandmother—whom he fired as one of those nannies after knocking her up—and my dad eked out a life in Horseback Hollow. Baxter's real family had nannies. They had private schools. They had everything that my old man didn't."

"I don't want a nanny," she said after a moment. "It never even entered my mind. But the baby won't be here for months yet, and I'm not exactly used to sitting around, whiling away my days waving a lacy fan and eating bonbons."

"You could use a few bonbons," he muttered. "You're still too thin."

"Gawky, skinny Amelia." She sighed. "Lucie got all the grace in the family."

"What the hell are you talking about?"

She shrugged dismissively. "It doesn't matter."

"You're the most graceful thing I've ever seen," he said in such a flat tone she couldn't possibly mistake it for a compliment. More like an accusation. "You're so far out of my league it's laughable. I still can't believe you danced with me that night, much less—" He broke off and shoveled his fingers through his hair, leaving the thick brown strands disheveled.

She tucked her tongue between her teeth, trying to make sense of his words. "You're the one who seemed out of reach to me," she finally said. Self-assured. Quietly confident. A man who'd held her and made her feel safe and beautiful and wanted.

His brows were pulled down, his eyes unreadable. "Baxter was the only one who wanted to buy the Rocking-U when my old man died." His lips thinned. "He'd buy it now, too, if I'd let him. Just so he could finally succeed in wiping away the evidence that anyone with his blood ever existed here."

"Forget about him! The man sounds hideous. And why would you want to sell the Rocking-U? That ranch is—" She broke off, trying to make sense of the nonsensical. "It's who you are," she finally finished and knew she had it right. Ranching wasn't merely something Quinn did. It was entwined with everything he was. The ranch was an extension of him just as much as he was an extension of it.

"It's the only way I can bring something equal to the table," he said through his teeth.

She pushed to her feet. "Let me get this straight," she said slowly. "You think the only thing you can offer this baby is *money?*" She laughed, but it sounded more hysterical than anything. "Money doesn't matter, Quinn! Good Lord, how can you think it would?"

"Because you've always had it," he said roughly.

"If I gave it all away would that make you happy?" Her voice rose. "Would that soothe your…your *ego?*" She swept out her arms, taking in the room around them. "How can you stand in this home that *love* so obviously built and talk that way?"

She snatched up the tabloid and threw it at his chest. "You should have sold the story," she said icily. "At least then you would have been the one to make a fortune on it. You know what? *Don't* sign the custody agreement.

I'd rather take this baby back to London than have him be raised by a man who can't recognize what's right in front of his face!"

Then, because tears were blinding her and her stomach was heaving, she fled upstairs.

Quinn started after her. She'd walked away the other day when she brought him that custody agreement and he wasn't going to let her walk off again.

He got to the top of the stairs just as she slammed the bathroom door shut and he started to reach for it.

"I would give her a little time," a calm voice said.

He looked from Amelia's mother, standing in a bedroom doorway, to the bathroom door. On the other side, he could hear Amelia retching, and his sense of helplessness made him want to punch a wall.

"Come." Lady Josephine walked toward him and tucked her hand around his arm, drawing him away from the door. "No woman wants to be overheard when they're in Amelia's state. Morning sickness is never fun." She smiled at him with unexpected kindness.

But he also noticed the way she subtly placed herself between him and the door.

"She's in there because of me." He wasn't only talking about her pregnancy. "She's upset."

"Yes." Lady Josephine's expression didn't change. Nor did her protective position or the steel behind her light touch on his arm. "It's been upsetting business. Come."

He reluctantly went with her back down the stairs and followed her into the parlor. She glanced out the window, then sat on the edge of a side chair, her hands folded in her lap, her long legs angled to one side. It was such an "Amelia position" that he had to look away.

"Mr. Drummond, please sit."

He exhaled and feeling like a kid called in front of the principal, sat on one end of the couch. "Call me Quinn. Lady Josephine," he tacked on hurriedly. Was it supposed to be Lady Chesterfield? Lady Fortune Chesterfield? He wished to hell he'd listened more to Jess's yammering about all that.

A faint smile was playing around the corners of the woman's lips. "And you may call me Josephine. We are a bit of family after all."

He could feel heat rising up his neck. "I suppose I should apologize for that. I wouldn't blame you if you wanted my head."

Her head tilted slightly. "Are you saying you took advantage of my daughter?" Before he could answer, she shifted slightly. "Amelia has a kind heart," she said. "She's always hated the attention our family is given back home. As if we're celebrities of some sort. Unfortunately, this business with Lord Banning got quite out of control and in hindsight, I wish I would have interfered early on. Perhaps I could have saved us all some of this embarrassment. But I've actually never witnessed Amelia allowing herself to be taken advantage of. In fact, she can be quite headstrong at times." Her blue gaze didn't allow him to look away. "I feel certain she was an equal participant in this situation."

"Lady—"

"Josephine."

"Josephine." He rubbed his hands down his jeans and stood, because just sitting there had his nerves wanting to jump out of his skin. "No disrespect, ma'am, but I'm not going to talk about that." He wasn't going to talk about having sex with Amelia to her mother. He wasn't going to talk about it with anyone.

"I've always thought that when two people who belong together are not, it's one of the saddest things there is."

He stared. "You think she belongs with *me*. I'm a small-town rancher, ma'am. I don't have a pot of gold. I've got one failed marriage and pots of cow manure."

Her lips twitched. "I forget how refreshingly frank you Americans can be." She rose gracefully. She was taller than Amelia, but no less slender, and Quinn knew when Amelia was her age, she'd be just as beautiful. "I had an unsuccessful marriage as well, Quinn. And then I met Amelia's father and I had a very, very successful one. I loved Simon with all of my heart and knew that he loved me equally. I want that for Amelia. I want that for all of my children. The past is past. And if you'll forgive an unintended pun, fortune isn't in gold. I hope you'll realize that for both your sakes."

She patted his arm as she passed him and pulled open the front door. "You don't have to love Amelia to be a good father to your child together. But if you don't love Amelia, be decent enough to allow her space to find someone who will."

Chapter Fourteen

"Come on." Jess dragged Quinn by the arm, pulling him toward the brightly lit building.

The Hollows Cantina was having its grand opening celebration and everyone in town seemed to have turned out for the festivities.

"Mac reserved a table for us," Jess continued, "and is waiting, and you are *not* getting out of coming just because you're a flaming idiot."

"Amelia's going to be there."

"No kidding, Sherlock." She dug her fingernails into his forearm the same way she'd done when she was an equally irritating teenager. "Maybe if you weren't so clueless when it comes to wooing a woman, you'd be with her instead of playing third wheel to me and my husband."

"I don't want to be here with you, either," he reminded. But she'd driven out to the Rocking-U and made it plain she wasn't leaving unless he came with her.

For the sake of a little peace and sanity, and only because he really didn't want to upset yet another pregnant woman, he had pulled on the only suit he owned and gone with her.

"I'll be just as happy to go back home again," he finished. There were strands of white lights strung around the Cantina's building, outlining not only the second story's open-air terrace, but the market umbrellas lining the street in front of it, and country music spewed out from inside. The festive atmosphere was the last thing he was in the mood for.

"Over my dead body," Jess raised her voice over the music and even though there were a couple dozen people lined up outside the entrance waiting to get in, she pulled him into the throng, waving at the familiar faces they passed. He knew everyone in Horseback Hollow, too, but she knew everyone from Vicker's Corners who was there as well, which made for slow going. But they finally reached the small table deep inside the first floor of the restaurant where Mac was already seated.

She slipped behind the table to sit next to her husband who shoved out the chair that had obviously been added to what should have been a two-person table for Quinn. He gestured with his half-empty beer mug. "Place is a madhouse," he said, leaning across the table so he could be heard above the noise. "Already put in orders for a beer for you."

Jess made a face and reached for her glass of fruit juice. "Some men might forgo alcohol in support of his pregnant wife having to abstain."

Mac grinned at her, obviously unfazed. "Baby, you're

pregnant so often, I'd never have another beer again if I gave it up whenever you're knocked up." He bussed her cheek. "I ordered you some hot crab dip," he added. "You can eat yourself silly on it."

Jess looked slightly mollified. "At least I know I won't have to share it with either one of you." Both Mac and Quinn detested crab. "You wouldn't know there had ever been any protests in town about this place opening." She was craning her neck around, openly gawking at the people crowded inside. "This is amazing!" She wriggled a little in her seat, clearly delighted. "I think every person from Horseback Hollow *and* Vicker's Corners must be here tonight."

Quinn was looking around, too, hopefully less noticeably than his sister.

But he hadn't spotted Amelia.

He knew she hadn't left town. Jess would've reported it.

A waitress wearing a stark white blouse and a black apron tied around her hips stopped next to their table and delivered a steaming crock of crab dip and crackers as well as two freshly frosted mugs filled with beer. "We have a special menu tonight," she told them as she dealt three one-page menus on the table. "Because of the grand openin' and all. I'll give you a chance to look it over and be back if you have any questions."

Quinn's only question was where Amelia was.

Not that he knew what he would say to her if he saw her. She was making a habit of walking away from him. The fact that he deserved it wasn't something he was willing to look at real closely.

And he was still feeling the bruises from her mother's velvet-over-steel dismissal the day before.

He lifted the beer mug, and angled in his seat so he could see around the restaurant more easily.

The staircase that led to the second floor was situated close to the center of the room; a wide iron and rustic wood thing that was as much a focal point as it was functional and the mayor, Harlan Osgood, was holding court at the base, recounting the steps taken to bring such a fine establishment to their little town as if he hadn't ever had his own doubts about it. Privately, Quinn figured it was a good thing Harlan's main job was as the town's barber, because a natural politician, he wasn't.

Marcos and Wendy Mendoza, the owners, were working the room, too. The young couple was eye-catching, to say the least. Wendy in particular looked more like she belonged on the cover of magazines than making the desserts that Julia claimed were out of this world. Quinn had to give the couple credit for seeming to give equal attention to everyone they stopped to speak with. They gave just as much time to Tanya and her folks, sitting at a table as crowded as Quinn's across the room, as they did the mayor.

"Mac, what are you going to have?" Jess was asking, tapping the crisp edge of her menu against the table. "I'm starving. I haven't had a speck of morning sickness in two days, and I am going to take advantage of it."

Mac chuckled. "I think I'm having whatever else it is you want to order so you can eat it, too."

Was Amelia still plagued with morning sickness?

Quinn pushed out of the chair.

Jess looked at him. "You're *not* leaving."

He leaned over her. "Stop bossing," he warned.

Then he kissed the top of her head and made his way toward the staircase. He knew the entire extended Fortune family was supposed to be there that night, and if they weren't on the bottom floor, maybe they were up top.

Getting there proved as slow-going as getting into the restaurant in the first place, though, because of all the people standing around on the stairs blocking the way. He could hear bursts of laughter coming from the upper floor and barely controlled the urge to physically move some of the roadblocks out of his way.

"Mr. Drummond!"

He looked over the side of the staircase to see Shayla waving at him excitedly, her orange ponytail bouncing, and he sketched a wave. But she was already worming her way around the mayor and up the steps until she was only a few below his position midway up. "It's so cool to see you," she gushed. "Is Lady Amelia here, too?"

The girl had helped them avoid Ophelia Malone in Vicker's Corners, so Quinn swallowed his impatience to get upstairs. "I'm looking for her now," he admitted. "How've you been? Do you still have a particular guest staying at the B and B?"

She widened her eyes dramatically. "Right? Miz Malone finally left this morning. My ma's not so happy—" she waved her hand behind her, presumably to indicate the presence of her mother somewhere in the madhouse "—'cause she paid the room on time and all, but I was glad to see her go. I can't believe what she got printed the other day." She wrinkled her nose. "So gross."

It was as good a definition as any and a lot milder than what Quinn still thought about the tabloid cover. "Did you and your mom already have dinner?"

"Nah. Not yet." She twisted her head around, looking

down on the patrons below. "Ma's over there talking to the Fremonts. They're all on the graduation committee for high school next year."

He automatically glanced over at the table he'd noticed earlier where Tanya sat with her parents. Shayla's mother's hair was just as orange as her daughter's. Either the color was real or they shared the same bottle of hair dye.

"Can't believe she did it," Shayla was babbling on. "Just so stupid, you know?"

He frowned. "What?"

"Tanya." Shayla rolled her eyes, looking disgusted. "Believe me, she's not one of *my* friends anymore."

God save him from teenage girl angst. He managed to edge up another step when the person in front of him moved slightly. "That's too bad," he said vaguely. Tanya had always been a hard worker for him and the dozen or so other people she also cleaned for in order to help supplement her family's strained income.

"Wow. You're nicer than I would be," Shayla was saying. She was practically shouting to be heard above the music. "Blabbing about your personal business to Miz Malone and all."

He went still, her words penetrating.

He went back down the step. "What did you say?"

Shayla looked suddenly nervous. "Uh—"

He nudged her to one side of the stairs so one of the servers carrying a stack of menus could get past them. "What do you mean about personal business, Shayla?" But he had the sinking feeling he already knew.

He'd tossed Amelia's pregnancy test in the trash.

Tanya cleaned his house.

Shayla shot a look toward the table below and Quinn

caught the pale expression on Tanya's face even from a distance.

"I don't think she meant to," Shayla said hurriedly. She might be willing to eschew Tanya's friendship, but she was obviously afraid of tossing her under the bus. "It's just Miz Malone kept talking to everybody and... and—" She lifted her shoulders. "Well, Tanya needed that car in the worst way or she's not gonna be able to get back and forth to Lubbock for school when she graduates next year and the money she gets cleaning houses is already used up on her ma's medicine. I thought you already knew."

Quinn sucked down his fury.

"I don't think she knew how bad it would be," Shayla finished. "Still." She made a face. "*I* wouldn't want her cleaning around my stuff. You're prob'ly pretty mad, huh."

Amelia's friend Molly hadn't done a single thing to betray her.

"It's okay, Shayla." He squeezed her shoulder and managed a smile even though he wanted to kick both Ophelia Malone and Tanya Fremont off the planet altogether. "I'm glad to hear the truth."

"Quinn!"

He looked toward the top of the stairs to see Liam beckoning.

"Go on and enjoy your dinner," Quinn told Shayla. "Once I find Amelia, I'll let her know you're here. I'm sure she'll want to say hello."

Shayla beamed. "You think?"

He nodded and started edging up the stairs again while she slipped through the people on her way down.

Liam clapped him on the shoulder when he finally

made it to the top. "Julia's done a helluva job here to-night with the Mendozas, hasn't she?" The man's face was proud. "We've got the whole family up here."

Suspicions confirmed, Quinn looked beyond Liam to the crowded tables spilling out onto the open terrace. Jeanne and Deke were sitting with Josephine and their brother, James Marshall Fortune. There was also another older couple sitting with them and he was pretty certain the man was the threesome's older brother, John. Which, according to Jess who always needed to know who was who, made him Wendy Mendoza's father. Aside from Jeanne and Deke's crew, spread out among the rest of the tables were a bunch of other faces he recognized from Sawyer and Laurel's New Year's wedding.

But Amelia was not among them.

"We've got extra reason to celebrate," Liam was say-ing. "Angie and Toby's adoption was finally approved."

His head was still banging with Shayla's news, but Quinn glanced at the man who seemed deep in conver-sation with his uncle James. Happiness radiated from his face. "That's great," he said. "Where's Amelia?"

Liam looked surprised for a moment, then glanced around. "Don't know, man. She was here earlier." He raised his voice even more. "Aunt Josephine, where'd Amelia go?"

In addition to Amelia's mother, Quinn suddenly found himself the focus of way too many eyes.

Josephine said something to her companions, then rose and worked her way through the tables toward him.

"I didn't mean to interrupt your dinner," Quinn said.

"You're not interrupting," she assured. She smiled slightly at her nephew. "Liam, I haven't had a chance yet to applaud your fiancée's efforts tonight. Is Julia going to be able to join us, or is she on duty all evening?"

"She's not on duty at all," Liam said, grinning. "But she can't keep from checking on things. She'll be 'round soon enough." He headed after the waitress that was circulating throughout the room with a tray laden with drinks. "Hey there, darlin', lemme take one of those off your hands."

Josephine looked back at Quinn. "I wasn't sure we would have the pleasure of seeing you tonight."

He wondered what she'd really like to say if she weren't so polite. Probably something more along the lines of hoping he wouldn't have the gall to show his face that night.

"I wasn't going to come," he admitted. He was glad he had, though, if only to hear what Shayla'd had to say. "Is Amelia all right?"

Josephine's expression was the same as it had been the other day when she'd essentially told him to put up or shut up. Calm. Seemingly gracious, yet still reserved.

"She's unhappy." She didn't attempt to raise her voice above the music to be heard, yet her words somehow managed to carry through anyway. "As are you, I believe." Then she sighed a little, her gaze following Sawyer and Orlando Mendoza as they moved among the tables. "I keep having to remind myself how entwined the Fortune and Mendoza families are," she murmured then looked back at Quinn again. "She went outside a short while ago. She said she needed some fresh air."

He stifled an oath. How had he missed her leaving the restaurant when he'd been on the damn stairs?

"Thank you." He started to turn and go back the way he'd come, but stopped. "La— Josephine."

She lifted her eyebrows, waiting.

"It wasn't Molly," he said abruptly. "You know. Who spilled the beans." He told her briefly about Tanya cleaning his place.

When he was done, he couldn't tell if she was relieved or not. He'd thought that Amelia's "royal face" was bad, but in comparison to her mother's, her expressive face was an open book.

"What do you plan to do about your young employee?"

"Fire her," he said flatly.

"Hmm." She nodded once. "Is that why you're anxious to see my daughter? To share this information?"

He could lie and say it was, even though he'd been looking for Amelia before Shayla's disclosure. As far as he was concerned, what went on between him and Amelia *was* between him and Amelia. "I don't know why I'm anxious to see her," he finally said truthfully. "I just know I have to."

It wasn't any sort of answer, but it seemed enough for her to smile just a little as she nodded once and headed back to her table.

He went down the stairs again where the sounds of celebration weren't as raucous, though the music was, and pretended he didn't see his sister trying to flag him down as he worked his way toward the entrance.

Once he got past the crowd still waiting to get in, he felt like he'd been shot from a noisy cannon into blissful peace.

The music was still loud. There were still dozens of people surrounding the tables beneath the colorful market umbrellas. But it was still *open* and he yanked off his suit jacket and hauled in a deep breath of fresh air.

The Hollows Cantina might well be bringing new jobs and new revenue to the area, and it wouldn't be crazy busy in the days to come like it was for the grand opening, but he was pretty sure he wouldn't be in any hurry to go back, no matter how good the food might turn out to be.

Bunching his jacket in one hand, he scanned the tables outside the restaurant. Amelia wasn't at any of them, so he walked past them until he reached the side of the building. She wasn't there, either, so he walked all the way around the building. And even then, he didn't spot her.

"Dammit, Amelia. Where are you?"

The whole of Horseback Hollow's businesses were contained in just a few short blocks and trying not to imagine her passed out cold in some shadowy corner, he started down the street, and then nearly missed her altogether where she was sitting on a bench in front of the mayor's barbershop.

The soles of his boots scraped against the street when he stopped in front of her and peered at her in the dark. Her skin looked white in the moonlight, her hair, eyes and clothing as dark as midnight. "You're not easy to find."

"I didn't know you were looking." She shifted slightly, given away only by the slight rustle of her clothes. "You've been in the restaurant?"

"Yeah." It was a warm night and he tossed his jacket on the bench beside her and started rolling up his sleeves. "It's a zoo."

She made a soft sound. "Yes. Too many people and too much noise for me."

"Were you feeling sick?"

She shifted again. "Not in the way you mean," she murmured. "What do you want, Quinn?"

"Molly didn't rat us out," he said abruptly. "It was Tanya. When she cleaned the house—"

"She found the test," Amelia finished slowly, dawning revelation clear in her tone. "Of course she did. I can't believe I never thought of that."

"I can't believe she talked to that woman," he said flatly. "I wouldn't have known if Shayla hadn't said something. Would've just kept paying the kid every Sunday to clean the bathrooms and mop the damn floors, never knowing any better."

"She's a girl," Amelia murmured.

"She talked about *our* business for the price of a car," he countered. "She won't be stepping foot in my house again. Or any others, if I can help it."

"Didn't you ever make a mistake when you were young?"

His lips twisted. "Why are you being so understanding? You were pretty upset thinking it was your mother's secretary."

"It's just all so…so sad, isn't it?" Her voice was soft. Oddly musing. "I'd say it was tragic except there are so many other real tragedies occurring every day." She sighed. "The press has been vilifying us ever since I came to Horseback Hollow. Ophelia used Tanya like a tool, no differently than she'd use a long-distance lens. Have you ever noticed how random it all is?" she asked abruptly.

He peered at her face but even though his eyes were becoming accustomed to the dark, he still couldn't tell if she was looking at him or not. "What's random?"

"If I hadn't decided to come to Horseback Hollow

with Mum for Sawyer's wedding over New Year's. If you and I hadn't danced when I came back again for Toby's. If James's father hadn't announced an engagement-that-wasn't. If any one of those things hadn't occurred, everything would be so different today."

"Maybe that's not random." His chest felt tight. "Maybe that's fate."

She shifted, her dark dress rustling. "You believe in fate." She sounded skeptical.

"I don't know what I believe, Amelia. Except I know I don't want you going back to London."

"I've told you and told you, you needn't worry about your place in the baby's life."

"What about a place in your life?"

She went silent for a moment, then slowly stood, walking closer to him until he could smell the clean fragrance of her hair and see the gleam in her dark eyes.

"Did you really want me to come back to Horseback Hollow after the night we shared? You said you did. And I...I thought you meant it. But maybe that's just what a person is supposed to say after a one-night stand. Protocol, if you will."

"It wasn't protocol," he said flatly. "I meant it."

He felt the weight of her gaze. "Why?"

The shirt button he'd left loose at his neck wasn't enough and he yanked another one free. "What d'ya mean *why?* I liked you. We had great—"

"Sex," she finished.

"*Chemistry* is what I was going to say."

"The end result is the same."

"Where are you going with this, Amelia?"

"I don't know." She sighed. "I've just been trying to

figure out how much I imagined about that night and what was actually real."

He didn't need light. He closed one arm around her waist and pressed his other hand against her flat abdomen, feeling as much as hearing the sudden breath she inhaled. "That is real."

"Yes." The one word sounded shaky. "But sex is not love. Having a baby doesn't mean love, either."

"Sometimes it does." He wanted to get out the words. But they felt stopped in his chest by a lifetime of disappointments. "Jess and Mac are having another baby. Trying again for a girl. So maybe she really had been in that hardware store to buy pink paint."

"I'm happy for them." Her voice was low. She gently patted his chest once. Then once more. "Think about it before you fire Tanya," she murmured. And then she stepped out of his arm and started up the street, disappearing into the dark.

Chapter Fifteen

Amelia's eyes glazed as she stumbled up the street.

"Amelia!"

Quinn was not going to come around. He wouldn't let himself, and she couldn't bear it.

"Don't walk away from me."

Her chest ached. She'd never understood that a heart breaking was a physical breaking, too. She could barely force herself to move when all she wanted to do was curl into a ball. She swiped her cheek and forced her feet to move faster. "What are you going to do? Throw me over your shoulder?"

"Please." Just one word. Rough. And raw.

Her feet dragged to a stop.

A block away, she could see the lights of the Cantina. Could hear the music playing on the night.

She didn't have to look back to see Quinn coming up

behind her. She didn't even need to hear his footfalls on the pavement. She could feel him.

"Toby and Angie's adoption was approved this afternoon. Did you know that?"

"Yeah. I saw him and your uncle James together. D'you think he's the one who gave him that money?"

"Aunt Jeanne wouldn't take the money he wanted to give her, so why not? He can afford it." She clasped her arms around her waist, trying to keep the pieces of herself from splintering on the road and nodded toward the festivities. "Everyone in there is celebrating," she said painfully. "Everyone in there is happy. Julia and Liam can walk into a room and light it up simply by looking at each other. Colton and Stacey are like two halves of a whole. I think Jude would lay down his life for Gabi and Christopher and Kinsley—" Her voice broke. "They're all happy. They're all in love. Is it so wrong to want that, too?"

"No."

She turned on her heel and looked up at him. "I could marry you, Quinn," she whispered. "Justice of the peace or a minister. It wouldn't matter. I could stand up in front of either and promise to love you for the rest of my days. And I wouldn't be lying." She sniffed but the tears kept coming. "But the marriage *would* be a lie, because I know you don't love me. And I can't live like that." She turned again, desperate to go somewhere, anywhere, for a little peace.

"And I can't live without you."

Had she gone so far over the edge that she was hearing things now, too?

"Don't leave me."

She sucked in a shuddering breath.

"Amelia." He closed his hands over her shoulders and turned her toward him. "Please." His low voice cracked. "Don't leave me." His fingers tightened, almost painfully.

"Quinn—"

He closed his mouth over hers, his hands moving to cradle her face. "Don't," he said hoarsely, brushing his thumbs over her cheeks. "I can take anything but that."

She could no more stop her hands from grasping his shoulders than she could stop loving him.

He kissed her again, lightly. Tenderly. The way he had that very first time. "If you leave me, I won't be able to take it. I love you," he whispered. "More than I've ever loved anything or anyone. And I am terrified. Okay?"

She wound her arms behind his neck, her heart cracking wide. "Nothing terrifies you."

"Not being good enough for you does." He dragged her arms away, holding them captive between them. "Not being a good enough father." He shook her gently, as if trying to convince her. "Not being a good enough husband. If I failed you or the baby—"

"You won't," she cried. "You can't fail me if you'd just love me. You think I'm not afraid? I don't even know how to make a baby's bottle. Infants can't eat peanut butter sandwiches!"

He folded her against him, tucking her head into his shoulder. "I know how to make a bottle," he said roughly. "Jess made me learn years ago. That's the easy stuff, Amelia. I'm talking about a life. What do I have to offer you?"

"Your heart," she said thickly. "Offer your heart! It's the only thing that matters. If you're afraid, be afraid with me. I can't bear it if you shut me out."

"Oh, my God," a voice said from nearby, startling them both. "Get a room or get on with it."

Amelia stared into the darkness, appalled when Ophelia Malone strolled closer. All of her pain, her uncertainty where Quinn was concerned, coalesced into a ball of hatred toward the paparazzo. *"You."* She started to launch herself at the dreadful woman, but Quinn held her back. "Haven't you done enough?"

"Evidently not." Ophelia sighed slightly. She held out her hands to her sides and Amelia spotted the camera she was holding.

She pulled against Quinn, but again he held fast. "She's not worth it." His voice was cutting.

"Why do you do this?" Amelia demanded of the woman. "Why do you go around making peoples' lives a misery? Is the money that good? Is it just that you enjoy tearing people's lives to shreds? What is it?"

"Oh, the money was good. Very, very good. But it didn't work anyway." Ophelia circled around them, giving Amelia's clawed fingers a wide berth. "Even knowing what sort of person you really are, Lord Banning *still* isn't giving my sister a chance."

Amelia shook her head, suddenly lost. "What?"

Ophelia sighed again. "You really are as dumb as a post," she mocked. "Your rancher there has more smarts than you do. At least he built that successful little ranch of his out of nothing but ashes. What have you ever done but smile pretty for the cameras while your mummy does all that charitable work that has people thinking she's such a saint?"

Quinn set Amelia to one side of him and snatched Ophelia's wrist with his free hand, making the other woman drop the camera. "Keep it up," he spat, "and I'll let her at you."

"Who's your sister?"

Ophelia shook off Quinn's hold and crouched down to pick up the two pieces of the camera. She held up the lens to the light from the Cantina, then tossed it off to the side of the road. "So much for that pricey little thing." She pushed to her feet. "Astrid," she clipped. She circled around Quinn until she was near Amelia again. "Astrid is my sister and if it weren't for *you* and your eminently suitable pedigree, Lord Banning would have chosen *her*. He would have gone against that decrepit father of his and married my sister whether she was a common shop girl or not!"

"You're insane," Amelia whispered, shocked to her very core.

Ophelia held out her arms. "Guilty as charged, no doubt." She suddenly tossed the camera at them and Quinn caught it midair before it could hit Amelia. "I don't have the stomach for this anymore. I'd like to say I hope you'll be happy together, but we all know I'd be lying." She turned on her heel and started walking down the street. "Taa taa, darlings."

Amelia pulled against Quinn's hold.

"Let her go," he muttered.

"She's. . .she's *vile!* I can't believe that woman is Astrid's sister."

He dropped the camera on the ground and turned her back into his arms, his hands sweeping down her back. "You know her?"

"Astrid? She sells coffee in James's building. And he's crazy about her. But he's had years to go against

his family and marry her. Now that he's the Earl of Estingwood, he could do whatever he wants. But he won't."

"Why?"

"Because she's a commoner," Amelia said simply.
"She's divorced. She has a child. Take your pick."

"I thought that stuff didn't matter anymore."

"It matters to the Bannings. And above all things,
James is loyal to his family."

He pressed his lips against her temple. "I don't want
to talk about James."

"Neither do I." From the corner of her eye, though, she
kept watch of Ophelia, long enough to see the woman
climb into an SUV and roar off down the street in the
opposite direction.

Quinn suddenly pushed her away from him. "Where
were we?"

Her throat tightened. "I don't know," she whispered.

"I do." Holding her hands, he abruptly went down on
one knee, right there in the middle of the street. "I think
this is the way it's supposed to go. Never did it before."

She inhaled sharply. "Quinn—"

"My heart is yours, Amelia Fortune Chesterfield. It
has been from the second you agreed to a dance with a
simple cowboy."

Tears flooded her eyes. "So is mine. Yours, I mean.
My heart." She laughed brokenly. "I'm making a mish-
mash. And there's nothing simple about you."

"Will you marry me?"

She nodded and pulled on his hands. "Yes. I don't
want you on your knees, I just want you by my side."

He rose and caught her close. "Preacher or a JP?"

She dragged his head to hers. "As long as it's soon, I
don't care," she said thickly, and pressed her mouth to

his. Joy was bubbling through her, making her feel dizzy
with it. "Take me home?"

He cradled her tightly, lifting her right off her feet.
"Kissing me like that is how getting you pregnant started
off," he warned. And then he laughed a little and swore.
"I can't. I don't have my truck. I rode here with Jess."

She groaned. "I want to be alone with you." She sank
her fingers through his hair, reveling in the realization
that she *could.* "I don't care how shameless that sounds.
I need to be alone with you."

"You're killing me," he said gruffly, and kissed her
so softly, so sweetly, that she would have fallen in love
with him all over again if she hadn't already done so.

Then he gently set her back on her feet. Kissed her
forehead. Her cheeks. "We'll go back and borrow some
keys from someone."

"And then you'll take me home?"

He lifted her hand and kissed her fingers. "And then
I'll take you home." They started back toward the Cantina, but Amelia suddenly ducked under his arm and ran
back to retrieve Ophelia's camera.

"What do you want that thing for?"

She pulled his arm over her shoulder once more and
fiddled with the camera as they continued walking back
to the Cantina. "There's got to be a memory card in
here somewhere." She held up the camera, squinting in
the light from the strands hanging in the trees. "Ah."
She spotted the storage compartment and freed the
tiny square inside before handing the camera to Quinn.
"Don't toss that aside either," she warned. "There might
be internal memory or something that will need to be
erased."

"Ophelia's gone." He brushed his hand down her hair. "Nobody else is going to care about that thing."

"Probably," she agreed, "But I'm not taking any chances." She went over to one of the umbrella-covered tables and reached for one of the candles burning inside short jars. "Mind if I borrow this for a moment?" she asked the people sitting there, and when there were no objections, carried it back to him.

Holding the jar between them, she dropped the memory disk onto the flame. "No more Ophelia Malone," she murmured, watching the thing begin to sizzle and melt, and feeling like the last load was lifting from her shoulders.

When the memory card was no longer recognizable as anything but a misshapen blob of plastic, she blew out the candle and carefully plucked it out of the wax.

Then she dropped it on the road and ground it fervently beneath her heel.

Quinn lifted the candle out of her hand and set it back on the table. "Remind me never to make you really mad," he said when she finally stopped grinding.

"I know how to fox hunt, too," she told him, looping her arm through his. She couldn't seem to get the smile off her face, but then she couldn't imagine a reason why she needed to.

Quinn Drummond loved her.

What she'd feared was only a dream was real. And she was going to treasure that for the rest of their days.

"Fox hunt," he repeated warily. But he was smiling, too, and he absently hooked the camera strap over his shoulder.

"My father taught us." She looked up at the balcony above the umbrellas and saw her mother there, talking with Orlando Mendoza and looking unusually animated. "Once upon a time my father was a pilot," she murmured, nodding toward the balcony. "The Royal Air Force."

Quinn pulled her close against his side once more, as if he couldn't stand even a few inches separating them. He tilted his head looking upward, his gaze sharpening slightly. "They look—"

"Cozy," Amelia finished.

"Interesting." He steered her toward the entrance of the Cantina that was no less crowded than it had been earlier. "Maybe Horseback Hollow will end up appealing to more of the Fortune Chesterfields."

As much as the idea delighted her, she was presently more interested in Quinn. "You promised something about keys?"

"Yes, ma'am," Quinn said softly and kissed her right there in front of the Hollows Cantina for all the world to see. Then he tugged her after him through the crowds. Jess and Mac were sitting all cozied up together at their small table, clearly unworried whether he ever returned or not. The stairs were still crowded and he exhaled impatiently. But Amelia dragged him through the swinging doors to the kitchen where there was another staircase.

Not grand. Not the center of attention. But entirely welcome. At the top, he threaded his way around the tables there.

Lady Josephine was sitting once more next to Jeanne Marie and Deke and her smile deepened when she saw them. "Have you figured out where your fortune is, then, Quinn?"

"Yes, ma'am," he said and lifted his hand linked with

Amelia's. "I surely have." His eyes met Amelia's. "Love's the fortune."

Her smile trembled and she leaned into him. "Keys," she whispered.

He threw back his head and laughed. "Keys." He spotted Liam. "Lend me your truck for the night and I'll *consider* selling Rocky."

Liam reached into his pocket and tossed the keys over several heads. Quinn caught them handily.

Amelia giggled, squeezing his hand.

And they raced for the stairs.

Epilogue

Quinn parked his truck near the tree house tree and went around to open Amelia's door. "Come on."

She tilted her head up toward his, a smile on her face below the bandana he'd tied around her eyes before they'd left the ranch house.

It had been a week since the Cantina's grand opening. A week during which they'd barely left one another's side. A week in which it was finally sinking in that Amelia was his.

She loved him. She wasn't going anywhere. She was filling the empty parts of him, and together they'd fill the empty rooms of their home.

"What are we doing?" Her voice was full of laughter.

"You'll see." He took her hands and helped her out of the truck.

"Not exactly." Her lips tilted. "Since you've blindfolded me." She turned her head from side to side as he drew her closer to the tree, obviously trying to get a sense of where they were. "Do I hear the creek?"

He moved behind her and slid his hands around her waist and kissed her neck below her ear, right where he knew it would make her shiver. "Good instincts."

She sighed a little, shimmied a little with that shiver, and covered his hands with hers, pressing them against her belly. She rubbed her head against his chest. "On occasion. I picked you, didn't I?"

"That you did." He kissed her earlobe. "Okay, you can look."

She tugged the bandanna off her head.

"I knew it," she said, laughing in her triumph. She peered up into the tree branches. "You've finished the floor! When did you have time to do that?"

He'd finished a lot more than that. "When you're lazing around in bed, snoring."

"I don't snore."

"You do." He kissed her nose. "Daintily. Like the lady that you are."

She rolled her eyes. "Oh, that makes it all right then."

He laughed softly. "It's safe for us to go up."

Her dark eyes roved over his face while a smile played around her soft lips. "*Us?* As in now you're going to let me climb a tree?"

His hands slid down her hips. "Only because I'm here with you. So do you want to go up or not?"

Her eyes sparkled. "What do you think?" She quickly yanked off the sandals she'd been wearing and tossed them onto the grass, then set her bare toes on the first foothold and deftly began climbing.

"Just go slow, okay? Be careful."

She looked over her shoulder at him, grinning and looking more like a teenaged girl than a pregnant woman. "Fine warning from the man who puts temptation in my path."

She continued up with Quinn standing below her, and between his distraction over the view of her bare legs beneath her summery pink dress as she went, even he had to admit that she seemed to know exactly what she was doing. "How often did you say you used to climb trees?"

She laughed. She'd reached the base of the tree house and pushed open the door in the floor. "Every day that I could get away with it." In seconds, she'd clambered through the hatch, and then there was only silence.

He imagined her up there, seeing the preparations he'd made early that morning while she'd been sleeping in his bed.

Their bed.

A moment later, she leaned over the high side boards that formed the walls of the tree house, her long hair hanging down past her shoulders. Her youthful grin was gone, replaced by a soft expression. "Are you going to stand around down there, or join me?"

He kicked off his own shoes and climbed up.

It didn't take him any longer than it had her, but in that brief time she'd still managed to slip out of her dress, and was laying on the thick blankets he'd spread out on one side of the structure.

He let out a breath.

She propped her head on her hand and smiled slightly, holding one of the daisies he'd stuck in a jar to her nose. She was wearing sheer panties and a bra the same pale blue color as the Texas sky. "This *is* what you had in mind, isn't it?"

He crawled through the door and dropped it back in place. "Yeah." He shucked his own clothes, pitching them in the corner.

Her lashes swept down and pink color touched her cheeks. "I'm wondering if Peter Pan ever got up to such mischief."

He knelt down beside her, and she rolled onto her back, her hair pooling out around her head. "Peter Pan was a boy," he murmured, sliding one strap off her shoulder and kissing the creamy skin there.

She ran her thigh against his as she bent her knee and dropped the flower in favor of closing her hand boldly around him. "And you're *no* boy."

He exhaled on a rough laugh and caught her hand in his, pulling it away. "Not so fast, Lady Fortune Chesterfield." He stretched out next to her and slid off the other bra strap, then unsnapped the tiny silver clasp between her breasts holding it together. "I have plans for you."

"That'll be Mrs. Drummond—" her voice hitched when he caught one of those rosy crests between his lips "—to you."

He smiled against her warm flesh. Already he could sense small changes in her body because of the baby inside her. Her breasts were fuller. Her nipples a deeper pink. "Soon as you finally say whether you want a minister or a justice of the peace, that's who you'll be." He kissed his way down her flat belly, anchoring her hips gently when she shivered and twisted against him.

"Minister," she whispered. Her fingers slid through his hair, clutching. "And soon."

He nuzzled his way beneath the sexy little panties that matched the bra. "Impatient to make this all legal?"

"Yes." She suddenly twisted, reversing their positions

and pinned him on the blankets. "And I want to say yes before I'm big as a house. But I want my brothers and sister here, too. And you'll need a suit since you lost your jacket at the Cantina the other night." She kicked off her panties and sank down on him, letting out a shuddering moan.

He clamped his hands over her hips. "You're not always gonna get your way like this, princess." He sucked in a sharp breath as she rocked her hips against him. "I'm only indulging this need for constant speed you've got 'cause—"

"You love me." She leaned over, rubbing her tight nipples against his chest, and kissed him.

"—you're pregnant and at the mercy of your hormones," he finished.

Then, wrapping his arm around her waist, he flipped her onto her back. Loving the color in her cheeks and the way her eyes went an even darker brown, soft as down and feeling like home.

"And because I love you," he said the words quietly. They were coming easier, but even when he didn't say them he wanted her to know he would never stop feeling them.

Her eyes turned shiny and wet. She laid her palm along his jaw and brushed her thumb over his lip. "If I'm a princess, you know that makes you my prince."

"I don't care what you call me, Amelia—" he sank into her "—as long as it means *husband*."

She gasped, and twined her legs around his hips, arching against him. "This...tree house is off-limits the second our son—"

"Daughter—"

"—hits puberty," she managed breathlessly.

He laughed and thumbed away the tears leaking from her big brown eyes. "Damn straight it is," he agreed. And then he kissed her and together, they flew.

*****

A sneaky peek at next month...

Cherish™

EXPERIENCE THE ULTIMATE RUSH OF FALLING IN LOVE

My wish list for next month's titles...

In stores from 20th June 2014:

❏ Her Irresistible Protector — Michelle Douglas

❏ A Bride by Summer — Sandra Steffen

❏ The Maverick Millionaire — Alison Roberts

❏ A Doctor for Keeps — Lynne Marshall

In stores from 4th July 2014:

❏ Million-Dollar Maverick — Christine Rimmer

❏ The Return of the Rebel — Jennifer Faye

❏ Dating for Two — Marie Ferrarella

❏ The Tycoon and the Wedding Planner — Kandy Shepherd

Available at WHSmith, Tesco, Asda, Eason, Amazon and Apple

Just can't wait?

Visit us Online

You can buy our books online a month before they hit the shops! **www.millsandboon.co.uk**

0614/23

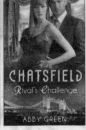

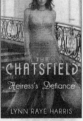

THE

CHATSFIELD®

Enter the intriguing online world of
The Chatsfield and discover secret
stories behind closed doors…

www.thechatsfield.com

Check in online now for your exclusive
welcome pack!

Join our *EXCLUSIVE* eBook club

FROM JUST £1.99 A MONTH!

Never miss a book again with our hassle-free eBook subscription.

★ Pick how many titles you want from each series with our flexible subscription

★ Your titles are delivered to your device on the first of every month

★ Zero risk, zero obligation!

There really is nothing standing in the way of you and your favourite books!

Start your eBook subscription today at www.millsandboon.co.uk/subscribe

Join the Mills & Boon Book Club

Want to read more **Cherish**™ books?
We're offering you **2 more** absolutely **FREE!**

We'll also treat you to these fabulous extras:

- Exclusive offers and much more!
- FREE home delivery
- FREE books and gifts with our special rewards scheme

Get your free books now!

**visit www.millsandboon.co.uk/bookclub
or call Customer Relations on 020 8288 2888**